Night Vision

**Center Point
Large Print**

Also by Randy Wayne White and available from Center Point Large Print:

Deep Shadow

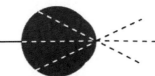

This Large Print Book carries the Seal of Approval of N.A.V.H.

Night Vision

RANDY WAYNE WHITE

CENTER POINT LARGE PRINT
THORNDIKE, MAINE

This Center Point Large Print edition is published in the year 2011 by arrangement with G.P. Putnam's Sons, a member of Penguin Group (USA), Inc.

Sanibel and Captiva Islands, and Immokalee, Florida, are real places, faithfully described, but used fictitiously in this novel. The same is true of certain businesses, marinas, bars and other places frequented by Doc Ford, Tomlinson and pals.
In all other respects, however, this novel is a work of fiction. Names, characters, places and incidents are either the product of the author's imagination or are used fictitiously. Any resemblance to actual persons, living or dead, or to actual events or locales is unintentional and coincidental.

The text of this Large Print edition is unabridged. In other aspects, this book may vary from the original edition.
Printed in the United States of America.
Set in 16-point Times New Roman type.

ISBN: 978-1-61173-047-0

Library of Congress Cataloging-in-Publication Data

White, Randy Wayne.
Night vision / Randy Wayne White.
p. cm.
ISBN 978-1-61173-047-0 (library binding : alk. paper)
1. Ford, Doc (Fictitious character)—Fiction.
    2. Marine biologists—Fiction. 3. Florida—Fiction.
    4. Large type books. I. Title.
PS3573.H47473N54 2011b
813'.54—dc22

2010052201

For my adored partner, Wendy Webb, and our eloquent, gifted Webb family: Sandy and Jim Phillips, Ben, Sarah, Tom, Janet, Luke, Jack, Mary, Joost, Jesse, Kelly, Ryder, Layla, and three ascending stars: Hannah, Phoebe and Zoë Webb.

AUTHOR'S NOTE

I learned long ago, whether writing fiction or nonfiction, an author loses credibility if he's caught in a factual error. Because of this, I do extensive research before starting a new Doc Ford novel, and *Night Vision* is no different.

However, a scene takes place in this book for which no research data was available. It concerns bottlenose dolphins that are surprised while foraging beneath mangrove trees, on land, on a starry, moonless night. As the author, though, I can vouch for the scene's accuracy and authenticity because I witnessed a similar event, and the details are as described, although viewed through the eyes of Marion Ford and Tomlinson.

Otherwise, thanks go to experts in various fields. These include Dr. Frank J. Mazzotti, wildlife biologist, and one of the country's foremost experts on crocodilians. Ryan D. Battis, of Laser Energetics, manufacturers of the Dazer Guardian. Peter Deltoro and Dr. Tim S. Sigman, both of whom provided invaluable help to the author.

Special thanks also go to my partner, Wendy Webb, my guardian, Iris Tanner, my partners and pals, Mark "Dartanian" Marinello, Coach Marty and Brenda Harrity, my surfing buddy Gus

Landl, my spiritual advisers Bill and Diana Lee, my battery and travel mate Don Carman, Stu "The Big Lefty" Johnson, lovely Donna and Gary "Twig" Terwilliger, and Dr. Brian Hummel, the author's intellectual compass and ever-faithful friend.

Once again, the early chapters of this book were written in Cartagena, Colombia, and Havana, Cuba, and I am indebted to friends who helped me secure good places to live and write. My thanks go to Giorgio and Carolina Arajuo for their help in Cartagena. In Cuba, my Freemason brothers Ernesto Batista and Sergio Rodriquez were particularly helpful, as were Roberto and Ela Giraudy, Rául and Myra Corrales and Alex Vicente.

Most of this novel, though, was written at corner tables before and after hours at Doc Ford's Rum Bar and Grille on Sanibel and San Carlos Islands, where staff were tolerant beyond the call of duty.

Thanks go to Col. Raynauld Bentley, Dan Howes, Brian "Boston Blackie" Cunningham, Mojito Greg Barker, the amazing Liz Harris, Capt. Bryce Randall Harris, dear Milita Kennedy, Kevin Filliowich, Kevin Boyce of Boston infamy, Eric Breland, Big Sam Khussan Ismatullaev, Olga Guryanova, lovely Rachel Songalewski of Michigan, Jean, Evan and Abby Crenshaw, Lindsay Kuleza, Roberto Cruz,

Amanda Rodriquez, Juan Gomex, Mary McBeath, tattoo consultant Kim McGonnell, the amazing Cindy Porter, "Hi" Sean Scott, Big Matt Powell, Laurie and Jake Yukobov, Bette Roberts and master chef Chris Zook, a man of complex talents.

At the Rum Bar on San Carlos Island, Fort Myers Beach, thanks go to Wade Craft, James Gray, Kandice Salvador, Herberto Ramos, Brian Obrien, lovelies Latoya Trotta, Alexandria Pereira, Kerra Pike, Christine Engler, Stephanie Goolsby, Danielle Gorman, Corey Allen, Nora Billheimmer, Molly Brewer, Justina Villaplano, Jessica Wozniak, Lauren Brown, Kassee Buonano, Sally Couillard, Justin Dorfman, Chris Goolsby, Patric John, Stephen Johnson, Manuel Lima, Jeffrey Lyons, Matthew and Michael Magner, Catherine Mawyer, Susan Mora, Kylie Pryll, Dustin Rickards, Brooke Ryland, Ellen Sandler, Dean Shoeman, Jessica Shell, Andrea Aguayo and Kevin "Stretch" Tully.

At Timber's Sanibel Grille, my pals Matt Asen, Mary Jo, Audrey, Becky, Bart and Bobby were, once again, stalwarts.

Finally, I would like to thank my two sons, Capt. Rogan and Lee White, for helping me finish, yet again, another book.

—Randy Wayne White
Casa de Chico's
Sanibel Island, Florida

Everything that has happened, everything that will happen, it all exists in this single moment, endlessly surfacing and submerging; natural order, perfect law. The word "coincidence" is an invention that defines our own confusion better than it describes a unique occurrence.

—S.M. TOMLINSON

One life is all we have and we live it as we believe in living it. But to sacrifice what you are and to live without belief, that is a fate more terrible than dying.

—JOAN OF ARC, 1412–1431

Night
Vision

ONE

ON AN EVERGLADES-SCENTED EVENING in March as I drove my pickup truck west, toward the Gulf of Mexico, my hipster pal, Tomlinson, reached to switch off the radio, saying, "Life is the best thing that can happen to any of us. And it's also the very worst thing that can happen to any of us. Problem is, our luck begins with mom's location when the womb turns into a slippery slide. That's why I self-medicate. It makes the shitty unfairness of it all almost bearable."

We had just dropped my chatty cousin, Ransom Gatrell, at Regional Southwest, and I was eager for a few minutes without conversation. I nodded toward the radio and told him, "Hey, I was listening to that. We can talk later."

"The Guatemalan girl deserves your full attention," Tomlinson reminded me. He leaned back in his seat and stuck his hand out the window, surfing the Florida night. "She's gifted. And she's in trouble."

He wasn't referring to Ransom, although my powerhouse cousin, and my other neighbors at Dinkin's Bay Marina, Sanibel Island, Florida, are a gifted, eclectic bunch.

"Your friends are always in trouble," I said.

"Your female friends, anyway. Percentages suggest the problem is *you*, not them."

"Tula isn't a female. She's an adolescent girl," he replied. "There's a big difference. Tula's at that age—a magic age, man—when some girls seem to possess all the wisdom in the world. They're not screwed up by crazed hormones and menstrual periods. They exist, for the briefest of times, in a rarefied capsule of purity. The window is very, very narrow, of course. It's afterward that most women go a little nuts. Hell, let's be honest. All of them."

"Uh-huh," I said.

Tomlinson pressed, "I'm trying to give you the background so you understand what we're dealing with. This girl traveled three thousand miles on freight trains, riding in the backs of semis, to get to Florida. Hell, she even hiked across a chunk of Arizona desert. It's because she hasn't heard from her mother in almost three months. Her brother, two aunts and an uncle are somewhere in Florida, too, and she hasn't heard from them, either. Something's wrong. Tula came here to find out what."

I said, "An entire family goes off and leaves a girl alone in the mountains of Guatemala? Maybe they're not worth finding."

"One by one," Tomlinson replied, "whole villages migrate to the States. You know that. They watch television at some jungle *tienda*.

16

They see the fancy cars, the nice clothes. Meantime, they don't even have enough pesos to buy tortillas and beans. All the volcanic eruptions and mudslides the last few years in Guatemala, how do you deal with something like that? The coffee crop has gone to hell, too. Another revolution is brewing, and there's no work. What would you do if you lived there, and had a family to feed? That's what I meant when I said a person's luck—good or bad—begins with where they're born. Are you even listening to me?"

An instant later, the man's attention wandered, and he said, "Holy cripes, another Walgreens. If they keep piling up the concrete, building more condos, this whole damn peninsula is gonna sink. Just like Atlantis. It could happen."

I downshifted for a stoplight, and I turned and looked at Tomlinson, the odor of patchouli and his freshly opened beer not as penetrating as the magenta surfer's shirt he wore. "Not listening, huh? The girl is thirteen-year-old Tula Choimha from a mountain village northeast of Guatemala City, not far from the Mayan pyramids of Tikal. Did I pronounce her last name right?"

"Choom-HA," Tomlinson corrected, giving it an Asiatic inflection, which is not uncommon in the *Quiché* Mayan language. He spelled the name, then added, "Does it sound familiar? It should. Choimha is mentioned in *The Popol Vuh*. She's the goddess of falling water."

17

He was referring to a book of Mayan mythology, one of the few written records to survive the religious atrocities of the Conquistadors.

I thought, *Oh boy, here we go,* but I pressed ahead, saying, "Tula just turned thirteen, you told me. Her mother's first name is something unpronounceable, so she goes by Mary. Or Maria. Tula arrived in Florida about eight days ago, and you met her—you *said* you met her—by coincidence at a trailer park the owners are trying to condemn so they can build condos. She lives with five other people in a single-wide."

"Meeting her wasn't coincidental. I would never say coincidental, because I don't believe in—"

I interrupted again. "But you didn't tell me the whole truth, did you? You didn't say that, about once a month, you cruise the immigrant neighborhoods, buying grass or fresh peyote buttons. The illegals smuggle in peyote from Mexico because it's safer than carrying cash they probably don't have in the first place. You used to drive your VW, but lately you've been taking your electric bike. *What?* You think it makes what you're doing less obvious? Just the opposite, pal."

I waited, glancing at the rearview mirror until I saw the man's smile of concession, before I added, "See? I *was* listening."

Tomlinson disappeared into his own brain as I

drove west, his right hand still surfing the wind, his left fist cupping a can of Modelo. *Disappeared* is a fitting description. Tomlinson has spent so many nights alone, at sea, he says, that he has constructed the equivalent of cerebral theme parks in his head for entertainment. Books, religion, music, whole communal villages populated, presumably, with Jimi Hendrix and Hunter S. Thompson types. All probably landscaped with cannabis sculptures trimmed to resemble objects and creatures that I preferred not to imagine.

Tomlinson is a strange one, but a good one. His perception of reality has, over the years, been so consistently tinted by chemicals that, my guess is, he has reshaped reality into his own likeness. And it is probably a kinder, brighter reality than the one in which most of us function.

Tomlinson is among the most decent men I know—if you don't count sexual misconduct, which I am trying to learn not to do. He's brilliant and original, something I can say only about a handful of people, and I count him among my most trusted friends—again, his behavior with women excluded. He had come into my little marine lab earlier that day asking for help. And when a friend asks for help, you say yes and save the questions for later.

It was later. Almost ten p.m., according to the Chronofighter dive watch on my left wrist.

March is peak tourist season in Southwest Florida, so beach traffic was heavy, both lanes a bumper-car jumble of out-of-state license plates punctuated by roaring packs of Harleys.

After several minutes of silence, Tomlinson's attention swooped back into the cab of my truck, and he said, "This place we're going on San Carlos Island, the trailer park's named Red Citrus. It's not far from the shrimp docks. And, lately, it's become a bitch of a dark space, man. I should have warned you before we started."

I said, "The shrimp docks? That sounds close to your new restaurant."

Tomlinson, the hippie entrepreneur, had opened a rum bar and grille on Sanibel, and another at Fisherman's Wharf, near the shrimp yards, bayside, Fort Myers Beach. I was one of the investors, as was my cousin, Ransom, who also managed both places, along with her two boyfriends, Raynauld Bentley, a Cajun, and Big Dan Howes. So far, Tomlinson's business acumen had showed no damage from his years of chemical abuse, so it had been a wise thing to do.

It was one of life's amusing ironies. Tomlinson, who claims to have no interest in money or possessions, is gradually becoming wealthy, boosted along, perhaps, by his own fearless indifference to failure. I, on the other hand, remain steadfastly middle class *because* of my indifference—not counting a cache of small, valuable treasures I have acquired over the years.

Jade carvings and amulets. Spanish coins of gold and silver. All will remain faithfully hidden away, barring an emergency.

"The trailer park's on the same side of the bay," he replied, "but a couple miles farther east. That's why I used to like cruising Red Citrus, it was close enough. I could moor my boat near the bar and use my electric bike. In the last year or so, though, the whole vibe of the place has changed. The aura, it's smoky and gray now like a peat fire. It's the sort of place that consumes people's lives."

I replied, "Isn't that a tad dramatic?"

He asked, "You ever lived in a backwater trailer park? You've spent enough time in the banana republics to be *simpatico* with the immigrants who live there—that's one of the reasons I asked you to come along. People in that park work their asses off, man, six or seven days a week, picking citrus or doing construction or busing tables at some restaurant. Then they wire half the money—more sometimes—back to their families in Nicaragua or El Salvador or the mountain regions of Mexico. Hell, you know the places I'm talking about, man. These people are always fighting just to survive. That's why the girl deserves our help."

It was true, I am *simpatico*. "These people" included illegals on the run, as well as the

21

"shadow illegals," men and women with green cards and work permits—sometimes forged, sometimes not. They live peacefully and work hard in this country, unlike the drug-fueled minority that gives the rest of them a bad name.

I knew "these people" well because I spent years working in Central and South America before returning to Florida, where I opened a small research and marine specimen business, Sanibel Biological Supply.

The illegals of Central America and Mexico are, in my experience, a gifted people. Strong, tough, smart and family-oriented. All the components required of a successful primate society.

However, *simpatico* or not, I am also pragmatist enough to understand what too many Tomlinson types fail to perceive or admit. In a world made orderly by boundaries, an unregulated flow of aliens into any nation makes a mockery of immigration law. Why wait in line, why respect legal mandates, if cheaters are instantly rewarded with a lawful citizen's benefits?

It is also true, however (as I have admitted to Tomlinson), there is a Darwinian component that must be considered. People who are sufficiently brave, shrewd and tough enough to survive a dangerous border crossing demonstrate qualities by virtue of their success that make them an asset at any country, not a liability.

Long ago, though, I learned I cannot discuss such

matters with anyone who is absolutely certain of their political righteousness. So, instead, I listened.

"The undocumented workers have it tough, man," Tomlinson said, as he stared out the window. "They've got to watch their asses from every direction. The only thing they're more afraid of than the feds are their own landlords. Say the wrong word, don't jump when the boss man says jump, all it takes is one vicious phone call. And the dude who runs the trailer park is about as vicious as they come. He's a body-builder. A great big bundle of steroid rage, full of grits and ya'lls and redneck bullshit."

I baited my pal, saying, "You're the expert on better living through chemistry," as I slowed and studied the road ahead. We had crossed the small bridge onto San Carlos Island. I could see the pterodactyl scaffolding of shrimp boats moored side by side, floating on a petroleum sheen of black water and Van Gogh lights.

On my right were fish markets and charter boats. To my left, a jumble of signage competing for low-budget attention.

As Tomlinson told me, "Just past the gravel drive, take the next left," I spotted a faded wooden sign that read:

RED CITRUS MOBILE HOME PARK
RVS WELCOME!
VACANCY

"A vacancy in March?" I said, slowing to turn. "That tells me something. It's got to be the only place around with a vacancy this time of year."

Sitting up, paying attention now, Tomlinson said, "Doc, I left out a couple of important details. One is that Tula—she's a thought-shaper."

I shot him a look.

"Of course, to a degree, we all have the ability to shape people's thoughts. This girl, though, has powers beyond anything I've ever witnessed."

Thought-shaper. It was another of Tomlinson's wistful, mystic fantasies, and I knew better than to pursue it.

"The second is: People at Red Citrus call her *Tulo.* So just sort of play along, okay?"

I said, "The masculine form?"

"You know how damn dangerous it is for a girl to cross Mexico into the States. Tula wants people to think she's a boy. She's a thought-shaper, remember? And the young ones, the adolescent kids from Central America, have more to fear than most."

I turned, shifted into first and proceeded beneath coconut palms and pines, weaving our way through rows of aluminum cartons that constitute home for many of the one million illegals in the Sunshine State.

When my truck's lights flushed a couple of peacocks, I wasn't surprised. Exotic fowl are common in the low-rent enclaves where migrant workers have adapted to living under the radar.

They depend on exotic birds, not dogs, to sound a private alarm when outsiders arrive.

The cry of a peacock is high-pitched. It is a siren whine that morphs into a series of honks and whistles. That's what I thought I was hearing as I parked the truck and stepped out into the summer-cool night.

It was a cry so piercing that I paused, ears alert, before turning to Tomlinson, who was visible in the glow of a security light as he pushed the truck's door closed. His hair was tied back with a red bandanna, which he was retying as we exchanged looks.

The scream warbled . . . paused for a breath . . . then ascended. As if reading my mind, Tomlinson said, "That's not a bird! It's a person—a man, I think!" and then he sprinted toward the source of the sound.

I hesitated, reached behind the seat, then went running after him, struggling to slide a palm-sized Kahr semiautomatic pistol into the pocket of my jeans.

TWO

A FEW MINUTES BEFORE THIRTEEN-year-old Tula Choimha heard the screams for help, a huge man with muscles pushed through the trailer door, stepped into the bathroom, then stood for a moment, grinning at what he saw.

The man finally said, "Hah! I knew you was a girl! By God, I knew it the first time I saw your skinny little ass from behind! It was the way you walked."

He paused to stare, then added, "Fresh little peaches up top. Nothin' but peach fuzz down below."

Tula, sitting naked in the bathtub, looked where the man was looking, hoping, as always, to find a miracle. But there was only her own flat body to see.

The girl recognized the man. He was the *propietario* of this trailer park, maybe the owner, too. The man scared her. But the man's wife—or girlfriend, maybe—a woman with muscles and an evil face, scared her more.

Automatically, Tula used her hands to cover herself. But then she took her hands away.

The man had fog in his eyes—most people did—and Tula decided it was safer to be still, like a mirror, rather than behave like a frightened vessel that could be taken by force, then filled.

The man, whose name was Harris Squires, looked at her strangely for a moment. It was almost as if he recognized her face and was thinking back, trying to remember. Then he tilted his head and sniffed twice, nostrils searching. He was a man so large that he filled the bathroom space, his nose almost touching the low ceiling. Squires's nose was flat and wide, like a gorilla's, but he was the palest man Tula had ever seen. A man so white that his skin looked translucent, blue veins snaking out from beneath his muscle T-shirt and tight jeans.

"Know how else I knew you was a girl?" he asked. "I could *smell* you, darlin'. Man-oh-man" —his grin broadened, showing teeth so even that it was as if they had been filed—"I can wind-scent a virgin from seven counties away. What's the word for virgin in Spanish?"

Harris Squires didn't speak Spanish, although he'd learned a few phrases. But his girlfriend, Francisca Manchon—Frankie—spoke bits and pieces of it. She had taught him some things to say. Frankie called male Mexicans *chilies*, or greasers. Women were *chulas*. Harris didn't understand what the last term actually meant, but he guessed it wasn't very nice, knowing Frankie.

"*No entiendo,*" Tula said to Squires. But she did understand. English was her third language. Spanish was the second—and even most Mexicans were unaware that her people, the *Indígena* of Guatemala, grew up speaking Mayan.

Gradually, Tula had acquired Spanish in the marketplaces of Tikal and Guatemala City. English had been learned from nuns at the convent where she and her brother had lived ever since their father was murdered and their mother had been forced north, to the United States, to provide money.

That was four years ago.

Six months earlier, Tula's brother had come north looking for their mother. Now he had disappeared, too.

El Norte—it was the way they spoke of the States in the mountain villages. *El Norte* was always said with a mixture of hope and dread because, in the ancient religion of the Maya, north was the direction of death.

The man stepped closer. "What'd you just say?"

"*Yo no comprende*," Tula repeated, shrugging her shoulders, feeling the man's eyes on her like heat. Squires leaned in.

He asked, "What's on those necklaces you're wearing? They'd look real nice on Frankie."

She didn't respond, hoping he wouldn't make a grab for the jade amulet and the silver medallion she always wore on leather straps, day and night, no matter what.

Instead, the man reached and began massaging the back of Tula's neck with his fingers. The girl didn't flinch. Instead, she found the bar of soap and began to lather her feet, her movements masculine and intentional, her expressions sullen, like a child.

The man stood, his smile gone. "Bullshit! You speak damn good English, you little liar. You and

old man Carlson was spying on me last night, weren't you, goddamn it? You and your special buddy—I snuck back here a few nights ago and heard you two whispering. You was speaking pretty good English, so you can stop your lying right now."

Harold Carlson was one of the few *gringos* who lived in the trailer park. Tula trusted him because she trusted her instincts. Carlson, already an old man at sixty, was also a drunk, probably a paint sniffer judging from the half-moon darkness of his eyes.

But, as Tula knew, the depth of a man's decency could sometimes be judged by the depths of his own despair. People who were kind, after years of being wounded by their own kindness, naturally sought ways to dull the pain.

Carlson was her *patron*. After their first conversation, she had thought of him that way. He would help her, given the chance, because that is what a God-minded person would do. After only eight days in the States, Tula felt confident because she had already acquired two *patrons*.

Her second *patron* was a man as well. He was a strange one, named Tomlinson, who did not have fog in his eyes. Even though he resembled a scarecrow with his straw-bleached hair, Tomlinson was one of the few people Tula had ever met whose kindness glowed through gilded skin.

Tula continued lathering. She had seen what Squires had done last night, but Carlson, the old man, had not. Squires had gone to the bed of a rumbling truck, lights out, and dragged something malleable and heavy across the sand, then down the bank into a little mangrove lake that was surrounded by garbage dumpsters and palm trees.

The sack had sunk in a froth of bubbles, Squires watching, before he returned to the truck.

It was a human body, Tula guessed. Something weighted in a sack. Tula had seen enough corpses being dragged through the streets of her village to know. They were old people who had ended their lives in a gutter usually but sometimes a young man who had died from drinking too much *aguardiente*.

Also, Tula had been old enough during the last revolution to remember corpses drying among flies in the courtyard.

Her father's charred body had been among them.

Tula hadn't intended to spy on Harris Squires last night. She had been sitting in the limbs of a ficus tree, listening to owls speak. There were two big owls, one calling from nearby, the other answering from across the water where the strange boats with metal wings were tied side by side.

The shapes of the boats—their triangular

30

silhouettes—had reminded Tula of the jade amulet she wore around her neck. And also of small pyramids that were covered with vines in the lowlands west of Tikal. These were familiar stone places that the girl often climbed alone in darkness so that she could listen to the great owl voices converse while she stared, unblinking, at a jungle that strobed with fireflies.

The owl voices and the sparking fireflies invited visions into the girl's head. At the convent, Sister Maria Lionza had taught Tula about this phenomenon, and the nun was seldom wrong about such things. Tula had been living at the convent, under the nuns' guidance, learning the healing arts, and also studying the Bible along with her other lessons.

Sister Maria was a fierce woman given to fits of epilepsy and kindness, and she was particularly kind to Tula, who was her favorite.

"My brave little Maiden of Lorraine," Sister Maria was fond of saying. "Our blessed saint spoke of you in one of my visions. And now you are here with us. A messenger from God."

It was only within the last year that Tula had begun to suspect that Sister Maria was actually preparing her to join the nunnery and, perhaps, the *Culta de Shimono*. It was a secret group—a mythical cult, some said—that caused the villagers to cross themselves at night while whispering of wicked nuns who were actually *brujeriás*.

31

The English word for *bruja* was "witch."

Thanks to Sister Maria's secret teachings, Tula had experienced many visions in the last four years. The most disturbing vision had come into Tula's head three times—all within the last few months—so she knew the vision would come true if she didn't act.

In the vision, Tula could see large white hands choking her mother to death, fingers white around her soft throat. In the vision, Tula's mother was naked. She appeared diminished by her submissiveness, a fragile creature clinging to life, while the big hands suffocated the soul from her body.

It was a difficult vision to endure.

Now, because Tula had yet to answer him, Squires leaned a shoulder against the bathroom wall, getting mad, but nervous, too. Tula could read his eyes.

He said, "Tell me what you saw last night, you little brat! You *were* watching me, weren't you?"

Tula didn't react, but she was relieved. If Squires had known for sure that she had watched him struggling to drag a corpse into the water, he would have killed her. He wouldn't be standing here, asking questions.

Not that that meant he wouldn't anyway. Tula guessed that he would invent some excuse, drive her to a quiet place, then befoul her body, as men did to young girls, and kill her. Or . . . or

he would ask someone else to do it. Fog covered the man's eyes, but fog didn't cloud the truth that Tula sensed: Squires was capable of murder—his spirit was already stained with blood, she suspected—but he was also a weak man tainted by the ugliness of people close to him.

Squires's wife, Tula sensed, was a poisonous influence. She had seen the woman only twice, but that was enough. The man called her . . . Frankie? Yes. She was a tall woman with large muscles, but her spirit was withered by something dark inside. Frankie was a man-animal, Tula was convinced, who enjoyed feeding on the weakness of smaller humans.

This man, Squires, was the same in that way.

For the weak, silence is among the few weapons available. Tula was using silence against Harris Squires now.

Squires tried his bad Spanish, saying, "Hear me, *puta*!"

He said it twice, but it didn't cause the girl to look away from her toes, so he returned to English, his voice softer. "I saw you, *chula*—you *know* that. I saw you sitting alone in a tree like a little weirdo. And you saw *me*."

It was true. At first, Tula didn't believe Squires could see her, sitting among branches, listening to owls, but then she realized he could. The man, after dragging the sack to the water, had leaned into the rumbling truck, then stood, holding binoculars to his eye. They weren't normal binoculars, Tula realized, as the man turned in a circle, searching the area, and then suddenly stopped, leaning to focus on the small space she inhabited.

When the man had jogged toward her, yelling, "Who the hell are you? Stay right where you are!" Tula had dropped from the tree and run, vaulting roots, then a wire fence at the boundary of the trailer park property.

Last night, she'd slept curled up on the floor of a bathroom stall, and she had spent most of the day in hiding, too, expecting Squires to appear. Now here he was.

Yes, Squires had seen her. His binoculars allowed him to see in darkness, like a night creature. Tula had heard rumors of such devices from women who lived in widow villages, created by the government after the last revolution for wives who had lost their men. In such villages, they knew about war, and the behavior of drunken soldiers, yet it surprised Tula that a man like Squires would own such a device for he did not look like any soldier she had ever seen.

"Was Carlson with you?" Squires demanded. "You two are buddies, don't try to deny it. The little weasel has been begging me for your mama's phone number the last couple of days."

Tula moved her legs, using the washcloth to hide some parts of her but to reveal others.

For a moment, Squires's expression signaled slow confusion, then he shook it and said, "You know, I just might know where she's living. I bet she's got some pretty little peaches on her, too—I wouldn't mind helping you find the lady. You want that phone number? Play your cards right, *chula*, I'm the man who can give you everything you want and more."

Tula sensed that Squires was lying about knowing her mother, so she ignored him, dipped her face into the water and washed.

Her eyes were closed, but she could feel what was happening when Squires dropped to his knees. His hips were against the rim of the bathtub as he grabbed a fistful of her hair. Then the man pulled her head back, saying, "Answer me, you little brat!"

The girl opened her eyes and sat still, muscles relaxed, letting silence communicate what she wanted the man to hear. Tula waited until he finally took his hand off her.

Slowly, Squires got to his feet and backed away. "What the hell's wrong with you? You a retard or what? You don't look even a little bit afraid. By God, I'll teach you! Just like I'll teach your whore of a mama to jump, once I find her!"

Tula's head snapped around when she heard that. Her eyes found Squires's eyes, and she said, "Don't talk about my mother that way. You have no right!"

That caused the man to smile, taking his time now, because he had finally won this game of silence. "See there?" he drawled. "By God, you speak the language as good as me."

The girl said, "Why be so mean? If you know where my mother is, you should tell me. This is a chance for you to do God's work."

"*God's* work?" Squires said, rolling his eyes and laughing. "You're a damn comedian. You think I keep track of every Mexican spends a few nights in this park? Besides, what do I care? Unless . . ." He paused to give the girl a theatrical smile. "Unless you're willing to give me something in trade. That's the way the world works, sis. Otherwise, why should I bother?"

Squires didn't expect an answer, but he got one.

"Because God is watching us," Tula told the man, looking into his face. It took a moment, but his expression changed, which pleased the girl. "The goodness of God is in you," she continued. "Do you remember how you felt as a child, full of love and kindness? God is still there, alive in your heart. Why do you fight Him so?"

Squires made a groaning, impatient noise. "You got the personality of an old woman. Christ! Save your God-loves-me speeches for Sunday school."

She could feel his anger rising again, and she knew she had to do something because she had broken the silence that protected her. Perhaps she had ruined the spell she was attempting as well.

36

Tula folded the washcloth, put her hands on the rim of the tub and got to her feet, water dripping. As she did, she looked into the fog that covered the man's eyes.

The man was a foot and a half taller than her, two hundred pounds heavier, but her confidence was returning as she cupped the jade amulet and the medallion in her right hand.

Then, closing her eyes, speaking softly in English, Tula began repeating the phrase that had comforted her these last few weeks, three thousand miles riding atop freight trains, in the trailers of eighteen-wheelers, dodging *Federales* who would have jailed her and the coyote gangsters who could have robbed and raped her.

As if praying, she chanted, "I am not afraid. I was born to do this. I am not afraid. I was born to battle evil, to smite the devil down. I am not afraid. I was born to do this . . ."

They were the words of her patron saint, a powerful spirit who communicated to Tula through the medallion she wore. The saint had died as a young woman, burned at the stake, yet she still came to Tula, sometimes at night in the form of visions, and during the day as a voice that was strong in Tula's head. The voice seemed to come to Tula from distant stars and from across the sea, where, long ago, a brave girl had put her trust in God and changed the world.

If the Maiden could vanquish the English

37

from France, certainly, with the Maiden's help, Tula could now vanquish this mean, weak man from her bathroom.

As Tula prayed, Squires made a sour face. "You was born to do *what?* You was born to be a pain in the ass, that's what I think."

He could feel the heat rising, no longer seeing an adolescent girl standing naked before him but imagining her talking to police, telling them about what she'd seen him do last night.

Squires grabbed the girl's arm and gave her a shake. "Get your duds on. You want to see your mama? We'll get in my truck and go see her now."

The man was lying again. Tula knew it. She could picture herself in the man's vehicle, the two of them parked in some dark place where no one would hear her screams.

Tula switched to *Quiché* Mayan and continued chanting, "I was born to do this . . . I am not afraid . . . I was born to battle evil and smite the devil down . . . ," as the man shook her so hard that her head snapped back, and then said, "Now! Let's go! Stop your goddamn jabbering and—"

He didn't finish. Squires's words were interrupted by a wild, wailing scream, and he let go of the girl's arms.

The man turned toward the sound, listening, then said to Tula as he went to the door, "I ain't done with you, *chula*. Don't you go nowhere!"

The screams came from a person who was terrified and in pain, the voice unrecognizable. But Tula knew instantly who the person was—it was Carlson, the old drunk with the good heart. The girl didn't understand how she knew such things but she did.

Without toweling herself dry, Tula pulled on her jeans, a baggy T-shirt and stepped into her sandals. On the kitchen table, among mole sauce, sodden nachos and an ashtray, was a bottle of tequila. She grabbed the bottle, hesitated, found a flashlight, too, then stuffed a kitchen towel into the back of her pants and went running out the door.

Tula Choimha felt sure and determined, emulating the behavior of the Maiden, who spoke to her now from across the ages. The voice was strong in Tula's head, instructions from a teenage girl who had lived a life of fearless purity six hundred years ago.

The Maiden's voice told Tula to be quick, that she could save the life of her friend. And the girl obeyed, as she always did when under the loving direction of the Maiden of Lorraine.

Tula's patron saint—Joan of Arc.

THREE

FOCUSING ON THE CRIES FOR HELP, I ran after Tomlinson, not gaining on him, through an area that consisted of maybe forty trailers packed tight into an area bordered by a low wire fence. Beyond the fence was a mangrove lake, where a crowd was gathering. The lake was fringed with coconut palms and a row of garbage dumpsters.

The place had probably been a homey Midwestern retreat back in the seventies, popular with Buckeyes who caravanned south each winter. But now smoldering cooking fires and a sewage stink communicated the demographic change and a modern economic despair.

Over his shoulder, Tomlinson yelled to me, "There's someone in the water!" which I could already see. At first I thought we had stumbled onto a brawl, that the fight had tumbled into the pond.

But the man's screams didn't communicate rage. The sounds he made signaled terror, an alarm frequency that registers in the spine, not the brain. His howling pierced the gabble of men and women who were peeking from their trailers, yelling questions and expletives in Spanish, as a dozen or so of the braver residents

—several of them children—ventured as a group, not running, toward the water's edge.

In his poor Spanish, Tomlinson yelled, "What's wrong? What's happening?" as I ran past him, hollering in English, "Call nine-one-one. It's a gator. A big one," because I could see details now in the pearl haze of security poles that rimmed the park.

I could see the alligator's tail, slashing water, an animated grayness edged with bony scutes that had not evolved since the days of stegosaurus. I could see the flailing arms of a man as he battled to stay above the surface of the water.

A likely scenario flashed into my mind: The man had stopped on the bank to urinate, or stare at what might have been a floating log—no one in their right mind would go for a swim in that cesspool—and the gator had snatched him.

It happens—not often in Florida—but it happens, and it had happened to a friend of mine only a few years before on Sanibel Island, where I live and run my small marine-specimen supply company. A good woman named Janie Melsek had been attacked while pruning bushes and she had died even though she had fought to the end, just as the man was fighting now. Even though in shock maybe he sensed that if the gator took him under, he would never surface again.

I hadn't been there when a twelve-foot gator took Janie into the water. I hadn't seen what had happened in the following minutes of terror. And things probably wouldn't have turned out any differently if I had. But maybe, just maybe, it was the memory of Janie that caused me to push through the slow phalanx of onlookers, as I jettisoned billfold, cell phone, then pulled the Kahr pistol from my pocket and lunged feetfirst into the water, unprepared for the knee-deep sludge beneath.

Jumping into the lake was like dropping into a vat of glue. My ankles were anchored instantly in muck, so my momentum caused me to slam forward, bent at the waist, face submerged, until I floundered to the surface and fought my way back to vertical.

The man was near the middle of the lake, only thirty yards away, screaming, "Help me! Grab my hand, I'm dying!" so maybe he'd gotten a look at me as I pried one slow right leg from the mud, losing my shoe, and then struggled to pull my left foot free. To do it, I needed both hands, so I pocketed the pistol and went to work trying to break the suction.

Behind me, someone had a flashlight, and he painted the pond until he found the alligator. I'd been right. It was a big one: four or five hundred pounds of reptile on a feed, creating a froth of lichens and trash that washed past me in waves.

It was a male. Had to be. Female gators seldom grow beyond ten feet and two hundred pounds.

The animal had its back arched, head high, and I could see that it had a frail-sized man crossways in its jaws, the man's buttocks and pelvis locked between rows of teeth that angled into a reptilian grin.

The alligator's eyes glowed ember orange; the man's face was a flag of white, and, for an instant, his eyes locked onto mine just before the animal slung its tail and rolled, taking him under, then bringing him back to the surface, the animal's eyes not so bright now because the angle had changed but the man still sideways in the thing's mouth.

Because the gator had him by the hips, the roll—a death roll, gator hunters call it—had not snapped his spine.

"*Please.* Take my hand!" The man coughed the words, stretching his arm toward me, his voice pleading as if trying to convince me it would be okay.

I wasn't convinced. I am neither stupid nor particularly brave. But I also know enough about animal behavior to feel sure that I wasn't being mindlessly heroic. There are certain predators—alligators, sharks and killer bees among them—that, once their sensory apparatus has locked onto a specific target, ancillary targets cease to exist.

I have swam at night among feeding sharks so

fixated on a whale carcass that my dive partners and I had nothing to fear. I once watched an Australian croc wrestle a feral hog into the water while an infant blackbuck antelope—a much easier target—drank peacefully within easy reach.

This alligator might worry that I wanted to steal the meal it had taken. But it wouldn't abandon a meal in its teeth to waste its time attacking me, additional prey.

I hoped.

I ducked beneath the water, dug at the muck until my left shoe popped free and then I surfaced as someone belly flopped into the pond next to me and began thrashing the water, racing toward the gator.

It was Tomlinson.

I pushed off after him, swimming hard, my head up, focusing on the bright, blurry horror ahead. I passed my friend after only a few strokes, watching as the gator turned and began ruddering toward the far shore.

The man's screams became whistled sobs, similar in pitch to the trumpeting of nearby peacocks, dark shapes that dropped from bushes and sprinted toward the shadows. Behind me, I heard a woman yell in Spanish, "Call for help, someone call the police!" but then heard a male voice hush the woman, saying, "Are you insane? Not the police!"

The gator appeared to be in no hurry now. The

animal knew we were in the water—gators possess acute hearing and the night vision of owls—but it didn't seem to care. Even so, it traveled deceptively fast over the bottom, and I was halfway across the lake before I was finally close to enough to make a grab for the thing. Before I did, I rolled onto my side long enough to find the pistol.

I took a couple of more strokes to catch up and then lunged to get what I hoped was a solid grip on the animal's tail. I expected the gator to slash its head toward me, a hardwired crocodilian response. For a few seconds, though, the thing continued swimming, pulling me along—me, an insignificant weight—but then its slow reptilian brain translated the information, and the animal exploded, its tail almost snapping my arm from the socket.

Because I expected the gator to swing its jaws toward me, I ducked beneath the surface, feeling a clawed foot graze my ear. I sculled deeper until my toes touched bottom, took a look toward the surface—it was like being submerged in tar—then swam a couple of yards underwater before angling up, hoping I didn't guess wrong and reappear within reach of the animal's teeth.

I didn't. Instead, I collided with something bony and breathing as I surfaced. The gator's belly, I thought at first. But then I heard a wailing profanity—the voice familiar—and realized I had banged into Tomlinson, who assumed he was being attacked from beneath.

My friend, I could see, had both hands locked on the gator's tail and was being dragged. The animal was swimming faster now, probably convinced we were competing gators, employing harassment, hoping it would drop its prey. It's a common gambit in the animal world, so the thing was trying to get into shallow water before dealing with us.

As I started swimming after them, I heard Tomlinson yell a garbled sentence, words that sounded like "You just scared the piss out of me! Do something, Doc!"

I planned to do something, even though I had no plan. I considered risking a shot at the animal's flank, but there were too many people around, and the slug would skip if it hit the water. No . . . I had to get closer.

It took longer than expected. Despite the gator carrying a man in its jaws and a second man clinging to its tail, I still had trouble catching the animal because I was palming the pistol in my right hand. A pound of polymer and steel is not an efficient fin.

Finally, though, I was close enough to throw my left arm over the animal's back, which wasn't easy because the creature was twice my size. The gator bucked its head at me in warning, its hard belly spasmed, but it kept going. I felt around until I had what I thought was a good grip on the far ridge of scutes, hoping the thing would continue swimming long enough for me to get my right hand up. Next, I would position the pistol flat against the bony ridge behind the gator's right eye.

Alligators have tiny brains, little more than a bulbous junction of nerve cells. However, their heads and jaws are also covered with thousands of bead-sized nodules that serve as remarkably sensitive pressure detectors. That's why a gator can sense a lapping dog, or the splash of a child, from a hundred yards away. Even if the bullet missed the brain, the shock might cause the animal to release its prey and dive or swim for safety.

As I pushed the pistol barrel hard against the gator's head, though, the thing rolled again. I was on the animal's right side. It slapped its tail and rolled to the left. The movement was as abrupt as the slamming of a steel trap, and I was vaulted over the animal, into the air, and lost my grip as I hit the water.

When I surfaced, I had no idea where Tomlinson was. But I knew the gator still had its prey because I could hear the man coughing water and I could see his dangling legs only a yard away in the flashlight's beam.

I had come up just behind and to the left of the gator's snout. Close enough to see the animal's bulging right eye, its pupil dilated within gelatinous tissue that cast an orange glow.

The gator saw me. No doubt about it, and I wasn't surprised when the thing slowed and swung toward me, opening its jaws, then slinging its head to release its prey, now fixated on me. It had been harassed enough. In the animal's mind, I was attempting to steal its meal. It had decided to fight.

I grabbed the man's leg with my left hand and pulled, trying to help him roll free but also using the resistance to lever myself close enough to throw my right arm over the animal's back. The gator shook its head again, maybe having difficulty tearing its teeth from the man's clothing, which provided me with the extra second I needed to get a grip on the reptilian neck with my left hand.

As its tail hammered the water, spinning toward me, I wrestled myself atop the gator long enough to steady the pistol barrel flush behind its right eye. My hold was tenuous, the positioning wasn't perfect, but I was adrenaline-buzzed and scared. I didn't hesitate. I fired two quick shots, the report of the pistol heavy and flat, muffled by the animal's keratin skin.

There was a convulsive, watery explosion that threw me backward. When I surfaced, the gator's tail was vertical, slashing the air like a wrecking crane, and I had to scull backward to keep from

being hit. A moment later, the animal rolle
the surface, still thrashing, and then submei
abruptly in a boil of bubbles and muddy detr
from the bottom.

I wasn't sure if I'd killed the thing or n
Alligators sink when dead, but they also su
merge if they're wounded or feel threatened.
the bullets had done only minor damage, the
the gator could be drifting to the bottom righ
now, tracking my vibrations as it regrouped.
didn't relish the possibility. To me, a known
quantity, however perilous the situation, is much
preferred to a vague unknown.

As I turned to search for Tomlinson, I hollered,
"Where is he? Did he go under?" meaning the
injured man.

I received an answer in the form of another
scream. It was a shredded plea in English, the
frail man hollering, "Help me! The animal has
me again!"

I pivoted toward the sound and started swimming.

FOUR

WHEN HARRIS SQUIRES PUSHED
through the crowd of little brown people and
realized what was happening, he grinned,
thinking, *Awesome!*

Because of his girlfriend, Frankie, it had been a rotten week. But seeing what he was seeing now made him feel hopeful. Two nights before, while shooting a homemade skin flick, the idiot Mexican girl with them had taken too much Ecstasy and stopped breathing just like that. There was no one around but them, thank God, but it wasn't until the next morning when Squires finally sobered up that even he had to admit the girl wasn't going to start breathing again. Meaning she was dead.

That was bad enough, but it got worse. The girl was a prostitute who belonged to a Mexican gangbanger named Laziro Victorino. Victorino was what the illegals called a coyote, meaning that for a price he would lead groups across the border into the States, then find them jobs, too —but for a percentage of their pay, which he collected weekly.

Victorino—V-man, his gangbanger soldiers called him—was a wiry little guy but a serious badass who carried a box cutter on his belt and had a teardrop tattoo beneath his left eye, along with a bunch of other gangbanger tats on his arms and back.

Squires was aware that the V-man had made a few films of his own, him and his boys. Snuff films. Kill a man or woman—or just torture them —and get it all on their iPhone video cameras.

Frankie had chided Squires, saying, "Why you

50

worried about some midget Mexican? You're twice that greaser's size. Besides, he's got some new girl with him every time he comes through here. He probably won't even notice she's gone."

Squires doubted that but didn't want to piss off Frankie by voicing his opinion. So he told her he'd never played a role in killing anyone before. And he didn't want to get in the habit of doing it.

That wasn't exactly true, although Frankie didn't know it. No one knew, and sometimes even Squires wasn't convinced it had happened.

Once, only once, alone with a pretty Mexican woman, Squires, naked, had taken the *chula* from behind, lulling her body into a thrashing silence, his hands around her throat, his body finishing and the *chula*'s life ending at a precise, constricting intersection that was euphoric beyond any physical sensation Squires had ever experienced.

He had been too drunk to remember details, though. And by the time he had sobered, the woman's body was already gone—into the lake near his hunting camp trailer, he guessed later— so it was as if he had imagined the whole damn thing.

But it had happened. The event—that explosive physical rush, a sensation of ultimate power— had rooted itself in Squires's brain. Occasionally, the memory flooded him with a horrifying guilt, which he mitigated by telling himself that it had only been a dream.

When he was blood-drunk on steroids, though, the roots of that memory propagated in the man's head. They snaked deeper into his brain, germinating into a fantasy that had become an obsession.

If he ever got the opportunity, if he ever got just the right girl alone, Squires would make that dream happen again.

Frankie had laughed when he had balked. "We've got nothing to feel guilty about. The stupid little whore did it to herself. It's one less stupid *chula* in the world. Good riddance. No one's gonna miss her and no one's gonna care. Now, do me a favor, clean up around here 'cause I've got that appointment in Orlando tomorrow. Make sure she's gone by morning—and you'd better never goddamn mention it again."

Which meant that Frankie was leaving the dirty work to him. That's just the way the woman was, and Squires had to wonder sometimes if Frankie's love of crazy, wild-sex kinkiness was really worth all her crazy, wild-bitch meanness.

For the first couple of years, it had been a toss-up. But now Harris was tired of the woman —a little frightened of her, too—and he was looking for a way out.

The reason had to do with something else

Squires had been wondering about: How had he gotten himself trapped into a relationship with a woman who reminded him more and more of his abusive, bullying mother?

Like his mother, Frankie had a nasty streak in her, particularly when it came to other women. Because of this, it was sometimes hard to tell if some of the things Frankie did were accidental or intentional. For instance, it wasn't exactly true that the Mexican girl had overdosed herself. Frankie had done it.

Frankie had dropped extra Ecstasy tablets into the girl's drink, doubling the dose she usually used when they happened to pick up a Mexican *chula* who was camera-shy and needed some loosening up.

This particular girl was unusually cute, with a sleek, sensuous body. When Frankie's hands were on a girl like that, her face flushed. Her body shook. It was a response that was part passion, part jealousy. It was like she never wanted to let the girl go. So maybe Frankie had decided to keep the *chula* by dropping in those extra tabs.

To Squires, it made what had happened seem less of a crime, the fact that a woman had done it to another woman. But that didn't stop him from going almost crazy with panic when he finally realized the girl was dead. Maybe he had killed that Mexican girl or maybe it was all a dream, but he'd never had to deal with a dead body before. Not sober, anyway.

They had a corpse on their hands. And they had to get rid of the thing without the Mexican gang leader, or the cops, finding out.

Not they, actually. *Him*. Frankie, who was sixteen years older than Squires, and a lot more experienced, would have nothing to do with getting rid of a dead body.

It wasn't the first time that something like this had happened while Squires was around, but it was the first time a girl had ended up dead instead of puking her guts out while Squires tended to her.

That's what really pissed him off when Squires took time to give the subject some thought. When would he learn not to leave Frankie alone with girls that were younger and prettier than her? And even if the stupid *chula* had done it to herself, who was going to believe it?

No one, that's who. Not with at least one eye-witness, maybe two, who had seen him drag the girl's body into the lake.

Now, though, Squires's future seemed to be improving, judging from what he could hear and see, out there on the lake, which was that Fifi had snatched one of the eyewitnesses, old man Carlson, into the water.

Fifi. That was the name of the twelve-foot gator that he and some buddies had trucked in from his hunting camp, east of Immokalee, way back off County Road 858.

Squires could see it happening and he liked what he saw.

The gator had that nosy little turd in her jaws and now looked like she was swimming him back to some dark hole where she could drown him. That's what gators like Fifi did. The ol' girl would probably leave the mouthy asshole underwater to tenderize a bit before finally chowing down.

No way could the cops blame Squires for something an animal did. It was perfect.

Squires wasn't sure if Carlson had in fact been an eyewitness, but, if he was, Fifi was now providing the solution. It had been a smart thing to move the gator here, where she could harass the Mexicans instead of the hunting dogs they sometimes used at his camp.

Squires's hunting camp—well, actually, the property belonged to his mother—was a big place, four hundred acres of cypress trees and saw grass that opened into flats of oaks and pines where feral hogs liked to feed. And where sometimes they'd kill deer and an occasional bear, too.

Once, in that same area, Harris had gotten a clear shot at a panther, but he'd missed.

Harris Squires loved that hunting camp as much as he hated tending his mother's three crappy little RV parks, this one, Red Citrus, being the only one even slightly fun. Red Citrus, at least, had girl tenants who weren't redneck hags with silver hair, big asses and little old titties shriveled like raisins on a vine. Brown girls, true, but at least they were young.

In Squires's mind, the younger the girl, the better—not something he would've admitted to Frankie, who was now in her forties—like the weird little *chula* who'd been pretending to be a boy and called herself Tulo. What was she, twelve, maybe thirteen years old? He'd been pretty down the last couple of days, but surprising "Tulo" in the bathtub had lifted his spirits.

Until that moment, Squires had been confused about how to handle the situation. Seeing the girl's body, though, all water slick and smooth, had changed that. It caused his secret fantasy to bloom bright in his mind.

He'd drive her to the hunting camp and show her around. Just him, alone. At the hunting camp, there'd be no one around to hear or see what he did. Not on a Tuesday night. It was a comfortable spot, private, with a big RV braced up on cinder blocks, generators, a cookshack, a shower and a wide-screen TV for video games and porn. A perfect place for a guy like him to make his fantasy come true with a little wettail.

Wettails, that's what Squires called them. He and Frankie had entertained a bunch of them out there at the camp, which was really more a second home than a camp. The place was comfortable enough to be fun but still wild enough for an ol' boy to get away, spread his wings and do just about any crazy thing he wanted without worrying about some cop or asshole ranger cruising by, asking questions.

Harris Squires hated nosy people. Do-gooders. If he and Frankie wanted to have some fun with a few young wettails, what harm were they doing? But try explaining that to a goddamn do-gooder.

Carlson was a prime example. Now Carlson was getting exactly what the little turd deserved.

Squires nudged a couple of short people out of the way as he edged closer to the lake. He could hear what was happening—Carlson screaming his lungs out, begging for help. It wasn't easy to make out details, though, because the mangrove pond was on the other side of the fence, in shadows cast by palm trees beyond the haze of security lights.

It made him wish he had his night vision binoculars. Those bad boys would've made everything bright as day, but they were behind the seat of his Ford Roush pickup, along with some other gear he usually carried: duct tape, an ax handle, handcuffs, condoms and sometimes a .357 Ruger Blackhawk when he wasn't carrying the gun in the glove box.

The handcuffs was something he carried for Frankie. The woman was crazy for bondage.

Squires turned toward the trailers, seeing kids' bicycles and rusting trucks, now seeing Tula push open her trailer door, then running toward him, carrying something in her hand. Squires squinted to see a . . . bottle of liquor?

What the hell?

Yep, she was carrying a damn bottle of tequila. Well, no one ever claimed that Mexicans were smart. But then he also saw that she was carrying a flashlight, which was exactly what he needed, so he yelled to her, "Over here! Bring me that damn light so we can see what's going on!"

The girl looked in his direction but ignored him. Because of that, Squires was about to yell something else, but that's when a big white guy came dodging through the crowd, speaking in Spanish, saying something that might have been, *"Excuse me, sorry. Let me pass."*

Definitely being polite, as the guy hurried to the lake's edge, kicking off shoes, shirt, then tossing his wallet and cell phone onto the ground before he jumped into the water. A second later, another white guy appeared. He was a skinny scarecrow of a hippie who was doing the same thing, stripping to go in the water.

What the hell were these two white dudes doing at Red Citrus?

Squires yelled to the hippie, "Hey . . . you!

58

What the hell you think you're doing?" but the hippie was busy pulling off his shirt and talking into his cell phone at the same time, before he dropped the phone on the ground, next to his wallet, and then he went into the water, too, but on his belly.

Using his cell phone? The asshole had probably just called 911.

Shit! This was all Squires needed. Fifi was in the process of solving a serious problem, but now here were a couple of solid-looking white citizens messing in his business.

Squires spat, "Goddamn do-gooders!" as he headed after the flashlight Tula was holding, pushing people out of the way.

A **moment later,** speaking into the hippie's cell phone, Squires was telling the 911 operator, "That's right, cancel the emergency, ma'am. We made a mistake here on our end. I know, I know . . . it's not the first time."

He'd checked PREVIOUS CALLS. When he'd seen 911, he knew he had to do something to stop the cops from showing up.

But then Squires had to whisper "Damn it" as he covered the phone so the operator wouldn't hear Carlson screaming across the water to the big white guy, yelling, "Help me! Take my hand!"

"Sir?" the operator said, raising her voice, "Who's yelling in the background?"

"Ma'am," Squires told her, being sweet, "I understand what you're asking. And at first we thought someone was in trouble. But, turns out, it's just a bunch of Mexican kids playing games. You know how girls squeal when they're running round, playing games at night?"

The woman asked, "Did you place the call? Is your name Tomlinson?"

Squires hesitated, aware that it was sometimes a mistake to lie to the cops before thinking it over. "Yep, that's my name," he said finally.

The operator told him, "We've already dispatched units to that address. Dispatched it to . . . to a Red Citrus RV Park, Guava Street, just off San Carlos Boulevard. That's near Fort Myers Beach, correct?"

Squires was getting nervous and impatient. He covered the phone and yanked the flashlight out of the weird little Bible freak's hand because she kept turning the beam toward the water, where there was now a lot of splashing and swearing going on.

"Damn it," he whispered to the girl, "pay attention!" as the operator asked him again, "Did you hear me? Is that the correct address, sir?"

Squires kept his voice pleasant and easy as he replied, "Well, if you reckon your people need to practice answering ambulance calls, ma'am, there's nothing I can do to stop 'em. I just wanted you to know this one is a false alarm. Everything's just fine here. Our folks are having lots of fun—it's a sort of party going on. So I guess I'm gonna have to apologize to your people again when they show up here for no reason."

The operator asked a couple more questions before Squires covered one ear, listening, until he suspected that the woman was convinced and had canceled the 911 call, no matter what she claimed. Then he hung up, as he swung the light toward the water, wanting to confirm the gator still had Carlson.

Fifi still had the guy, all right. But Squires could see the big white guy was swimming hard to catch up, which caused him to wonder, *Who the hell is that crazy son of a bitch?*

Well . . . there was an easy way to find out.

From the hippie's billfold, Squires removed a wad of cash. It looked like a bunch of crisp twenties. He stuffed the money into his jeans, then retrieved the big guy's billfold. There wasn't nearly as much cash in it but enough. Yep, these two dudes were solid working citizens —plus, there were some other interesting things to see in this second billfold.

Squires's eyes shifted from the pond to what he was holding. He used the flashlight to go through credit cards, business cards and IDs that showed a nerdy-looking guy with a jaw and glasses.

Marion D. Ford, Ph.D.
Sanibel Biological Supply
Dinkin's Bay Marina

Marion. What kind of name was that for a man?

The guy was a damn scientist or something, apparently. What the hell was a scientist doing at a trailer park full of *chilies* and wettails? Squires put one of the man's business cards into his back pocket before he went through the other stuff, paying special attention to a couple of unusual IDs.

Yeah, the dude was a scientist, but there was some other stuff that worried Squires. Could be the asshole worked for the feds, too, because one of the IDs gave this guy, Marion Ford, unlimited access to something called the Special Operations Center at MacDill Air Base in Tampa.

What the hell was that about?

And there was another plastic ID for a military base in Cartagena, Colombia. But that one was mostly in Spanish, so there was no telling what it meant.

The dude, Ford, Squires guessed, must be some small-time scientist who worked for the feds. But he wasn't really in the military—not according to what Squires was looking at in the billfold, anyway. Just maybe hired by the military, for some reason or another.

Could that mean the hippie and the nerd were actually with the Department of Immigration? Squires gave himself a few seconds to think about it. At first, that made some sense to him. Why else would they come snooping around a trailer park ass-deep in *chilies* and *chulas*?

But then Squires got a sinking feeling. What if the two dudes were actually with the DEA instead? What if they had come here trying to set up some kind of drug bust on the small steroid operation Squires was operating?

Squires whispered "Son of a bitch" as he glanced toward the pond, where he could see the gator rolling in a spray of water, and he thought, *Eat that bastard, Fifi! Kill them both!*

Squires was pretty sure he had seen the hippie, Tomlinson, before, cruising around the park in some shitty old Volkswagen that had to be twenty years old. Sometimes a girlish-looking electric bike, too. Which wasn't that unusual. Dopers often cruised the parks because they knew that the *chilies* arrived from Mexico carrying baggies of weed or peyote buds in their pants instead of cash.

Hell, Squires had bought grass from them himself, although, more often, he just took the shit when he wanted it. Sometimes, he'd yank a guy up by the ankles and shake him, like shaking quarters out of an old pair of jeans. What the hell could a Mexican do about it? Call the cops?

That was one of the good things about managing a place like Red Citrus. No one on the whole goddamn property wanted the cops around, especially Squires and Frankie, so that made it a safe place to be. Which is why, in their newest double-wide trailer, Squires had set up a smaller version of the cookshack they had out there at the hunting camp. It wasn't the sort of cook-shack where he actually cooked food. What he cooked up was home-brewed steroid gear like testosterone enanthate, and equine—which was a horse steroid called EQ—plus winstrol and deca-durabolin.

"Gear" was bodybuilder slang for steroids, almost always purchased illegally.

Squires had become good at rendering high-grade veterinarian powders into injectable muscle juice. The kitchen was well supplied with Whatman sterile filters, 20-gauge needles, sesame oil, benzyl benzoate and everything else needed to produce a first-class product.

Squires had started small, producing just enough gear for himself and Frankie, who had, at one time, been one of the top female body-builders in the country. Then he began to sell to a few guys he trusted, and that's how they got started.

It was Frankie who noticed how fast the cash was piling up just from selling to friends. So the two of them had expanded the operation, thinking they could make more money dealing gear than they could ever make running his mother's shitty trailer parks or teaching yoga classes, which Frankie sometimes did. They bought vials by the gross. They bought two vacuum machines and a label maker, too.

Turned out, they were right about making money.

Dopers thought a fresh peyote button was expensive? Ask a bodybuilder about the price of a vial of Masteron or high-grade Testosterone-E. Frankie could walk into any gym in South Florida where muscle freaks congregated and make an EQ horsey whinnying noise and that would bring them running.

Juicers knew exactly what the lady was carrying in her gym bag and they were damn eager to buy. Because of the feds, dependable gear was so goddamn hard to get, Squires and Frankie were now making a small fortune, all in cash, selling their home-brewed goodies in kits, complete with pins and syringes if that's what the bros wanted.

Their little organization was becoming so well known, and their products so trusted, that gym rats in South Florida had come up with a nickname for the stuff. They called it Gator Juice. As in, "You tried the Gator Juice Tren? Or the Gator Juice A-bombs? Gator Juice is goddamn grade-A shit. Good to go, man. As in *G-two-G*."

Squires's eyes kept swinging from Ford's billfold to the drama taking place out there on the lake. A couple of *chilies* had come through the crowd carrying a big military-type light called a Golight, so Squires pocketed the scientist's cash, then handed both billfolds to one of the *chilies*, saying to him, "Hang on to these, will ya, *amigo*? Now, give me that goddamn light."

With the Golight, Squires could see that it was getting interesting out there on the water where Ford was doing something that would've been hard to believe if it wasn't actually happening. Ford had his left arm slung over the gator's back while Fifi struggled to swim, still carrying Carlson sideways in her mouth. What Ford was trying to do, Squires realized, was climb onto the gator's back.

Un-by-God-believable!

Into Squires's mind came the image of the big Australian, the crocodile hunter guy who he used to like to watch on TV, which made what was happening easier to comprehend. But once the scientist got onto the gator's back, then what?

Squires placed the big spotlight on his shoulder to steady the thing, then leaned to focus the beam on something the scientist had in his hand.

What the hell was the dude carrying?

A hammer, maybe, that's what it looked like. No . . . not a hammer. It looked like Ford was trying to steady an itty-bitty pocket pistol behind one of Fifi's eyes—which was a stupid goddamn thing to try. At least, Squires hoped it was a stupid goddamn thing to try.

Suddenly, he could feel that sickening feeling in his stomach again, worried the crazy do-gooder was going to find a way to free Carlson and screw up the only good luck Squires had had in a week. But it was pointless, what the guy was trying to do . . . *wasn't it*?

Squires hoped it was true. There was no pussy pistol in the world with enough stopping power to . . .

WHAP-WHAP!

Squires jumped when he heard the gunshots. Then he stood straight, realizing that the man had managed to get a couple of rounds off.

Behind him, the crowd made a collective *Ooohing* noise as they watched the alligator's tail slam sideways, then tilt upward like a crane. The tail stood there for an instant, before the big animal rolled and then sank from sight.

Shit! Where was Carlson?

Squires fanned the light back and forth, searching. Maybe the nosy old turd had gone down with the gator. No . . . no such luck. Carlson was still out there, floundering to stay on the surface while the hippie swam toward him.

Sons a bitches!

Squires felt an acidic surge move from his abdomen toward his head, the signal that he was becoming seriously pissed off. It was a steroid charge that he had experienced many times but seldom as strong as tonight—which would have made sense, if he'd stopped to think about it. Tuesdays and Saturdays were Squires's pin days—"pinning" being bodybuilder talk for steroid injections.

That morning, he had flooded two syringes with testosterone, equipoise, trenbolone and decanoate—all oil-based, veterinarian-strength gear—and injected it into his thighs, but only after heating the oil under a hot spigot to make the sticks faster and less painful.

As a special treat—because it had been such a shitty two days—he had also eaten five tabs of dianabol, a hundred milligrams.

D-bombs, man—nothing else hit Squires quite as hard as dianabol, although he preferred the injectable version. Juice was easier on the liver than pills. But he was out of D-bomb oil until he made his next trip to the hunting camp.

Squires lived for that full-on testosterone buzz. He loved the evening of a pin day, when his blood levels were so hormone drunk that he could track the oil moving through his veins like heat. It caused his muscles to twitch and swell beneath his skin, the fibers feeding so furiously on hormone soup that Squires could feel the mass of his body changing.

"You got your monster face on tonight," Frankie

would sometimes say to him as they elbowed for space before their weight-room mirror, Frankie usually posing naked, but Squires wearing a thong because steroid gear shrunk his nuts so small it was embarrassing.

"I love it," the woman would tell him, "when you got your monster face on."

Because of the D-bombs, and because of what was happening, Harris Squires had his monster face on now.

He paused long enough to kick one of the cell phones toward the water, hoping it belonged to the guy named Ford—the damn do-gooder dude who'd just shot his alligator, Fifi. Then Squires batted a couple of *chilies* out of his way, as he began to pace, still carrying the spotlight, waiting for the bastard to make it to shore—if he ever did.

As Harris Squires knew from years of hunting the Glades, big alligators died hard.

FIVE

WHEN I HEARD THE FAMILIAR VOICE yell, "Doc! Help me get this guy in!" I spun around to see Tomlinson's silhouette only a few yards away, but that's all I could see because someone onshore was blinding me with a powerful spotlight.

69

I waved my hand and yelled in Spanish, "Get that thing out of my eyes!"

But nothing happened. So I yelled louder, in English, adding, "You dumbass!" for emphasis.

For an instant, the light swung skyward, and I could see that Tomlinson had the injured man in a cross-chest carry, trying to swim him to shore. He was having trouble, though, because the guy was fighting him, swinging his fists, trying to get a solid elbow into my friend's face. The man apparently thought the alligator still had him.

There was no telling how badly the guy was hurt, but he was obviously in shock. I swam closer, my head up, got a hand under the man's arm and pulled his ear close to my lips, yelling in Spanish, "You're safe! Stop fighting!"

I repeated it several times before his head rolled toward me, eyes wide, and he whispered, in English, "Am I dreaming this? Am I dead? This is a terrible dream if I'm not dead."

Yes, he was in shock . . . a small man with a gaunt drunkard's face that was a saprophytic gray in the glow of security lights. His voice was incongruous—he spoke with the rounded vowels of a Virginia gentleman.

I asked him, "What's your name?"

He continued babbling, telling me, "I don't know what happened! I walked down to look at something floating in the water. Next thing I know, something was dragging me in . . . like it

70

was trying to squeeze the guts out of me. I heard something snap . . . something way inside my body."

The man looked at me, eyes blinking, and I heard what he must have sounded like as a child when he asked, "Am I badly hurt? I don't want to die, I really don't."

I replied, "Lay back. Get some air in your lungs. We're taking you to shore." I could see there was an open slash on the man's forearm, and his legs looked as dead as wood, the way they floated on the surface.

As Tomlinson positioned himself to support the man's other arm, he asked me, "Did you kill it?" meaning the alligator, and I could tell he hoped I hadn't hurt the thing.

"Let's get out of here before we catch a damn disease," I told him. "Start swimming, I'll keep his head up."

Truth was, I still didn't know if the gator was dead. Judging from the way the animal's tail had periscoped to the surface, at least one of the bullets had done damage to the neuro system.

Either way, a wounded gator was the least of my worries. The most dangerous animals in Florida's backwaters aren't reptiles. They aren't amphibians or fish. I was more concerned about microscopic animals that, as I knew too well, thrived in stagnant lakes like the one we were in.

The injured man might survive the wounds the gator had inflicted only to die from bacteria that lived in the animal's mouth. Or from a single-celled protozoan that all the commotion had kicked free from the muck below.

The injured man wasn't the only one at risk—Tomlinson and I were in danger, too. There are varieties of single-celled animals that don't need an open wound to slip through a primate's skin armor. The amoeba *Naegleria* can travel through a man's nostrils, into the brain and cause an encephalitis that is deadly. It's rare, but I knew from my professional journals that this same microscopic animal had killed at least four healthy young men in the last few years.

The water temperature of the pond felt warmer than the injured man's flesh. It stunk of sulfur and garbage, and as Tomlinson and I began sidestroking toward shore my fingers noted the water's protoplasmic density. The density was created by microbes and muck held in suspension.

It was a brackish water mangrove lake, not much larger than a baseball field, surrounded by a trailer population that probably used the place to dump all kinds of refuse—natural, man-made and chemical. It caused me to wonder why a quarter-ton alligator would choose such a stagnant, public place to live.

The probability was, the animal didn't live

here. More likely, the gator had been traveling cross-country—they often do during the spring mating season. My guess was, the thing had only recently arrived, stopping for a few nights to feed. If a gator that size had been a permanent resident, someone at the trailer park would have reported it to Florida Wildlife cops and demanded that the thing be removed.

Or would they?

I thought about it as we swam sidestroke, Tomlinson on one side of the injured man, me on the other.

Maybe not, I decided. I remembered Tomlinson telling me that the only thing park residents feared more than law enforcement was their own landlord.

That made sense, combined with what I knew about the people who lived in places like Red Citrus. I had spent enough time in Central America, and had lived long enough in Florida, to learn not to underestimate the tenacity of the descendants of the Maya and Aztec. They could endure just about anything with a stoic calm that was all but impossible to read, and just as impossible not to respect.

People like this could live their lives, day by day, next door to an aggressive gator, or next door to a crazed neighbor, and never say a word in protest. Living under the radar meant surviving quietly no matter what.

We were drawing close to shore. The injured man had stopped fighting, but the muscles of his arms remained contracted, his breathing was rapid. To Tomlinson I said, "When we get to the bank, don't try to stand. The bottom's like quicksand."

He asked me, "Do you have shoes on?"

I said, "I was just thinking the same thing. There's probably broken bottles and all kinds of crap on the bottom. We're going to need some help."

To the injured man I said, "What's your name? Can you talk?"

The man groaned, and said again, "Please tell me I'm dreaming this. What happened to my legs? I can't feel my legs."

I thought, *Uh-oh,* and squeezed his arm to reassure him as I looked toward shore. I could see shapes and shadows of several dozen people watching us. But I couldn't see clearly because my glasses were hanging around my neck on fishing line, and also because the spotlight was blinding me again.

In Spanish I yelled, "Take the light away from that person, I can't see! Shine it on the ground. We need some help. Four or five people, hold hands and make a chain so we can pull this man out. But don't come in the water. Stay out of the water!"

I could see people moving toward the bank,

74

including the man who was carrying the spot-light, a huge silhouette capped by blond curls and shoulders in a muscle T-shirt.

It was the landlord. Had to be.

I called to him in English, "Get that goddamn light out of my eyes! I'm not going to tell you again."

In reply, I heard a surly Southern twang shout, "What'd you just say to me, *asshole?*"

The drawl was unmistakably redneck Florida.

Trying to keep it reasonable, I told him, "You're blinding me. We've got an injured man here!"

I saw the man quicken his pace and heard him bellow, "You don't give the orders around here, you do-gooder son of a bitch! I give the orders! Now, get your ass out of my goddamn lake. You're trespassing! What the hell you doin', trespassing in my lake?"

I glanced at Tomlinson. His face was orchid white in the harsh light, and he rolled his eyes. "The landlord," he replied. "He's the jerk I told you about. Something Squires. He's a mama's boy. She's the one with all the property."

Tomlinson had described the guy as all grits and redneck bullshit, plus a full helping of steroids. It matched with what I was hearing.

The water was so shallow now that I was using my left hand to crab us over the bottom, the muck gelatinous between my fingers. It was

75

frustrating. I had no idea how badly that man was hurt, but I knew we couldn't waste time getting him out of the water and treating his wounds. It was impossible to hurry, though. Try to stand, we'd sink to our waists in slime.

"Did you call nine-one-one?" I asked Tomlinson. I couldn't look directly into the spotlight, the thing was too bright, so I was using peripheral vision to keep track of Squires as he descended on us, pushing people out of the way. I noticed that the men who had been attempting to form a human chain scattered from his path.

"We should be hearing sirens by now," Tomlinson replied, "or maybe not. It was only about five minutes ago that I called. But they'll be here." Then he surprised me by calling out in a cheery voice, "Hey! Hey, Tulo, it's me! Tell some of the men we need help getting out of here. We need about five people!"

Tomlinson used the masculine form of the name, but I realized he was yelling to the teenage girl he had mentioned, the girl we had come to help. Tula Choimha.

I saw a slim, luminous figure appear, backlit by the spotlight. The girl had a flashlight, which was pointed at her sandals, and something else in her hand. A bottle, it looked like.

To Tomlinson I said, "Watch the guy's head—he might have a spinal injury."

My pal replied, "Then maybe I should stay

in the water with him until the paramedics arrive."

I was thinking about the killer microbes, not the alligator, when I replied, "No, we've got to get him out of here. You, too."

"Dude," Tomlinson muttered, "I don't even want to ask what that tone of yours means." He glanced over his shoulder. "You think the gator might come back?"

I said, "I'll climb up the bank, and we'll try to pull him out without moving his head. These people aren't going to help, they're afraid. Oh . . . and for God's sake, don't even try talking to that landlord. You'll just make him madder. Let me do the talking."

Tomlinson's attention remained on the girl, mine on Squires, who was still shouting threats at us and not slowing as he lumbered toward the water. I knew we had to hurry, but it would be worse to misjudge the situation. Steroid drunks, like pit bulls, are an unpredictable demographic. If the guy was as furious as he sounded, anything could happen.

I laced my fingers into the knee-high weeds that grew along the bank and pulled myself out of the water, hand over hand, trying to time it right. Friends sometimes chide me about my obsessive attention to detail and my hyper-awareness of my surroundings—particularly if the environment is populated with strangers.

Sometimes, I am tempted to reply, "I'm still alive, aren't I?" but never do.

Fortunately, my hyperwariness paid off. Again.

Just as I was getting to my feet, blue jeans muddy, a slimy mess, Squires appeared. He took a quick jump step, grabbed me by the left arm and stabbed the huge light into my face as I stood. He was screaming, "Can you see any better now, you son of a bitch! Who do you think you are, coming 'round here, giving orders!"

I pushed the light—a military Golight, I realized—out of my eyes and tried to back away, but the man's hand was like a vise. In an easy voice, I said to him, "Calm down, Squires. We have a guy who needs medical attention."

It didn't help. "Screw you!" the man yelled, his breath hot in my face. "Who the hell died and made you boss, you goddamn do-gooder prick? You're giving *me* orders?"

I kept my voice even. "When the police arrive, what are they going to think when I tell them you tried to stop us from saving this man's life?"

Squires was trembling, he was so mad. He roared, "You're not telling the cops nothin', asshole! How you gonna talk to anybody after I snap your damn head off and use it to feed my gator?"

His gator? It was an unexpected thing to hear, but it told me something.

I was gauging the man's size and his balance. He was about six-five, six-six, probably two-eighty, but weight-room muscle is among the most common cloaks of male insecurity. To test his balance, I rolled my left arm free of his grip. At the same time, I gave him a push with the fingers of my right hand. It wasn't an obvious push. It was more of a blocking gesture, but he didn't handle it well.

Clumsy people have a difficult time with simultaneous hand movements, and this guy was clumsy. The little push turned his entire body a few wobbly degrees to the left. It was all the opening I needed, but I didn't take it.

Now was not the time for a brawl. Besides, Tomlinson and I needed this guy's cooperation if we were going to save the injured man. The illegals who lived in the park weren't going to risk helping us—not if their blustering bully of a landlord disapproved. And I couldn't blame them. They had to live here. I didn't.

I squared my body to Squires's, and said, "This is my last try to be reasonable. We've got an injured man and we intend to help him. Get out of our way and behave like an adult."

That's all it took. Squires screamed at me, "Or you'll do what?" and he jammed the light toward my face again.

I had no choice, I ducked under the light and then drop-stepped beneath the landlord's extended right arm. From the sound of surprise he made, the move was the equivalent of a disappearing act. Where had I gone?

I had disappeared behind him, that's where. Years ago, in an overheated wrestling room, I had practiced hand control and simple duck unders day after day, week after week, year after year. I had practiced the craft of grappling so relentlessly that I had pleased even our relentless perfectionist of a coach, a man named Gary Fries. Fries was a wrestling giant, all five feet seven inches of him, and he would not tolerate mediocrity.

Thanks to that coach, I've never been in any physical confrontation in my life where I didn't feel confident I was in control of the outcome. That doesn't mean I have always won. I certainly have not. But I've always felt as if I *could* win if I picked my shots and made the right moves.

Like now, as I came up behind Squires, saying into his ear, "You've got a big mouth, fat boy," because now his anger could be used to my advantage. I wanted him so mad that he lost control. When the big man tried to pivot, I laddered my hands up his ribs to control his body position and leaned my head close to his shoulder blades so he couldn't knock me cold with a wild elbow.

When Squires realized he couldn't maneuver

free, he stuttered, "Hey . . . get your hands off me, asshole!" and tried, once again, to face me.

I was ready because that's exactly what I wanted him to do. I let Squires make half a turn and then stopped his momentum by ramming my head into his back as I grapevined my left ankle around his left shin. An instant later, I locked my hands around his waist and moved with him as he tried to wrestle free.

Our backs were to the mangrove pond. With a quick glance, I confirmed that Tomlinson and the injured man weren't directly behind us—it was a dangerous place to be if things went the way I planned. Then I used my legs to drive Squires away from the water. Instinctively, the man's feet dug in, then his legs pumped as he tried to drive us both backward. Squires was taller, heavier and stronger than I. His energized mass soon overpowered my own.

The timing was important. I waited a microsecond . . . waited until I felt the subtle transition of momentum.

When it felt right, I dropped my grip a few inches lower on the big man's waist. I relocked my hands, bent my knees and then maximized Squires's own momentum by lifting as I arched my back.

I waited another microsecond . . . and then I heaved with all my strength as we tumbled backward.

In wrestling jargon, the move I'd executed was a *suplex*. As I arched backward, I used a two-handed throwing technique, not unlike a Scottish gamesman throwing a fifty-pound rock over a bar. In this case, though, the weight was closer to three hundred pounds. Squires had amassed considerable momentum, and it was his own momentum—not my strength—that sent him flying.

I guessed he would land near the pond's edge, which is why I had checked behind me before setting up the *suplex*. I couldn't have guessed, however, that a man Squires's size would sail beyond the bank and land on his shoulders in a massive explosion of water.

I got to my feet, cleaning my hands on my jeans. I found the spotlight and aimed it at Squires's face when he surfaced. He was disoriented and floundering. I watched him splash to vertical, as he spit water and swore. Mostly, he swore at me, ordering that I get that goddamn light out of his eyes.

I told him, "Come up here and say that, fat boy," and watched the man jam his feet toward the bottom, which is precisely what I hoped he would do.

It was his second mistake of the night.

For a few seconds, Squires stood tall in waist-deep water, as he struggled to find footing. Then he began to sink. The more he struggled, the

more suction he created and the deeper he went into the muck.

Squires wasn't a wrestler, and he wasn't much of a swimmer, either. He couldn't manage the delicate hand strokes necessary to sustain positive buoyancy. Soon the man was so deeply mired in mud that he couldn't move his legs. Water was rising toward his shoulders, and it scared him.

"Goddamn it!" he shouted to the migrants watching. "Help me. Get a rope! Somebody go get a rope and pull me out of here."

Drowning was terrifying enough, but then another thought came into Squires's mind. I could tell because of the wild look in his eyes as he glanced over his shoulder, yelling, "Hurry up, before that gator comes back! Does anybody have a gun? Someone break the window of my truck and grab the gun from the glove box. Shit! Hurry up!"

Automatically, my right hand touched my sodden pocket to confirm the Kahr 9mm was still there. It was.

No one moved except for a frail, luminous figure that I recognized. It was the teenage girl Tomlinson had been calling to, Tula. I watched her step free of the crowd, then walk toward me, her eyes indicating Squires as she said in English, "Do you think he might drown?"

I replied, "That's up to him. If he keeps air in his lungs, he'll stop sinking."

I watched the girl, impressed by her articulate English, but more impressed by the way she carried herself and the respect park residents accorded her. When she spoke, even the men watching her went silent.

"Will the animal come back?" she asked me. "Did you kill it?"

I was moving toward the injured man and Tomlinson as I told her, "I wounded it, maybe. I don't know," and was tempted to ask, *Why are you worried about that jerk?*

I listened to the girl tell me, "I used your telephone to call the emergency number. Or maybe it was his."

She glanced at Tomlinson, who was on his knees in the water, cradling the injured man, and then explained, "The angry *propietario* told the emergency police not to come. But they are coming now."

The angry *propietario* was Squires. Apparently, the girl had heard him cancel Tomlinson's 911 call. How else could she have known?

In Spanish, I said to people milling in the shadows, "We need three or four men to help get the injured man out of the water. I think his spine is hurt. We have to take care not to move his head. We need towels and ice and disinfectant . . . and a board of some type for him to lie on. Plywood would work."

As I spoke, I had to raise my voice to be heard

above Squires, who was now raging, "Why aren't you people moving? Goddamn it, I need a rope! And one of you bastards fetch my gun! How'd you little shits like to be homeless again? I'll call the feds on your sorry asses if you don't move now!"

The man was panicking in his rage, his attention focused on shadows behind him where the gator might be lurking. As long as he kept his lungs inflated, the muck wouldn't overpower his own buoyancy. But now, I guessed, Squires was hyperventilating, and in real danger. I was considering going in after him myself when the girl called in loud Spanish, "Do what the landlord says. Get a rope, but not his gun! Help him! Would God want you to allow a helpless man to drown?"

God allowed helpless men to drown daily, but her words got people moving. A couple of guys went jogging toward the trailers, while others moved toward Tomlinson, awaiting instructions. As I approached the bank, I told the men to stay close, we'd need them soon. I was also searching the ground, looking for my shirt, because I wanted to clean my glasses.

Beside me, Tula said, "Use this," and handed me a towel, which she pulled from the back of her jeans. "He's my friend," she added, indicating the injured man. "His name is Carlson, and he has a good heart. When you get him out of the

85

water, I will pray. Will you help me pray to heal his wounds?"

The girl's syntax was odd, I noticed, whether she spoke in English or Spanish. It was formal in an old-fashioned way, which made no sense for someone her age.

Carlson was listening from only a few feet away. He was semiconscious, looking up at the girl, a sleepy, dazed smile on his face.

I said, "My friend will be glad to help you pray. Won't you, Tomlinson?" and handed the towel back to the girl before I told one of the men to hang on to my feet when I gave him the word. Then I got down on my hands and knees and crawled to the water.

It wasn't difficult to lift Carlson ashore. He was all bone and skin, couldn't have weighed more than a hundred and forty pounds. Once we had him on the slick grass, we maneuvered a piece of plywood under him, then sledded him to higher ground.

Through the entire process, I held the man's head steady. From the way he'd described the cracking sound "deep inside him," I guessed the gator had broken his spine. I didn't want to turn a paraplegic into a quadriplegic.

Tula comforted the man as we moved him. She stroked his head, told him he would recover quickly, and also chanted what I guessed to be a prayer in her native language. I can speak only enough *Quiché* Maya to thank the person who brings me a beer, so I had no idea what the girl was saying.

When we had Carlson safely away from the water, I checked his injuries. His forearm showed puncture marks, as did his waist and buttocks, but the bleeding wasn't bad.

His legs, though, had a pasty, dead look that suggested I'd been right about the broken spine. As I took note of the wounds, Tula tapped me on the shoulder and said, "I'll hold his head while you use this." She was holding a bottle of cheap tequila, waiting for me to take it.

Tomlinson had found his sandals and seemed to be looking for something else but stopped long enough to grab the bottle and take a long swig.

"It's not for drinking," the girl told him, her tone communicating disapproval. "It's to clean your wounds."

"That's exactly how I'm using it," Tomlinson replied, then took another long belt, before he said to her, "Tula, while we work on your friend, would you do me a favor? Ask around and find out who has our billfolds. I found the phones, but our billfolds are gone."

But then he told her, "Never mind," as a man approached, billfolds in hand.

Tomlinson thanked the man, saying, "*Muchas gracias, compadre,*" but I could tell that something was wrong as he opened his billfold, then mine.

Tula stared at him for a moment before saying, "Your money is gone. I can see it in your face."

The girl turned toward the water, where Squires was struggling to reach a rope some men were trying to throw him. "He has your money. The *propietario*. No one but him would have robbed you."

In the peripheral glow of the Golight, I looked at the girl closely for the first time. She had a cereal-bowl haircut, and a lean angularity that didn't mesh with the compact body type I associate with Mayan women. Yet there was nothing masculine about her. She was boyish enough to pass for a boy, but her demeanor, while commanding, was asexual. In the truck, Tomlinson had said something that sounded strange at the time but now made sense. He had said, "She's an adolescent girl, not a female," which described her perfectly.

Thirteen-year-old Tula Choimha, I decided, was a child who handled herself like an adult. It was unusual, but probably less uncommon in girls than boys. Besides, the girl had spent the last few years living on her own, without family, which had no doubt contributed to her maturity.

"They're coming to help you," Tula whispered into Carlson's ear as she gauged the direction of distant sirens. She took the bottle of tequila from

Tomlinson, soaked the towel with liquor, then dropped to her knees and began to wash the puncture wounds on Carlson's arm and then his buttocks, unconcerned that I had pulled the man's pants down to access his injuries.

"I can't feel my legs," the man told her again. He had said it several times in the last minutes, his reaction ping-ponging between horror and shock.

"Your legs are healing," I heard the girl tell him, her right hand gripping a necklace she wore. "Your wounds are healing now. You must have faith."

I watched her pause, head tilted, and the rhythm of her voice changed. She told him, "Our strength comes from faith. But our faith is sometimes eaten away by little things that God hates. If we lack faith, though there be a million of us, we will be beaten back and die."

I exchanged looks with Tomlinson, wondering if he, too, suspected her singsong syntax suggested that the girl was reciting something she had memorized.

My friend was nodding his approval. Personally, I felt a chill. To me, the robotic passion of the devoutly religious is disturbing. Too often it is a flag of surrender to fear and the exigencies of life. Maybe my assessment is unfair, but I associate religious fervor with pathology. Tomlinson, of course, does not.

"Squeeze my hand and put your faith in God," Tula whispered to the man, as she scrubbed at the puncture wounds on his buttocks. "Remember the godliness that you possessed as a child? It will return to you. God will make your body whole again."

Someone had brought a Coleman lantern, so I switched off the Golight and placed it on the ground. I was looking through my billfold, seeing that someone had rearranged my IDs and credit cards, seeing that all my cash had been taken, as I also watched the girl pour more tequila on Carlson's wounds, then scrub harder with the bloody towel.

"Do you feel this, *patron*?" she asked him. "Can your legs feel the heat of God, trying to enter?"

Once again, Tomlinson and I exchanged looks, as Carlson's eyes widened, and he said, "Maybe . . . maybe I can . . . I'm not sure . . . but something's happening. Wait . . . yes! I do feel it. Yes, my skin is burning! I can feel your hands, Tula!"

"They are not my hands, *patron*," Tula told him, not surprised. "It's the warmth of God's love you feel. He is in your body now. He has traveled from my body into your legs."

The man's face contorted into tears, and I watched him move one pale foot, then the other.

Carlson was crying, "Tula, you're right! I can feel my legs!"

I was pleased to know that I had been wrong about the man's broken spine. Shock, or a damaged nerve, might explain the temporary loss of feeling in Carlson's legs. But my interest in an explanation was short-lived because nearby I heard a man yell in Spanish, "It is back. The alligator is back. Someone shine the light!"

I swung the Golight toward the lake, where I saw a reptilian wake, and two bright red eyes riding low in the water.

The huge gator, still alive, still determined to feed, was gliding toward the bodybuilder, who was already screaming for help.

SIX

SIRENS DESCENDING ON RED CITRUS RV Park was bad enough, but when Harris Squires saw red eyes breach the water's surface, glowing twenty yards behind him, he felt a charge of panic beyond anything he had ever experienced, aware that he was about to lose one of his legs, maybe worse.

Squires understood what those eyes meant because of all the nights he'd spent hunting in the Everglades or getting stoned and plinking away at gators in ponds that dotted his four hundred acres.

Fifi was back. The biggest damn gator Squires

had ever seen in his life was still alive, watching him, her eyes glowing in the light of a lantern that someone had brought so the two white guys could give first aid to that nosy old drunk, Carlson.

Squires tried to scream, but his voice managed only a high-pitched yelp, as his legs and arms went into hyperflight, trying to free himself from the muck. It was like one of those sweaty damn nightmares he sometimes had when he stacked testosterone and Tren. Nightmares in which he'd try to run, or call for help, but his body was dead, unable to respond.

Mired up to his thighs in mud produced the same sickening terror. He was desperate to run and he was trying . . . he even managed to get his right leg free. But then Squires felt a tearing pain in the back of his leg and realized he'd pulled a hamstring muscle.

The pain brought his voice back, and he yelled to the cluster of men, only a few yards away on the bank, "The gator! The gator's after me! Throw me that goddamn rope again!"

Suddenly, someone on shore turned on the Golight. The dazzling beam confirmed that the gator was swimming toward him, and Squires felt like vomiting, he was so scared.

Four times, the Mexicans had lobbed coils of clothesline to him. But each time the rope wasn't strong enough, or the men weren't strong enough, and the rope had broken or pulled free.

This time, though, a Mexican with some brains had produced commercial-grade nylon with a weight taped to the end. When he lobbed it, the coil went sailing over Squires's head but landed close enough for him to grab the rope before it sank.

As Squires looped the rope around his chest, he risked another glance over his shoulder, and there was Fifi, gliding closer. Her eyes were a ruby pendulum, swinging with every stroke of her tail.

Squires whirled toward the bank and hollered, "Pull, you dumb-asses! Don't you see that god-damn gator? For God's sake, pull!" He began to thrash with his arms, trying to help the men tractor him the few yards to safety.

At first, there must have been a dozen Mexicans on the bank willing to help him after the Bible-freak girl had ordered them to do it. When the sirens became audible, however, half of the little cowards had gone scrambling. Now there were only four little men onshore, in jeans and ball caps, all hitched to the rope, and they leaned against Squires's weight.

"Pull! Get your asses moving!" Squires screamed. "Jesus Christ, she's coming faster!"

The first heave of the rope yanked Squires forward. Another heave flipped him onto his back so that his eyes were fixated on the alligator when his left shoe finally popped free of the mud and he began to float toward the bank.

Now Squires's mind returned to nightmare mode, and everything happened in terrible slow motion. He was flailing with his arms, screaming for the men to move faster, while sirens and lights converged overhead, filling his head with a chaos so overwhelming he could barely hear his own voice. The night sky echoed with throbbing lights that were the exact same piercing red as the alligator's eyes.

Fifi was so close now that Squires could see the black width of her head. The animal pushed a wall of water ahead of her that lifted his body as she closed on him, which caused Squires to roll his body into a fetal ball, preparing himself for what was going to happen next.

"Get me out of here, *goddamn you!*" Squires voice broke as he pleaded, and he rolled to his stomach, unable to watch as the gator's mouth opened to take him, the animal a massive darkness only a few yards away.

As he turned, he realized he was close enough to touch the bank, where weeds were knee-deep. He lunged, got a fistful of grass in both hands and tried to pull himself out. He was too heavy, though, and roots ripped away from the earth, causing him to fall back into the water butt first.

As Squires hit the water, everything was still happening in slow motion. He got a snapshot

look at three figures running toward him. It was the Bible-freak Mexican girl and the two white guys, the hippie two steps ahead of the guy named Ford. Ford appeared to have stopped for some reason, maybe to fish something from his pocket, but the girl and the hippie were coming fast. But then Squires didn't see anything else because he closed his eyes as he fell backward and landed on Fifi, who felt wide and buoyant in the water.

An instant later, Squires endured a watery explosion beneath him. He floundered for a few seconds, then he felt bony hands on his shoulder and realized someone was trying to drag his weight up the bank but wasn't having much success.

Squires used his fingers to claw at the sand as he crawled out of the water, picturing the gator opening its jaws again to snap off one of his legs, but it didn't happen because then he heard: *WHAP-WHAP!*

Two more gunshots.

Several long minutes later, Squires was on his knees, breathing heavily, aware that headlights of an ambulance and two emergency vehicles now illuminated the area like a stage.

He heard men's voices calling sharp orders, one of them yelling, "Put the weapon on the ground. Step away and show me your hands. Do it

now!" Then he heard the same voice, louder, say, "Show me your goddamn hands and walk toward me!"

An asshole cop. It had to be—no one but a cop could mix contempt and authority in quite the same way. But Squires realized they were yelling at the big guy, Ford, not him, which was a relief. It gave him some hope.

The hippie was trying to help Squires to his feet, but Squires yanked his elbow away, saying, "Get your goddamn hands off me!" but then winced when he tried to take a step. He hissed, *"Shit,"* because the back of his right leg was knotted and hurt like hell because of the pulled hamstring.

The hippie said to him, "Are you okay? Did it bite you? That was damn close, man!"

Squires put some weight on his leg and took a few experimental steps, watching the big guy walk toward a semicircle of cops and EMTs, holding his hands high. Then he listened to Ford say in the distance, "The injured man's over there, he needs attention right away. An alligator grabbed him, I don't know how bad. Then it came back after the big guy. That's why I had to use a weapon."

It had been a bad night so far, but Squires decided this might be a chance to turn things around. He pushed the hippie away and started toward the cops, limping barefooted, straighten-

ing himself, trying to look respectable despite his slimy knee-length shorts and muscle T-shirt.

He waited until he was sure the cops were looking in his direction before saying, "I'm the manager, I own this place. I was hoping you boys would show up. That asshole right there"—he pointed at Ford—"almost got me killed, the way he was banging off rounds from that little pistol of his. Hell, maybe he did kill someone. We should have a look around. Check on the units and make sure one of my tenants isn't hurt."

Squires made a point of ignoring Ford, who was staring at him now. For some reason, the scientist had a quizzical expression on his face, not amused, not pissed off, but *interested,* like Squires was some kind of bug.

It was weird the way the man appeared so relaxed, not the least bit worried, despite the guns the cops had now lowered, which caused Squires to remember that maybe Ford and the hippie were part of some DEA sting. Maybe they were even friends with these cops, who might be playing some kind of game.

Cops did shit like that all the time when they had their sights set on busting an underground steroids lab. Or so Squires had read on the Internet bodybuilder forums. It was law enforcement's way of sticking their noses where they didn't belong.

When one of the cops said to Squires, "Stop

right there, no closer," Squires did, then listened to the man ask, "What's your name?"

Squires told him, deciding suddenly it was better to be friendly if Ford was DEA, which is why he added, "But I got no hard feelings against the dude. Maybe he was just trying to help me save that poor drunk over there—"

Squires looked toward the bank, where EMTs were already working on Carlson. There wasn't a *chilie* or a *chula* around now, he noticed. They'd all disappeared except for the weird little Jesus freak, who was pestering the EMTs about the old drunk, probably getting in their way.

Behind him, Squires heard the hippie call to the cops, "Why the hell do you have your guns out? Big tough guys—you're afraid of a couple of unarmed men and a little kid?"

The hippie said it in an irritated, cop-hater tone, which, to Squires, was more proof that these guys were working undercover for the feds.

Squires used the opening as an excuse to snap at the hippie, saying, "Shut your mouth, these guys know what they're doing. Let them do their damn jobs!" which might earn him some brownie points with the cops.

Squires hoped so. He felt a welling chemical anxiety inside his head, probably caused by steroids mixing with adrenaline, no doubt the result of that goddamn gator coming so close to biting his ass off. Plus, there was the not-so-small

matter of the dead Mexican girl's body some- where on the bottom of the lake.

Christ, when he remembered the dead body, Squires felt like he might vomit again, he was so nervous.

The bodybuilder stood there, shifting from his bad leg to his good leg, trying to appear as calm as the nerdy scientist. He watched carefully as the cops talked to Ford in a low voice, and then he felt another jolt when Ford not only lowered his hands but then shook hands with someone who stepped out of the shadows. Another cop, maybe, although the man wasn't wearing a uniform.

As the two uniforms holstered their weapons, Squires thought, *Oh shit,* and took a look around. The hippie was walking toward the cops, a pissed-off expression on his face until he saw that the cops had put their guns away, which caused the hippie to relax a little. It gave the skinny dude time to reassess, which is probably why he turned his attention toward Squires.

"What kind of lost soul are you?" the hippie asked, walking toward him. "What do you mean, we helped *you* save that man? You didn't do a damn thing but interfere! We just saved your life, and this is how you act?"

The hippie was talking loud enough for the cops to hear if they wanted, but they appeared to be busy with Ford.

Squires decided it was better to deal with the hippie privately before someone started paying attention. So he limped toward the dude, who looked ridiculous, in Squires's opinion, with his droopy surfer shorts, his skinny little muscles and his ribs showing.

When he was close enough, Squires said to him, "Look, I don't want any more trouble here. You play nice, I'll play nice. How's that sound to you?"

A confused expression appeared on the hippie's face as he replied, "If that's supposed to mean something, man, I don't follow. What the hell you talking about?"

Squires told him, "I'm willing to cooperate," his voice low now. "I know who you are. I think I know why you're here. I'll help set the bust up, if that's the way you want to play it. You think those cops wouldn't like to take down a major supplier? Hell yes, they would. One word from me, it could happen."

Squires was thinking of giving the feds Laziro Victorino, the gangbanger who sold dope on the side, which seemed like a smart way to kill two birds with one stone. Plus, the V-man had shot those snuff films, too, which was a hell of a lot bigger deal than busting a small steroids operation like his.

Maybe the hippie would admit he was DEA, maybe he wouldn't. Squires was watching the man's reaction to see.

The expression on the hippie's face changed from confusion to mild concern. "Who've you been talking to? Did you bully your tenants into giving information about me? Turned them into narcs?"

When Squires didn't answer immediately, the hippie almost lost it. "That sucks, man! It really sucks. There's nothing lower than a damn narc, in my opinion. These people come here with zero money, they need to make a buck, so what's it matter to you? That's really small-time bullshit —and I just helped save your ass. You could be dying right now! Getting your bad-karma ticket punched for hell. Instead, you're threatening me!"

It took Squires a moment to realize what the hippie was saying. He put the words together with all those crisp twenties in the hippie's billfold and started smiling. Squires couldn't help himself. The damn hippie didn't work for the DEA. The dude was worried about getting busted himself!

Suddenly, Squires felt back in control. Well . . . sort of. He still had his girlfriend, Frankie, to worry about, and that gangbanger Victorino. The V-man was scary, but Frankie scared him more. There was no telling the amount of crap the woman would dump on him once she'd heard the cops had been snooping around the lake.

The lake. What lay on the bottom of that lake

was Squires's biggest worry. It caused him to look toward the water, where the mangrove trees looked yellow in the bright ambulance lights, the water black as asphalt. What if they wanted to recover the alligator's body and decided to drag the pond?

Squires's smile faded for an instant but then returned. Nope, they wouldn't need to drag the pond. Because now Squires noticed two cops, one of them lying on the bank, trying to get a rope around something that Squires realized was the gator's tail.

Good! Fifi was dead—the fat pig deserved it, after attacking him. Shit, after all the times he'd fed her chunks of pig, once a whole yearling deer? And then the animal turns on him!

The scientist probably couldn't shoot worth a shit, but he'd finally gotten lucky with his little lady's pistol. True, Squires had been counting on the gator to get rid of the dead girl's body, and maybe Fifi already had, which struck him as an encouraging possibility.

At first it did, anyway—until he thought it through.

What if the cops took the gator to the Wildlife people? What if the Wildlife cops opened Fifi's belly to have a look?

Damn it!

Squires hadn't thought of that and he felt sick again. What if the gator had eaten the Mexican girl's body? Or even a few pieces? The cops would come storming back here with search warrants and handcuffs, and that would be the end of him.

Jesus Christ, he couldn't let that happen. Not with the Bible-freak girl still around to testify that she'd seen him drag that heavy sack to the water. If it wasn't for her, it would be easy enough to play dumb and let the cops blame the V-man. Or any one of the hundreds of other drunken Mexicans who lived in the area. That would be the natural direction to go. Wetbacks killed wettails, right? It happened all the time.

Squires took a look around. The girl had disappeared. Where? She had been kneeling by Carlson. Didn't seem the least bit concerned that the cops could ask for her ID, find out she was an illegal and take her skinny ass into custody. Not just illegal but underage at that, which meant she'd probably end up in some state orphanage.

Stupid little Mexican.

Squires felt pressure building in his head again as he fumed about the girl, a nobody wettail who could have him jailed if she decided, maybe even send him to the electric chair. It made him furious to think that one little Mexican had so much power over him.

Squires became even more determined to fulfill his fantasy . . .

A voice interrupted. "Why were you staring at

103

that child? What's going on in the twisted brain of yours?"

Squires realized the hippie was talking to him. He turned, surprised, and a little pissed off. He studied the hippie, seeing the seriousness in the guy's Jesus-looking eyes, also seeing how scrawny the dude was, easy enough to snap the man's body in two if he wanted.

"She's a chick, not a child, you dumbass," Squires said to him, and then enjoyed the guy's reaction.

"You don't know what you're talking about," the hippie said, but in a sort of testing way.

"Bullshit, I don't. You ever seen a boy with pretty little knockers so firm they could poke your damn eye out?"

The hippie took a step toward him. "Why would you even say something so disgusting?"

Squires was loving the look of outrage. "Because it's true," he told the guy. "Tonight, that little girl and me had a nice conversation while she was in the trailer taking herself a bath. That's some tight little ass she's got for a wettail that young."

The hippie said, *"Wettail?"* then started walking toward Squires, the dude's eyes a little crazy. "You lay a hand on that girl, I'll see you in prison. You stay away from her or I'll . . ."

"Or you'll what? Try and scratch my eyes out?" Squires used a *Screw you* smile to make the guy madder, hoping the dude would take a swing at him while there were plenty of witnesses right there watching.

"Have an illegal Mexican girl squeal to the cops?"

The look of frustration on the hippie's face was an awesome thing to see. "Go ahead, tell the cops I was watching the girl take a bath. Let's see how long it takes for them to ship your little pal's ass back to shithole Mexico."

Squires flipped his middle finger at the dude, turned and made a quick trip to his double-wide, where he hid the cash he had stolen from the hippie and the hippie's asshole friend.

He stuck the money under the false bottom of a drawer, with stacks of twenties, fifties and hundreds he and Frankie had amassed from selling Gator Juice. Probably more than fifty thousand there.

Frankie would know the exact amount. Harris Squires seldom had the patience to count it.

An hour later, with all the lights and cameras and Florida Wildlife vehicles arriving, Harris was thinking that killing an alligator was a bigger deal than killing a person.

He had overheard one of the cops telling a reporter that unless it was a life-or-death situation, harming or harassing a gator could mean a year in jail and up to a four-thousand-dollar fine.

Good. He hoped they took Ford away in hand-cuffs.

It didn't look like it was going to happen, though, the way the cops had been treating the bastard. They'd hauled the drunk, Carlson, away in an ambulance, but not before Carlson had told them that Ford and the hippie had saved his life. Carlson was probably the only witness the nerd needed, but the little Bible-freak girl had seen the whole thing, too. Not that she'd stuck around long after the ambulance left.

Where was she? Squires was getting nervous, thinking that maybe the girl would grab her things and disappear from Red Citrus. Or maybe the cops had taken her away to question her privately.

Damn it! That was a possibility. Could be she was telling them right now what she'd seen Squires doing the night before.

No telling how long before the little brat talked, if it happened. It was something he would have to deal with later, though, because what Squires was doing right now was sitting in the backseat of a squad car, answering questions. There were two cops, a chunky guy in uniform and a Latin-looking woman wearing a white blouse tucked into a dark skirt, a regular professional ball breaker. Squires knew it the moment he set eyes on her.

The woman cop, whose name was Specter, was

making notes as Squires told her his version of what had happened. In his version, he had been the hero, not Ford, which didn't get a response from the woman, and that worried him. Had they put him in the squad car to ask about the gator? Or to question him about what he had dumped into the pond the night before? Or maybe, just maybe, one of the nosy cops had taken a peek into his double-wide trailer and seen the steroids kitchen with its propane tanks and chemical jars everywhere.

Squires was feeling twitchy as the woman finally sat back to comment instead of just asking questions. She turned toward the backseat and said, "It's strange—the man the alligator attacked? The victim had no recollection of you being involved in any way, Mr. Squires. Dr. Ford and Dr. Tomlinson both tell stories that are very different from yours. I'm wondering why that is."

The hippie was a doctor, too?

Jesus Christ, Squires thought, *there must be colleges out there giving diplomas away to any idiot who can fill out the forms.*

Squires told the woman, "Let me tell you about that guy, Carlson. He's lived here for more than two years. He's a drunk and a paint huffer. He's out of his mind most the time. You know what a paint huffer is?"

The woman wrote something on a pad before she replied, "We've got another problem. Do

107

you have any idea what that problem might be?"

Squires could feel his heart pounding in his chest. He looked out the window, seeing a tow truck in the bright lights, where a Wildlife cop was taking video as the crane winched Fifi slowly off the ground, all twelve or thirteen feet of her.

Squires was wondering if the back door of the squad car had locked automatically. If not, maybe the smartest thing he could do right now was make a run for it. Hide out for the night, then call Frankie and have her take him to the hunting camp, a place where he could hide and think things over in peace.

Squires put his hand on the door handle, thought about it another few seconds, then changed his mind. Once Frankie heard what had happened, she'd flip out. Hell, the woman would probably turn him over to the cops herself. Besides, how far would he get with a pulled hamstring?

Squires rubbed at the back of his leg and said, "All I know is, if I don't get some ice on my leg, I'm not going to be able to walk tomorrow. How screwed up is that? I help save the life of one of my drunken tenants and I end up crippled for a week. I'm a professional athlete, which I don't expect you to know. I'm training for the Mr. South Florida, which is in Clearwater Beach, this June, so an injury like a pulled hammie can be pretty serious if I don't take care of it."

The woman cop said, "Just a few more questions, Mr. Squires. There's something else I want to ask you about, this problem I mentioned—"

Squires felt himself getting mad, which he knew wasn't smart, but he couldn't help himself from cutting her off, saying, "Miz Specter, we've all got problems. All I know is, I need some ice. I save a man's life, now you're talking to me like I'm some kind of criminal. I don't want to get tough about it, but you're on my private property. And if I need medical attention—a bag of ice, I'm saying—then I should be able to—"

The male cop interrupted, sounding like a wise-ass, telling him, "You own a trailer park and you're a bodybuilder. That's a handy combination."

What the hell did that mean?

Squires was telling himself, *Stay cool, don't let the prick make you mad,* as he corrected the guy, saying, "I own three mobile home parks, not trailer parks. A trailer's something you use to haul stuff, not live in. We offer manufactured homes and RV sites. It's what I do in my spare time."

"You're the owner?" the cop asked. "I called the address in, and it came back a women named Harriet Ray Squires owns this place."

"Same thing," Squires replied. "But we're trying to get out of the business, which you can probably understand, seeing the type of shit we have to put up with. Three acres of back-bay waterfront, only a couple miles from Fort Myers Beach. That'll be some serious money once we clear these units off and sell the place."

The cop wasn't done badgering him, though. "So you work for mom when you're not earning a living doing the muscle shows. What steroids are you stacking?" The cop said it, trying to sound like he knew something about the subject.

The cop continued, "The show you're training for is in June?"

"Mr. South Florida," Squires replied.

The cop said, "Four months away from a show, you're still on your bulking cycle, right? Let me guess, you're doing about a thousand milligrams of testosterone mixed with, what, D-bol? Primo? I hear anavar is big with you guys once you start cutting."

What Squires wanted to do was tell this know-it-all asshole, *Primo is for pussies,* which was true, in his opinion, even if it was one of Arnold's favorite steroids.

Instead, he calmed himself with a familiar lie, saying, "I tried that crap a few years back, but the side effects scared the hell out of me. Plus, they do urine tests now. Steroids are illegal. Or maybe that's just for us professional athletes. I've got no reason to follow it. But, to me, the crap's not worth the risk. I've heard it gave some guys brain cancer. If you've got the right genetics, who needs the shit?"

"A health nut," the cop said, proving he really was a prick, but then the woman took over by silencing the man a look.

"Back to that problem I mentioned," she said to Squires. "Someone robbed Dr. Ford and Dr. Tomlinson. They took almost two thousand dollars from their billfolds. Cash."

That quick, Squires felt like he could breathe again. Hell, he'd almost forgotten that he'd hidden their damn money in his double-wide. Even if the cops had searched him and found the cash in his pocket, it was no big deal. Not compared to a murder rap, anyway, or running a steroids operation.

Squires asked what he thought was a smart question: "Did the guys leave the billfolds in their vehicle? That's not very smart, you ask me. Not around here."

When the woman replied, "No, they tossed them on the ground before they went into the water," Squires let them see that he was thinking about it.

"I don't want to sound like a racist," he said after a few seconds, "but I've got a lot of Mexican tenants. And the way they are around any kind of valuable property, especially cash money, that's just a fact of life. The little bastards will steal you blind, give 'em a chance. There's something else to think about, too. Or maybe I shouldn't say anything, because I'm not one to stick my nose into other people's business. I hate people like that."

The woman said, "Oh?"

Squires made a show of it, giving it some more thought, before saying, "It has to do with that hippie-looking dude, Dr. whatever his name is. Think about it, that's all I'm saying. A guy who looks the way he looks, carrying that much cash."

"Tomlinson," the woman said. "He and Dr. Ford are from Sanibel Island. You've never met them before?"

"The Tomlinson dude, no, but I've seen him cruising my park plenty of times. About once a month he shows up. Like I said, I don't know the guy, so I'm not making any charges here, but that's another fact of life. The drug dealer types come through my park all the time. They know that the—"

Squires caught himself. He'd almost said *the illegals*.

"—they know that the migrant workers who live here sometimes have grass and peyote to sell. They bring it with them from Mexico when they cross the border. Maybe the guy, Tomlinson, is a drug dealer. Why don't you search their vehicle? You might find something that would surprise you."

That didn't play too well, but Squires didn't

care. The cops didn't know about the dead girl's body in the lake. And they didn't know about his steroids kitchen only a block away.

Not yet, anyway.

Harris Squires was looking through the squad car window, seeing the tow truck lower Fifi onto the bed of a truck, its big tires flattening beneath her weight. The vehicle was about the same size as the stake truck he and his buddies had used to bring Fifi to Red Citrus.

Seeing the gator, he couldn't help but worry about what the Wildlife cops might find in the animal's belly. Squires was also thinking, *I've got to get my hands on that little Bible-freak girl before she goes blabbing to the law.*

Half an hour later, when the cops had released him, after he'd showered and iced his bad hamstring, Squires opened a fresh pint of tequila and began to make the rounds.

The little brat wasn't at the trailer where she usually stayed. But that was okay. The girl had left behind her only clean shirt, a ratty little book and a framed photo of what was probably her Mexican family.

She couldn't have gone far.

The bodybuilder took a moment to study the photo. His eyes moved from the girl—who looked about eight or so when the shot was taken—to what must have been the girl's mother, who was wearing an Indian-looking shawl over

her head. The angular noses were similar, the line of their jaws.

Why the hell did they both look so familiar?

Hell . . . all Mexicans looked the same, Squires decided. The important thing was to find that damn girl.

SEVEN

AS WE WALKED BENEATH MANGROVE trees toward my little home and laboratory on Dinkin's Bay, Sanibel Island, Tomlinson couldn't help fixating on the subject of Tula Choimha.

It was understandable. The girl had vanished shortly after the ambulance hauled her friend to the hospital and we'd failed to find her even though we had spent more than an hour searching.

"Doc," he said for the umpteenth time, "I know damn well what happened. How often am I wrong when I feel this strongly about something?"

I replied, "You're wrong most of the time, but you only remember the times you're right. Stop worrying about it."

"How can I stop worrying when every paranormal receptor in my body is telling me that Squires grabbed our girl for some reason? She wouldn't have just disappeared like that. Not without saying something to me. Damn it,

114

compadre, we should have stayed right there until we found her."

I said, "Do me a favor. Take a deep breath. Then make a conscious effort to use the left side of your brain for a change. Squires is a jerk, but why would he kidnap a thirteen-year-old girl? There's no motivation, he has nothing to gain. It would be the stupidest time possible to crap in his own nest. He grabs the girl when cops are swarming all over the place?"

After a few quiet paces, I added, "We'll check in again tomorrow morning, but we're done for tonight. We did everything we could."

True. After being questioned by county deputies, then Florida Wildlife cops, and after refusing interviews with three different reporters, we had spent more than an hour at Red Citrus, hunting for Tula.

This was after I'd insisted that we both take an outdoor shower and then used the rest of the tequila to kill whatever microbes that might have been searching our skin for an entrance.

At the trailer where Tula was staying, we had found some of her extra clothing—boy's jeans, a shirt—a book titled *Joan of Arc: In Her Own Words*, plus a family photo in a cheap frame. The photo showed a six- or seven-year-old Tula, an older brother, her father and mother standing in front of a thatched hut somewhere in the mountains of Guatemala.

Like Tula, the mother wasn't short and squat like many Guatemalan women—which, to me, suggested aristocratic genetics that dated way, way back. The mother wore traditional *Indio* dress, a colorful *cinta*, or head scarf, and a blue *robozo*, or shawl. The lady had a nice smile in the photo, but there was an odd anxiousness in her expression, too. She was an attractive woman, slim, with cobalt hair and a Mayan nose. Not beautiful but pretty, and looking way too young to have borne two children.

If children had not been in the photo, I would have guessed the mother's age at less than seventeen.

Tula might have gone away and left her clothing, but she wouldn't have left the photo. It suggested that the girl was still in the area. I also found it reassuring that the people with whom she was staying were less concerned than Tomlinson. They were among the few who knew that the unusual boy was actually a girl.

"It is something the maiden does at night," a Mayan woman had told me in Spanish. "She goes to a secret place where no one can find her. She says she goes there to be alone with God. And to speak to angels who come to her at night. Every night the maiden disappears, so tonight is nothing new. Sometimes during the day she disappears, too. We respect her wishes. She is very gifted. Tula is a child of God."

I found the woman's phraseology interesting and unusual. The translation, which I provided Tomlinson, was exact. *Doncella* is Spanish for "maiden." *Hadas* referred to woodland spirits that are common in Mayan mythology, the equivalent of Anglo-Saxon faeries or angels.

It is a seldom used word, *doncella*. In Spanish, "maiden" resonates with a deference that implies purity if not nobility. Again, I was struck by the respect adults demonstrated for the child. It bordered on reverence, which was in keeping with the small shrine the locals had erected outside Tula's trailer. The shrine consisted of candles and beads placed on a cheap plaster statuette of the Virgin Mary.

"Tula has been in the States just over a week," Tomlinson had explained to me, "but already word has spread that a child lives here who speaks with God. Tula didn't have to tell these people anything about herself because she's a thought-shaper. One look at her, her people knew that she's special. Word travels fast in the Guatemalan community. Their survival depends on it."

"In that case," I'd said, trying to get the man off the subject, "park residents will naturally keep track of her movements. They think she's special? Then she'll attract special attention. Someone around here is bound to know where her secret place is."

But no one did. Finally, Tomlinson and I started going door-to-door, but the neighbors were so suspicious of us, two *gringos* asking questions, that they probably wouldn't have told us where the girl was even if they had known.

My guess, though, was, they didn't know.

Now, two hours later, as Tomlinson and I walked toward my rickety old fish house, we discussed what I was going to make for dinner. It was my way of changing the subject. I was hungry, and it had also been several hours since Tomlinson had had a beer. It was an unusually long period of abstinence for the man, so it was no wonder his nerves were raw.

I was relieved to be home. My house and lab are more than a refuge, although they have provided refuge to many. The property, buildings and docks that constitute Sanibel Biological Supply are a local institution, second home to a trusted family of fishing guides, live-aboards and an occasional female guest.

Of late, though, I'd been going through a period of abstinence as well—not the liquid variety. So I was ready for a few beers myself. It had been one hell of a crazy night, and Tomlinson wasn't the only one who felt a little raw.

There are fewer and fewer houses like mine in Florida. The place is an old commercial fish house built over the water on stilts. The lower level is all dockage and deck. The upper level is wooden platform, about eight feet above the water. Two small cottages sit at the center under one tin roof, and the platform extends out, creating a broad porch on all four sides.

I use one of the cottages as my laboratory and office. The other cottage is my living quarters, complete with a small yacht-sized kitchen and very un-yacht-like wood-burning stove that is a good thing to have on windy winter nights.

When we got to the first flight of steps, I paused to turn on underwater lights I had installed near my shark pen. Underwater lights, to me, are more entertaining than any high-tech entertainment system in the world. The drama that takes place between sea bottom and surface is real. It is uncompromising. There is no predicting what you might see.

Tonight turned out to be a stellar example. Even Tomlinson went silent when I flipped the switch, and the black water beneath the house blossomed into a luminous translucent gel.

Simultaneously, a school of mullet exploded on the light's periphery, and we watched the fish go greyhounding into darkness.

Beneath my feet, under the dock, spadefish the size of plates grazed on barnacles that pulsed in feathered ivory colonies like flowers, raking in microscopic protein. There were gray snappers and black-banded sheepsheads, circling the pilings.

In a sand pocket beyond, I noticed meticulous shadowed bars—a small regiment of snook, their noses marking the direction of tidal flow. I also saw a lone redfish, with copper-blue scales, dozing next to a piling, while, above, dime-sized blue crabs created furious wakes as they sprinted across a universe of water, oblivious to the danger below.

"Doc . . . you see that? Over there—see it? There's something moving."

For some reason, Tomlinson whispered the question, and I followed his gaze into shadows of mangrove trees at the shore's edge. My friend's tone communicated curiosity, not danger, so I took my time.

I removed my glasses and cleaned them before replying, "I don't see anything." But then I said, *"Wait,"* and began walking toward shore because I saw what had captured the man's interest.

There was something lying on the sand between mangrove trees and the water. It was a man-sized shape, gray and glistening in the ambient light. Then another shape took form, this one animated and suddenly making a lot of noise as it crashed through foliage.

The shapes were alive, I realized. They were animals of some type.

Red mangroves are also called walking trees because their trunks are balanced on rooted tendrils that create a jumble of rubbery hoops

120

growing from swamp. Whatever the animal was, it was having trouble getting through the roots to the water.

Tomlinson whispered, as if in awe, "My God, Doc—this can't be happening!" Apparently, he had figured out what was in the mangroves, but I still had no clue.

I jogged down the boardwalk as my brain worked hard to cross-reference what I saw with anything I had ever seen before.

Nothing matched.

At first, I thought we'd surprised two stray dogs, from the way one of the creatures tried to lunge over the roots. But no . . . the shapes were too big to be dogs.

Feral hogs? A couple of panthers, maybe?

No . . .

For a moment, I wondered if I was seeing two large alligators. They often strayed into brackish water, and we occasionally even find them Gulf-side, off the Sanibel beach.

Wrong again. Gators don't lunge like greyhounds. And they don't make the clicking, whistling noises I was hearing now.

It was one of the rare times in my life when I wasn't carrying some kind of flashlight, which I regretted, because the creatures began to take form as I got closer. When my dock lights had first surprised them, one of the creatures had been on the bank, several feet from the water.

The other had been in the mangroves, many yards beyond.

I watched, transfixed, as first one, then the other animal, finally wiggled its way back into the shallows. Soon, the crash of foliage was replaced by a wild, rhythmic splashing as both creatures hobbyhorsed toward deeper water.

Visibility wasn't good in the March darkness, but I could see well enough now to finally know what we were looking at. Particularly telling were the fluked tails and the distinctive pointed rostrums of the two animals.

From the deck, I heard Tomlinson whoop, *"Wowie-zowie, dude!"* then laughed as he called, "This is wild, man! Have you ever seen anything like that in your life?"

No, I had not.

I had stopped running because I wanted to concentrate on what was happening. I watched intensely, aware that it was one of those rare moments when I knew that, later, I would want to recall each detail, every nuance of movement, in the scene that was unfolding.

The two creatures we had surprised were mammals. But they weren't land mammals. They were members of the family Delphinidae, genus *Tursiops*. They were pure creatures of the sea— at least, I had thought so until this instant.

I watched until the pair of animals had made it to deeper water, where they submerged . . .

reappeared . . . then vanished beneath a star-streaked sky.

After a moment, I walked in a sort of pleasant daze to the house, where Tomlinson stood, grinning. He held out an arm so we could bang fists and said in a soft voice, "Bottlenose dolphins. I wouldn't have believed it if I hadn't seen it for myself. Completely out of the water, feeding on dry land."

I was smiling, too. There are few things more energizing than the discovery of something profound in a place that is so familiar, you think all its secrets have been revealed.

Tomlinson was feeling it, too. "My God," he said, his head pivoting from the mangroves to the bay. "How could anyone ever get tired of living on the water? This place is magic, man, it's just pure-assed *magic*. Dolphins foraging beneath the trees while Sanibel Island sleeps. The freaking *wonder* of it all. Wow!"

He paused, both of us listening to the distinctive *Puffffft!* as the dolphins exhaled in synch, out of sight now but their images still clear in my mind.

Tomlinson asked me, "Have you ever in your life heard about something like this happening? Not me. Never ever. And I know *a lot* of devoted druggies who see crazy shit all the time."

Tomlinson was so excited that he was talking too fast, thinking too fast, and I wanted to slow everything down.

I replied, "Hold on a second, I'm trying to think this through. We don't know for sure they were feeding. That's an assumption." My mind was working on the problem, delighted by the challenge.

Tomlinson tried to interrupt, but I shushed him with a wave of my hand.

I said, "Granted, it's the first explanation that came into my mind—that they came ashore to feed. But we need to take a look in the mangroves. A *close* look. And photograph the entire scene, too. If they were feeding, they might have left something behind. I'll get a flashlight."

Tomlinson repeated himself, saying, "In all the literature, in all the crazy dolphin stories I've heard, this is a first. What about you?"

His reference to crazy dolphin stories was an unusual thing for someone like Tomlinson to say, but he was spot-on. Bottlenose dolphins are the unwitting darlings of every misinformed crackpot who has ever yearned for a mystical link between humans and the sea. That includes more than a few misguided biologists who have credited the animals with everything from paranormal powers to the ability to heal children stricken by disease.

Dolphins—and these were *dolphins*, not porpoises —are brilliantly adaptable pack animals. Intelligent, true, but they are still pack animals, which includes all the ugly mob behavior that

124

the term implies: assault, gang rape, occasionally the attempted genocide of competing species.

Dolphins are brilliantly adapted for survival—and they survive relentlessly, as all successful species do.

I waved for Tomlinson to follow me toward the house as I answered, "In Indonesia, I heard stories, maybe Malaysia, too, from people who claimed to know people who said they'd seen dolphins foraging in the mangroves, feeding on crabs. But it's never been documented—not that I know of, anyway. I just figured it was part of the dolphin mythology. You know, the sort of stories that date back to mermaids—bull dolphins sneaking ashore to have intercourse with virgins. That sort of baloney."

I left the man there and went up the steps, two at a time, to fetch flashlights. Mentally, I was assembling a list of dolphin experts I could call, pleased not only because of what we had just seen but because it had taken Tomlinson's mind off the Guatemalan girl.

When my pal is fixated on a subject, he becomes repetitive and tiresome. I had invited him to dinner earlier in the day, so there was no getting out of it, and I didn't want to have to endure his brooding theories about what had happened to Tula Choimha.

I believed that he was underestimating the girl. She had managed to travel solo, with very little money, from the mountains of Guatemala to Florida on her own with no problems—none I was aware of, anyway. The territory she had crossed included some of the most dangerous country on earth—particularly the migrant trails of Mexico, where outlaws and warring gangs prey on travelers. Robbery and rape are commonplace.

The fact that Tula had negotiated the trip successfully, and alone, said a lot about her character. But it said more about her instincts. The girl was street-savvy. I thought it unlikely that she would have allowed herself to be victimized in the markedly safer environment of a Florida trailer park, Harris Squires or no Harris Squires.

Inside the house, I grabbed two potent little Fenix LED flashlights, hesitated, then decided, what the hell, first I would change into clean shorts and a shirt. The dolphins wouldn't be coming back, so there was no hurry now.

I leaned outside and told Tomlinson he should do the same. In the lab, I found a 500-milliliter bottle of reagent-grade propyl alcohol. I tossed my clothes outside, doused myself good, ears included, then placed the jug on the deck for Tomlinson to use.

As I changed, I checked my phone messages. One was from a state biologist whose name I had heard, but I'd never met. Her name was Emily Marston.

Emily—common nicknames included Emma, Milly and Em. Probably because it had been a month since I'd had a serious date, I wondered if any fit.

"Dr. Ford, in the morning I'm leading the necropsy on the alligator that was killed tonight. Since we're working at the park station on Sanibel and since you were involved, I thought you might like to join us. But only if you're interested personally. This is not an official request."

I found the woman's voice attractive, and her last sentence an alluring addendum that was, at once, both welcoming and dismissive.

Yes, I was interested.

I made note of the lady's name, her number, the time of the necropsy, then went out the door after slipping a little Kodak point-and-shoot camera into my pocket.

As I did, my mind returned briefly to Tomlinson's assertion that the bodybuilder Harris Squires was responsible for the Guatemalan girl's disappearance. Was there even a small possibility that he was right?

I'm a careful man—particularly when a child is involved and when my own conscience is on the line. I gave it some more thought.

"Every paranormal receptor in my body is convinced that the guy grabbed her," Tomlinson had told me, or something close to that. It summarized his entire argument. Everyone else at the trailer park had told us that she disappeared at night all the time. If they weren't worried, why should we be? But just in case, while I was at the necropsy tomorrow morning, I decided I'd make sure Tomlinson went back to the trailer park to dig around.

EIGHT

WHEN HARRIS SQUIRES TOLD TULA, "your friend, Carlson, must be in a lot of pain because he wants you to come to the hospital," she knew he was lying, but the voice in her head told her to get into Squires's big, rumbling truck anyway and go with him.

This was early the next morning, several hours after the EMTs had refused to let Tula ride in the ambulance, and after many more hours that she had spent in hiding.

The girl knew it was unwise to linger near the lake, inviting questions from the police. So she had wandered off to her tree to speak with the owls, but the owls were not calling, possibly because of all the noise and flashing lights.

Even so, she waited, sitting alone in the high limbs of the banyan, where she could observe the actions of her second *patron*, Tomlinson, and his friend, the large man with eyeglasses, who was speaking with police.

Tula focused on Tomlinson, who was talking to Squires. She sensed her *patron*'s good heart and godliness, and also that he was angry about something. He was angry at the landlord, perhaps, who had used God's name to blaspheme them even though they had saved his life.

Yes . . . the man was angry at Squires. T had watched Tomlinson walk toward the h landlord, and, for a moment, she thought might strike him. Instead, the two men exchang loud words that weren't always loud enou for her to hear, but she heard enough. Tula kne they were talking about her and she listene carefully.

Soon, she felt ashamed because she realized that the landlord was telling the *patron* about seeing her naked in the bathtub. The girl felt her face become hot, and she felt like sobbing.

No man had ever seen Tula naked before, and very few women. Sitting in the tree, she had vowed to herself that it would never happen again. *Ever.* Not as long as she lived—unless, of course, the voice in her head, the Maiden's voice, told her that she should marry. But that seemed unlikely, and, even then, Tula would not want it to happen.

The Maiden had gone to her death a virgin Tula knew this was true, just as she knew eve detail of the saint's life because, at the con Sister Lionza had given her books about J

Arc. Tula had read those books so many times that he knew them by heart.

He favorite book was a simple volume that included only words that the Maiden had written in r own warrior's hand or had spoken before witnesses. Tula loved the book so much that it a one of the few things she had brought with her from the mountains of Guatemala. Its entries panned the saint's childhood, included her lionhearted testimony at her trial and, finally, her last words as flames consumed her body: Jesus! *Jesus!*

There was no intrusive scholarship in the book. No third-party guessing about what the Maiden had thought or felt.

That small book was pure, like the Maiden herself. Tula carried it everywhere and had read it so often that her own patterns of speech now naturally imitated the passionate rhythms of the girl who had been chosen by God.

Tula knew that imitating the Maiden's style of speaking caused some people to look at her strangely, but she took it as an affirmation of her devotion. The book had been a great comfort to Tula on the journey from the mountains to this modern land of cars and asphalt by the sea.

Tula had memorized several favorite passages. There were many that applied to her own life:

hen I was thirteen, a voice from God came n me govern myself. The first time I heard it, I was terrified. The voice came to me about noon; it was summer, and I was in my father's garden. I had not fasted the day before. I heard the voice on my right. There was a great light all about.

Soon afterward, I vowed to keep my virginity for as long as it should please God . . .

Tula had not been in her father's garden, of course, when the Maiden's voice first came. Her father had been murdered by the *revolucionarios* as Tula, age eight, watched from the bushes. The memory of what she had seen, heard and smelled was so shocking—her father's screams, the odor of petrol and flesh—that her brain had walled the memory away in a dark place.

Little more than a year later, when Tula began to feel at home at the convent, the dark space in her soul had opened slowly to embrace the Maiden's light.

Another favorite line from the book was: *I would rather die than to do what I know to be a sin.*

When Tula whispered those words, she could feel the meaning burn in her heart. She had whispered the phrase aloud many times, always sincerely, as an oath to God. The words were clean and unwavering, like the Maiden's spirit. Tula could speak the phrase silently in the time it took her to inhale, then exhale, one long breath.

I would rather die than to do . . .

. . . what I know to be a sin.

Tula longed for the same life of purity, for it was the Maiden's writing that had first sent her into the trees to seek her own visions. The Maiden, Tula had read, had often sought God's voice in a place called the Polled Wood, in France, where she had sat in the branches of a tree known as the Fairy Tree.

Tula doubted if she would ever see France, but Florida had to be more like Orléans than the jungles of Quintana Roo.

It was strange, now, to sit in a Florida banyan tree so far from home, watching the flashing lights of the emergency vehicles. The Maiden's visions, Tula remembered, were always accompanied by bright light, which caused the girl to concentrate even harder on what she was seeing.

The lights pulsed blue and red, exploding off the clouds, then sparking downward, rainlike, through the leaves. The lights were brighter than any Tula had ever seen, lights so piercing, so rhythmic, that they invited the girl to stare until she felt her body loosen as her thoughts purified and became tunneled.

Soon, Tula slipped into a world that was silent, all but for the Maiden's voice—Jehanne, her childhood friends had called the young saint. Jehanne's voice was so sure and clear, it was as if her moist lips touched Tula's ear as she delivered a message.

It was a message Tula had heard several times in the last week.

You are sent by God to rally your people. The clothing of a boy is your armor. The amulets you wear are your shields . . .

Fear not. I speak as a girl who knew nothing of riding and warfare until God took my hand. We drove the foreigners away because it was His will. He provided the way.

You, too, are God's instrument. You will gather your family in this foreign land, and free them from their greed. You will lead them home again, where they can live as a people, not slaves, because it is His will.

Trust Him always. He will provide the way for you.

Tula loved the solitude of trees. She loved the intimacy of this muscled branch that was contoured like a saddle between her legs. Once, as the saint's voice paused in reflection, Tula found the nerve to whisper a question with a familiarity that she had never risked before.

"Jehanne? Holy Maiden? I think of you as my loving sister. Is this wrong? I have to ask."

I am the God-light that lives within you, the Maiden's voice replied. *We are one. Like twins with a one soul.*

Sisters? Tula hazarded, thinking the word but not speaking it.

Forever sisters, the Maiden replied. *Even when you leave this life for the next.*

• • •

For more than two hours, Tula had sat motionless in the tree as the Maiden spoke to her, providing comfort and the governing voice of God. She was only vaguely aware when her *patron*, Tomlinson, walked beneath the tree, calling her name, followed by the large man with eyeglasses. Whose name, she had learned, was Dr. Ford.

There was something unusual about her *patron*'s friend, she realized vaguely, as the two hurried past. Something solid and safe about Dr. Ford . . . But the man was cold, too. His spirit filled Tula with an unsettling sensation, like an unfamiliar darkness that was beyond her experience.

The girl didn't allow her mind to linger on the subject, and she was not tempted to call out a reply because she was so deliciously safe. Her body and heart were encased by the Maiden. The Maiden's lips never left her ear.

Even when the flashing lights vanished from the tree canopy, Tula continued sitting because Jehanne continued to speak, whispering strong thoughts into Tula's head.

The Maiden's words were so glory filled and righteous that Tula thought she might burst from the swelling energy that filled her body. It caused blood to pulse in her chest, and in her thighs, until her body trembled. It was a throbbing sensation so strong that she felt as if she might explode if the pressure within didn't find release.

You are sent to rally your people. You are sent by God . . .

The first time Tula had heard those words was only seven days ago, her first night in Florida. She had been sitting on this same thick branch, new to the large banyan tree.

Those words had been a revelation.

Tula had come to *El Norte* to find her mother and family, yes. But in her heart she knew there was a greater cause for which God had chosen her. Why else would the Maiden risk guiding her to *El Norte*, the direction of death?

On that night one week ago, Tula had been so moved by the revelation that, as she returned to her trailer, she had stopped to address adults who, every evening, collected around a fire to drink beer and laugh.

It offended Tula the way the adults were behaving because she feared her mother had behaved similarly after she had abandoned her own family. Even so, the girl had stood silently, feeling the heat of fire light on her face, listening and watching.

Gradually, Tula became angry. The Maiden had ordered her soldiers and pages not to drink alcohol or to sin with loose women and dice. She had counseled her followers to pray every day, and to never swear.

These adults weren't soldiers, but they were all members of the same mountain people. They were Maya, they were *Indígena*, like her. And Tula knew it was wrong for them to be living drunken, modern lives so removed from the families they had left behind in the cloud forests.

Tula stepped closer to the fire. She cleared her throat and waited for the adults to notice her. Soon, as voices around her went silent, Tula let the French Maiden guide her Mayan words.

"If your children could see you now," the girl asked in a strong voice, "what would they think? What would your wives and husbands think? I am speaking of the families you left behind in the mountains. Your *real* families. Do you think they are consorting with drunken neighbors, lusting after money and flesh? No. They are asleep in their *palapas*. Their hearts are broken and lonely from missing you."

Tula was surprised by her own confidence, but more surprised by the angry reaction of the adults. Men sat in a moody silence for a moment, then began to jeer and wave her away as if Tula's opinion meant nothing. The women were indignant, then furious. They swore at her in Spanish, calling her a stupid boy who had sex with animals. And the matron of the group—a squat, loud woman—picked up a stick and threatened to thrash Tula unless she ran away.

Tula had stood her ground, looking into the woman's eyes as she approached. Tula was unafraid, for, in that instant, she experienced something strange. She sensed the Maiden melding into her body, bringing with her a heart so strong that Tula felt a profound and joyous confidence that she had never before experienced.

"Sisters?" she had asked the Maiden.

Yes. Even when you leave this life for the next.

Tula had doubted the promise at first but now she knew they were Jehanne's own true words.

As the matron drew near, Tula had smiled, saying softly, "Strike me if you wish, but I will only turn the other cheek. First, though, tell me why you are so angry. Do you hate me for what I said? Or do you hate me because what I said is true?"

The matron had sworn at her and swung the stick in warning but then stepped back because Tula did not flinch. Still smiling, Tula had said to the woman, "Do you remember the goodness of God that you felt as a child? He is still there, in your heart. Why do you fight Him so?"

That stopped the matron, and she listened more closely as Tula told her, "You came to *El Norte* because you love your family. God knows that. It is the same with everyone here, is it not? Only you know how painful it is to be a mother or father who cannot afford food for their children's table.

"But do you also understand how hurtful it is to lose your mother in exchange for a bundle of pesos sent weekly from the United States? Children need their parents more than money or food—that's why I'm here. I have come to lead my family home."

Then Tula had asked the woman, "Who did you leave behind? A son? A daughter?"

The woman's expression transitioned from anger to uncertainty. "What business is that of yours, stupid child?"

Tula was aware of the Maiden inside her, exploring the woman's thoughts, but the Maiden did not share what she was learning.

"You left behind a husband and children," Tula guessed, feeling her own way. "You planned to return, but here you are. How many years has it been?"

It took a full minute before the matron spoke, but she finally did. "Two children," the woman replied, sounding weary now and a little unnerved. "Our first child, she died, so there were three, not two."

The woman looked at the group as she added, "I must stop saying that I have only two children. My third child, her name was Alexandra, but only for nine days. She is with God now. I should have told you this."

Tula had glanced at the man with whom the woman had been sitting and knew he wasn't her husband. The woman was an adulteress, but Tula did not say it. For some reason, she felt kindly toward the woman despite the woman's sins and respected her sadness.

Instead, Tula said, "You are a good women, I feel that is true. It has been several years since you have seen your family, yet you have not abandoned them. I know I'm right, I can see God's own goodness in your eyes. You are a devoted mother. How many times a month do you send money?"

The woman replied, "Every week, I cash my check at the Winn-Dixie, then pay cash to the Western Union clerk at the cigarette counter. At Christmas, I send three checks. In four years, I have never missed a week. Even though my husband has taken another woman, I still send the money."

As an aside to the adults the woman added, "I've heard that my children now call this new woman mother. It is something I have been ashamed to share. I don't know why I am telling you now."

When Tula reached to place her hand on the matron's shoulder, the woman shrugged the hand away, getting angry again—angry not at Tula but because she was so close to tears.

"Leave me alone," the woman said. "We are adults, we've worked hard all day in the fields. Now we are relaxing, what business is this of yours? Go play with your little *penga* instead of harassing good men and women."

"Maybe you know my family," Tula had pressed. "My mother's name is Zabillet. Here, people call her Mary. My brother's name is Pacaw, but sometimes Pablo. He left home six months ago. I have two aunts and an uncle in Florida, too, but I don't know where."

The woman seemed to be paying attention as Tula added, "My mother came to *El Norte* four years ago, when I was only eight. Like you, she sent money every week. There is a phone booth outside the *tienda* in our village, and every Sunday night I was there, waiting, when she called. Two months ago, though, my mother stopped calling. And the number to her cell phone no longer works."

"It's because of the coyotes and the field bosses," a man sitting nearby explained. "They control us by controlling our telephones. Everyone knows that, unless you're stupid. You must be stupid. Why does that surprise you?"

Tula replied, "It doesn't surprise me. Not now. Not since I've learned how the Mexican coyotes cheat us. They charge us pesos to come to *El Norte*. Then they charge us dollars to provide us with work and a place to sleep, and a telephone that they can disable at any time. But when my mother stopped calling, I knew something was wrong."

Sounding impatient, another man said, "We

were enjoying ourselves before you interrupted. Now you stand here, asking rude questions. Our *Indígena* sisters and brothers arrive in Florida every day, but we don't ask their names. We mind our own business. If you have lost your mother, go to Indiantown and ask the *Indígena* there. Or go to Immokalee. It is only an hour's drive in a truck.

"If your mother is in Florida," the man continued, "the Maya of Immokalee and Indiantown will know—there are many thousands of us in those villages. Now, please get out of my sight. I did not work all day in the sun to have my beer interrupted by a disrespectful child who criticizes his elders."

Immokalee.

Tula had heard of the town, of course. It was one of the last places her mother had lived prior to her disappearance. Tula had heard of Indiantown, too. Everyone in Guatemala knew of these villages because they were the largest Mayan settlements in Florida. In these places, Tula had heard, the *Indígena* sang the old songs and spoke the ancient language, not the bastard tongue of the Mexicans.

Tula said to the man, "I appreciate your advice, but you are wrong about me being disrespectful. I said what I said, but the words are not mine. You do not understand who I am. Look at me closely, perhaps you will."

141

"The nerve of this *mericon*!" one of the men chided. "He is a dirty little faggot. See how he poses and struts, as if he is more important than his elders?"

"Doubt me if you wish," Tula said in a firm voice, "but I will not listen to your profanities. Look at me. Don't just use your eyes, use your heart also. I have been sent here by my patron saint. I am unworthy, just a stupid child. But I am also an instrument of God. So be careful how you speak to me."

There! She had finally said aloud what she had never had the courage, or conviction, to share with anyone. Tula was afraid for a moment how the people would react.

She could feel the adults looking at her, their faces suspended above the fire as brown as wooden masks worn at festival time in the Mayan mountains. As the men and women stared, Tula felt her body transforming as she stood erect, chin angled, and she wondered if the adults would correctly perceive the changes that were taking place within her.

It was something that Sister Lionza had been teaching Tula at the monastery, the art of projecting thoughts—the first hint that the nun was preparing her for membership in the *Culta de Shimono*.

Thoughts are energy. Our thoughts are sparks from God's eyes. Devote your thoughts to an image. Picture that image with all your heart. Soon others will see, with their eyes, the image that lives in your mind.

In Tula's mind, as she posed by the fire, she envisioned a precise picture of herself the way she *yearned* to look. Her jeans and ragged shirt were armor molded to her body by firelight. The amulet and medallion that she clutched were now a glittering shield.

Yes, Tula decided. The adults saw that her body had been transformed. A few of them, anyway. It was in their eyes, both respect and wonder. She felt sure enough to say, "I'm only a child from the mountains, but I have been transformed by my patron saint. Don't be uneasy, don't be afraid of my strange dress. The Maiden speaks to me and she speaks through me. She provides me words for you that I believe are words from God."

Voices around the fire muttered, asking about the Maiden—what did the name mean?—while Tula continued speaking.

"The Maiden has told me that this land will never be our home. Our home is in the cloud forests of the mountains. It is in the jungles where our ancestors built pyramids that rivaled the greatness of Egypt. She has told us to think back and remember our home. And the love we have for it. It is true that we do not have shiny red pickup trucks in our yards. Or televisions with large screens. But what good is a red truck when it cannot drive you to your family?"

Tula sensed emotion in the people her words touched just as she could also hear the whispered grumblings of those who did not see or believe —men mostly, but also a few women who got to their feet, speaking insults and a few whispered profanities.

The matron, however, was not among them. She had stared at Tula with glistening eyes.

"You speak to God?" the woman asked. "How do we know you are not lying?"

Jehanne had been asked this same question many times by her inquisitors, so Tula used the Maiden's own words to answer.

"I do not speak to God. He speaks to me. Any other way would be improper. Who am I? I am a poor, stupid child. The voices that direct me come from Him. I believe this truly in my own heart. I am his instrument; only a messenger instructed by the words of my patron saint, the Maiden."

The woman, near tears, replied, "I don't know why I believe you, but I do. It must be true, for you looked into my heart and told me what I was feeling. I miss my children. I miss my village, and the cooking fires and the odors of my girlhood. What did you say to us about God being in us as children? I can't remember your exact words—"

"I asked you to remember how you felt as a child. When you felt the goodness of God inside you. God is still there, alive in your heart. I asked, 'Why do you fight Him so?' "

From the shadows beyond the fire, a man's voice chided Tula, saying, "Next this boy will be telling us that he also speaks to the goats who bugger him! Why is he wasting our time. Go away, little turd, or I will bugger you myself!" Grinning, the man had stood and pretended to unsnap his belt.

Tula was surprised that only a few people laughed at the insult, and she was comforted by the realization that very few of these people would ever laugh at her again.

When Tula had finally left that fire circle, seven nights before, some of the adults had watched her in a silence that was a mixture of fear, awe and longing. On that very same night, someone placed a statuette of the Virgin Mary outside her trailer.

The next evening, after the day's work was done, the matron and two neighbor women appeared at Tula's trailer, seeking to speak privately.

The next night, a small line formed outside Tula's door. Each night afterward, the line was longer. Some people came from as far as Indiantown, Miami and Immokalee to speak with the child who was said to be an emissary from God.

News of the unusual child traveled at lightning speed through the cheap cell phones of the Guatemalan community.

Sometimes, women and men wept as they asked for Tula's guidance and advice. Many attempted to kneel and kiss her hand, but Tula refused their adulation, just as the Maiden had refused the worshipping gestures of her own followers six hundred years before.

"We are sisters?" Tula had questioned Jehanne, hoping desperately that it was true.

Even when you leave this life for the next, the Maiden had promised.

Tula was now more determined than ever to be equal to the honor of being chosen by Jehanne.

To every person who came to her, Tula challenged them with the same parting question: "Do you remember the goodness of God that was in you as a child? He is still there, in your heart. Why do you fight Him so?"

Much had changed since Tula had spoken to the fire circle a week before. The respect with which her neighbors treated her was beyond her experience, yet she handled it comfortably and exercised her new power only for good—to spread the word that she was searching for her family, and, tonight, to order the adults to help save her *patron*, Carlson, and also the landlord, Harris Squires.

Something else that had changed, Tula realized, was that she had lost her anonymity. The eyes of her neighbors followed her everywhere she went. Which is why she had waited long after the ambulance and police cars had left to finally climb down from the tree and retreat to her trailer.

She didn't stay long, though, because the memory of Harris Squires's words scared her. She knew the giant man would come looking for her soon. So she had gone to the public toilet, curled up in a stall and had tried to sleep.

Too much had happened, though, for Tula's mind to relax. She fretted about Carlson—would he live?—and also regretted not speaking with the strange man, Tomlinson, who Tula barely knew but who she had immediately accepted as her second patron and protector.

Early that morning, still unable to sleep, Tula had returned to her tree to speak with the owls and watch the sunrise, she told herself. But it was really to invite that pulsing, trembling feeling into her body. As she straddled the limb, which Tula thought of as a saddle, the Maiden had floated into Tula's body almost immediately, but only for a short time.

Suddenly, then, without farewell, the Maiden's voice was gone. It was replaced by the distant inquiries of morning birds—the owls had remained silent—and then the sound of approaching foot-steps.

Tula had been weeping, as she always did when the Maiden left her, yet she was crying softly enough to hear the crack of twigs and then a man's voice say, "Lookee, lookee, what I see. It's getting so I know where to find you. What do you think you are, *chula*? Some kind of bird?"

Tula looked down to see Harris Squires staring at her through the strange binoculars that allowed him to see in the night like an animal.

It wasn't until the giant had grabbed Tula, clapping his hand over her mouth to silence her, that the Maiden's words returned to comfort the girl, saying, *Stop fighting, go with him. You are in God's hands. God will show you the way.*

Now, sitting beside Squires in his oversized truck, Tula said to the man, "What do you call these bracelets on my wrists? They're hurting me. Will you please take them off?"

Squires made a noise of impatience as he drove. He had been trying to focus on his sex fantasy, but the girl kept talking.

"Why don't you answer me?" the girl said, irritated. "I have every reason to be angry at you. Instead, I am speaking to you politely. You should at least answer when I ask you a polite question."

Squires made another groaning sound.

She didn't stop. "If I had wanted to run from you, God would have given me the strength. Instead, He told me to come with you. That's why I am here. There's no need for you to chain my hands."

Squires was aggravated, but also surprised by the girl's calm voice, her matter-of-fact manner.

"They're called handcuffs," he told her, because it was obvious that she wouldn't shut up until he answered. "It's a safety precaution. If you did something stupid, like open the door and jump, who'd you think would get the blame?"

"I just told you," the girl replied, "God wants me to be with you. God must care about you or He wouldn't have told me to save you from the alligator last night. I wouldn't be with you this morning. Do you remember me ordering my people to help you?"

Her people? Who the hell did she think she was?

The girl had something wrong with her brain, Squires decided. Maybe she was some rare variety of retard—he had seen things on TV about kids like that. Or maybe just crazy. It had to be one of the two because of course Squires remembered the girl yelling at the crowd of Mexicans, ordering them to help him. He also remembered the little flash of hope the girl's voice had created in him as that big goddamn gator swam toward him fast with those devil-red eyes.

Why would the little brat try to help him? It made no sense for her to save his life after he had forced his way into the bathroom, then played around with her while she was naked.

Crazy. Yeah. She had to be.

As Squires drove, he looked at the girl, who was fiddling with the handcuffs, acting like they were hurting her skinny wrists. Close-up, she was a tiny little thing, her fingers long and delicate with dirt beneath the nails. The vertebrae on the back of her neck were visible beneath the Dutch-boy hair, like something he'd see on skinny dogs.

Compared to Squires's own bulk, the girl was a sack of skin and bone, which Squires found galling. The weirdo was nothing but a worthless little *chula*, yet there was also something oddly big about her, too, the way she handled herself, full of confidence. It was disconcerting.

In a bar, Squires could flash his shit-kicker monster face as fast as any other brawler, but, truth was, he'd never felt confident about anything in his life. Not compared to the way this little kid acted, anyway.

What really burned his ass, Squires realized, was that all the women in his life were the same way. Frankie and his ball-busting witch of a mother both had that same know-it-all confidence.

No . . . not exactly the same, because the girl didn't use the same nasty-mouthed meanness that his mother and Frankie both used to make him feel like a pile of shit most the time. But

150

even though the girl was different, in her way, she was just another bossy female.

Tula said to him now, "You *do* remember that I helped save you. I can tell. Just now, you were thinking about the big alligator coming to eat you. But it didn't eat you because we all helped you. So you should trust me. I'm not going to run away. I'm here because God wants me to be with you. Perhaps He wants me to be your protector every day, not just last night. It's possible."

"My protector!" Squires laughed. "Take a good look at me, *chula*. Why the hell would I ever need your help?"

He glanced away from his driving long enough to touch his right bicep, which he was flexing. "You ever seen another man in your life built like me? Not down there in some Mexican shithole, you never did, I'd bet on that. I don't need protecting from nobody because there's not a goddamn thing in the world I'm scared of."

A moment later, he said, "Okay, in a minute or so I'm going to pull up to a garage and I want you to do what I tell you to do."

They were in East Fort Myers now, bouncing down a long driveway toward the river, horses grazing in a pasture to their right.

The giant man continued, "We're gonna switch vehicles—it's where my mom lives, but the bitch isn't home. She's off on some cruise someplace with one of her boyfriends. But if you see someone coming down that goddamn driveway, you honk this horn, understand? I'll leave the truck running until I get it in the garage."

No one came. Leaving Tula chained in the truck, Squires even took some time to go inside the house, make a protein shake and pack a bag of ice for his sore leg. He also found a pint bottle of tequila, which he kept on the seat next to him.

Soon they were on the road again, but in an older truck with huge tires that smelled of dogs and beer and the tequila the man was nipping at. His hunting buggy, Squires called the vehicle, which had an even louder engine than the truck they had left behind hidden in his mother's garage.

Tula knew that Squires was lying about taking her to the hospital to see Carlson. But what she had told the giant was true. Even though the man had forced her into the truck—leaving her few possessions behind at the trailer park—she wasn't going to attempt to escape. Not unless the Maiden ordered her to.

The handcuffs were heavy on her wrists, though. And Tula felt vulnerable, sitting on the floor with her hands bound, unable to see out the window. The man was a fast driver, weaving through morning traffic, braking hard for red lights. Or maybe it just felt as if they were going fast because she was on the floor and Squires had the windows open, the roar of the truck's mufflers loud in Tula's ears.

This was even more frightening than climbing onto the top of a freight train, riding exposed to wind and rain through the mountains of Mexico. On the train, at least, Tula had been able to watch for dangers ahead.

But not here, riding on the floor. She was unaccustomed to this kind of speed and she feared a collision. Tula imagined impact, then being trapped, unable to use her hands, especially if there was fire.

Fire terrified the girl. She had watched her father die in flames, smelled his clothes burning, heard his screams, and the vision still haunted her.

Even the Maiden had feared fire. In the little book Tula had left back in the trailer were Jehanne's own words:

Sooner would I have my head cut off seven times than to suffer the woeful death of fire . . .

Tula bowed her head and began to pray, speaking in English loudly enough to be sure that the giant landlord heard her, hoping to irritate the man into action.

"Dear Lord my God, I ask in Jesus' name all blessings on this man who is driving too fast and drinking liquor at the same time. I ask that he look into his heart and understand that he's scaring me, the way he's got my hands locked.

Even though the police might stop us at any time and arrest him and take him to jail! Make him know I am not going to run away because I am his friend. And a friend does not leave a friend . . ."

The girl went on and on like that.

The louder the girl prayed, the bigger the gulps Squires took from the tequila bottle. After a while, even liquor didn't help, and Squires couldn't stand it anymore. He glanced down at Tula, then turned on the radio, wanting to drown out her voice. It was AC/ DC doing "Black Ice," but it only caused the girl to pray louder.

Shit. The little brat was maddening.

Squires found all her talk about God disturbing, an upset he felt in his belly. Truth was, he didn't want the girl to talk at all. Even if he didn't make his fantasy come true by raping her, he still had to kill her when they got to the hunting camp— what choice did he have? And the more she talked, the more girlish and human she seemed, which Squires didn't like.

It irked him that she had brought up the gator attack to make him feel guilty. She was just making it harder for him, using guilt like a weapon, which is the same thing that Frankie and his mother did on a daily basis.

The realization that this little girl was no different provided Squires with a sudden, sweet burst of anger that immediately made him feel better about driving her to the hunting camp, where he was going to get her drunk, get her clothes off and have some fun.

"Why can't you just sit there and shut up," he said to the girl as he screwed the top back on the bottle. "Do you want to see your drunken friend, Carlson, or not? I'm trying to do you a favor! So instead of whining about your wrists and asking God for a bunch of stupid favors, you should be thanking me for going out of my way to help you."

"But what will the policemen say if they stop us and see what you've done to me?" the girl replied, sounding more like an adult than a girl. "Or if we get in a wreck and the ambulance comes? They'll see that you've handcuffed me and take you to jail. How will God be able to help you in jail?"

Squires said it aloud this time—"Shit!"—as he turned hard onto a shell road, then parked behind some trees in a chunk of undeveloped pasture, where he removed the girl's handcuffs.

It was probably a smart thing to do, because it was midmorning now, he had to pee, and if the girl was going to try to run an empty pasture was better than a 7-Eleven or some other place where strangers could see.

But the girl didn't run. When Squires returned to the truck, he yanked Tula up onto the seat beside him, and said to her, "There! Happy now? You got no more excuses for whining."

It didn't shut her up, though.

"You should wear your seat belt," the girl reminded him when they were on the road again. "God cares about you. You keep forgetting. And if you got hurt in a crash, what would happen to me? I have no money and no extra clothes."

"Do you ever think about anyone else but yourself?" Squires snapped.

A few seconds later, he said, "God cares?" and managed to laugh, although it wasn't easy. The suggestion that anyone cared about him was idiotic. His head ached from too much tequila, last night and already this morning. And Frankie was pissed at him—yet again. Someone must have called her from the RV park last night when the cops arrived because the woman had left five messages on his cell between ten and two a.m. The last message was a rant so profane that Squires had deleted it before getting to the end.

"I ask you to do one simple thing and you completely fucked it up—as usual," Frankie's message had begun, and then it got nasty from there.

Well . . . that was enough of Frankie's bullying ways, as far as Squires was concerned. He had had it up to *here* with the woman's bullshit. That's why before leaving Red Citrus he had cleaned out all the important stuff from their double-wide just on the chance he could summon the nerve to leave and never see that bitch again.

The important stuff included bags of veterinarian-grade pills and powder that were in the locked toolbox in the bed of his hunting truck. And also about sixty thousand cash from steroid sales, which was in a canvas bag bundled with rubber bands along with the Ruger revolver. The whole business was under the driver's seat, safely inside a hidden compartment that he had made himself using hinges and a cutting torch.

Frankie was mad now? *Christ.* The woman would go absolutely apeshit when she realized the money was missing.

Squires was also worried about Laziro Victorino, the badass Mexican with the box cutter and teardrop tattoo under his eye. If cops found a piece of a woman's body inside an alligator from Red Citrus, the V-man would know instantly it was one of his prostitutes and he was going to be pissed. Someone would have to pay, because that's the way it worked with the Mexican gangs.

You kill one of them, they killed two of you. That's why Victorino made snuff films. To remind people.

First person the V-man would suspect was him and Frankie because everyone knew they had a thing for videoing Mexican girls, sometimes as many as three at a time. They were videos that Frankie posted on her porn website but also sold to Victorino's gangbangers, which was another way she made money when she wasn't dealing gear. Not that Squires and Frankie ever appeared on camera. No, the videos were for profit but also a way for Frankie to have fun behind the scenes.

Mostly, though, Squires was worried about the dead alligator. What would cops find in her belly when they cut the thing open? That would probably happen this morning, from what he had overheard the Wildlife cops saying. That reminded Squires to switch the radio from AC/DC to a news station.

In Florida, a dead alligator that had eaten a girl would be big news.

Even with the radio loud, it was hard to think his problems through. It was because the weird little Bible freak never shut up. She asked questions about the truck's air-conditioning. And the CD player, then about his iPhone, which was plugged into its cradle next to the gearshift. It was like the stupid kid had never been out in the world before.

The girl also kept giving him updates from God.

This God talk was getting old.

"Think back to when you were a child," she was telling Squires now as she sat upright beside him, looking at something near the gearshift— his iPhone, maybe. "Do you remember how safe you felt? Do you remember the love and good-

ness you felt? That was God's presence inside you. And He is still there, so why do you fight him so?"

They were on Corkscrew Road, driving east through bluffs of cypress trees, past orange groves and grazing cattle, toward Immokalee, the gate to his hunting camp only half an hour beyond that little tomato-packing town.

Because of what the girl was saying, Squires's mind slipped back to when he was young—he couldn't help himself even though he tried—and he was surprised to realize that the noisy little brat was right.

Truth was, he really had felt *different* as a child. He had felt safe and full of kindness, unless his witch of a mother was screaming at him, calling him a "worthless little bastard" or saying, "You're even stupider than your faggot father!"

It was strange how things had changed since he was a kid. Maybe because of the tequila, or maybe because of the guilt the girl had caused him to feel, the realization struck Squires as important. He took a swallow from the bottle and let his mind work on it until he thought, *I'll be goddamned. What the brat says is true.*

Somehow, the world and his life had become mean and dangerous and dirty.

How? When had it happened?

That was a complicated question that took some time. The man wrestled with the issue as he

159

drove. Had it started when he'd first discovered tequila and weed? Up until then, he'd been kind of a quiet, shy kid.

No . . . no, that wasn't the reason he felt as shitty as he did right now. His life had really taken a turn for the worse when he met Frankie. That was almost four years ago, him being twenty-two at the time, Frankie thirty-eight but still with a body on her. And the woman was a regular hellion when it came to games in bed.

Sex—Frankie was addicted to it, and not plain old regular sex, either. The woman liked it rough, sometimes violent enough that Squires's nose and lips would be bleeding when they were done—once even his dick, which was having problems enough of its own because of the way steroids affected it.

The woman liked hurting her partners, especially if they were female.

Yes, it was when he'd met Frankie that things had really begun to change. That's when his life had switched from living a hard-assed guy's life, hanging out with other bodybuilders, to living a life that was small and mean . . . yes, and dirty, too.

It was strange thinking about stuff like that now while driving to his hunting camp, where, until that instant, Harris Squires had fully intended to punish this noisy little freak by raping her.

But *damn* it. Now all this talk about God was deflating his enthusiasm, not to mention his dick. Worse, it was adding to his gloom. It threatened to bring back the withering guilt that kept welling up about accidentally murdering that Mexican woman.

Trouble was, unlike with the Mexican woman, Squires had no choice about the girl. She was an eyewitness. She had to go.

Because it made him mad thinking about what he had to do, he said to the little brat, "Do you have any idea how crazy you sound? You're in the United States now, *chula*. In Florida, they'll throw you in the loony bin for saying crazy crap like that."

Reaching for his iPhone for some reason, the girl replied, "Where are we going? I know you're not taking me to the hospital. You can trust me, so why not tell me? It's always better to tell the truth."

"Why, because God is watching us?" Squires laughed, pushing the girl's hand away. The time on his iPhone, he noted, was 10:32 a.m. They still had to get through Immokalee, another hour of driving ahead of them.

"If God really is watching," Squires told her, sounding both angry and serious, "the dude had better perform one of his miracles pretty damn quick. Or it's out of my hands, *chula*. Hear what I'm telling you?"

Because of the caring, wounded expression that appeared on the girl's face, Squires added, "No one can blame me. What happens next, I can't control. And that is the *truth*."

NINE

THE NEXT MORNING, I WAS UP BEFORE sunrise, 6:30 a.m., because I was supposed to meet the necropsy team at eight a.m. sharp. I wanted to get a quick workout in first, though.

Lately, I had been nursing a sore rotator cuff, but was still doing PT twice a day, taking only an occasional Monday off. I knew I'd feel like crap if I didn't get a sweat going and have a swim. When a man gets into his forties, he has two choices—invite the pain required to maintain his body or surrender himself to the indignity and pain of slow physical decomposition that, in my mind, would be worse than death.

I wanted to make this one fast but tough.

I punished myself with half an hour on a brutal little exercise machine called a VersaClimber. HIT—high-intensity training. Thirty seconds climbing the machine at sprinter's speed—about a hundred feet per minute—then thirty seconds at a slower pace. Over and over, nonstop, after a five-minute warm-up.

I couldn't use the pull-up bar, so did a hundred sit-ups, a hundred push-ups, then jogged Tarpon Bay Road to the beach. The swim out to the NO WAKE buoys and back was painful, but it didn't hurt as much as the mile-and-a-half run home.

When I lumbered, huffing and puffing, down the shell road, Mack, who owns Dinkin's Bay Marina, was having a meeting with Jeth, Nels and the other fishing guides. So I stuck around long enough to tell them about the dolphins we had seen in the mangroves—I knew they wouldn't believe Tomlinson—then headed for the shower. Tomlinson himself was already on his way back to Red Citrus.

An hour later, I was standing over the remains of the alligator I had killed. The thing was stretched out, belly-up, on a tarp beside dissecting trays, a lab scale, and an assembly of knives, jars and a single stainless-bladed saw.

It was not something I felt good about, looking down at the dead gator. This inanimate mass only hours before had been a tribute to the genius of natural selection and the animal's own survival skills. The rounds I'd fired had put an end to a life that had probably spanned sixty years.

Emily Marston's team consisted of herself, a sullen man who didn't offer his name and a graduate student from Florida Gulf Coast University who was assigned to document the necropsy on video.

The sullen man, I soon decided, had been romantically involved with the woman biologist, but the relationship had ended recently and unpleasantly.

It wasn't a guess and it wasn't intuition.

The situation was easily read in the tension between the two, the curt questions, the man's surly tone and the woman's defensive body language.

Judging from his age, the man might have been one of Marston's professors a few years back. In the field sciences, it's not unusual for female students to bond with male teachers—ironic that the romantic habits of scientists often mimic the behavior of the animals they study, but it is true.

Emily Marston certainly wasn't icy to me. She was warm and deferential. The way her eyes sought to communicate with mine caused me to wonder if her invitation to the necropsy had been more than professional courtesy. We probably had a few mutual, peripheral friends, but we'd never met. I wondered why.

"Dr. Ford, I've read so many of your papers— some of them a couple of times," Marston had said, greeting me as I'd stepped from my truck. "I guess you'd call me . . . well, a sort of fan. Except now you'll just think I'm an even bigger nerd than I am."

She was a large woman, late twenties, with an angular Midwestern face that suggested the

164

automotive crossroads of Michigan—part German with a touch of Pole and Irish, I guessed. She struck me as the librarian type: a woman who camouflaged her body beneath baggy, masculine clothing that only served to emphasize a busty, long-legged femininity.

Right away, I was interested in the woman physically. I couldn't help myself. I prefer the closet beauties, the private, introspective types who share their physical gifts only with a few. But I also reminded myself that, by Dinkin's Bay standards, I had been abstinent for a long, long time. And seducing women who are on the rebound from a relationship is a repugnant behavior employed only by the lowest form of predatory male.

Even so, I noticed that incidental physical contact between us was more than occasional. It seemed accidental, though it seldom is. Shoulder bumps shoulder, elbow brushes breast. It is the oldest form of human cipher, the secret language of females and males, a language that no one acknowledges but every man and woman on earth employs and understands.

Like now as I stood next to Marston, who had changed into rubber boots, gloves, safety goggles, coveralls and a heavy lab apron that she pretended to be having trouble tying.

"Do you mind," she asked, touching fingertips to my arm before turning her back to me.

"Sure, happy to help," I said, and tied the thing, aware of the nasty look her former lover was giving us.

When I was done, I managed to make the situation worse by letting my hand linger on the woman's shoulder as I told the little group, "This my first necropsy. For an alligator, anyway. You know Frank Mazzotti, the saltwater croc expert? I almost had the chance to watch him work, but I had to leave the country for some reason. I really appreciate the invitation."

"Well," the woman replied, sounding a tad breathless, "it's always nice to be the first at something in a person's life. Paul"—she looked at the sullen man—"did you read his paper on filtering species in brackish water environments? It was in the *Journal of Aquatic Sciences*, wasn't it, Dr. Ford? Really an excellent piece. Your writing style reminds me of the late Archie Carr, the turtle master. Formal, very orderly, but readable. No bullshit academic flourishes when clear, concise sentences will do the job."

I told the woman I wasn't in Carr's league and meant it. Then added, "Let's make a deal. Call me Ford. Or just plain Doc—which is a nickname. It has nothing to do with what I do. Having a degree, I mean."

I tried not to sound like a self-satisfied jerk, but I bungled that, too.

Now I felt like an even bigger ass as I let the

woman pat my shoulder while she continued speaking to Paul. "In the article, he referenced a necropsy on a manatee that had died during a severe red tide. Wasn't that at Dinkin's Bay where you live, Doc? He was the first to make the association between dinoflagellates and toxicity in sea-dwelling mammals."

"How nice for Dr. Ford," Paul said, ignoring me—not that I blamed the guy. I really didn't, although he was pushing the limits when he added, "And let's not forget that we also have Dr. Ford to thank for providing us with a dead alligator to work on this morning. Very, very thoughtful of you to kill such a beautiful animal. What did the police report say?"

The man looked at a clipboard, before reading, " 'The alligator was subdued by four shots at point-blank range from a nine-millimeter Kahr handgun.'

"Subdued," the man continued, sarcasm creeping into his voice. "I guess that's police jargon for slaughtered."

He looked up from the clipboard and spoke to the graduate student. "I've never understood why some men feel inadequate unless they're carrying a gun. I'm not talking about you, of course, Dr. Ford," he added, his sarcasm undisguised. "It's the rednecks and hicks I'm referring to. The right-wing bumper-sticker types. I'm unfamiliar with handguns. Is a Kahr one of those famous pistols that heroes use in the movies? Maybe you're carrying it now concealed somewhere in your pants. I bet Emily would love to see it."

I had been watching the woman's face color, but the guy had finally crossed the line. She snapped, "Paul! Enough! Stop what you're doing right now! Dr. Ford's my guest, and I won't allow you to—"

The man cut her off, saying, "Your days of telling me what I can and can't do are over, Milly dear. The courts took care of that, remember? It was your decision, not mine. And, frankly, I couldn't be happier. Didn't we come here to work? I have other things to do."

Which, from Marston, earned the man a chilly "Don't we all have better things to do, Paul? You're the one who insisted on coming along."

"I volunteered to help. And, of course"—for the first time the man looked directly at me—"I wanted to see why you were so determined to meet the famous Dr. Marion Ford. I thought maybe I'd understand once I saw him. But, sorry, I just don't get what the fuss is all about."

I had taken a step back to remove myself from the conversation. Long ago, I learned not to participate in quarrels between lovers— particularly if I happened to be one of the lovers. So I stood there, feeling embarrassed for both people, as they argued, Drs. Paul and Emily, two intelligent people who had once been in love.

It went on for a while. The barbs they exchanged exhibited a practiced familiarity that proved these two people had become expert at hurting each other. But it ended abruptly when the woman finally called a truce, saying, "Paul . . . Paul, I'm sorry, Paul! I was wrong to let you come. It was mean of me. It was thoughtless, and I'm sorry. I truly am."

The man, Paul Marston, Ph.D., I would learn later, responded by throwing his apron and clipboard on the ground as he said, "Yes, your behavior has been very mean and thoughtless. For once we agree. And how refreshing to have you finally admit it, for a change."

Then the man turned, strode to his Subaru and drove away.

"Damn it," Emily said when he was gone. "I'm so sorry you two had to witness that. Paul isn't like that. Not really. And neither am I. But we signed our divorce papers less than two weeks ago, so it's an emotional time. I'd hoped we could continue our professional relationship, but clearly . . ."

The woman allowed silence to trail off.

The grad student, who had pretended to be busy organizing her camera gear, spoke for the first time, saying, "I think they both behaved like jerks, Dr. Marston. What is it about men?"

It took me a moment to realize that the girl had included me. What the hell had I done besides allow myself to be used as a foil? Even so, I decided it was time to try to reverse the dark momentum on this pretty spring morning.

"There's a lesson for ladies everywhere," I said to them both. "The male of the species is equipped with a prick for reasons that exceed the demands of basic human reproduction." I looked at Marston. "If you come up with an explanation, I'd like to be among the first to hear it."

I was hoping to see a pair of smiles. It took the grad student a moment—maybe we both shared the same physical awareness of Emily Marston.

Finally, though, the girl gave in.

Fifteen minutes later, I was saying to Emily, "I'm particularly interested in seeing what's in the animal's stomach."

She was wearing a digital headset. She nodded and said, "An animal this age, you never know what you're going to find." She nodded again to the grad student as a cue, touched the POWER button on the mini-recorder, selected a knife and then began dictating as she started the necropsy.

"The specimen is an adult male alligator. Length and weight have already been noted. Scutes at"—she was looking at the ridges on the animal's back—"scutes seven and ten show distinctive scarring, but I judge it to earlier

170

injuries. There is no evidence the animal has ever been tagged or documented. We'll begin by making a standard Y-cut from the animal's sternum to its cloaca."

The woman looked at me, adding as an aside, "There's no scalpel big enough for something like this. So I use a Gerber Gator Serrator. Really. That's the name of the knife. I found it at some outdoors store and couldn't resist."

The tool in her hand looked like an oversized pocketknife, and it was sharp. I watched her saw through the dense scale work of the gator's belly as the grad student moved to a better angle with her video camera.

Marston was good. She worked with speed and a minimum of wasted effort. I watched her remove and weigh, in precise order, the animal's heart, its liver and other vital organs, before she said, "Next we open the stomach. As I told Dr. Ford, you never know what you're going to find, particularly with an animal this age."

She looked at the grad student with concern before adding, "How are you doing? I know, the smell can be tough to deal with. Are you okay?"

The student had gone a little pale. "Maybe if I get a bottle of water," she said, "that might help. Mind if we take a short break?"

With Marston's permission, the girl hurried off to the shade, where there was an Igloo filled with ice and drinks.

The smell of the alligator didn't bother me. I found it heavy and distinctive. There was a musky sweetness that reminded me of the way a fresh tarpon smells—a delicate, vital odor that was mixed with an acidity that I presumed to be cavity fluids and blood.

I said, "Do you mind if I use that extra pair of gloves and help you with the stomach when you get it open?"

"Sure," the woman replied. "You sound more than casually interested. Are you looking for something in particular? Last night . . . the person the gator attacked, he didn't lose any—"

"No," I said. "The man still has all his parts. Just puncture wounds."

She was nodding. "That's what I thought or the police would have insisted on being here. Or EMTs would've opened the belly last night."

I said, "What I'd expect to find is the stomach empty. Or almost empty. We're only, what, a month or so away from their dormant season?"

"The last real cold front was in January," Marston corrected me. "This animal has certainly eaten since then."

"Even so," I said, snapping on a surgical glove, "he had to be pretty hungry to attack a full-grown man. Not only that, he came back and tried to attack a second man, even though I had already wounded the thing. What I'm interested in finding is those rocks I've read about. The

172

ones you find in a gator's belly. Gastroliths? I've never seen one."

"How's the man doing?" the woman asked, meaning Carlson. "I haven't heard anything since last night. In fact, I'd love for you to tell me the whole story sometime—if you ever have time. I've been studying alligators for seven years and I can't imagine anyone jumping into the water at night and wrestling around with something this size. I certainly wouldn't have tried it. That takes a very unusual man, in my opinion."

I caught the friendly implications. I also sensed that the woman was providing me with an opening to ask her out. It was in the airy way she said it—something I would act upon but later. In reply, I told her I hadn't gotten an update on Carlson and turned the conversation back to gastroliths.

"We still don't know for certain that alligators swallow rocks for ballast," the woman told me, sounding more relaxed and in charge now. "But I can't think of any other reason they'd bother. In an animal this size, I would expect to find quite a few. They don't look like much until you clean off the patina. But then some of them can be quite interesting."

She was right. With the grad student filming, Emily slit the animal's stomach lining, then held it open as I fished my hands in. At first, I thought there was nothing to find. But then,

173

closer to the intestines, I found several hard, globular objects. I removed one that was about the size of a baseball and handed it to Emily. She appeared pleased.

"This is one of the larger gastroliths I've seen," she told me as she used the knife to scrape part of it clean.

I used a paper towel on my glasses, then knelt beside her to see. I'm not a geologist, but there was no mistaking the crystalline facets of the rock, soon glittering in the morning sunlight. It was a chunk of gypsum.

Marston caught the significance immediately.

"This is very strange finding a stone like this," she said softly, studying the thing.

"That's what I was thinking."

The grad student had zoomed in on the rock. "I don't understand what you're talking about," the girl said. "It's pretty—sort of. But what's so special about a rock?"

Emily asked me, "You found this animal in a pond on San Carlos Island, right? It's really is quite surprising."

I told her it was a brackish lake, only a few miles from Fort Myers Beach, before telling the grad student, "In Florida, the only gypsum I know of comes from the highland regions in the north and central parts of the state. Alligators travel, I understand that. But is it possible this thing could have crossed a hundred miles of swamps, then crawled through cities, across highways, this far on its own?"

The woman was thinking about it, lips pursed. She was wearing safety goggles, and I liked the nerdy dissimilarities of her elegant jaw, the sweep of autumn-shaded hair. Only a male biologist is capable of undressing a woman with his eyes and then completing the fantasy by projecting how she would look naked, sprawled on white sheets, all the while kneeling on a tarp beneath buzzing flies, his hands slick with gastric fluids.

That's exactly what I was doing. But then my conscience intervened by reminding me that this woman had been divorced for only a couple of weeks. No matter how confident Emily Marston appeared, she was vulnerable, probably an easy target for just about any decent-looking, unprincipled jerk who came along. Although I am, admittedly, an occasional jerk, I do embrace the conceit that I am a jerk with at least a few principles.

I listened to the woman say, "If the gastrolith was a lot smaller, and when you consider how old this animal must be, I wouldn't have a problem with the distance. Over a period of thirty or forty years, yes, it could have traveled a hundred miles on its own. But my guess is, only a large alligator would ingest a rock this size, which suggests to me that someone may have transported the animal—"

The grad student, still filming, interrupted, saying, "Maybe a dump truck hauled a load of gravel to the beach. You know, from around Lake Okeechobee, as fill or something. That would explain a chunk of gypsum being this close to the Gulf of Mexico."

I smiled at the girl, pleased by her quick reasoning, and I told her exactly that as I fished my hands into the gator's stomach again.

I removed several more gastroliths. Then I found a chunk of what appeared to be a turtle skull. Then several more bones, bleached white from acid, that were not so easily identified.

Not at first, anyway. It wasn't until I had placed the bones on the tarp in an orderly fashion that I began to suspect what we had just found. Collectively, they resembled the delicate flange of a primate's hand—not necessarily a human hand, because feral monkeys are common in Florida.

I became more certain they were primate bones when I added a radius bone and pieces of what might have been metacarpal bones.

"My God," Marston said, voice soft, "I think we need to call the police. This isn't fresh, obviously. It has to have been in the gator's stomach for at least a few months, but even so . . . ."

I told the woman, "Wait. There's something else."

I had been holding my breath while I felt around in the animal's stomach and started

breathing again as I leaned into the stomach, t|
placed yet another bone on the tarp.

This one was unmistakable. The grad stud|
stumbled for a moment, almost dropped t|
camera, but then she leaned to zoom in on wh|
we all could identify.

It was a wedding ring. Cheap and brassy, b|
set with a minuscule stone that may or may n|
have been a diamond. The ring had been crushed
probably by the gator's teeth, so that it wa|
crimped into the bone of what had once been |
human finger.

"A woman's hand," the female biologist said,
and had to work hard to keep emotion out of her
voice.

"A woman's ring, anyway," I replied, holding
the bone close to my eyes, seeing what might
have been a bit of inscription. "The medical
examiner will know."

At sunset, I was on my back porch, lathering
beneath the outdoor shower, when I felt the
vibration of unfamiliar footsteps. Tomlinson was
in the house, probably guzzling the last of my
beer. Plus, the snowshoe slap of his big bare feet
is distinctive. It wasn't him.

The person approaching was decidedly female.
Wearing hard-soled shoes, I guessed, possibly
high heels.

With a bar of soap, I attempted to cover what I

could cover as I turned to see Emily Marston, although I didn't recognize her at first. True, I wasn't wearing my glasses. True, I only got a glimpse before the lady sputtered an apology, then ducked behind the corner of my house. Still, I did not associate the long glossy hair and a white tropical suit with the boot-wearing biologist I had worked with that morning.

When I heard the woman call, "Sorry! I'm really . . . sorry," I recognized the voice, though.

My reaction was immediate and adolescent— which is to say, I did what most men would do under the circumstances. I made a quick visual survey of my personal equipment, hoping I had been enhanced, not diminished, by the sun-warmed water in the rain cistern overhead.

First impressions are important. Particularly in the primate world, where proportions are emblematic.

Not bad, I decided. Not bad at all. Yet I attempted to deepen my voice as I called to the lady, "The house is open, go on in. Make yourself at home. There's a bottle of red wine, maybe some beer—if there's any left."

She would discover, soon enough, that I had company.

I reached for a towel, then my clothes, taking my time at first until I remembered that every minute I lingered was another minute that Emily Marston would be alone inside with Tomlinson.

It was a risky combination. A divorcée on the rebound and my randy pal.

Even sober, my boat-bum friend has the sexual discipline of a lovebug. By now, seven p.m., he was already a six-pack and a couple of joints into this balmy March evening. Stoned, there are no depths to which the man will not sink in hope of luring fresh prey to his sailboat and, at the very least, getting the lady's bra off.

As Tomlinson is fond of saying, "There are few experiences in life more satisfying than unveiling a pair of fresh breasts."

Speaking of women as if they were festively wrapped presents—a metaphor that, for Tomlinson, made every new day a potential Christmas morning.

As I came into the house, though, Emily was sitting primly at the galley table, looking elegant in a copper blouse and white linen jacket, while Tomlinson talked about the phenomenon we had witnessed the night before—the two dolphins we had seen charging out of the mangroves. That was probably a good thing because he had been obsessing about the Guatemalan girl, who had yet to reappear. He had called me earlier that day to report no luck and that he was coming back. I wasn't sure what else to do, but we had decided to keep the problem running in the backs of our heads to see if something came up.

"Sorry to show up uninvited, Doc," Emily said as I knelt at the refrigerator, looking for a beer. "I should have yelled. Or rang the bell . . . or something. But I did knock—"

"I had my earbuds in," Tomlinson explained, motioning to some kind of miniature device that played music. "I was listening to a new download. A four-hertz theta frequency, trying to get my head straight."

Emily looked at him, interested, as she continued speaking to me, saying, "So I walked around to the back of the house because I could hear someone humming—"

Tomlinson interrupted, "Doc was humming?" as if he didn't believe her.

I said, "Isn't that what people do when they shower? Sing, hum. I was showering."

Emily said, "Yes, you were," sounding as if she approved, her eyes locking onto my eyes. "I hope you aren't pissed—and you certainly shouldn't be embarrassed. I was restless tonight —we had ourselves quite a day, didn't we?"

Yes, we had. Emily and I had spent all morning together, waiting for the county forensic team to arrive, and then most of the afternoon answering questions, first from the authorities and then from a couple of reporters.

I avoid media types. It's an old habit. Putting my name or face out for public scrutiny is unwise when you've lived the life I have lived. When a guy has determined enemies, he protects his privacy with determination.

The woman, though, didn't have a problem with it. She had handled the reporters politely and with just the right amount of professional reserve. I was impressed.

"That's why I had to get out and go roaming tonight," she was explaining now. "I decided to risk surprising you to see the amazing Dinkin's Bay"—she smiled—"where bottlenose dolphins walk by moonlight."

The woman glanced at Tomlinson, and I could tell that she hadn't expected me to have company —for good reason. I had dropped more than a few hints during our hours together, telling the lady that I lived alone, wasn't dating anyone special, and that I usually worked late in the lab —if she ever happened to be in the area.

Not that I had anything sexual in mind.

Right.

Now here she was, and her uneasiness was palpable.

Tomlinson has an uncanny ability to read people. He helped the woman relax by making her laugh, saying, "Know what the weird thing is? When I tell people about the dolphins, they don't believe me. But the moment Doc says it, it's like gospel. I just don't get it."

He leaned toward Emily. "From what I've heard, you're an educated woman. Any insights

into how some people can be so damn misguided?"

Emily laughed, then asked if we'd take her outside to see the area where the dolphins had come
ashore. She was wearing hard-soled shoes, not
heels, but I told her it was a bad idea.

"It's all muck and mangroves," I explained.
"Your clothes would be a mess. Plus, the
mosquitoes. It's no place for a lady at night."

That earned me a smile and another potent
look. "Thanks for noticing. After the way I was
dressed this morning, I went out of my way to
look like a woman tonight."

For an instant, I wondered if the woman wasn't
being a little too obvious, then decided it was
okay. I liked her, she liked me and was letting
me know it. Nothing wrong with that. "You
succeeded," I told her.

"Then I've already had a good night," she
replied. She held my gaze for a moment, then
turned to Tomlinson. "Doc told me that you
found pieces of crabs' legs and carapace when
you checked the area. But, to him, that wasn't
enough proof the dolphins were feeding. What
do you think?"

Tomlinson had been doing some staring of his
own, and I was relieved to hear him say, "I
always defer to Doc in matters that require a
brain but not much heart. But what I really think
is, I need to get going. It's sushi night at the

Stone Crab. And Rachel told me they just got in some fresh conch from Key West."

"But wait," Emily said as she watched him get to his feet. "You mentioned something I wanted to ask about. Were you practicing deep theta-wave meditation? I wanted to hear more."

Now she definitely had Tomlinson's attention. "It sounds like you know something about the subject."

"At home, I've got a few four-hertz theta tracks. But I prefer the higher frequencies." She included me in the conversation with a look. "The higher frequencies are associated with brighter colors, feelings of well-being. After what we found in that gator's stomach, I went straight home, showered and put the headsets on."

Tomlinson was smiling, and I could sense that his determination to exit courteously had been replaced by a growing interest in Emily.

"Biofeedback and brain harmony," he said. "We are chemical-electric beings, grounded only by spirituality. Kindness and passion in most of us. Lust in a few cases, too. Quite a few, from what I've seen in this part of the world."

I said, *"Lust?"* aware that Tomlinson was an expert at planting subliminal suggestions into the heads of unsuspecting females.

Emily was laughing, a smart lady who apparently had pretty good antennae of her own because she took control of the conversation, saying, "I'll

discuss the subjects of passion and lust with Doc
—*if* he's interested. But not in mixed company,
thanks. The thing I wanted to ask about is, if you
were listening to a theta track, I'm guessing
you're upset about something. Doc told me a little
bit about what happened last night. The gator
attack and the girl disappearing. Not everything,
of course. He's a hard one to get to open up. He
mentioned he had a best friend. That's you, I
take it."

Tomlinson grinned, and said, "It requires
someone who's forgiving. And not easily bored."

"Then it is you. How do you get him to talk?"

Tomlinson came close to winking at me as he
replied, "I fed him psychedelic mushrooms once
—by accident, of course. And once I got him
stoned on some very fine weed—same thing, by
accident. At best, even when high I would describe
him as vaguely chatty. But in a very careful way."

Emily was having fun with this, but I felt like
they were teaming up when she asked, "You
don't smoke, Doc? Or is he kidding?"

I had opened a Diet Coke because all my beer
was gone. Compliments of Tomlinson, of course.
I shook my head slowly, *no*, took a sip and
listened to Emily talk.

"I guess I'm surprised—that's not a judgment,
by the way. Personally, I can't believe it hasn't
been legalized. It makes me feel all loose and
relaxed. I laugh a lot. And act stupid. I think it's

184

good for people like us to act stupid sometimes. Don't you . . . Doc?"

Now the expression on Tomlinson's face was telling the world *I'm in love*, which is why I spoke up, saying, "You mentioned sushi night at the Stone Crab? They close at nine, don't they? You've only got two hours."

The restaurant was only five minutes away on a bike. He knew exactly what I was telling him.

Tomlinson countered, "We could all go. I could tell Emily about Tula. Maybe later we can even drive across the bridge to Red Citrus and have another look around. I like this woman, Doc. What's your last name?"

"Marston," Emily said, watching my friend's face. "Emily Marston. Or Milly. Or Em. Or whatever you want."

Tomlinson let that settle, retreating into his brain to think about it. "Marston, that's not very tribal-specific. You have olive eyes . . . no, gray-green. Polish, maybe, which tells me Chicago, or maybe Detroit. A bit of Irish, too, plus some German? Doc," he said to me, "this person is intuitive. She has a gift. I think she can help us find the girl—after I fill her in."

Once again, the woman took charge, making me her ally by saying, "Nice try, but Marston isn't my maiden name. Another night, maybe. Until then, Doc can fill me in just fine. We have a lot to talk about."

"*Well* . . . all righty, then," Tomlinson said, aware that he'd just been dismissed. His inflection, though, suggested a truce but not capitulation.

"Doc could use some downtime," Tomlinson offered, getting to his feet. "The dude has been pretty restless himself lately. He doesn't have to say anything. Everyone at the marina can tell. He spends time looking at maps and listening to foreign news on his shortwave. He works out harder, he drinks fewer beers. The one sure sign?" Tomlinson gave me a knowing look. "His lab begins to smell of a very specific kind of oil that folks like me don't associate with fish and boats."

"Oil?" Emily said, confused, then sniffing. A moment later, I was taken aback by the look of recognition on her face. *"Oil,"* she said. "Yeah, I can smell it. Very faint, but it's there."

I stood and opened the screen door. "If you think of it, you might stop by the 7-Eleven and buy some beer. See you in the morning—but not too early. *Okay?*"

Tomlinson was laughing as he headed out the door but turned to say to the woman, "Or maybe I'll see you two at the Rum Bar later. We just got in a shipment of twelve-year-old Fleur de Caña from Nicaragua. Really superb stuff."

I was heartened by Emily's green-eyed gaze and by her response: "It's entirely Doc's call. Whatever he's up for, I'm with him."

● ● ●

Whatever concerns I had about Emily Marston's vulnerability were set free when she slipped her arm through mine as we walked toward the marina and she told me, "I didn't divorce Paul because I was unhappy with him. I did it because I was unhappy with myself. Oh, I pretended it was his fault. Came up with all sorts of reasons why we had to end the relationship and move on. He'll always be the professor. To him, I'll always be the student. And another big problem was . . ."

I waited through several seconds of silence before I told her, "Talk about it or don't, that's up to you. I was impressed by the way you stood up for him, after your argument this morning. That was nice. Unusual for an ex-wife or -husband to do."

It was as if she didn't hear me because she picked up the thread, saying, "For some reason, I want to be honest with you about what happened, Paul and me. One of the problems was, he doesn't enjoy physical contact—not really. Not with me, anyway. But not with anyone, I think. I'm amazed at how many people dislike being touched. Aren't you?"

No, but I didn't say it. Instead, I walked and listened, giving the woman time.

It took a while. Finally, she asked, "Know what I was doing, Doc? I was making excuses. I was using a device that doesn't make me look very damn nice at all. I blamed Paul to justify what I did. The truth is, I ended the marriage because I wasn't happy and I wanted out. Blaming him was a way of getting what I wanted."

I replied, "I think it's common for the species Sapiens to do whatever it takes to justify pleasure by manipulating our own guilt. Don't be so hard on yourself."

"But that doesn't make it right," Emily countered. "Seriously, I'm not trying to punish myself. For me—and it drives me nuts some-times—for me, the way my mind works, it's important to get the facts straight. My dad used to say something that was cute at the time, but now it makes sense. He'd say, 'You lie to your friends and I'll lie to mine, but let's not lie to each other.' I try not to lie to myself, Doc. I think that's maybe what he meant."

I smiled and said, "The age difference between you and Paul wasn't a factor?"

"Fifteen years is just about perfect," she replied. "It puts the male and the female at about the same level of maturity."

"You're not joking."

The woman said, "Maybe twenty years. It depends on the guy," but didn't hit it too hard, which told me the subject was unimportant to her.

We were walking through the shell parking

lot, toward the marina docks, after stopping to admire the lady's new car. It was a mid-sized Jaguar, black and tan, that didn't mesh with her occupation or her probable income. Now I could see boats moored in rows, windows glowing, and an American flag at the end of the dock, flapping in a star-bright breeze.

I said, "Are you always this frank?" letting her know that I appreciated it.

"Doc," she replied, "I'll be twenty-eight in October, and I plan on living to be a spry and very active ninety. I don't want to live a screwed-up, unhappy life. Or a selfish life. We receive peace in exchange for helping others. I really believe that." Then she grimaced and said, "Jesus, I didn't mean that to sound so naïve and girlish. Did it?"

"You have it all planned out," I said.

"It's not being selfish," she replied, "to take responsibility for our own lives. And that's the only plan I have. This morning, when you laid that poor woman's bones on the tarp and I saw that ring, I felt so goddamn sad I wanted to cry. Did it show?"

I lied. "No."

Emily said, "It was my wedding ring I was looking at. That's the way it felt. *My* ring finger, and I had been swallowed by something as predatory as any alligator that's ever lived."

"Predatory?" I said.

"By fear," she said. "I think fear rules unless we fight it. But not many people do, you think? We just go with the flow, doing what's expected. Letting our lives drain right down into the gator's belly."

"Some, maybe" I said. "I'm in no position to judge."

"Well, that's not for me. I'm going to try my damnedest to live a life that matters. Cut the safety net and throw it away. Which sounds idyllic, but it's actually scary shit when I think it through. That's what I plan to do, Doc. In fact, I'm already doing it. Starting two weeks ago." She leaned her breast into my arm. "If I have regrets later, it's not because I was afraid to, by God, try something new."

I patted the lady's hand and steered her past the bait tank, toward the bay, where dock lights were tethered to black water, golden shards roiled by wind. The fishing guides were in, their flats skiffs rocking in a buoyant line, and a whisper of big band music seeped from one of the sleeping yachts, out of sync with the tapping flag-pole halyard.

It was a little after seven p.m. on a Wednesday. A quiet time at Dinkin's Bay.

I was feeling good. The decision that Emily would come to my bed had just been made without even discussing it—an exchange made via silent subtext. The unspoken dialogue that takes place minute to minute between fertile males and females, generation after generation.

This female had not only said yes. She had fronted the wordless invitation. She had also put me at ease by allowing me to fish for answers to unspoken questions.

Was she emotionally stable? *Yes.*

Did the age difference matter? *No.*

I was enjoying the moment, aware that it was among the rarest of transitional times. I would soon undress this woman. "Unveil her," in Tomlinson terms, for the first time. And there would never be another first time for Emily and myself.

There was no rush, no need for more complicated sexual maneuvering. I could luxuriate in what was to be. I'm no romantic, but I do love women. Hidden beneath a cotton blouse, bound by elastic, what would Emily's breasts look like unveiled in the back-bay light of my bedroom? Her hips, her thighs . . . and what subtleties of layered coloring in the lady's shadowed triangle?

"Did you hear what I said, Doc?" Emily asked, nudging me. "You just disappeared on me. Where'd you go?"

I noted the lady's intuitive smile, which told me she knew full well where my mind had gone —probably because her mind had been there, too.

Yes, I was right, because she turned to a subject

that had all the freeing implications of seeing the bones of a dead woman's hand. The bawdiest of sexual behavior can be excused—even celebrated —by reflecting on unexpected tragedy, the inevitability of death.

As I had told Emily: *People do whatever it takes to justify pleasure by manipulating our own guilt.*

"I was thinking about the Guatemalan girl," she said. "I asked if you'd read the story in the *Naples Daily News* last week. It was about human trafficking. I'm interested because I joined the Florida Coalition Against Human Trafficking. I've been to only two meetings, but I'd like to get a lot more involved."

I said, "A biologist doing social work?"

"I can't think of a better cause."

I said, "When I put that together with your new car, it suggests to me you're wealthy. Isn't that an oxymoron? Wealthy biologist?"

"Normally about now," she smiled, "I would get very self-righteous and ask what money has to do with a social conscience. But you guessed right, our family has money. My father did well for himself. Maybe I should have mentioned it. He's an ornithologist."

I replied, "A wealthy bird-watcher. Another oxymoron."

"Oh, that is the least of the mysteries about my dad," the woman said, giving me a searching

192

look. "He gets a big kick out of telling people that bird-watching was an inexpensive hobby—as long as you had a passport and your own private jet."

I was struck by the mix of her inflections. Emily said it in a joking way, but she also seemed to be baiting me with information that invited further investigation.

Because I couldn't discern her purpose, however, I dodged the temptation. "So your paternal family has money," I said.

Emily replied, "My grandfather left me a trust fund when I turned twenty-one. Not a ton of money but enough. Paul had a problem with that. He's a nice man. He really is. But he has ego issues. Would you have a problem if your wife had a lot more money than you?"

I found the word "wife" startling so shrugged and dodged that question, too. "The human-trafficking thing," I said, "I've always had an interest. Probably because I worked in Central America for several years. I spent some time in Africa, too. Tell me what you know."

A moment later, I had to ask, "Why are you smiling?"

"Because you're funny," Emily said. "The way you guard your secrets by asking questions. Your interest is real, though—that's makes it okay for some reason. You care about people. I can tell. By the way, you left out the time you spent in

Southeast Asia and Indonesia and a bunch of other places, too."

Before I could reply, the woman told me, "I know more about you than you realize—including all the traveling. I already told you, I've read your research papers. In your writing, the really interesting stuff is always between the lines. Like when Tomlinson mentioned the smell of oil in your lab. I recognized it. I know what kind of oil it is. Do you want me to tell you?"

It was gun oil and specialized solvent. Tomlinson had surprised me by mentioning it. He had never mentioned it before.

"The pumps and aerators in my lab require special lubricants," I said. "There's no mystery about that."

Emily replied, *"Really?"* to let me know that she was aware that I was lying. "You became sort of a hobby of mine, Dr. Ford. Paul embarrassed me so bad this morning when he mentioned it— which was precisely what he intended to do. Not that there's a lot out there about you. Only two photos. That's all I could come up with on the Internet. And I'm pretty damn thorough when I get on a research binge. Does *that* bother you?"

"Money and the attention of a beautiful woman," I said, turning to face her. "Why would that bother anyone?"

"I'm not beautiful," Emily said, her face tilting suddenly downward. "You don't have to say

194

that. We're both pragmatists. People like us prefer the truth. I might be handsome on a really good day, but I'm not beautiful. I never have been. So there you are. I came to terms with it long ago."

I replied, "I'll be the judge of what's beautiful and what isn't. If you don't mind."

The woman hesitated, wondering if I was going to kiss her. She gave it a moment, looking into my face, then she took my hand and tugged. Suddenly we were returning to my stilt house, walking faster than before.

After a minute or so, she was talking again, back on a safe subject. "Trafficking is big business," she began. "A lot bigger than the average citizen realizes." Because I was momentarily confused, she explained, "You asked, so I'm telling you what I know. More than a thousand undocumented workers, men, women and children, arrive in Florida daily. They're smuggled in by Mexicans, mostly. And a lot of the smugglers are Latino gang members. Coyotes—that's what they're called in the trade. But you know about all this. Of course you do."

I was thinking about recent headlines that detailed the gang wars now going on in Mexico and California. Mass murders, men, women, and children pulled from their beds and shot in the back of the head execution style. Eighteen near Ensenada. A dozen gangbangers killed the same way in Chiapas. "Ceremonial-style murders," as one survivor had described it.

I replied, "I've never learned anything in my life while my mouth was open. Keep going. You just filled in a couple of blanks."

"Okay," she said. "If that's what you want. Coyotes are usually in the drug business, too. It's a natural. Prostitution and pornography, those are the other primary sidelines. The people they screw over . . . it makes me furious to even talk about it because the people they use have nowhere to turn for help. They're slaves by every definition of the word. The way coyotes and their gangs abuse women and children is beyond despicable."

Emily started to continue but then hesitated. "I'd rather not go into some of awful things they do. It's really upsetting to me. Not if you already know."

Along with the news stories, I had also read Florida Law Enforcement reports that detailed how traffickers recruited sex slaves and controlled them. Fear was the common weapon. One gang, the Latin Kings, had videoed a live vaginal mutilation. They showed it to new recruits to keep them in line. There had been at least one ceremonial beheading, the perpetrators all wearing bandannas to cover their faces, their tattoos hidden by long-sleeved raincoats.

Cell-phone video cameras. It was what they used.

"No need for details," I told Emily. "Keep it general."

The woman let her breath out, relieved. "I'm not going to tell you why I appreciate that, but I do. Okay . . . so come up with the very worst punishments you can imagine and that's the daily reality for a lot of small brown women and boys. These are people we see every day working in the fields, riding their bicycles, hanging out at the supermarket and cashing their checks to send money home."

I said, "That's why Tomlinson's so worried about the girl. Me, too."

"Tula Choimha," Emily said. "Is that how you pronounce it?"

I said, "The girl . . . she's a very different sort of thirteen-year-old. Religious, but religious to a degree that borders on hysteria. You know what I mean? For the wrong sort of egotistical asshole, she'd be an inviting target. Humiliate the saintly little Guatemalan girl. There's a certain breed of guy who'd stand in line to do that."

"That's a volatile age. For girls especially it can be a nightmare," Emily said, sounding like she had lived it. "Fantasies range from sainthood to whoring. A scientist from Italy published a paper that gives some credence to what's called poltergeist activity. You know, crashing vases, paintings falling from the walls—all caused by the turbulent brain waves of adolescent

197

girls. Which all sounds like pseudoscience to me, but who knows? Maybe there's a grain of truth."

I had stopped tracking the conversation when Emily mentioned poltergeists. I was reviewing what Tomlinson had told me earlier on the phone. He had returned to Red Citrus, but Tula was nowhere to be found. Her few personal possessions were still in the trailer, untouched since the night before. But it looked as if her cot *had* been slept in.

Tomlinson had called and asked me to join in the search. But, at the time, Emily and I were stuck at the necropsy site, waiting for the medical examiner's investigator. So he had driven his beat-up Volkswagen, hopscotching from one immigrant haven to another searching for Tula, but no luck.

"Did he stop at churches?" Emily asked me now, regaining my attention.

"Tomlinson didn't mention it. You're right, that would've been smart. Maybe the girl was afraid of something. Or someone. And ran to the nearest Catholic church for protection. She couldn't risk turning to the authorities."

The woman said, "Please tell me your friend contacted the police, right? Her safety's more important than her damn legal status."

"Of course," I said. "I called, too. Tomlinson insisted."

"Because he was afraid the police wouldn't take him seriously?"

I said, "It wouldn't make any difference. The state has a whole series of protocols that go into effect when a child is reported missing. Illegal immigrant children included. There's a long list of agencies, from cops to the Immigrant Advocacy Center, that get involved. Tomlinson thinks they're going to issue an AMBER Alert tonight, if they haven't done it already. It's the best system in the world for protecting kids. But it's still an imperfect system."

I continued, "The problem is that people at her trailer park—the family Tula lives with?—they don't believe the girl's missing. At least, that's what they told the cops as recently as this afternoon. They say she goes off by herself for hours at a time. Police will do more interviews tomorrow. We may not like it, but that's the way it is for now. An AMBER Alert, of course, if it happens, will change everything."

Emily asked, "Do you think she was kidnapped? It's a possibility, I hate to say it. The coyotes, the things men like that do to young girls and boys . . . I don't even want to think about."

I said, "She left behind a family photo that she'd carried for three thousand miles. That bothers me. There was a book we found, too. And some clothing. So, yeah, I think something happened."

"A book?" Emily asked.

"Not a Bible," I said. "It's a book of quotes from Joan of Arc. I took a close look. A lot of dog-eared pages and fingerprints. Some underlined passages. She kept it with her for a reason."

"Joan of Arc," the woman nodded as if that somehow made sense to her.

I gave it some more thought. "A church could be the answer," I said. "It's plausible. She got scared and ran. There were cops all over the place, so she probably scooted off to the nearest church so she wouldn't be questioned."

I wasn't convinced, though, and neither was Emily. Why hadn't church authorities contacted state authorities if they had a runaway girl on their hands?

"Doc?" Emily said. "If you're going back there tomorrow to check the churches—let me come with you. My Spanish is pretty good. Your friend was right. I think I can help."

I found it interesting that she seemed to intentionally avoid using Tomlinson's name. Was it to reassure me that she had no interest? Whatever the reason, I found it endearing.

From my pocket, I took a little LED flashlight. I clicked it on, took Emily's hand and led the lady down the mangrove path to the boardwalk that crosses the water to my house. When we got to the shark pen, I switched off the underwater lights and pocketed the flashlight.

We stood for a moment in the fresh darkness, listening to a waterfall of mullet in the distance, seeing vague green laser streaks of luminescence thatch the water.

"Enough talk about coyotes and kidnappings, and every other dark subject," I said, putting my hands on the woman's shoulders.

I felt Emily's body move closer, her face tilted toward mine. She was ready and smiling. "Is that why you turned off the lights? To brighten the mood?"

"No," I said as I slid my hands down to her ribs. I took my time, stopping just beneath her breasts, my index fingers experimenting with a warm and weighted softness.

"I was starting to wonder if I'd have to make the first move," Emily Marston said—said it just before I kissed her.

TEN

LATE WEDNESDAY AFTERNOON, LAZIRO Victorino was sitting at Hooters in Cape Coral with a tableful of wings and low-level Latin King brothers when the news lady came on the television, reporting from a swamp near Fort Myers Beach, about a dead alligator that had a human hand in its belly.

Probably a woman's hand because they had also found a wedding ring.

Victorino recognized the place immediately. It was Red Citrus trailer park. Hell, most of the *Indígena* who lived there, he'd personally arranged for their transportation to Florida and jobs, which meant that he *owned* those people.

He'd probably also owned the woman the hand had belonged to.

Victorino wasn't the only one paying attention to the news lady. One by one, his Latin King *pandilleros* turned to look at him, not staring but letting him know they weren't stupid.

In the last few months, Victorino—the V-man —had mysteriously lost three, maybe four, *chulas*, and, goddamn it, it had to stop. Next, his homeys, his *pandilleros hermanos*, would do more than just stare at him. They would be laughing behind his back, making jokes that the *jefe* had lost his balls.

Victorino had suspected for months who was stealing his girls. Maybe selling them, maybe starting a prostitution business, maybe killing them, too—not that he cared, not really. There were always plenty of immigrant girls to choose from. But he couldn't tolerate a public display of disrespect, and the bony hand of one of his dead *chulas* on the six o'clock news was as public as it could get.

This bullshit had to stop. Laziro had worked too hard building an organization, recruiting soldiers, disciplining his *Indígena* girls, sometimes even his *pandilleros* when a soldier got out of line.

Yes, it had to stop. And Victorino knew exactly who to see to make that happen.

He stood, dropped a fifty on the table from a turquoise money clip, then threw his homeys a hand sign before pushing his way to the door—two fingers creating devil horns. He paused for a moment to confirm the nods of deference he deserved. Then he drove his truck to Red Citrus trailer park, where he expected to find Harris Squires. The *gringo* giant was all muscle but no backbone. V-man had bullied the shit out of the dude more than once, so no problem. He was looking forward to cutting this white boy down to size.

Instead, he found the dude's hard-assed lady. Victorino had done business with her, but he had never tried to push her around because the *puta* was pretty scary herself.

The woman's name was Francis-something, but everyone called her Frankie. The woman was old, which was intimidating to begin with. Probably early forties, and she had muscles like a man from shooting up all that gear shit the couple made to sell. She had a hoarse steroid voice like a man's, too, but everything else was all woman, particularly her store-bought double-D *chichis*, which she showed off braless, wearing muscle T-shirts and tube tops, probably trying to look

203

like the muscle-magazine covers she'd posed for ten or fifteen years ago.

Mix the lady's *chichis* with a body covered with tats, dyed scarlet hair, pierced tongue and her nasty attitude, it was no wonder that even Latin King soldiers watched their behavior, and their asses, around Frankie. Harris Squires probably believed they showed the lady respect because of him and his muscles. But the dude was wrong.

Frankie was the scary one, which is why even the V-man had never crossed her. How you gonna win, crossing a *gringa* ballbuster who was six feet tall with biceps the size of his own calves?

That was about to change.

Standing outside a new double-wide, Victorino got up on his toes, looking through a bedroom window into Squires's private trailer. The place was a mess. Closet and drawers ransacked, clothes on the floor, a suitcase lying open on a bed that hadn't been made, so at first the V-man thought, *Shit! They're already gone.*

It made sense they'd run off, and not just because of the six o'clock news. There were cops all over the place, which is why Victorino hadn't turned into Red Citrus. Instead, he had parked his truck at the shrimp docks down the road near a rum bar. Then he had walked through what reminded him of a boat graveyard and jumped the fence, saw a squad car and two unmarked

SUVs waiting by the garbage dumpsters, where, he guessed, they would soon be dragging the lake, looking for more pieces of the dead girl. Or maybe dead girls.

Three of Victorino's ladies had gone missing, so the timing was about right. It was a year ago that Squires and Frankie had started shooting porn up there at their fancy hunting camp, small-time at first, but then with a special video room with lights, a water bed and all kinds of weird black leather contraptions hanging from the ceiling.

Neither Squires nor the redhead had appeared in any videos that Victorino had seen. But he'd heard they both got off behind the scenes, enjoying all kinds of kinky shit. The couple had taken a special interest in the V-man's girls once they got seriously into the business. They'd hired more than a few *Indígena* as talent, and several Mexican cuties, too.

About ten months ago, Victorino's first *chula* had disappeared. After that, about every three months, he'd lose another one. The V-man had suspected them for a while, but bones inside the belly of that redneck asshole's pet alligator was the final proof he needed. His *pandilleros* realized it, which is why they'd given him those looks at Hooters.

Maybe the cops suspected, too. No wonder the pair had split before police started asking questions, so the V-man figured he'd missed them. But then he saw Frankie walk into the room, carrying an armful of folded clothes, a joint between her lips, curling smoke, and he felt better about the situation. The woman hadn't finished packing, so maybe Harris was still here, too.

No . . . the white giant was gone. Victorino confirmed it when he circled the trailer and saw that the dude's big V-8 Roush Ford monster truck was gone. Squires wasn't smart, but he wouldn't have loaned that sweet ride to nobody.

Victorino checked a couple more windows, then went to the door where a sign read NO ENTRY! in Spanish and English. He tested the knob and was surprised to find the door unlocked.

A moment later, he was standing inside, seeing a big-screen TV and stereo equipment, then a kitchen that didn't look like most kitchens, but that was no surprise to the V-man. On the counters were four big gas-burner plates, each with its own canister of propane. The shelves were lined with a mess of medical-looking shit, bottles of oil and chemicals, and measuring beakers that looked like they belonged in a lab. Which was exactly what this place was—a lab for cooking steroids.

Jesus, just a spark, the whole place would explode like a bomb—maybe not a bad way to handle the situation, Victorino decided, if he could get Frankie and her muscle boy into the trailer at the same time.

Victorino had seen a kitchen like this before, only a lot bigger. It was at Squires's hunting camp, where Victorino and his *pandilleros* had partied themselves on a couple of occasions. They weren't invited often, but, when they got the call, the V-man and a few of his boys made an appearance because it was a mutually beneficial business association.

Squires and Frankie ran three trailer parks, which provided handy instant housing for newly arrived illegals. On the side, they shot porn, which the Latin Kings also made and marketed as a sideline, and that put money into everyone's pocket.

Victorino's soldiers pedaled the videos to dumb little *Indígena* dudes, who'd probably never seen a naked woman in their pathetic little lives. The *gringo* couple needed girls for their movies, of course, which meant they also needed weed and blow, which put cash right back into the V-man's pocket.

Not that Victorino trusted the *gringos*. No way. It was business, nothing more. The couple treated him like just another wetback. To them, there was no difference between him, a Mexican stud and some scrawny little *Indio* from Guatemala or El Salvador or some Nicaraguan *pendejo*.

A wetback was a wetback, to most *Americanos*. That's how clueless they were. But the V-man never let it show that it bothered him. When he looked into a *gringo*'s eyes and saw the contempt or indifference, all he did was smile his great big gold-toothed smile, pretending to be their Mexican *amigo*. But he was really thinking how goddamn stupid they were.

These two especially, an old woman with wrinkles on her muscles and her redneck boyfriend, the two of them acting like big-money hotshots until the cops finally took them down.

Which would happen. If the V-man didn't get busy and take them both out first.

The V-man wasn't smiling now as Frankie came into the room, stumbling because he surprised her, then yelling at him in her deep voice, "What the hell are you doing in my home?"

Then she caught herself because she recognized Victorino as the V-man yet didn't sound any friendlier when she added, "Oh. It's you. What the hell are you doing in here without knocking? I'm in a hurry. We don't need any more grass or shit today. Get out. Get out of here right now."

Victorino let the woman watch him react slowly, making her wait as he turned his back to her. He made sure the door was closed but unlocked in case he wanted to get out fast. He pivoted to face her, then snapped on the surgical gloves he had brought along for effect.

First the left glove. Then the right.

Then he surprised the woman again by flashing the box cutter he was palming and asked, "You don't want any smoke or blow—but what about girls? You don't need any more of my pretty little *chulas*? The way you been killing my girls off, I thought you'd be in the market by now."

The V-man expected the woman to squat right there and piss her panties, she should have been so scared, seeing the rubber gloves and the razor. Instead, it was the woman's turn to surprise him.

Frankie balled her hands into fists and took a step toward him, shouting, "I'm trying to figure out just how goddamn stupid you are! You come in here, cops all over the place, looking like a faggot or a fucking serial killer, with those gloves, your bandanna and your pissy little knife. I should slap the shit out of you right now, then tell the cops you tried to rape me."

Victorino had to smile at the woman's *cojones*.

"Me?" he said easily. "I'm the stupid one? They found pieces of one of my girls in your bigass alligator today. What you call that fucking lizard, Fifi or something? On *your* property. It was just on TV, bitch, and you're calling *me* stupid?"

209

He bounced the razor in his hand, not believing how the *gringa* was handling this. No wonder his soldiers were spooked by the woman.

The woman's face changed. "You're kidding me, on television news? You've got to be shitting me. What did they find?"

Victorino told her. "Bones of a human hand. You pretend you don't know that? Had a fucking ring on the finger! A woman's hand."

Now Frankie's resigned expression read *Sooner or later, it was bound to happen.*

"Half an hour ago," Victorino continued, "I was sitting at Hooters, enjoying some chicken wings with my boys. Why you think I hurried over here, leaving behind all that fine food?"

He held up the box cutter. "You better listen to what I'm saying, *chinga*. You and your jelly-boy boyfriend disrespected the V-man. All the times I was nice to you both and this is how you thank me? Now I got no choice but to leave a few marks on that body of yours. As a warning to other dumbasses. Cut off an ear, then slice my initials into your face, that might get my point across. Or maybe cut one of those big titties and listen to the air leak out."

He pointed the razor at her, wanting the woman to pay attention to the blade. But she didn't. Instead, Frankie was suddenly preoccupied, thinking about something else, acting like the V-man wasn't even in the room.

Victorino raised his voice. "You hear what I just said to you . . . *puta*?"

The woman made a waving motion with her hand. "Quiet," she said. "I'm trying to figure out how to handle this." After a moment, she added, "And don't fucking call me a *puta*."

Jesus, this wasn't going the way things usually went when Victorino waved a blade in a girl's face. He was staring at the woman and he couldn't believe that her face showed no fear. Instead, when Victorino reached to grab her elbow, the woman yanked the elbow away and got madder.

"Keep your greasy hands off me. Haven't you got any damn sense?"

Victorino took a step back, his grin fading, then moved between the woman and the door, thinking she might run for it. Hoping she'd make a move, actually, which would give him an opening. He'd forgotten how goddamn big Frankie was, so he might have to tackle her, get her on the ground, then stuff something into her mouth before going to work with the box cutter.

But the woman didn't run. She returned to her packing, throwing clothes into the suitcase. "You have any idea how much shit I have to do?" she said. "The cops are bringing in equipment to drag the pond, you dipshit. Two or three hours at the most, the boat, or whatever it is they use, gets here. Next thing, they'll be banging on this door. One of your idiot whores OD's, falls in the water, who you think they're gonna blame? They're gonna blame *you*, dipshit. And I'll be here to give them your name unless I can get this cookshack cleaned up and get our shit out of here. So leave me alone!"

Jesus. This woman had balls. Hell . . . maybe she really *did* have balls. Hard to tell with the sweatpants she was wearing. Victorino had never thought about getting a look at the lady's goodies before, but now it crossed his mind.

He stood there, thinking about it. Two or three hours before the cops went to work dragging the lake?

They had some time.

He let the woman see him retract the razor and put the box cutter into his jeans. "Where's your asshole boyfriend?" he asked. "That jelly boy should be here helping you, not letting you do all the work."

Frankie said, "Don't even mention that prick's name to me." Then she nodded toward the hallway and told him, "Out there in the main room, I've got two more suitcases. Go get them. And hurry up."

Victorino didn't like that. A Latin King captain didn't take orders from some *gringa*. Even for her to try to give him orders was offensive. On the other hand, it wasn't likely that an old white woman knew crap about the respect a *pandillero* captain deserved. And the woman did have nice-looking *chichis*.

"Did you hear me?" she said. "Run and get those suitcases."

"Hey, you about to get your face slapped, lady," Victorino replied. "You want a favor, you ask the V-man nice. You say 'please' and you say 'thank you.' Or you can kiss my Mexican ass."

"Okay . . . *please* get my goddamn suitcases. And be quick about it—unless your Mexican ass wants to go to jail."

When Victorino returned to the room carrying the suitcases, he asked about Squires again, saying, "When's your boyfriend coming back? Does he know the cops are here? That would piss me off, my man running away with all this shit going down."

"That asshole isn't a man—he's an overgrown mama's boy," Frankie snapped. "You know what he did? He ran out on me early this morning. He stole fifty-nine thousand dollars cash from our box and packed his shit. Then the dumbass stuck around long enough to take some little teenage brat with him."

Victorino said, "Teenage?" not following but very interested in the cash the lady had just mentioned.

"Some underage little bitch!" the woman yelled. "I know because some state asshole officials were nosing around here an hour ago,

213

asking about a missing kid. Harris figured the cops were going to arrest him, so he ran and took along something to play with. But I'll find him. I know exactly where he's going and I'll catch him there."

Victorino was trying to unsnap one of the suitcases but having a tough time. "A white girl?" he asked, curious because he had heard that Frankie enjoyed *chulas* a lot more than the redneck.

"No, some little Mexican brat who everyone thinks is a boy. But not me. I knew better—even Harris didn't believe me when I told him. She's probably not even thirteen yet, but you know what a perverted asshole Harris is. So he apparently figured it out."

After thinking about it for a second, the woman sounded fairly perverted herself, adding, "Her name's Tulo-something. You remember her? Kind of pretty, with a Dutch-boy haircut with bangs, and always quoting the Bible. But a cute little ass on her."

Victorino said, "A girl, you sure about that?"

Frankie ignored him, too busy packing to listen.

Victorino said, "Maybe I know the one, a skinny kid, got here 'bout a week ago. Kinda tall, for a Guatemalan, and real quiet. Had a fucked-up haircut, like someone used a bowl on his head."

"Not a he, a *she*—a sneaky little tramp of a girl," Frankie said. "I knew it right away."

The V-man was employing his thoughtful-businessman expression. "A little *chula*, huh? I'll be go-to-hell. That Guatemalan *puta* lied to me. I'm gonna have to do something about that."

The woman made a snorting noise.

"And Harris, too. The way I've been losing *chulas* lately?" the V-man said. "I've got to cut someone's balls off for this, then stuff them down his goddamn throat! My homeboys will be laughing behind my back, wanting to steal my shit, everything I've built. I take this personally."

Folding a blouse, Frankie told him, "I don't give a damn how you take it. You're gonna have to wait in line if you want to kill Harris and that little wettail." Then she stared at the bed for a moment before saying, "You haven't figured out how to open that goddamn suitcase yet?"

The V-man was doing his best, getting frustrated with the cheap-assed little gold snaps, as he replied, "I won't kill the little bitch. But I've got to find her and make an example. I'm a businessman. Killing a girl that age, where's the profit?"

Frankie slapped Victorino's hands away from the suitcase, saying, "A regular genius, that's what you are. A regular Wall Street tycoon," as she popped the locks with her black fingernails, then returned to her packing.

The V-man was thinking, *Smart-ass white bitch,* but pretended to be unruffled, not pausing as he continued, "Wall Street or Main Street, business is still business—when you get to be a man in my position. You say she's, what? Twelve, maybe thirteen? That means I own her for four or five more very profitable years. It's sort of like owning a fine racehorse, understand? Or a nice limo you rent out."

Frankie said to the V-man, "You mind moving your ass?" then pushed by him to get to the closet. No . . . a table, where she found a lighter, then stood tall in front of the window and relighted a joint that the bitch didn't bother to offer him.

From the smell of the smoke, the V-man guessed it was shit his *pandilleros* had sold her. Fine Mexican weed laced with cocaine. Yes, the woman was inhaling deeply, smoking what the homeboys called a *banano,* so no wonder she was so jazzed.

The V-man kept talking, saying, "I start her out by selling her virginity five or six times to some of my best clients. Top dollar. Dudes down here from New York, Chicago, real-money players who the V-man deals with only *personally.* Then put the *chula* to work, doing private parties. Buy her some clothes, show the bitch how to use lipstick and protective condoms 'cause pregnant *chulas,* they very hard to market. Maybe next year, on the street. Or six months, depending on

216

how she holds up. Unless one of my clients wants to rent her full-time as a maid or a cook —I'm still making money on that."

The woman stood and looked at Victorino for a moment as if an idea had just come into her mind. "Do you know who that dead hand belonged to?"

"The one in the alligator?" Victorino said. "It was one of my *chulas*. Had to be."

Frankie asked him, "What makes you so sure?"

"Three of my ladies went off, left their shit, their money," Victorino said. "Hell, they even left their *shoes* and never came back. Not all at once, of course, but I ain't dumb. Went off and left their fuckin' *shoes*, I'm saying. Even a crazy woman wouldn't go off and leave her shoes. Why you think I come straight here when I finally got me some proof? You two been fuckin' around with my *chulas*, everyone knows that. But I figured you was selling them on the street—"

"Harris killed them," the woman interrupted.

Victorino stopped talking and tried to read the woman's face. Was she telling the truth?

"You got my attention," he said slowly.

"I just told you, Harris murdered all three. Maybe more—I was never around when he did it. He'd get screwed up on blow or triple his testosterone dosage by accident—he's always forgetting his needle days—and that just makes him even crazier. Or he'll drop a handful of D-bombs, which makes him even worse."

The woman continued, "You want to cut someone's balls off for disrespecting you? Harris Squires is the guy you're looking for—if you can find his balls. Because of all the juice he shoots, he's got a dick the size of a Vienna sausage."

Victorino enjoyed that so much, he had to smile. He found it encouraging, just the two of them alone, suddenly sharing secrets, in this brand-new double-wide that smelled pretty good, like carpet, marijuana smoke and fresh vinyl.

He said to the woman, "All three, huh? You sure of this?"

"I just said it. Pay attention, I don't make a habit of repeating myself."

"He fed 'em all to that bigass alligator?"

The woman said, "Harris and some buddies loaded that stinking animal into a truck, drunk as hell, playing Crocodile Hunter one night, and brought the gator here to scare your wetbacks. We planned to sell this place to developers once his asshole mother dies—if she ever does. All the legal bullshit from pissed-off renters would have slowed things up. To Harris, the boy genius, it seemed like a smart thing to do."

Victorino was giving it some thought as he said, "That *pendejo* snuffed out three of my

218

ladies, huh?" not loud, letting the woman know that he was angry but cool about it, a professional boss man who knew how to deal with situations such as this. "How'd he do it? Use a gun? He don't have the balls to take his time and make it enjoyable."

The woman said, "He's got a thing for rough sex. It's the only way he can get off. He'd load their drinks with Ecstasy, then choke them while he was banging them. Or maybe they just OD'd on their own. How would I know?"

That's exactly what Victorino was thinking: How could the woman know these details unless she was involved?

It also crossed his mind that a woman her size, with all those muscles, she might even be talking about herself, not about her boyfriend. He had heard the rumors that Frankie liked doing women even better than men. It was because of all that steroid shit she shot into her body.

Victorino motioned to the kitchen. "That shit you cook up, it makes a dude's thingee shrink?" Because the woman ignored him, he decided to add, "Think it would bother you watching me cut Harris's little thingee off?"

That got the *gringa*'s attention. Frankie Manchon gave the man a weird look like she'd love to watch him cut Squires's nuts off.

Man, this was one scary lady. But kind of

sexy, too. It was the way her blue eyes got a real shiny, eager glow. . . .

Sexy, yeah, the V-man decided, in a real dirty way, which might be fun. Victorino was thinking maybe he should take a few seconds and lock that outside door so the two of them could enjoy their privacy.

That's exactly what he did.

But then she spoiled it.

"Take off those fucking rubber gloves," she told him. "They make you look like a janitor."

That did it. This woman needed to learn some respect.

He said, "You say your jelly boyfriend drugged three of my ladies and killed them? You think that's a big deal? Like he's a badass or something?"

Frankie tried to interrupt him, probably with some smart-ass remark, but Victorino kept talking, saying, "I'm a fucking Aztec, *chinga*. You understand what that shit means? One time, I cut a dude's heart out, the thing still beating in my hand. That's the last thing this dude saw—his eyes wide open, staring at his fucking heart. That was before I cut the dude's neck open. Cutting his neck was my way of being *kind* to the dude, understand? Because he had been my loyal brother up until an unfortunate thing he did. But I got no personal relationship with you and your redneck boyfriend. You hear what I'm telling you?"

The woman was listening now, looking at him with her shiny blue eyes, but not showing much.

"But when some woman disrespects me, what I do is I start cutting pieces off her body until she begs me to stop. Then I feed those pieces to the damn dogs and make her watch them eat her ears, her fingers, maybe a chunk of her tongue if the fool has a big mouth like you.

"Rednecks use alligators? My boys and me, we prefer dogs. Pit bulls we keep for the fighting ring. And it's been a while since any of them got some white meat. Do you know what I'm saying?"

The woman took a moment before she replied, "Yeah, you're a hardass and you like talking about it. You made your point."

Victorino wasn't so sure, so he pulled up his left sleeve to show the woman his Diablo tattoo, eight teardrops beneath it, six blue, two red. "Know what these are? These are my stripes. In the Kings, you don't wear this paint, *chinga*, unless you earned it. Take a look for yourself."

For some reason, that impressed the woman, and Victorino realized that she wanted to prolong this talk of killing. It made her breasts stick out, her breath coming harder, as she took a step to get a better look at his arm.

"Why the different colors?" she asked. "I don't think I've ever seen sloppier tats in my life. You want some good work, I've got a man in Key West who's an artist."

Frankie touched Victorino's arm, her black stiletto fingernails with glitter on them denting his skin. "These tattoos, they look like your guy used a sewing needle and Easter-egg dye."

The V-man jerked his arm away, saying, "That's 'cause I did 'em myself! The blue is for six dudes I wasted, two in Chicago. Both of them Crips—but here I am."

He tapped at the red teardrops. "These the ones you need to pay attention to. One of my girls doesn't obey me, I give her one warning only." And he took out the box cutter.

Yeah. Frankie was impressed now, her chest moving faster, her blue eyes bright. She came closer, her arm lifting toward him, and then—
Whap! The slap caused Victorino to drop the razor, he was so surprised, and the next thing he knew the woman was on him, trying to claw his eyes out with her fingernails. Yelling at him, too, saying, "You think you're man enough to get my panties off? Do you? Huh? *Do you*, you skinny little shit? It took three of my cousins my first time —and they were Vermont studs, not wetbacks."

She kept repeating it as she flailed at him, her voice low and hoarse, breathing fast, as Victorino got behind her, then spun her down on the bed.

And for a while, that was all Victorino remembered.

An hour later, 6:30 p.m., the V-man was in his pickup truck, following the woman's Cadillac convertible to Harris Squires's hunting camp, where she'd promised they would find the redneck, the money and the pretty little girl who'd been pretending to be a boy.

Before leaving, Frankie had unpacked a bottle of Crown Royal and a baggie of grass that one of Victorino's soldiers had sold her. In their vehicles, they each had a plastic cup and a joint —sweet-smelling *bananos*, fine weed laced with coke. By now, they were both feeling good.

Victorino certainly was. The woman was a goddamn animal in bed. He'd never experienced anything like it in his life. No other woman had come close to doing what Frankie had done to him. And, *man*, Victorino had, by God, gotten off on it, feeling crazy wild afterward.

Already, the V-man was ready for more. He had heard old women were best in the sack 'cause they were so damn appreciative, but it was more than that with Frankie. The woman had a monster in her. Something black and glossy with claws that lived inside her head, looking out through those blue eyes of hers.

"I want to watch when you use that razor blade on Harris," Frankie had said to him, her voice still flushed.

"Sure," Victorino had replied, meaning it. It would be a chance for him to show off a little and also prove to his *pandilleros* he was still a hardass. He had decided to invite some of his brothers along and maybe video the whole thing.

Not sure all this was going to take place, though, he then had to ask Frankie, "But what you got planned to do with your boyfriend's body once we done? That can be a problem. That big lizard of yours, she's dead now."

The woman noticed Victorino looking at the row of propane tanks in the kitchen as she replied, "You just stick to your business and let me do the thinking." Then added, being even more serious, "But the little girl—you can't touch that girl. I want you to promise me that."

Giving a Latin King captain orders again, but it was okay. It was pretty clear to Victorino what Frankie wanted. She wanted that little girl-boy virgin for herself.

But that was okay, too. The *gringa* woman, being the way she was, she'd probably get off a couple of times on her own and then invite the V-man to join the party.

ELEVEN

EMILY MARSTON AND I WERE TAKING A break, curled up naked, spooning on my narrow bed, when I heard Tomlinson trotting up the boardwalk, the distinctive slap of his feet telling

224

me he had something important going on. Why else would he be in such a hurry?

As Emily stretched and yawned, I turned my wrist to see the glowing numerals of my Chrono-fighter watch. It was still early, only 9:30 p.m.

"The house is shaking again," she joked. "My imagination?"

I leaned to kiss the woman's cheek, then behind her ear, feeling a welling sensation within my chest that was not unknown to me but so rare and long ago that I was startled. I was also dubious, instantly on alert.

That same thoracic response is probably why sappy poets associate the heart with love. I had just met this woman, knew very little about her. To feel what I was feeling, after only a few hours together, was irrational. Not that love is ever rational.

"It's Tomlinson," I said. "Something must be wrong."

There was.

"Tula sent me a text," Tomlinson told me as I pushed aside the bedroom curtain, shirtless, buckling my belt.

I noticed that his hand was shaking as he combed fingers through his John Lennon hair. "He's got her, Doc. Harris Squires, I was right. And the goddamn cops told me they're already doing everything they could. Those *assholes!*"

Adjusting my glasses, I took his cell phone,

saying, "Maybe if you lived in a country where there were no cops, you might have a little more respect."

Tomlinson began to pace, his ribs showing, now shirtless, wearing red surfer baggies. "If you called downtown, it might be different," he said. "You know a lot of guys on the force. We've got to do something, Doc!"

The text was in English. I sat next to my short-wave radio, turned on the lamp and read, "Safe, in his truck. In God's hands. 22 miles from Im."

I said, "I don't doubt it's from her, but are you sure? Where did a Guatemalan kid learn how to use a cell phone?"

"It's the first thing they learn when they get here," Tomlinson replied, sounding impatient. "That, plus the best food is always at Taco Bell."

I said, "She didn't finish the message, so okay . . . yeah, of course it's from Tula. I remember you saying she had your number in case of emergencies."

"She sent it from Squires's phone," he said, chewing at a strand of hair. "I called and recognized his voice. I didn't say anything. Do you think I should have? He wouldn't have let her send me a text, and I was afraid I'd set him off, make him suspicious. So I just hung up. You know, like a wrong number."

"Did he call back?"

"No . . . Jesus! If he sees that text she sent, I'd hate to even think what a guy like that would do to Tula."

On a pad of paper, I copied Squires's number, then spun the swivel chair to face Tomlinson, who was now leaning into the refrigerator, moving stuff, then saying, "Jesus Christ, Doc, don't you ever go to the store? We're out of beer again. What a night to be out of beer!"

I said, "Tula was in the middle of writing 'Immokalee.' I-M—what else could it be? Twenty-two miles from Immokalee, but she was interrupted."

Tomlinson used his hip to bang the refrigerator door closed as I added, "Which means she saw a road sign—the distance is precise. Unless Squires told her, which seems unlikely. Why would he tell the girl where she is? She's only been in Florida for a week, so she couldn't have guessed the distance from landmarks. But why would he take her to Immokalee?"

Tomlinson replied, "Everyone in Guatemala has a relative living in Immokalee. Or Indiantown. Or maybe the guy has a place down there, who knows? Rednecks have hunting camps sometimes."

I was trying to project a reason why Squires would drive Tula Choimha to a Guatemalan stronghold. I said, "He could be taking her there to look for her mother, but that makes no sense.

I don't associate acts of family kindness with Harris Squires."

"The girl's a thought-shaper," Tomlinson reminded me. "She can get people to do things they normally wouldn't. Tula can project ideas in a way that makes people think they came up with it on their own."

I ignored him, saying, "He might do it if money was somehow involved. Or sex and money— the world's two most powerful motivators. A thirteen-year-old girl and her mother. There's no money in that combination. Which leaves—"

I left the sentence unfinished as I returned my attention to the girl's text to see if there was more to learn from the few words she had written.

Listening, Tomlinson used his heel to shut the fridge. He was carrying a tumbler filled with ice toward a bottle of Patrón tequila on the counter as I continued, "They've done some traveling, that's obvious. Maybe he stopped at a 7-Eleven or something and left his phone in the vehicle. That gave her an opening to use the phone, but Squires interrupted Tula before she could finish the text. And her hands aren't tied—they're not taped, anyway. That's a positive. But why not call you instead of type a message?"

Tomlinson had already figured it out. "Because she couldn't risk holding the phone to her ear. You're right, probably a 7-Eleven. Someplace he could keep an eye on her through a window. So she hid the phone in her lap and texted. That would have been safer. And there's less chance of him checking for texts, then checking recent calls. Tula's very smart, I already told you."

"Do you know what kind of truck he drives?" I was leafing through my private phone book, many of the names written in my own form of code. As I picked up the phone to dial a police detective friend of mine, Emily appeared from behind the curtain, combing her auburn hair with a brush, wearing one of my baseball jerseys buttoned down to her thighs.

"We meet again," she smiled, looking at Tomlinson. "I was just getting acquainted with your best friend. Your timing could be better, you know. But . . . it also could have been a lot worse."

Tomlinson stopped chewing at his hair long enough to say, "It looks to me like someone just finished touching all the bases."

The woman had a nice smile, ironic and tolerant. "A baseball metaphor," she laughed, tugging at my jersey. "It works, but not entirely accurate. I was counting on extra innings."

As Emily said it, she moved past me, trailing an index finger along my shoulder. I saw the way Tomlinson's eyes followed her, focusing first on the abrupt angle between breasts and abdomen created by the baggy baseball jersey, then on her long hiker's legs, calf muscles flexing.

Clearing my throat, I burned my pal with a look that read *Don't even think about it.*

Emily noticed, which caused her to grin, charmed apparently by our adolescent sparring. Then she rewarded me with a look that read *You've got nothing to worry about.*

That thoracic glow again. It was in my chest.

On the telephone, a detective acquaintance, Leroy Melinski, was telling me, "I've got the report up on the screen right now. Thirteen-year-old Tulo Choimha, an undocumented Guatemalan national. He, uh . . . he was reported missing last night, but it didn't get official until a couple of hours ago when a full AMBER Alert went out. So maybe your beach-bum pal's pestering did some good. Is he still the strung-out cop hater I remember?"

Looking at Tomlinson as he came through the door with two quart bottles of beer—I'd remembered there was beer stowed on my flats skiff—I said to Melinski, "If anything, he's worse. I think the man's personality evaporates as he ages. It's causing his weirdness to condense right before my very eyes."

"Personally," Melinski replied, "I don't think cop haters are funny. I'd slap the shit out of that hippie prick if he gave me a reason."

The bitterness in that caused me to raise my eyebrows, and I said, "As entertaining as that sounds, I called to talk about the missing child."

"The kid," Melinski said. "I know, I know. But there's another piece of news first I think you'll find interesting. Our guys finished dragging that lake this afternoon. Where you shot the alligator?"

As I listened, I signaled Tomlinson to pay attention. "You found more bones?" I asked.

"No, they found a different body. A fresh one. Another female. Latin, probably mid-twenties, but both of her hands were right where they belonged. The only thing missing was the girl's life. Someone put her in a garbage sack, then used wire and concrete blocks to sink her. Dead two or three days at the most, according to the guys on the scene. Which is a guess, of course, but they've seen enough floaters to come close. No obvious injuries, so no telling how she died. We're still waiting on the medical examiner's report."

To Tomlinson and Emily I said, "It's official, there's an AMBER Alert out on Tula. And they found another dead girl—unrelated to the bones we found in the gator. They finished dragging this afternoon."

Tomlinson threw his head back, fists against his temples—a silent scream—while Emily shook her head, smile gone.

To Melinski I said, "That hand belonged to someone. They found nothing else down there that was human?"

"I was told they did a pretty thorough search,

231

but maybe they'll try again tomorrow. One of the medical examiner's guys told me the bones you found might be a month old or a year old. Maybe more. But it definitely wasn't a fresh kill—assuming the victim died. And they're not sure it's female, despite the wedding ring. They're trying to narrow it down. That's a job for the forensic lab."

I said, "Which means it's even more important to find that missing kid. The killer—that's the guy we think abducted her, Leroy. He's a steroid freak. With a real nasty temper."

I had already given him Squires's name, his number and told him about the text Tomlinson had received. The detective had passed the number along to his staff, and we were awaiting confirmation that the cell phone belonged to Squires.

"You don't need to convince me about hurrying," Melinski said. "When a kid goes missing, there's a forty-eight-hour window. I don't have to tell you what usually happens if the search goes longer than two days. Problem is, this morning the family the kid lives with told officers that he wandered off by himself all the time but he'd show up. He always did. So it wasn't considered a priority until this afternoon. No father, no mother to push for a search, which I'd like to say hasn't happened before. But it has."

I corrected him. "You must have misheard,

Lee, this is a girl we're looking for. Tula, not Tulo. She's been pretending to be a boy since she left Guatemala because she's smart. You know how dangerous that border crossing is. The family she lives with knows the truth. And probably a few others but not many. I'd consider it a personal favor if you called out the cavalry on this one. Like I said, the guy she's with is a chemistry freak. He goes from cold to hot real fast."

I could picture the detective reading through the computer files as he replied, "If that's true, then this whole damn report's wrong. If the family knew it was a girl, why didn't they say something? He . . . *she* was reported as a suspected abductee late this afternoon. The AMBER Alert went out at twenty hundred hours. All the missing-child protocols are in effect, but our people have been looking for a damn teenage boy, not a girl."

"Last time I saw her," I told him, "she was wearing jeans and a baggy blue T-shirt, so most people couldn't tell the difference." Then I gave the man the best physical description I could, pausing to pass along details that Tomlinson provided as he paced back and forth.

I could hear Melinski's fingers tapping at a keyboard as he said, "That's something to go on, at least. The problem is—and this is a good example—people in these kinds of places, the immigrant trailer parks, they're scared to death of our guys. So some of the state agencies, the Immigrant Advocacy people, will be sending people around asking questions. Maybe they're on it now. Christ, I hope so. We have almost no information on the kid."

I could hear his frustration as he added, "For more than an hour, we've been looking for a boy. Who knows, maybe some cop stopped them, then turned her loose, not knowing."

I said, "But at least you can narrow down the search area. Maybe they're in Immokalee by now. Or somewhere close."

Melinski said, "You said she didn't type out the whole word. She wrote: I-M."

I replied, "What else could it be? Did anything come up on Squires?"

I listened to Melinski typing as I watched Emily busy herself in my little ship's galley of a kitchen. She was listening, eyes moving from the teakettle to me, the concern showing on her good-looking face, that jaw and nose, autumn-colored hair swinging loose.

"There are thirteen Harris Squires in this state," Melinski said after a moment, "but there's only one whose mother owns trailer parks. A rich kid, from what I'm seeing. A rich mother, anyway. She owns three mobile home parks . . . a house on the beach . . . taxes almost thirty grand a year. And four hundred–some acres of undeveloped land in the Everglades east of Naples."

Immokalee was northeast of Naples about thirty miles. Tomlinson's remark about rednecks liking hunting camps came into my mind.

"Any houses or cabins on that property?" I asked, thinking a hunting camp would be a good place to disappear with an abducted girl.

"Uhhh, nope . . . I don't see anything here. Nothing that's been permitted, anyway," he replied, then began to read from Squires's file.

"He got bumped once for possession of marijuana, no conviction, back when he was a kid. Get this"—Melinski paused, and I could picture his face in front of a computer screen as he read—" 'The informant regarding the minor in question was the minor's mother, Mrs. Harriet Ray Squires. Mrs. Squires had to be restrained by officers when she confronted said minor the morning after his arrest.'

"Christ, Doc," Melinski laughed, "the guy's own mom narced him out. If he's one of those crazies who only goes for young girls, maybe it's because his mom was such a hardass. He looks for women he can control."

I said, "That's the only thing on his record?"

"No," the detective said, "but he's not what I'd call real dirty. Not compared to most of the losers who come through here. There's a DUI arrest, which his lawyer somehow got tossed out when he was nineteen. Then about five months ago he was banged for speeding—doing a hundred and ten on I-75, Pinellas County. If this is the guy we're after, he's got a vehicle that can do that and more. It's an almost new Ford Roush pickup truck. That's one of those tricked-out specials. Big engines and big tires for guys with egos and—"

I interrupted, "What's the license number? And the color?" I was leaning over a notepad, making notes.

There was a pause before Melinski let me know how patient he was trying to be, saying, "Doc, come on, now. You know I'm not allowed to do that. Even if I was allowed, I wouldn't do it because the last thing we want is some civilian playing detective, upsetting people and probably getting his ass into trouble. Meaning you. Frankly, you've got a history of it. No offense."

I said, "It was just a question, Lee."

"A few months back, you were the suspect in a murder rap, Doc. So excuse me for being careful. I shouldn't even be talking to you."

I said, "I called because I want to help, not get in the way."

"Please tell me you don't plan on looking for this guy, Doc. There's an AMBER Alert on the kid, what more do you want? What can you do that a state full of trained professionals can't?"

I said, "I know . . . you're right, but—" then

listened to Melinski say, "From what you said, this guy Squires is a bad actor. Driver's license has him listed at six-six, two forty-five, and he has a concealed weapons permit. No weapons registered to him, but that doesn't mean diddly-squat. In this state, you can buy freaking grenades if you know who to talk to. Why risk inviting that kind of trouble? What's this girl to you?"

I was looking at Emily as I told him, "Like you said, the girl has no parents around. No one to act as her advocates. I've spent a lot of time in Guatemala. I speak the language and I like the people. So why not? The point is, I don't give a damn about Squires—arrest him or don't arrest him, that's your business. But I care about the girl. If I can help find her by asking around, talking to people in the Guatemalan community, what's wrong with that?"

Melinski said, "Hang on a second," sounding impatient. A moment later, he said, "Okay, here it is. The number that sent Tomlinson the text? It's his phone, Harris Squires's. As of now, every cop in the state will be looking for that fancy-assed truck of his. And we'll find him. I can guarantee you that."

To Tomlinson and Emily I whispered, "It was Squires's phone," as Melinski continued, "My next move is to contact our hostage-negotiation guys and ask them how we deal with this. Risk calling Squires and asking him if he's got the girl? Then try to talk him down, convince him the smartest thing he can do is turn himself in. Or keep everything under the radar until we locate the truck. I'm not the officer in charge of this, but I know who is, and she'll listen to me."

I said, "If you have the right kind of person talk to him, someone trained—definitely not the tough-guy type—it could work."

"But what if it *doesn't?*" Melinski asked me, sounding angry or frustrated—a man who had been in a tough business for too long. "Jesus Christ! A thirteen-year-old girl a thousand miles from home. No family to look after her, and some steroid freak jerk grabs her. These Latin American kids, man-oh-man, Doc. The undocumented girls, particularly, they're the easiest targets in the world—you're right about that one.

"Some of these gangbangers," he continued, "the Mexican coyote types. To them, snatching female illegals is like a sport. Like hunting rabbits or doves—something soft and harmless that can't bite back. And the sad thing is, hardly anyone even knows this shit takes place every day. Let alone cares."

To Melinski I said, "I don't envy you guys the choices you have to make."

I meant it.

"Doc," the detective said, "I'll give you my cell number, if you want. And I'll call you the

238

moment we get anything new. But I don't want you nosing around, asking people questions about that girl. And I don't want you messing with this Harris Squires dude. Give me your word?"

I replied, "I have no interest in finding Squires. I don't ever want to see the guy again. I'll promise you that."

A few minutes later, we were in the lab, discussing ways to help find the girl, which, of course, meant finding Harris Squires. Try as I might, there was no separating the two.

My lab is a wooden room, roofed with cross-beams and tin sheeting. The place smells of ozone and chemicals, creosote and brackish water that I could hear currenting beneath the pine floor as Tomlinson lectured us.

My friend was trying to hurry us along, doing his best to sound rational and reasonable, telling me, "It's not even ten yet, and it takes less than an hour to drive to Immokalee. Faster, if we knew someone who had a big fancy car. We could be there way before bar closing time. Right on Main Street there's a good barbecue place, too, that stays open. I wouldn't suggest it, but they have a salad bar."

He turned to give Emily a pointed look, obviously aware that her Jag was parked outside the marina's gate. But if the lady noticed, she didn't react. She was going through a file I had started years ago, a file on bull sharks that inhabit a freshwater lake one hundred and twenty-seven miles from the sea in Central America.

We had gotten on the subject of sharks earlier in the evening when I was showing the lady a gadget I was testing that might repel attacking sharks. Laser Energetics of Orlando had sent me the thing, a palm-sized tactical light called a Dazer. Its green laser beam was hundreds of times more powerful than a legal laser pointer and could drop a man to the ground with one blinding blast. A test victim had described the pain as "like a screwdriver in the eye," which is why a special federal license was required to possess it. If the Dazer affected sharks the same way, it might save sailors, pilots and divers who found themselves in a bad spot.

On the file Emily was holding I had written in ink *Sharks of Lake Nicaragua*.

"You have some fascinating stuff here," Emily told me, looking at a black-and-white photo of a fisherman I had interviewed a few years back. He was missing a scarred-over chunk from his right thigh. Attacks in Lake Nicaragua are not uncommon. Water is murky, private bathing facilities are rare and backwater bull sharks have the feeding instincts of pit bulls. Males of the species, *Carcharinus leucas*, have a higher concentration of testosterone in their blood than any animal on earth.

In the background of the photo, tacked to a wall, were several sets of shark jaws. The largest of them was opened wide enough to cut a man in half.

The fisherman I'd interviewed had lost his thigh as a kid and had dedicated his adult life to getting even. The fact that Japanese buyers paid top dollar for shark fins only made his work sweeter—until he and other fishermen had all but depleted the landlocked shark population. The man was dead broke when I met him but still thirsty for revenge. By then, though, a rum bottle provided his only relief.

I know a quite a bit about Central America and the varieties of sharks that thrive there—finned predators and two-legged predators, too. For several years I had lived in the region, traveling between Nicaragua, Guatemala and Masagua during the endless revolutions. I was in the country doing marine research—a fact that I made public to anyone who asked because I was also working undercover on assignment for a clandestine agency composed of a tiny, select membership.

By day, I did collecting trips, wading the tide pools, and I maintained a fastidious little jungle lab. By night, I shifted gears and did a different type of work. I attended village celebrations and embassy functions. I wore a dinner jacket and went to parties thrown by wealthy landowners. I wore fatigues and trained with a counterinsurgency group, the *Kaibiles*. Less often, I roamed the local countryside on the hunt for gangster "revolutionaries" who, in fact, were little more than paid bullies and assassins.

On those occasions, I carried a weapon for a reason.

I've spent my life doing similar work in other Third World countries—Indonesia, Southeast Asia, Africa, Cuba. The study of marine biology has served me well in my travels, both as my primary vocation and as a believable cover. When a stranger inquires about local politics, residents are instantly suspicious, and for good reason. But when a stranger asks about the local fishery— where's a good place to catch sharks?—he is instantly dismissed as just one more harmless, misguided fisherman.

I've never really confided in Tomlinson, but he's perceptive, so knows more about my background than most. And he probably suspects that I'm still involved in that shadow world of hunter and hunted—which I am. But he doesn't know the truth and he never will.

No one ever will.

I was looking at Emily, thinking about the complications my sort of life brings to a relationship, as Tomlinson intruded again by saying with exaggerated patience, "I don't expect your full attention. You both have the same rosy glow, which tells me you've had yourselves a really fabulous first date, so congratulations. But have you heard even a single word I've said?"

Emily looked up from the folder, her expression empathetic. "I know you're worried about the girl. I don't even know her and I'm worried. But I'm going to follow Doc's lead on this. Something tells me he's got better instincts than most when it comes to these things."

She looked at me as she added, "Trust me, I understand what it's like to have a family member go missing."

Tomlinson gave her a curious, questioning look, as if trying to decipher the implications. Then he got back to business, saying, "Okay, I agree with Doc. If every cop in Florida is looking for Tula, what good can we possibly do? It's a valid point. But here's another fact that's valid: Cops aren't welcome in immigrant communities. How many times have we talked about this? Why not at least go to Immokalee and have a look around? An hour in a car together—a four-beer drive, depending on traffic, and traffic shouldn't be bad on a Wednesday night that far inland. Hell, it could be fun."

Emily was studying my face, her expression now asking me *What do you think?*

She had dressed, but looked less formal in her white slacks, copper blouse, because her jacket was still hanging in my bedroom closet. I hoped it would stay there for the rest of the night—along with the woman—if we could manage to get rid of Tomlinson.

The trouble was, Tomlinson was right. Guatemalans would probably talk to us, but they would vanish the moment police appeared. If Squires had indeed taken Tula to Immokalee, someone would have noticed a big *gringo* with an *Indio* child. Why he would risk doing something so stupid, I had no idea. But if he had, the locals might trust us with the truth, which we could then pass along to police.

I said to Tomlinson, "It's been a while since I've been to Immokalee, but I remember it being farther than an hour."

Tomlinson was sitting at my desk computer. He'd been doing a lot of typing and printing as I showed the lady around the lab, enjoying her reaction to rows of aquaria that contained sea anemones, snappers, filefish, sea horses, scallops with iridescent blue eyes and dozens of other brackish-water creatures that I had collected from the grass flats around Dinkin's Bay.

"Immokalee seems like a long way to you because your truck's so slow," Tomlinson replied, not looking up from the keyboard.

"Have you ridden with this guy yet?" he asked Emily. "Like an old lady, he drives—no offense to old ladies, don't get me wrong. I love women of all ages. But top speed in that old Chevy of his, it might be sixty. Not that he's ever pushed it that hard. I keep telling him to buy a new vehicle, but he's too cheap. In that truck of his, he's right. It would take us forever."

I asked Emily, "Have you ever been there?" meaning Immokalee.

I got the impression she had, but the lady shrugged, open to fresh information.

"It's inland, southeast of Sanibel—saw grass and cattle country. Tomatoes, citrus and peppers, too—all crops picked by hand. It's only forty-some miles, but you have to take back roads because it's off the tourist path. The town's not big, maybe twenty thousand people, and the population is mostly Hispanic."

I looked at Tomlinson, expecting him to correct me, as I added, "Back in the nineteen eighties, a Mexican crew chief brought in a truckload of Kanjobal Maya from Guatemala to work in Immokalee's tomato fields and another place, Indiantown, which is north. That began the connection. Now those two towns have become sort of the Mayan capitals of Florida. That's where all the Maya head when they're looking for family. Or if they get into trouble."

Tomlinson did correct me, saying, "It was nineteen eighty-two, I've got it right here on the screen. Now half the population of Indiantown is Mayan. This article doesn't say how many Guatemalans live in Immokalee, but the Latin population is almost eighty percent, which means there has to be ten or fifteen thousand *Indios* in Immokalee—which makes it bigger than most of the cities in Guatemala.

He continued, "I don't blame those people for not wanting to be documented. They're mostly political refugees, on the run from their government because they did something or said something to piss off the big shots in Guatemala City. Their government still uses firing squads, don't they, Doc?"

The man said it in an accusatory way as if I were somehow responsible.

"Up against the wall, asshole," he added, shaking his head, "which is typical of a bunch of right-wing Nazis."

Right wing, left wing, it made no difference in Central America . . . nor anywhere else, for that matter, because the power hungry all gravitate toward the same dangerous interstice on the political wheel.

Even so, I said nothing as Tomlinson continued paraphrasing from what he was reading on the computer.

"In the seventies, Guatemalan exiles tried building a little village just across the border in Mexico. But their own army had a bad habit of sneaking across and shooting the *Indígena* on sight. Finally, Guatemalan military wiped out the whole village.

"Florida was a whole ocean away, and the really desperate refugees decided this was a safer choice. Now about thirty thousand Maya live in south Florida, which historically makes for a very nice symmetry, when you think about it."

I saw that Emily had missed the connection, so I explained, "He's talking about the original inhabitants of Southwest Florida. It was a major civilization. They were contemporaries of the Maya, a people called the Calusa."

I suspected that the woman knew Florida history, but she listened intently as Tomlinson told her, "The Calusa and the Maya had too much in common for it to be accidental—in my opinion, anyway. The Calusa built shell pyramids and courtyards. They were led by ancestral kings, not chiefs—just like the Maya. They were here thousands of years before the Seminole."

He studied the woman long enough to confirm she was interested before confiding, "Some nights, I anchor off one of the islands near here —Useppa Island—where the shell mounds look like small mountains. I smoke a doobie or two, and those pyramids come alive, man. People march around the mounds in wooden masks, carrying torches. Cooking fires burn, babies cry —real live vignettes. Teenagers screwing in the bushes, old men taking dumps knee-deep in water—scenes like that. When the wind's just right, I can hear hard men talking war. It's a very heavy connection for me. The Calusa are still here, man, when moonlight chimes the right notes."

Emily was smiling, charmed by Tomlinson's childlike sincerity. No surprise there. I had seen that smile on the faces of hundreds of women, maybe thousands, in the last ten years.

My pal continued, "Archaeologists may call them by a different name, but the Calusa were Maya. They were oceangoing people who got around. It's sad but kinda funny now that the Mayan people are considered illegal immigrants even though they've been on this peninsula five thousand years longer than anyone else."

Tomlinson looked up from the computer screen, done with his monologue, and glanced at his watch, eager to get going, a familiar stoned smile on his face. It had been fifteen minutes since I had told Detective Leroy Melinski that I would not search for Harris Squires, but now we were planning to do just that.

But then something unexpected happened. I watched my pal focus on Emily, studying her face, and then the smile faded as he looked at something that had just appeared on the computer screen. Whatever it was troubled him.

After a moment, the man motioned toward me as he said to Emily, "You're serious about this guy, aren't you."

It was a statement, not a question.

Confused, then amused, Emily replied, "What a strange thing to say. I'm not in the habit of picking up strangers at alligator necropsies. Maybe the average girl does, but not me. I wouldn't be here if I wasn't interested."

Tomlinson's expression changed, a look that was all too familiar. I call it his Sorcerer's face. His eyelids drooped, his eyes appeared glazed by what he was seeing, the details he was absorbing, his attention focused laserlike on Emily Marston.

"What I'm saying is, you've been interested in Doc for a while. In your head . . . in your brain, there's a whole little room devoted to Dr. Marion Ford, isn't there? That *is* unusual."

Emily's smile hardened, a defensive posture, but she continued listening.

Tomlinson's eyes were almost closed now as he said, "You've done a lot of thinking about this guy. I can sense the vibes, it's becoming very clear. But it took you a while to find a way to meet him. A proper way to meet him, I mean. Someone told you about Doc a long time ago, maybe. Someone who was. . . . who was *important* to you."

He took a breath, his eyes open now as he asked, "Am I right?"

Emily turned to me. "Does he guess weights and birthdays, too?" She laughed the words, but her discomfort was visible.

I understood why. After we had made love for

249

the second time, I had taken her out in my flats skiff, a twenty-one-foot boat. We had drifted from Woodring Point almost to the marina, lying on the deck, looking up at the late-sunset sky. I'd learned a lot about the woman by the time we'd returned to my stilt house an hour later and made love yet again.

As I knew, Emily was uncomfortable because what Tomlinson had just said was all too close to the truth. She had heard about me a couple of years before from her own father, whom she adored.

Had Emily told me her maiden name, I would have made the connection much earlier.

The highly regarded amateur ornithologist who could afford to travel to Third World places had mentioned my name several times to his daughter—usually when she was dating some guy her father didn't deem worthy.

I could admit to Emily that I knew that man, but that was as far as I could go. She willingly shared her secret, I could not.

I became even more uncomfortable when she told me that her father had disappeared thirteen months ago. I had met the man only twice—under circumstances that are still classified—so I knew without doubt that bird-watching was to him what marine biology is to me. It was an effective cover story for the dangerous intelligence work he did.

From past experience, I also suspected that Emily's father was dead. If I ever disappear from Dinkin's Bay, the same will be true of me.

It was a strange situation to be in. In a way, I knew things about Emily's father that she would never know. She described him as "sweet, sensitive and generous."

I didn't doubt that was true, but I also knew the guy had to have a dark side or he would not have survived as long as he had in the business. I covered my discomfort with a silence that communicated an interest in the woman's past. My interest was genuine.

Now Tomlinson had pried into our private conversation with yet another of his uncanny guesses. What irritates me is that he always does it in a way that gives the impression he possesses supernatural powers, which, of course, he does not.

It took me a couple of years, but I finally figured out how he does what he does, although I may never understand how he does it so well. Tomlinson is extraordinarily perceptive. He has a genius for reading nuances of speech, body language and facial expressions. He then ties all those tiny bits of datum together to make plausible and often accurate projections.

It requires an intellect of the first magnitude, yet it is still a magician's trick.

I said, "Knock it off, Tomlinson. She has to

work tomorrow. We can take my truck or your VW. Either way, we've got a long drive. If we're going, let's go."

Emily stood, neatening papers to return to my *Sharks of Lake Nicaragua* file. "We'll take my car," she said. "He's right, my Jaguar's fast. As in, scary fast. I'll call my office in the morning. I can take a personal day if we don't make it back tonight. Is there a hotel near this place we're going?"

I said, "Yes. Sort of," remembering a Bates Motel–looking place at the edge of town called Sawgrass Motor Court. I felt like I should offer her another chance to beg off but didn't want to risk it. Instead I said, "Immokalee's only an hour, maybe forty minutes, in a decent vehicle. Don't worry about it, we'll be back here before one-thirty in the morning. Probably earlier."

"Or we could stay at my cottage," she offered. "It's not Sanibel—but what is? You'll like it, though. It's an old Florida Cracker house"—she was looking around my lab—"sort of like this. All yellow pine. Wood so hard, you can still smell the turpentine sap when you drill. I have two bed-rooms, and it's close to the Interstate—on the river, near Alva."

Tomlinson was standing at the printer now, waiting for something to finish. His eagerness to get on the road, all as his nervous energy, was suddenly gone.

He handed me several printouts. One was a map of Immokalee, churches and restaurants marked. Another was a Google Earth satellite photo. It took me a moment to realize it was the four hundred acres that Melinski had mentioned. According to tax records, it was owned by Harris Squires's mother.

I was using a magnifying glass on the satellite shot, seeing what might have been an RV hidden in the trees, as Tomlinson said, "Doc, can I talk to you for a minute? Alone."

I replied, "If it has something to do with Emily, go ahead and say it." Then I had to wonder why my normally talkative pal suddenly went very quiet.

It took several seconds before Tomlinson finally said to Emily, "I don't want to upset you, but I get premonitions sometimes. That's why I was asking you about Doc. I wanted to see if your karmas are connected."

Emily said, "Our karmas?" as if she didn't understand but was willing to listen.

"I'm a psychic sensitive," Tomlinson told her, pouring himself another shot of Patrón. "An empathetic, too. In fact—and this is something I don't share this with many people—I was employed by our own damn government as an expert on what they called remote viewing. I'd have never done it if I'd known who was paying me. Ask the good doctor if you don't believe me."

I nodded a confirmation. While still in college, Tomlinson had worked for the CIA during a time in history when the Soviets and the U.S. had recruited people who, after completing a very bizarre military test, were believed to have paranormal powers. The CIA called the project Operation Stargate. Stargate was fully funded by Congress until 1995, when wiser heads prevailed.

Tomlinson was looking at the woman, his voice soft, as he continued, "I just found something that gives me a very bad feeling about Emily making this trip. For Doc and me, it doesn't matter. We've lived and died a dozen times. But you . . . you're fresh, you're new. I've got a feeling something bad's going to happen tonight if you go to Immokalee. It's because of your karmic linkage with Doc and me."

"Are you stoned?" Emily asked him, serious.

"I was," he replied, giving it some thought. *"Cannabis interruptus*—the girl's disappearance has completely screwed up my schedule. On a lunar scale, I'd say I'm closer to the Sea of Crises than the Sea of Tranquillity. We can share a spliff if you want—but later. Right now, I'd like you to take a look at this."

Emily's expression asked me *Is he for real?* as she reached for a photo he was handing her, something he'd just printed from the Internet. I intercepted the thing and took a look. It was a pen-and-ink drawing from the time of the Spanish Inquisition. A Mayan pyramid in the background. In the foreground, a woman, tied to a ladder, was being tilted toward a roaring fire by Conquistadors.

I passed the drawing to Emily as I asked, "What does this have to do with her, for Christ's sake? You're getting her upset for no reason."

"Look at the face," Tomlinson replied, voice calm now but concerned. "I don't know why it caught my eye, but it did. There's a connection. I'm not sure what, but I don't think Emily should go with us."

"You think this woman looks like me?" Emily asked. "I'm flattered, I guess. We're both dressed in white, is that what you're saying? If it wasn't for the gown, she could be a nice-looking boy."

After a moment, she added, "Our cheekbones, I guess, are similar, and . . . she has a sort of plain face, like mine. But don't most women have plain faces? And the hair's completely different."

The image of the adolescent girl, Tula Choimha, came into my mind. I wondered why Tomlinson didn't make the association, it was so obvious. But why lend credence to a preposterous assertion by asking a pointless question?

Emily handed the drawing back to me as she said to Tomlinson, "It's sweet of you, but, come

255

on, be serious. I don't believe in this sort of thing. If you don't want me tagging along, just say so. All of that pseudoscience nonsense— precognition, astrology, clairvoyance, numerology. Sorry, I've never been able to take that sort of thing seriously."

The woman put her hand on my shoulder. "Doc, talk some sense into him, would you?"

Tomlinson replied, "It's called tempting fate when we ignore our own instincts."

He turned to me. "I really don't think she should go, man. Something bad's going to happen. I can feel it. If you want, stay here with her, I'll go to Immokalee on my own. It has something to do with fire, I think."

He took the drawing from my hands, giving it serious thought. "That's what came into my mind when I saw this. Fire . . . and pain. Something terrible. Why risk it?"

I felt ridiculous, caught in the middle. Emily was waiting for me to agree with her—we were both scientists, after all. Tomlinson, my pal, was asking me to respect his instincts.

To me, it was more than that. Intellectually, I knew there could be no rational linkage between a random drawing and what might or might not happen to Emily on this very real Wednesday night in March.

Logically, it was absurd. Emotionally, though, I couldn't let go of the fact—and it is a fact—that

Tomlinson's intuition, although often wrong, is also more than occasionally right.

As I took the drawing from Tomlinson's hands, saying, "Let me see that again," Emily gave me an incredulous look that said *You can't be serious?*

I looked at the thing, paying no attention to the details because I was carrying on an argument in my head. Debating Tomlinson in the comfort of the lab, or sitting over beers aboard his sailboat, is one thing. But human certitude is an indulgence that can be enjoyed only in a cozy and safe environment.

It irritated me to have to admit it to myself, but, wrong or right, Tomlinson had asked a reasonable question: *Why risk it?*

As I placed the drawing on the dissecting table, Emily said to Tomlinson, "We're not being fair to Doc. I can almost see his mind working. Choose between his best friend or agree with a woman he's just met? That's not something he'd do to us, so I'll make it simple. I withdraw. I'll see you guys tomorrow evening for drinks, if you want. You can fill me in."

I thought I noted some mild sarcasm until the woman slipped her hand beneath my arm and gave a squeeze. I thanked her by placing a hand on her hip and pulling her closer. Truth was, she had a point. Would I back a lady I'd just met? Or remain loyal to an old friend?

I backed Tomlinson, of course. Sort of.

"Here's what I think," I said, looking at Tomlinson. "Three *gringos* driving an expensive car will attract too much attention in Immokalee. In a place that small? Especially at this hour. My Spanish is better than yours, and I speak a little *Quiché*. Emily's not dressed for barhopping. And frankly, Tomlinson, you wouldn't be an asset, either. There are some cowboy types down there in Immokalee who aren't real fond of hippies."

I felt a perverse jolt of pleasure at the surprise on the man's face. I interrupted as he tried to protest, telling him, "You say Emily is in danger tonight? It's not rational, but I'm not going to argue. Which means she should stay here. Either that or you should follow her home just to make sure she gets back safely. I'm going to Immokalee by myself."

Tomlinson appeared nonplussed, his expression asking me *Is this some sort of test?*

In reply, I smiled and said, "If I can't trust my best friend to look after a lady in danger, then who can I trust?" To emphasize my point, I stood and squeezed his scarecrow shoulder almost hard enough to make him wince.

"But I have to go!" he said. "I'm worried sick about that little girl."

"Then drive your VW back to Red Citrus and have another look around," I told him. "Splitting up makes more sense, anyway. We can stay in touch by cell phone. But *after* Emily is safely home. If I hear something, I'll call. You do the same."

Giving me a look of approval, Emily said to Tomlinson, "Sounds like your pal has made up his mind. Any objections to me coming here tomorrow after work? This is an interesting little marina you have. I bet you two have some stories."

I said, "I'm counting on it," as Tomlinson took a square of paper from his breast pocket, unfolded it to reveal a pencil-thin joint.

He said, "You've gotta love this guy, don't you? The freaking earth could be wobbling off its axis, anarchy loosed upon the world. But good ol' Doc will still be trying to do the right thing, in the most rational possible way, wanting the best for all concerned."

He held the joint so Emily could see it. "In the meantime, us *human* humans have time for a couple of hits. Care to join me outside for the pause that refreshes?"

I was a little surprised that Emily nodded her head. Tomlinson was baiting me, that was apparent, so I ignored them both.

As I went out the screen door, down the steps toward my shark pen, I was already busy deciding what equipment to take just in case I got lucky and got a lead on the missing girl. The odds were slim, but that was okay. The fact was, it would be a relief to be on the road alone. No more talking, no more debates.

That feeling stayed with me, even after I had kissed Emily goodbye and I was bouncing down Tarpon Bay Road in my old pickup truck, a canvas backpack sitting square and heavy beside me, traffic sparse.

In the bag was a Sig Sauer 9mm semiauto pistol, plus the pocket-sized Kahr that is fast becoming my favorite handgun. There was an odd assortment of other gear that I usually carry only when outside the country: gloves, a black watch cap, a handheld GPS, a Randall attack/survival knife and a MUM night vision monocular mounted on a headband.

Just for the hell of it, I had also included the tactical laser light, the Dazer. I hadn't done enough testing to have confidence it would work on feeding sharks. But the company that made the thing, Laser Energetics, had invested years, and a lot of money, to prove that a small, blinding laser beam could disable a human attacker.

Had Emily been along and gotten a peek into that bag, she might have been shocked.

Or would she?

It was something to think about as I drove across the causeway bridge, the Sanibel Lighthouse strobing to my right, a black fusion of water and stars to my left.

Maybe not, I decided, judging from who her

father was . . . or had once been. The man couldn't have confided even in his daughter, but it was possible that Emily had been inquisitive as a girl and had done some snooping.

As I passed beneath the tollboth onto a fast four-lane, I checked my watch. It was 10:05 p.m. on this Wednesday night. Tula had been under the steroid freak's control for at least twelve hours.

It was an unsettling fact.

Unless somehow related, grown men kidnap young girls for only one reason. Once their sexual fantasy is satiated, they usually panic and choose murder as a way to obliterate their lesser crime. The only variable is how many hours before the kidnapper has had enough?

One thing was certain: In twelve hours, the girl had already been victimized.

But was she still alive?

TWELVE

JUST BEYOND A SIGN THAT READ Immokalee 22 miles, Harris Squires locked the gate to his hunting camp behind him, then banged the truck into four-wheel drive, telling himself, *Shoot the girl in the back of the head. Stop thinking. Get it over with.*

After what he'd just heard on the radio, about

261

cops finding human bones in the dead alligator's belly, he had no choice but to do it.

And he would.

It was almost noon on Wednesday. The craziness of the previous night—the alligator, the flashing police lights—seemed like a month ago, which might have had something to do with the pint of Cuervo Gold Squires had killed on the ride. Mixed with Red Bull and a Snickers bar, he should have had a good buzz going. But instead his brain felt raw and skittish.

Beneath his seat, in the hidden compartment, Squires had the .357 Ruger Blackhawk revolver in a canvas bag that was also packed full of cash money.

The gun was the long-barreled model, chrome with black grips. The cartridges were as thick as his pinkie finger. They were hollow points that would blow the back side out of a watermelon after neatly piercing its rind.

An unsettling image of the girl's head came into Squires's mind of how her face would look after the bullet exited. Skin without a shell and lots of blood. But this wasn't pretend, there was no going back. Fifi may have missed her chance to kill him, but that fat toad had found a way to totally screw up his life.

Squires had felt dizzy as the radio announcer's voice drilled the details through his skull. Then he'd felt physically sick, a nauseating panic deep in his chest that made him want to jump out of the truck and run screaming into the cypress shadows that lay ahead.

The bones had to belong to the *chula* Frankie had killed. The one he had bundled into a garbage bag, weighting the body with wire and cement before dragging it to the lake. Squires kept telling himself that, even though he knew there was a chance that the gator had eaten a different dead girl months earlier. The Mexican girl from his sex dream—if the sex dream was real. Which could prove to cops that he was the murderer, not Frankie.

If it had really happened.

It was a dream, Squires told himself now, because that's what he wanted to believe. *I didn't do anything wrong. Or I would remember dragging a body to Fifi's pen. The Mexican girl probably ran off while I was asleep.*

That made Squires feel a little better. That goddamn Frankie was entirely to blame for this mess. Her with her love for kinky sex, the way she got off on using and abusing Mexican girls. It was some kind of sick power trip . . . or maybe Frankie's way of punishing younger, prettier women for the saggy way her own body was aging.

Squires realized that he had never allowed himself to acknowledge just how dangerous the woman was. If he did, then he'd have to

263

admit to himself that the dead *chula* he had sunk at Red Citrus probably wasn't the first girl Frankie had killed. There might be at least two others, maybe more.

It was just a guess, Squires couldn't prove it because, until they had trucked Fifi out of the hunting camp, Frankie had handled all her personal *chula* problems on her own.

Frankie might be getting up there in years, but that woman was still big and strong as hell. She could have stuck a dead *chula* under each arm and carried the bodies down to Fifi's pen, no problem.

That's why Harris Squires had stayed out of the woman's way and didn't ask questions. In his mind, if he ignored the shit Frankie did, it was like it never happened. Plus, on the rare night when a girl disappeared, he was always so screwed up on tequila, grass and crank that it all seemed blurry and unreal, anyway. Sort of like his sex fantasy dream . . .

Until now. Everything in Squires's life had changed as of last night, and this morning. Now he'd probably go to jail—even the electric chair —because of all the sick and nasty shit Frankie had done.

Tula had been listening to the radio, too, and paid close attention to how the giant man beside her reacted. She saw Squires's face mottle, then go pale. It was a rancid color, like the faces of sunbaked corpses she had seen on village streets as a child. That caused her to think of her father, the way he had been murdered, and Tula had placed her hand on the giant's hand, her first instinct a desire to comfort Squires rather than abandon him to the misery of his own fear.

Tula had felt real fear before. Not the common everyday sort that everyone feels but the variety of fear that sweeps people over the abyss, then sucks them downward. It was while sitting in a tree near the convent, reliving her father's death, that she had experienced a wave of panic so dark that Tula felt as if her heart might explode. Immersed in the memory of what she had witnessed, of what she had lost, it was then, her brain numb with fear, that Tula heard the Maiden's voice for the first time.

That moment had changed everything.

No matter what happened to Tula in the future, the girl felt a serene confidence that fear of that magnitude could never overwhelm her again. The scars from that night were like armor. Thanks to the Maiden, Tula believed she was now immune.

"You should breathe into your belly," she had told Squires as he switched off the radio. "It sometimes helps."

After studying the man's face for a moment, she had added, "God is with you if you need Him. Ask and He'll come into your heart. The goodness that was in you as a child is still alive inside you. Just ask God and He'll help you."

When the girl touched him, Squires had yanked his hand away, drawing it back to slap Tula, but something stopped him.

"Just shut your damn mouth—" he said, biting off the sentence. "Don't you say another word to me. Understand? Not another damn word or you'll be sorry!"

Squires found the girl's calm demeanor infuriating, and he almost did slap her when she replied, "There is no sin so terrible that God won't forgive you. Two nights ago, when I watched you at the lake, I knew what was in the bag that you put into the water. I knew it was the body of a dead person. But, even so, I prayed for you."

Squires could barely speak, he was so incredulous, but managed to ask, "You *admit* that you saw me?"

"Of course," Tula replied, and then repeated a familiar phrase: "I would rather die than to do something I know to be a sin. I will never lie to you. It's an oath I have made to . . . to someone important. On the radio, the man said the bones they found were probably from a woman's hand. Because of the ring she wore. Why would you murder a young woman?"

Squires couldn't believe what he was hearing. She would rather die than tell a lie? Jesus Christ, the girl was *begging* for it.

"I didn't kill her!" Squires yelled, leaning toward Tula. "You hear me? I didn't goddamn kill her! All I did was get rid of the body! So why did you have to be there, snooping around?"

Tula said to him calmly, "Why do you use such terrible words—taking God's name in vain? That's a sin. I won't listen to you anymore if you use profanity."

Squires pushed his face toward the girl, his eyes glassy as he bellowed, "Kiss my goddamn ass! Do you realize what this means, you idiot? Why'd you have to be there watching? Now I got no goddamn choice! Do you even understand what I'm telling you?"

As Tula began to answer, the man drew his hand back again to slap her and roared, "I'm warning you for the last time! Shut your mouth!"

Tula could see that Squires was crazy with anger, and she sensed that he was on the brink of an emotional explosion. The man appeared near tears.

When she tried to comfort Squires, though, by patting his knee, it only caused him to moan in frustration, then swear at her, using a word Tula had never heard before but she assumed was profane.

By then, they were at the gate.

Now Squires was wrestling the truck over a rutted trail that tracked for a half mile through pine flats, cypress and myrtle to where an RV and his steroid cookshack were anchored with hurricane stakes, the building hidden beneath trees near a cypress pond that looked cool and inviting to Tula.

Focusing on the cypress trees helped keep Tula from weeping—that's how badly she felt for the man. She was also beginning to feel frightened for herself. During the hours since they had left the trailer park, the Maiden had not come into Tula's head to speak with her or to calm her.

Tula knew that the Maiden would not abandon her. There was no possibility of that. But where was the Girl of Lorraine now when Tula sensed so much danger?

I must find a tree, Tula thought. *If I can sit peacefully in a tree and breathe into my belly, the Maiden will return and tell me what I should do.*

Tula could think of only one reason why the Maiden would order her to travel with this giant, angry man who might also be a murderer. It was the Maiden's way of providing Tula with a vehicle and a driver to go in search of her mother. Tula had became convinced of this when she saw the sign that read IMMOKALEE 22 MILES. But how could she make Squires understand that the Maiden wanted him to help with the search?

Yes, Tula needed guidance. It seemed unlikely that the man would react kindly if she asked to be left alone in a tree. Not until he calmed down a little—then, perhaps, Tula could reason with him, and possibly even win him over as a friend.

So instead of asking to be allowed to walk into the cypress grove, Tula said, "Why have we come here? You should eat some food, it's no wonder your body is trembling. We haven't eaten all morning. And I have to use the bathroom."

Squires had pulled into the shade of a tree near a medium-sized trailer, white with green trim, its paint fading. Unlike the trailers at Red Citrus, this trailer was also a motor vehicle, with tires jacked off the ground on blocks and a windshield covered with shiny aluminum material. There were also a couple of wooden structures that looked homemade, one of them with locked shutters and a heavy door.

Squires switched off the engine and said to Tula, "Get out of the truck and shut up. I don't want to hear nothing else out of you. Just do what I tell you to do. We're going for a walk."

There was something strange about the man's voice now. It was a flat monotone, all of the emotion gone out of it. Tula could smell the alcohol on his breath, but his eyes looked dead, not drunken.

"Walk where?" she asked, trying to be conversational. "It's very pretty here. There are trees down by the water that look good for climbing. And lots of birds—egrets with white feathers, I think. Do you see them up there?"

The man's face colored, but he got himself under control before saying, "I'm going to tell you one more time and I want you to listen. No more talking. You've got nothing to say that I want to hear, so shut up and follow me. That's exactly where we're going, to look at all the pretty birds."

"But I need a bathroom," Tula insisted as she watched Squires lift the driver's seat and then open what appeared to be a hatch in the floor. He removed a canvas bag that was heavy, judging from the way he handled it.

Squires turned and began walking toward the cypress pond where Tula could see white birds suspended like flowers among the gray limbs, some on nests in the high branches.

"Get moving," he said without looking at the girl. "And I'm warning you—I don't want to hear another goddamn word out of you."

Tula got out of the truck and realized that her legs were shaking. Staying calm when the man was angry had not been easy, but this different voice, so flat and dead, was scaring her. She walked around the back of the truck, wondering if she should risk telling the man that her bladder was so full that she feared wetting herself. But Tula stopped after only a few words when her voice broke, afraid that she would start crying.

The Maiden had never cried, even when

tortured by her tormentors. Even as flames had consumed her, the brave saint had not wept, but, instead, had called out the name of her Savior.

"Jesus," Tula whispered now, her right hand clutching her amulets, as she followed Squires toward the trees. "Please protect and keep me, Jesus," she said in Mayan, and continued repeating the phrase as they walked along the edge of a pond that was cooled by cypress shadows and moss. The giant kept walking, far into the tree shadows, so far that Tula's abdomen began to cramp because of the pressure in her bladder.

Finally, Squires stopped beside a tree at the edge of the pond, where water black as oil was flecked with leaves, white-feather down and long-legged insects that skated on the surface beneath cooing birds. For a time, the man stood with his back to her, and Tula realized that he was taking something from the canvas bag.

"Turn around and look at the water," Squires said to her in the same flat dead voice. "Do it now."

"Can I please go to the bathroom first?" Tula asked the man, frightened but also angry at herself because tears had begun streaming down her face.

Squires was looking over his shoulder at her. "No. Just do what I tell you to do. This won't take long. Turn your back to me and look at the water. Hurry up."

Tula could see that Squires had something in his hand. She got a look at it when she pivoted toward the pond.

It was a large gun, silver with chrome.

Tula had seen many guns during the fighting in the mountains, but she had never seen a gun so shiny before. The metal was hypnotic, it was so bright, which scared her.

Tula's chest shuddered, and she couldn't help herself. Urine dribbled down her leg as she began crying, but silently, keeping her weakness to herself as she sensed the giant walk up behind her, the gun in his hand that was soon a silver reflection on the black water, the man on the surface huge, the size of a tree.

"Get down on your knees, child," said a voice in Tula's head, and Tula obeyed instantly, overwhelmed with relief, because it wasn't a man's voice. It was the Maiden. The Maiden had returned to her in her moment of need, and Tula knew everything would be okay now.

Get down on your knees, the Maiden counseled, *and pray.*

Behind Tula, as she whispered a prayer, the giant stood in silence. A minute passed. Then two minutes, then three.

In the water's reflection, Tula could see that Squires was pointing the pistol only inches from the back of her head. Occasionally, he would lower it, but then he would raise the pistol again. But Tula was no longer frightened.

Once again, she felt a serene immunity from fear. The amulets she clutched in her hand provided strength. What happened would happen. She was with God and she was content. The Maiden would not allow her to suffer pain, and, ultimately, Tula would be reunited with her mother, her father and family again, which was something the girl wanted more than anything she had ever wanted in her life.

Be at peace, child. I am with you always, the Maiden said, speaking as softly as the muted light inside the girl's head.

For another minute, Tula waited, her head bowed. She felt so confident and content that she decided to help the man along by saying, "If this is what you must do, then I forgive you. If it is God's will, then you are doing the right thing. Don't be afraid."

Tula waited for so long in silence that she had resumed praying before the man spoke to her, "It's what I have to do. I don't have a damn choice, and it's your own fault. You'll tell the police what you saw and they'll arrest me. Even though I didn't kill that girl, they'll charge me with murder. Do you understand?"

His voice wasn't so empty of emotion now. It gave the girl hope, but she was inexplicably disappointed, too. She had felt so peaceful and free kneeling there, waiting for it to end.

Tula considered turning to look at the man but decided against it. Looking into the barrel of the silver gun might bring her fear back, and she didn't want that to happen. She didn't want to risk crying or losing control of her bladder again.

"I understand," she said to Squires. "I'm sorry I saw what I saw. I didn't mean to be in the tree watching you, but I was."

Tula glanced at the water's mirror surface and saw that Squires was leaning toward her now. Then she felt the barrel of the gun bump the back of her head as the man said, "You told me yourself you don't lie. Even if you promised me you wouldn't tell the cops, I wouldn't believe you. Do you understand now why I have to do this? Unless you promise me—I mean, *really* promise me—and mean it."

The man's voice was shaking, and Tula knew he was going to pull the trigger. She closed her eyes, pressing her chin to her fingers, as she replied, "I can't promise you, I'm sorry. If the police ask me, I will have to tell them the truth. I won't lie to you and I won't lie to them. It's because of another promise I have made."

In Tula's ear, she heard a metallic *Click-Click* and she knew that the man had pulled back the revolver's hammer. On her cheeks, she felt tears streaming, but she wasn't afraid. She was ready for what happened next.

What happened next was, in the high cypress limbs above them, there was a squawking, cracking sound. Then the fluttering of wings as a bird tumbled from the tree canopy and thudded hard on the ground nearby. Tula looked up, surprised. Then she was on her feet and running toward it without even thinking, tucking the jade amulet and silver medallion into her T-shirt as she sprinted.

"It's a baby egret!" she cried, kneeling over a thrashing bird that looked naked because its feathers hadn't come in yet. "I think it broke its wing."

Carefully, the girl cupped the fledgling in her hands, using her thumb to try to steady the bird's weak neck. And she stood, saying over her shoulder to Squires, "That must be her mother up there. See her?"

Tula motioned to a snowy egret that was hovering overhead, its yellow feet extended as if to land, excited by the peeping noises the baby bird was making.

"Yes," Tula said, "its wing is broken. At the convent, we took care of many sick animals. We can help this bird, I think." Then she looked at Squires, adding, "I can't stand it anymore. I have to go to the bathroom now."

Then she stopped because of what she saw.

Harris Squires was sitting on the ground. He was rocking and crying, his hands locked around his knees, making a soft moaning sound in his misery. If the gun was somewhere on the ground nearby, Tula didn't see it.

The scene was even stranger to Tula because, the way the man was sitting, slope-shouldered and huge, reminded her of a bear she had seen begging for peanuts at the zoo in Guatemala City.

The bear had struck the girl as being very sad, an animal as repulsed with itself as it was humiliated by its captivity. The scene was even stronger in Tula's mind because her father had taken her to the zoo the day before he was murdered.

Slowly, the girl walked toward Squires. She was embarrassed for him and sad in the same way that she had felt sad for the bear. She placed the little bird a safe distance away, in case the big man moved, and then hesitated before touching her fingers to Squires's shoulder.

Tula patted the man gently as she might have patted the bear, given a chance. And then said to him kindly, "I must go behind a tree and use the bathroom. I can't stand it anymore. *Please.* But promise me something. It's important. Promise me you won't look. I know that you have seen me without clothes. But I don't want a man ever to see me that way again. Do you promise?"

Rocking and sobbing, the giant nodded his head.

Tula said to Squires, "My mother had a little doll like this. She wore it pinned to her blouse. Even the same color, bright orange and green, instead of blue like most of them. They're called worry dolls in English. At night, you tell your worries to the doll and put it under your pillow. The next morning, all your worries are gone."

The girl sniffed the doll, knowing it couldn't be her mother's—not way out here, so far from where a woman could get work cleaning houses or mopping floors in a restaurant—but, then, Tula had to wonder, because the odor of raw cotton was so familiar.

Maybe it seemed familiar because everything else inside this man's trailer was so foreign.

Squires had started the generator, and they were inside the RV that smelled sour and stale like the ashes of a cold cooking fire. Tula had found the doll, only an inch tall, mounted on a brooch pin in a strange room where there was a camera, lights on tripods and a bed with a strange black leather contraption hanging from the ceiling.

The doll was on a table piled with photos of naked women. The women were frozen in poses so obscene that Tula had looked away, preferring to focus on the miniature Guatemalan doll in traditional Mayan dress.

The photos were of Mexican women, judging

from their features, but a few Guatemalan women, too. Tula didn't linger over details and closed the door to the room behind her, feeling as if the ugliness of that space might follow her.

Squires was sitting in a recliner, looking dazed, eyes staring straight ahead as he drank from a pint bottle of tequila. He had found the revolver, which was now lying in his lap, and Tula sensed that he was rethinking what had happened out there in the cypress grove. She had witnessed his breakdown and he would begin hating her for it soon, the girl feared, if she didn't get his mind on something else.

After pinning the worry doll to her T-shirt, Tula went to the kitchen, where she found cans of beans and salsa and meat but no tortillas. There was a can opener, too, and plates, and a cheap little paring knife with a bent blade, but sharp.

"You need food, that's why you feel so tired. I'll cook something," Tula said to Squires as she carried a pan to the stove. A moment later, she said, "We have a gas stove at the convent, but I can't get this one to light. Unless I'm doing it wrong."

Squires blinked his eyes, seeming to hear her for the first time. It took a while, but he finally said, "You're a nun?"

"Someday, when I'm older," Tula replied. "I am going to dedicate my life to God and to helping

278

people. My patron saint is Joan of Arc. Have you heard of her?"

After a few beats of silence, Tula added, "I am modeling my life after the Maiden. That's what the people of France called her, the Maiden. But to her friends, she was called Jehanne."

"The gas isn't on," Squires said to the girl but didn't get up from the chair. His indifference suggested he didn't care about food. But he did appear interested in the convent Tula had mentioned because, after several seconds of silence, he said, "You live with nuns? No men around at all, huh? That's got to be weird. Not even to fix shit?"

"The convent is where I live and go to school. I work in the kitchen, and the garden, too. That's how I learned to speak English and to cook using a stove."

Tula had been twisting the dials for the burners without success. Now she was searching the walls, looking under the stove, hoping the man would take the hint and make the gas work. He needed food, not tequila, and Tula wondered— not for the first time—why so many men preferred to be drunk and stupid rather than to eat hot food.

The giant took a sip from the bottle and told her, "I was raised Catholic. I used to be, anyway. But then all that stuff about priests cornholing little boys—and the goddamn Pope knew about it 'cause he was probably screwing boys himself before he got old. Little boys are in big demand in the Catholic religion. That's probably the problem with you. You've been brainwashed by all that sick Catholic bullshit. Why else would you pretend to be a boy?"

Tula wondered if Squires was trying to upset her, give himself a reason to get angry again and shoot her. So she changed the subject by saying, "I've been thinking of a way to solve your problem. I don't want you to go to jail. There's another way, I think, to keep the police from arresting you."

That surprised the man, Tula could see it, so she added, "I believe you when you say you're not a murderer. Just looking into your face, you couldn't do something like that—not by yourself, you couldn't. I don't want to tell the police what I saw. That's why I've been thinking about this problem."

"My guardian angel," Squires said in his flat voice, not bothering to attempt sarcasm. "I forgot. You were sent by God in case I get into trouble. Lucky me."

He took another drink, and Tula could feel the anger building in the man.

Getting irritated herself, the girl turned away from the counter where she had the salsa open and had used the sharp paring knife to cut the meat into slices. "Listen to me!" she said, frowning at the giant. "I want to find my mother and brother. That's all I care about. I want to go home to the mountains. If I'm home in the mountains, your policemen can't ask me questions. That's why I've been thinking of a way to help you."

That made Squires snort, a sound close to laughter. "What do you want me to do, buy you a plane ticket?" he asked. "Drive you to the airport and wave good-bye? That easy, huh? I don't think so, *chula.*"

Tula felt the Maiden flow into her head, giving instructions, which is why she calmed herself before crossing the room, where she placed her hand on the giant's curly blond head. "You may not believe it, but it's true," she said. "I wouldn't be here unless God wanted me to help you. He loves you. He wants you to come back to Him. You can believe me or not believe me, but you can't deny the goodness that's in your heart."

The girl didn't say it, but her recent words came into Harris Squires's mind. *Do you remember the goodness that was in you as a child?*

The girl patted the man's head as he stared down into the tequila bottle. Tula could feel Squires's brain fighting her, but she continued, "The Maiden has told me how to help you. We must go to Immokalee and ask the people there about my mother and my brother. I have two aunts and an uncle somewhere, too. When we find them, I want you to come home with us to the mountains. In your truck, you can drive us."

Tula looked around the room, seeing the stained walls, the carpet, a peanut can filled with cigarette butts, sensing in the next room the obscene photos staring up at the ceiling tiles.

She said, "This place has sin and ugliness all around. It's no wonder you're unhappy. You should leave this dirty life behind while you still can. You would like the mountains. We live closer to God in the mountains. It is cool there, even in summer, and the rains will begin soon. You can stay a week or a month. Maybe you will like it and want to build a home. The police won't find you if we leave Florida. They can't ask me questions."

"Drive you clear to Mexico?" Squires said like it was a stupid idea. But at least he was thinking about it. Tula could see that his mind was working it through.

"Guatemala, not Mexico," Tula corrected him. "It's much more beautiful than Mexico. And the villages aren't so dirty. Most of them, anyway."

Yes, Squires was giving the idea some consideration because he asked, "Where's Guatemala? Is it farther than Mexico? Mexico's a hell of a long way."

"I'm not sure of the exact distance," Tula said, coming as close to lying as she could allow herself.

"But it's farther than Mexico, that's what you're telling me."

Tula replied, "What does distance matter when there are roads and you own a truck? You can drive the whole way. Or take a train, once we're across the border. I hear the coaches are nice. I've never been inside a train, but I rode on the top of boxcars from Chiapas to San Luis Potosí. Three different train lines, I had to board."

"You're shitting me. You climbed up and rode on the top of a train when it was moving? Christ, what do those things do, fifty, sixty miles an hour?"

Tula replied, "One night, an old man told me we were traveling almost three hundred miles an hour, but I think he was drunk. It's the way even adults travel if they want to come north. Sometimes, riding on top of the train was nice. We could pick green mangoes if the trees were close enough, and it only rained once.

"In Chiapas, though, it was dangerous. There are a lot of Mexican gangs there that wear bandannas and tattoos. At three stops, they robbed some of the men. And I think they attacked two girls who were on one of the cars behind me."

Tula started to add that she hadn't seen it happen, but she had heard the girls screaming. Her voice caught, and she couldn't continue with the story.

Mentioning gangs and tattoos reminded Squires that the police weren't the only ones looking for him. Laziro Victorino would be cruising Red Citrus the moment he heard about the alligator with a dead girl's bones in its belly. Victorino was a little guy, but he was all muscle and attitude, a scary little shit who enjoyed killing people. Cutting them up with that box cutter of his or shooting them behind the ear and feeding them to his dogs.

Squires had heard the stories and he had seen a couple of the V-man's snuff films. The teardrop tattoo beneath the dude's eye was so weird it was scary.

What Squires hoped was that Victorino would run into Frankie, who might well kick the shit out of that vicious little wetback. Or vice versa. Either way, it was okay with Squires. He hoped he never saw either one of them again in his life. He was sick of the whole goddamn business.

A question formed in Squires's head as he reviewed his predicament: Why the hell did he have to stay in Florida?

The answer was simple: He couldn't think of a single goddamn reason.

Not the way things were now. Almost everyone he knew was an asshole or a drug dealer or a crackhead killer like the V-man. The girl, Tula, was a weirdo Jesus freak, but she had hit the nail on the head when it came to the life he was living. It was a dirty life. It made him feel dirty —Squires could admit that to himself now that he was on the run from a murder rap. So why not make a change before it was too late? Maybe going to Mexico wasn't such a bad idea.

He said to the girl, "I drove to New Orleans once and it took me twelve hours. How much farther is the border? I think you have to drive clear across Texas, too."

Squires placed the tequila bottle, then the revolver, on a magazine stand, and sat up a little as he tried to picture the geography of the southern United States. In his mind, everything south of Texas was just a hazy design, with curves and bulges bordered on both sides by oceans.

"First," Tula reminded him, "we must go to Immokalee and ask about my mother. I'm not going home without my family. People call her Mary. Mary Choimha. Or Maria sometimes, too. She lived at your trailer park for a while, that's why I went there first."

"Every *chula* in Florida is named Mary or Maria," Squires said. "I can't keep track of everyone who rents at my place. You Mexicans are always coming and going."

Tula said, "Then you lied to me. You said you had met her, that you could take me to her. You told me that at the trailer park last night."

Squires shrugged. "So what? We're not all perfect like you."

285

"You would remember my mother," the girl insisted. "She's very beautiful—much prettier than me. Carlson said, last year, he saw your wife talking to my mother. That she gave my mother a cell phone . . . or maybe you gave it to her, Carlson wasn't sure. But the phone stopped working two months ago, which is why I came here. My mother would have called me if her phone was working."

Squires told the girl, "I don't have a wife, especially not the bitch you mean," as he leaned back to think about what he'd just heard.

The information was disturbing. All kids thought their mothers were pretty—Squires all too aware that he was a rare exception, because his mother was a chain-smoking witch. But why would Frankie give Tula's mother a cell phone unless Frankie had something to gain?

Squires had given dozens of cheap phones to Mexicans, the cell phones that charged a flat fee with a limited number of minutes. Usually, he gave them to men who were good workers—and it was always for selfish reasons: It was a way of controlling the guy, make him indebted, and a little scared, too, that the phone would be taken away or the service canceled.

Christ, Frankie had run so many Mexican girls through the hunting camp and their double-wide at Red Citrus, he would have needed a calculator to keep track.

Was it possible that this kid's mother was one of the *chulas* Frankie had used? Squires considered the girl's age, which would put the mother in her mid- to late twenties, Mexican girls being prone to marrying young.

The possibility was too upsetting, though, and Squires decided that it wasn't something he wanted to think about. He stared at the girl intensely for a moment, then looked away, suddenly aware there was something eerily familiar about the girl's eyes and high cheekbones.

"Why would you listen to that crazy old drunk, Carlson?" Squires said to the girl. "I don't want to hear any more about your mother. Understand?"

Aware of the man's sudden mood change, Tula said, "Let me fix you some food while we talk. You need to eat for strength if we're going to drive to Immokalee."

The man laced his fingers together—Tula had never seen hands so huge—and sat up in the recliner. He was trying to remember how many Marys and Marias he or Frankie had screwed or used one way or another. But then felt a withering guilt descending, so he stopped himself. Instead, he let his mind shift back to the girl's idea about leaving Florida.

Squires had thought of traveling to Mexico many times. Most of the big steroid manufactures were there because it was legal to make and sell gear. Hell, the place was bodybuilder heaven. In fact, Squires's first supplier, before he got into the business, was an Internet place called mexgear.com. Mexgear's shit was good to go, and they had good prices. Squires had bought Test C, Tren, EQ and Masteron from the online Mexicans there for less than fifty bucks a vial, and they'd always thrown in some extra gear if it was a big order.

The fact was, he didn't need Frankie to continue his steroid operation. He could set up an underground lab just about anywhere, plus he spoke English, unlike the Mexgear guys, which always made it a pain in the ass to deal with them.

Speaking English was definitely to his advantage, Squires decided, even in Mexico. Most bodybuilders were Americans or lived in Europe, so it would be a smart way to expand and maybe make a lot of money. He couldn't wait forever for his rich mother to die.

"Go to Mexico for a few months," Squires said aloud, testing the idea on his ears.

He looked toward the little kitchen as if he'd just awakened from a doze. "I don't need any food. Not now. But I could us a little pick-me-up. Come with me—I'm not taking my eye off you for a second. If you want to cook, that's up to you. Here, I'll show you how to turn on the gas."

Tula watched the giant get down on his knees

and open a cabinet beneath the sink. He told her, "There's a red knob under here and an emergency-cutoff switch. But first check and make sure you turned the burners off or one spark and this whole place could go up."

Squires stood, the trailer creaking beneath his weight, and Tula followed him out the door, past the peeping baby egret that she had placed in a box after feeding it water and a few drops of condensed milk with an eyedropper. Squires had refused to help her catch and mash up minnows from the pond, which is what Tula believed that baby egrets ate, but maybe later he would.

Or maybe the mother egret, which was still flying around, occasionally landing near the box, would figure it out and bring the fledgling some food.

A few seconds later, Squires removed two padlocks from the homemade-looking wooden building. He lifted a steel bar, and soon Tula was inside a dark space that smelled of chemicals and propane.

When her eyes adjusted, she saw a row of gas burners on a counter that were connected by hoses to tanks beneath. It explained the propane smell, just as shelves filled with bottles and stacks of paper filters explained the odor of chemicals.

"What do you make here?" the girl asked Squires.

"You ask too many questions. Forget you ever saw this place, that's my advice to you," the man replied as he touched a switch, neon lights flickering overhead. That done, Squires took a pack of syringes from a drawer, then opened two small boxes that contained rows of unmarked vials.

Out here, the propane burners had steel manual lighters, like lanterns the girl had used. She stood against the wall, out of the way, as the man put a pot of water on, flame low.

"I always heat my vitamins first. It's cleaner, plus it shoots smoother," he told the girl as he loaded a syringe with oily-looking liquid from three different vials, then dropped the syringe into the water.

"I got a shot once," Tula said, pleased they were having a conversation. "A doctor came to our village. He was British, I think, but still a nice man. The needle was a vaccine for mosquito bites, he said, not vitamins."

"Vitamins keep me strong and healthy," Squires replied in a tone that told Tula he was lying about something, she wasn't sure what.

Fascinated by what she was seeing, Tula watched as the man stripped off his shirt, then rubbed what smelled like alcohol on his left shoulder. Never in her life had she seen such huge muscles. Squires really was a giant. He looked as if he had been carved from stone, gray stone,

the sort her ancestors had used to build pyramids.

"I saw a movie once in Guatemala City," Tula told the man, aware of a strange feeling in her chest. "My father took us, my brother and me. The movie was about Hercules, the strongest man in history. He was so strong that he pulled down marble columns and defeated the Centurions who killed Jesus. But I think you are stronger than him. You are much larger."

For the first time since she had met Harris Squires, a pleasant smile appeared on the man's face. In that instant, Tula could see how the giant must have looked as a little boy. He had been a sweet child, probably, maybe a little shy. It caused the girl to wonder what had happened in this man's life to make him mean and to do dirty things such as take photographs of naked women.

Squires replied, "Hercules, no shit? Well, it's all about living clean and using the right vitamins," as he plunged the needle into his bicep and emptied it.

He wasn't done. He used two more syringes —one to load the steroids, a second needle to inject—and pinned a darker oil into the cablelike muscle that angled from his neck to his shoulder.

"Dianabol," Squires said, sounding dreamy and satisfied, rolling his shoulders. "By God, I love a big hit of D-bomb. I don't need any food now, I'm good to go."

Tula watched the man, wondering what that meant as he added, "It's twenty-some miles to Immokalee, but I don't expect there to be much action on the streets. Not on a Wednesday. But if that's what you want, let's do it."

Tula felt a thrill as the Maiden came into her head again, instructing the girl what to say next.

"We'll go to the churches," she told Squires. "On a Wednesday night, people will be praising God and singing. We will find people there who might know about my mother."

Squires was shaking his head. "Where do you come up with this crazy crap? People don't go to church on Wednesday nights, not even Catholics. Unless it's to play bingo or some kind of shit. At least, they didn't back when they made me go."

"The Maiden speaks to me," Tula told him, interested in the man's reaction. "If she says it's true, then it will happen."

Saying it, the girl felt as if she was sharing a secret with Squires, something that increased the weight on her chest and gave her an odd sensation in her abdomen. It was a warm feeling, standing close enough to the giant now to touch her head briefly against his elbow just to see how he reacted.

This time, he didn't yank his arm away. So Tula took another chance by placing her fingers on the man's huge wrist as she told him, "We can

292

trust the Maiden. Whenever I need guidance, she is always there for me."

It felt strange to the girl, her fingers on a man's skin, but Tula decided that she liked it.

Squires turned off the burner, then the lights, before padlocking the door closed. As they walked toward the RV, he said, "The Maiden . . . ? You mean that saint you mentioned? Don't ever tell a shrink what you just told me. They'll throw you in the damn loony bin. Which is probably where you belong."

"Joan of Arc is my patron saint," Tula said, her voice firm. "She *does* speak to me. Usually at night—that's when the visions come to me."

Irritated, Squires said, "Night visions, too. You're even screwier than I thought. Listen, I don't want to hear every damn detail. You talk too much."

"But it's true," the girl said. "I see things that will happen in the future. Sometimes I see things during the day, too. But it's better if I'm alone. For me, sitting in a tree is a nice place."

Remembering that the girl had spied on him from a tree caused Squires to feel the dianabol he'd just injected accelerate to his temple, vessels throbbing. It created a blooming chemical anger in him, and he clenched his fists as he reconsidered what was happening.

Why the hell was he being nice to this crazy little *chula*? He brought her out here expecting to strip the girl's clothes off, then have some fun. The little brat could send him to Raiford Prison if she wanted. At the very least, he should kill her.

It's not too late. I can take her out to the pond, shoot her in the back of the head, then drive to Mexico on my own. I don't need her. Why put up with any more of her crazy talk?

But from the sick feeling Squires got just thinking about it, he knew he couldn't do it. Maybe later but not now. The reasons had to do with the girl's irritating kindness . . . and also the haunting familiarity of her face.

Even so, it pissed him off the way this know-it-all wettail kept chattering away, so Squires decided to shut her up by saying, "I don't want to burst your bubble, *chula*, but that Joan of Arc bullshit, it's all just fairy-tale crap. You're talking about the girl who carried a sword and dressed like a dude? It's total bullshit."

Instead of waiting for the girl to answer, he continued, "She's a goddamn cartoon character, for Christ's sake. Like Santa Claus and the Easter bunny. The Disney World people probably came up with that Joan of Arc stuff. What in the hell ever convinced you that she talks to you?"

Tula was a couple of steps behind Squires as they walked toward the RV, but she hurried ahead and grabbed the man's wrist, which caused Squires to stop and peer down at her.

"Don't ever say that again," Tula told him, her expression fierce. "The Maiden is real. I can show you in the history books! She led King Charles's army, carrying her banner and sword. She forced the English sinners out of France. At first, even the king didn't believe that she was sent by God, but the Maiden proved it to him."

Tula gave the man's wrist as shake. "She was a great leader and her soldiers loved her. The Maiden lived a *pure* life. She died a virgin, as a woman without a husband should. Have you committed so many sins that you don't want to believe such a good person could exist?"

Squires didn't know what to say. He felt ridiculous, allowing himself to be lectured by this skinny little teenager with her boy's haircut, breasts just beginning to blossom.

"And something else," the girl continued, giving the man's wrist another shake. "Stop calling me a *chula*. My name is Tula. Please show me respect. And no more profanity! It hurts me when you use those words. Why do you intentionally hurt me when you know I care for you? I want to help you to be happy again, but then you say such awful things!"

Harris Squires got a funny feeling in his throat when the girl said that. It was stupid to react that way, he knew it, but there it was.

He stood silently as he watched the girl march off toward the truck, then turn with hands on her hips before saying to him, "If we're going to Immokalee, let's go. But you can't go like that—not into a church. You have to change your clothes."

Squires growled, *"What?"* He was carrying his shirt in his hand, wearing baggy shorts and flip-flops.

The girl didn't back down. "If you hadn't thrown me into your truck this morning without even asking, I would have brought my extra shirt. But you have clean clothes hanging in the trailer. I saw them."

Squires thought about arguing, maybe even threaten to slap the girl's face to let her know who was in charge. But then he thought, *The hell with it.*

The little brat was exhausting. Besides, it wouldn't kill him to get cleaned up a little. It might even make him feel better, because his shirt was soaked with sweat—he could smell its hormonal stink—and he hadn't showered since almost having his ass eaten off by Fifi the night before.

"You mind if I take a little nap first?" he said to the girl, being sarcastic, but he meant it. He was suddenly very tired despite the fresh D-bomb juice and testosterone pulsing through him.

"Will you put those steel things on my wrists again, the handcuffs?" the girl asked. It made her nervous, the idea of being alone with the man in the trailer. He might start drinking again. Drink himself into a different mood, and Squires might even try to force her into his bed —Tula would have preferred a bullet in the head to the horror of a man's hands on her body.

But then she studied the giant's face, seeing how empty and tired he looked, and decided no, he would not hurt her. Not now, at least. So the girl added, "If you think you have to chain me, I won't fight you. If it will allow you to sleep for a little while, I think it's what you should do. I won't mind."

The Maiden had been imprisoned in chains, and Tula felt an unexpected thrill at the thought of sharing the experience. It was exciting, the prospect of being locked up alone, but safe with God and Jehanne in her head, while the giant slept nearby.

But the man disappointed her by saying, "If you promise to shut your mouth for a little bit, I don't care what you do. Run off and get eaten by panthers, that's your decision. Just stop your damn talking for a while. My ears are starting to hurt."

Four hours later, when Squires exited the trailer wearing slacks and a polo shirt instead of shorts and flip-flops, his hair wet and slicked back, Tula tried to compliment him by saying, "You look very nice. Blue is a nice color, it shows your eyes. When you were sleeping, you looked so peaceful, I hated to wake you. But it's getting late."

The girl was nervous because Squires was carrying the iPhone she had used an hour ago to type a quick message to her *patron*, Tomlinson, while the giant slept. She had done it just to let him know that she was safe and not in trouble. It was the first text Tula had ever attempted and she had hit the send button accidentally before she was done.

Would the big man notice?

Tula watched Squires glance at the phone, then held her breath as he looked at it more closely.

"That's weird," he said, swiping his fingers over the screen. "Usually, I don't get service out here at the camp, but it looks like someone called. No message, though—probably because of the shitty reception."

Tula relaxed a little when the man swore again softly, adding, "It was Frankie, I bet. I bet she is one pissed-off chick. If I'm lucky, I won't never see her again."

As they approached the truck, the redheaded woman with muscles was still on Squires's mind because he asked the girl, sounding serious, "Tell me something. At Red Citrus, you ever talk to Frankie? Did she ever try to get you off alone?"

"I saw her at the trailer park twice," Tula said. "I had a bad feeling about her, though. So I stayed away from her."

Squires was interested. "A bad feeling? What do you mean by that?"

"A feeling that there is something dark in the woman's brain. That's the only way I can explain it. She scared me. I'm glad you don't want to see that woman again. I think she is a bad influence for you. And she's too old, anyway. A man who looks like Hercules could choose any woman in the world. You should marry a nice woman. A young girl who cares about you and can cook you food."

Realizing how that sounded, Tula threw her hand over her mouth, embarrassed.

But Squires didn't appear to notice. Sounding like it was hard for him to believe, the man said, "That surprises me. Frankie never said even a single word to you?"

"Her eyes watched me when she saw me," the girl replied. "I could tell she wanted to speak with me, but I didn't give her the chance. Her eyes are very blue. I felt like she was trying to see through my clothing. And that there might be something bad inside her. Maybe evil, I'm not sure. So I stayed away."

The man appeared satisfied, maybe even relieved. "Good," he said. "That was real smart of you. Never ever let that bitch get you alone."

Squires grunted as Tula, getting into the truck, tried to buoy his spirits by saying, "There's no need to worry about the redheaded woman now.

The Maiden is my protector. Now she is your protector, too."

"Sure, yeah, right," the man replied. "Whatever you say, sis. But if you really want to impress me, try shutting that mouth of yours for a while."

"You'll see," Tula insisted. "Jehanne is right about the churches tonight. We will find people there who can help us. And that woman— Frankie? Even if she is evil, you and I have nothing to fear."

By the time they'd spent a couple of hours in Immokalee, with its Circle Ks, tomato-packing warehouses and migrant housing, Squires had stopped trying to figure out how the weird little Jesus freak had gotten so famous among all these Mexicans who came out of the woodwork to see the girl, once word got around that she was in town.

Squires knew that the *chilies* back at Red Citrus had built some kind of voodoo-looking shrine to Tula. Why? He had no idea. But how did these Mexicans know about the girl way out here in cattle-and-tomato country, sixty miles from the Gulf beaches and his trailer park? Christ, Tula had been in Florida for only a week or so. Now here she was with strangers fawning over her like she was some kind of damn rock star.

Something else that surprised the man was that the Maiden—whoever the hell *she* was—

300

was right about churches being open on a Wednesday. Not all, but a couple.

More likely, though, credit went to the strange little girl who heard voices but sat quietly, hands in her lap, during the twenty-mile drive from the hunting camp to this city linked to the outside world just by train tracks and a winding road.

The only time Tula had stirred was once when they passed a state trooper's car going the other way. When the girl saw Squires's knuckles go white on the steering wheel, she stroked his forearm and said, "If a policeman stops us, don't worry, I'll tell them you're my friend. And that we're looking for my mother. They'll believe me. Know why? Because it's the truth."

Squires had tried to catch the news on the radio, hoping for an update on the dead woman they'd found. It was also in his mind that Tula could have been reported missing and that the cops might make the connection.

Hell, for all he knew, Frankie had blown the whistle on him herself, once she discovered that all their cash missing. Blame the dead girl's body on him, that would be easy enough for Frankie to do—and maybe even try to prove it, the bitch was such a good liar.

But no luck with the radio—there were only FM stations out here in the boonies. So Squires decided, screw it, he would just go with the flow and stick with the girl. He couldn't make

301

himself kill his crazy little eyewitness, so maybe he was better off joining her. For now.

At the edge of the Everglades, the open highway became Main Street, with palm trees and gas stations, and lots of small brown people, some of them women, wearing what looked like colorful blankets. And lots of scrawny, bowlegged Mexican men, too, wearing straw cowboy hats.

At a supermarket named Azteca Super Centro, Squires turned right past Raynor's Seafood & Restaurant, then drove backstreets, zigzagging through a residential area, because that is what the girl told him to do.

The man had never been in a town so small with so many wetback churches. Iglesia Bautista Jesucristo. Pentecostal Church of God. Evangelica Redimidos por la Sangre de Jesus. Amigos en Cristo.

It was like being in a foreign country, the names were so strange. A lot of Spanish praying went down on this plateau of asphalt and lawns bleached brown by the Florida heat, the entire city opened wide to an Everglades sky above.

Not all of the churches were busy, but a couple were, with parking lots full—pickup trucks and rusting Toyotas—church doors open, with people inside singing hymns or shouting out wild words in Spanish.

Squires could hear all this, as they idled along

in his truck, windows down. A few blocks later, they came to an adobe-colored brick building with a tin roof, Iglesia de Sangre de Cristo, and the girl told him to pull in. She'd start here.

"I'm staying in the truck," Squires said, giving Tula a look that told her *Don't bother arguing.* "But remember this: If you try running out on me, there'll be hell to pay. That ain't a profanity, it's a promise."

Tula stared at him a moment, the door open, her wounded expression asking the man *When will you ever learn?*

Then she jumped down to the ground, a girl not much taller then the truck's tires, saying, "If the priest will let me, I'm going to talk to the congregation. I would like you to come in and listen. I wouldn't feel as nervous if you were with me. Please? I can speak in English for you. Most of them will understand."

Squires shook his head, and kept his eye on Tula until she was inside. After half an hour, though, he did get out and peek through a window, because it seemed strange the way people off the street were suddenly hurrying across lawns to get to the church. The place was already packed, but more people kept coming, some of them chattering on their cell phones, excited expressions on their faces, as they jogged along.

What Squires saw through the window caused him to wonder if Frankie had slipped some

303

Ecstasy into his fresh batch of steroids, the stuff he'd just injected.

That's how surreal the scene was.

What he saw was Tula, the skinny little girl dressed like a boy, standing at the altar, speaking Spanish in a strong voice, as the priest—a fat little dweeb with no hair—looked on adoringly. Which caused Squires to think maybe the asshole really believed Tula was a boy. But the priest wasn't the only one giving the girl his full attention.

Sitting squashed together on wooden pews, some of the women were bawling silently into hankies, moved by what the girl was saying. And a line was forming near the altar, Mexican men with farmer's tans, short little women—some on their knees—apparently waiting to meet the girl when she was done speaking.

But why? Squires moved to a window that was closer to find out.

It made no sense, but what the people wanted to do, he discovered, was kiss the girl's hand, or hug her, or maybe ask her to say a prayer for them, which Tula appeared to do several times, touching her hand to a person's head while she muttered words toward the ceiling.

My God, even the priest got in on it, hugging the girl while she touched his dweebish bald head and said something that Squires was close enough to hear but couldn't understand.

Dumbass, the man thought to himself. *Why the hell didn't I ever learn Spanish?*

It was frustrating hearing but not understanding, especially because he was trying to figure out why the girl commanded such respect from so many adults, all of them strangers.

Maybe Tula sounded smarter in Spanish. That might explain it, which caused Squires to spend some time weighing the possibility. It had to be true, he finally decided. In English, the girl came off as pretty damn strange, maybe even nuts. In Spanish, she must have sounded a lot smarter.

Right or wrong, it gave Squires a funny feeling to witness how famous the girl had become. He guessed it was something to be proud of, hanging out with a celebrity, even if the girl's fans were all Mexicans.

What he was witnessing was impressive, Squires had to admit it. Being with a celebrity was new in his experience, unless he counted Frankie, which he didn't of course. Fifteen years ago, Frankie had been a minor bodybuilding star —Miss South Florida U.S.A. once and Miss Vermont Bodybuilder three times in a row— which the bitch never stopped reminding him when they got into arguments over which steroids were best for different kinds of cycles.

But being with Tula, the strange little Jesus freak, was an entirely different experience. Squires had never seen anyone look at Frankie the way these adoring people kept their eyes glued to that little girl.

Yeah, sort of proud—that's the way he felt. And he would have continued watching if a few tough-acting Mexicans—or were they Guatemalans?—hadn't slipped out the church door to give him their hard-assed beaner glares.

"What you lookin' at, man?" one of the *chilies* said to Squires as they walked toward him, all three taking out their gangbanger bandannas, he noticed.

Squires turned to gauge the distance to his truck where he'd stored the Ruger Blackhawk beneath the seat. Not that he needed a gun to deal with these little turds—even with a pulled hamstring—but it was good to know he had options.

He waited until the trio was closer before he said to them, keeping his voice low and confidential, "Hey, I gotta question for you boys. What's that little girl in there saying that's so important? Man, even the priest is hanging on every word. How'd she get so famous?"

Squires was trying to be friendly, strike up a nice conversation with these hard Mexicans. But no luck.

The head *chilie* was easy to pick out. He was the one tying on his blue colors, low over the eyes, as he said something that sounded like, "Choo tryin' to be funny or what, man? 'Cause choo ain't funny," his Mex accent strong.

Not quite so friendly now, Squires told the dude, "You'd be laughing your ass off if I wanted to be funny, douche bag."

The two beaners moved closer to the head gangbanger, standing shoulder to shoulder, as their leader replied, "We know who you are, man. We know all about the shit goes on out there at your damn hunting camp, too. So get the hell out of here, back to your trailer park that smells of *mierda*. This here's a damn church, man. Why you wanna bother us here with your presence?"

Squires was surprised, at first, that the Mexican knew so much about him, but then he wasn't. Hell, maybe all three of these dudes had lived at Red Citrus for a while. That wouldn't have surprised him, either, because most of the illegals sooner or later showed up at one of his parks.

"Let me offer you some friendly advice," Squires said to the men, motioning for them to lean closer. "Pay attention or I'll rip your ears off and stick 'em up your ass. I asked you a polite question. I expect a nice answer. That girl in there is a friend of mine. Why's the priest letting her stand up there and talk to the whole audience?"

"Right-t-t-t," one of the *chilies* said, feeling around for something in his pocket. "That girl in there, if you say you know her, you lying *coño*. She's a saint, man. So you better behave yourself with respect or we'll run your white ass outta here."

"Is that what she claims?" Squires asked.

"She talks to God and God answers her back," the Guatemalan replied, sounding defensive, but pissed off, too. "What proof you want? God is telling her we should return to our homes in the mountains. And not put up with *gringo* assholes like you. For what? Live in a shithole trailer park like yours? Drive a fancy truck that takes half my pay every month?"

The word "mountains" registered in Squires's memory, which caused him to say, "I hear it's pretty nice where some of you Mexicans come from. Even in summer, I heard it's nice 'n' cool up in those mountains. That true? What's a big house and a few acres sell for?"

"A jelly boy like you moving to Guatemala?" the *chilie* said to him. "Man, don't even think about it. We don't want your kind dirtying up our home." He took a step. "You say you a friend of this girl? I think you full of bullshit, man."

Squires was looking through the church window again, trying to gauge how pissed off Tula would be if he caused a disturbance out-side. No, he decided. He wasn't going to do it. The girl had already gotten mad at him once today, giving him a look that had made him feel sort of low, like he'd disappointed her. Once was enough. He didn't want to have that feeling again.

Squires held up his hands, palms out. "Stay cool, *amigos*. Only reason I'm here is to help the girl find her mama. Ya'll just run along before the little saint in there makes you come back and apologize to me. Because when she was talking to God, the big guy didn't send her to *you*. God sent her to *me*."

Smiling, Squires limped back to his truck and waited. The three gangbangers looked at one another for a moment, their faces unfocused, then they obviously decided *Fuck it!* and went inside the church.

While he was messing with the radio, trying to find some decent news, his phone rang once, but no one was there when Squires answered, saying, "Hello . . . *hello?*" during a long silence.

A wrong number, he decided. It had to be.

An hour later, a little after eleven p.m., Squires and the girl were back at the hunting camp, walking from his truck toward the RV, as frogs chirred from a spatial darkness that was bordered by cypress trees and stars. He had been feeling pretty good about things up until then, but, suddenly, Squires didn't feel so good anymore.

Shit!

Frankie was at the trailer, waiting for them. Laziro Victorino, too, along with some of his gangbanger soldiers, who came out of nowhere so fast they had their hands on Tula before Squires had time to do anything about it.

309

Up until then, though, it had been the best night he'd had in a while. The big man had been feeling better and better about helping the strange little girl instead of shooting her in the back of the head. And Squires had never seen the girl so happy.

On the drive from Immokalee to the hunting camp, she had sat in the passenger seat, chattering away, sounding excited because she had found out where her aunts and brother were living. Maybe her mother, too. Or so she thought.

But when Tula told Squires about it, he wasn't so sure.

"Aunt Vilma and Isabel are working on a tomato farm in a city called Ocala!" Tula had exclaimed as she exited the church, waving a piece of paper. "I have Aunt Isabel's phone number. And my brother, he picked oranges this winter. He was always so lazy, but it must be true."

As they drove down Main Street, Immokalee, out of town, the girl was laughing, telling Squires, "Pacaw has moved around a lot, but he might be living outside a city that is named Venice. He had trouble finding work because he's younger than me, only twelve—but he acts older. Everyone I met at the church thought he was at least sixteen. The people I met tonight, they are wonderful."

Squires had to ask. "Did they say anything about me? Some tough Mexican dudes came outside and gave me some of their tough-taco shit. But you were . . . you know, in the middle of your speech. I didn't want to cause no trouble."

The big man said it expecting the girl to appreciate his thoughtfulness. Maybe she did, but he had hoped for a more positive reaction.

Squires gave it some time before he glanced at the girl and asked a question that had been on his mind: "You could have run out on me tonight, sis. You could've had your new friends call the cops. Why didn't you? I was sitting here in the truck, wondering about it."

The girl had looked at the giant, shaking her head, and didn't bother to speak the words her affectionate expression was telling him.

Instead, she said, "I'm very hungry. One of the women—she was so sweet. She asked for a lock of my hair but didn't have any scissors. She told me there is a very excellent restaurant not far. It's called Taco Bell. You must be hungry, too."

They used the Taco Bell drive-through, and Squires listened to the girl chomp down about half her weight in junk food as he drove—Tula, beside him, eating like it was the best Mex she'd ever had in her life.

Squires had the taco salad and an unsweetened iced tea. He was an athlete, for Christ's sake. In his business, diet was everything, even during a bulking cycle. The perfect male body wasn't built in the weight room, it was sculpted in the kitchen—Squires had read that someplace.

Ten miles from the hunting camp, the girl had gotten onto the subject of her missing mother, a conversation that Squires had tried to postpone because he already suspected where it was going.

"I keep trying to tell you the best news," the girl had said to him. "My mother was working in restaurants and cleaning houses. But then she went to work for a very rich man and has been traveling a lot—which is probably why I haven't heard from her. She didn't tell anyone the man's name. But she told someone's niece that the man's company makes movies. That she was going to become an actress! This was about two months ago, which is probably why she had to get a new telephone. My aunts or brother will know more when I talk to them. Didn't I tell you that my mother is beautiful?"

Squires thought, *Uh-oh* . . . understanding immediately why Tula's mother hadn't told anyone her employer's name. Either no one had revealed the name to her or the woman was too ashamed to admit it. Every Mexican in Florida knew that Laziro Victorino was a badass gang leader and the only films he had an interest in were porno and snuff films.

That gave Squires a sick feeling in his belly. She *could* have been talking about some other guy who made movies—but he strongly doubted it.

Tula's mother must have been damn hard up for money to make such a decision, which wasn't unusual for Mexican women who sent money back home. But to go to work for the V-man? It had to be more than just needing cash, Squires decided. Maybe she'd gotten hooked on crank or crack. No telling, but a lot of Mexican girls did after getting into porn or prostitution.

Squires remembered the little girl sniffing the little doll she'd found and saying her mother had one just like it. It didn't prove the girl's mother had been entertained by Victorino or Frankie, sitting in their trailer, drinking margaritas laced with Ecstasy. But it sure made it a strong possibility.

There was also an even more disturbing possibility, but just thinking about it made Squires feel queasy. That he'd been the one who'd entertained Tula's mother—the Mexican *chula* in his sex dream. So Squires had changed the subject by handing Tula his iPhone, saying, "Call your aunt what's her name. Tell her you're okay. Where'd you say they're living? Do it now because we're going to lose reception the moment I turn off the road to my camp."

"We're not going back to the trailer park?" the girl asked, surprised. "That's what I told the priest. That's what I told everyone, that we're returning to Red Citrus." She hesitated. "I would feel better if I could sleep on my own cot and

313

get my things. I have a book there I read every night before I turn off the light."

Squires shook his head. "The camp's closer, and I need a drink. We'll get your things tomorrow."

Guessing what the girl was worried about, he added, "Don't worry, you'll have your own bed. And all the damn privacy you want—as long as you promise to stop talking so much. What about calling your aunts?"

As Tula giggled in her seat, excited to be dialing her aunt, Squires thought about details. He wasn't good at geography, but he'd done body-building shows all over Florida. Tula had mentioned Ocala and Venice. They were both north, off Interstate 75, which was right on the way if they were driving to Mexico.

Damn . . . it was a big decision. Leaving the country had seemed like a smart thing to do earlier when he'd been drunk and scared shitless. Now, with the girl laughing and chattering in Spanish to her aunt, it suddenly seemed all too real. Like the idea was closing in and smothering him.

How would he feel riding with a bunch of wetbacks all that distance? His truck was a double cab, so there'd be enough room. Hell, Mexicans were like folding chairs. You could pack twenty of them into a Volkswagen. And it wasn't like he'd be breaking any laws, since he'd be driving a load of illegal immigrants back to where they belonged. Still, the prospect seemed so foreign to him that he began searching for an alternative.

But no matter how Squires viewed his situation, he couldn't get around the fact that if the cops questioned Tula about the dead Mexican girl, they'd arrest him for something, probably murder. Laziro Victorino was in the back of his mind, too.

Then Squires thought about the way the girl had described her village. It was quiet and clean, she'd said. A place that was high in the mountains where it was cool, and closer to God.

Squires told himself he didn't care anything about God. But he was sure sick of Florida, where he'd been doing stupid, illegal shit, always feeling guilty—*a dirty life*, Tula had described it, and the girl was right.

All his problems would be solved, though, if he took Tula and her family to Mexico. No more murder rap, no worrying about cops busting his steroid business, no more of Frankie's bullying, and of her sick, twisted ways.

Squires reminded himself that he had around sixty grand in cash—plus a few grand more he'd stolen from the two white guys last night. That was more than enough money to kick back at some Mexican beach resort for a month or two.

And if he liked the place, maybe he'd invest some of that money in starting up a first-class steroids lab—a place where it was legal to use and make gear. Hell, he could hire Tula and her family to keep the place clean and do office work. The girl was strange, but at least he knew that she'd never steal from him or lie to him about the books.

Okay, Squires thought to himself, *Mexico it is.*

Goddamn, that felt good! He'd finally made a decision. It put a little smile on his face until Tula handed him his cell phone as if the thing was broken, telling him, "I can't hear what my aunt Isabel is saying anymore. She was right in the middle of telling me something important when we got cut off."

"I told you, we don't have good reception out here," Squires replied.

"But I wanted to hear what she was telling me!"

As the man slipped the phone into his pocket, he paid attention because the girl sounded so serious, which is why he asked her, "What'd she say that's got you so riled up?"

Tula replied, "My aunt said an important woman called her tonight. A woman who works for the government helping immigrants. She was very worried because she said the police are looking for you and me."

Squires felt his heart begin to pound. "Your aunt said that?" he asked.

"No, that's what I'm trying to tell you. The woman said they've been talking about us on the radio and television all night. Some kind of special alert for children. It has a color in the name."

Squires whispered, "Shit! An AMBER Alert."

Reacting to the expression on the man's face, Tula added quickly, "Yes—but it's okay, don't worry! The first thing my aunt will do is call the woman and tell her that you are my friend. She's probably talking to the woman right now. Telling her that I'm very safe and happy. My aunt promised."

Squires said, "Jesus Christ, an AMBER Alert. What next?" but was listening, wanting to hear better news.

Tula told him, "Then my aunt will call the church and speak with the priest—she knows him very well because she picked tomatoes in Immokalee for a season. His name is Father Jimenez, and she will ask him to telephone the police tonight and tell them the same thing."

"Talk slower," Squires said. "Tell the cops what?"

"That I'm with you because I *want* to be with you. So no one will be worried. My aunt was so relieved to hear my voice, she was crying. But she promised me, so I know she will do it."

Tula held up the paper she was carrying. "In the morning, I will call the woman myself. I have her number here, too."

Squires took a deep breath, letting it out slowly,

before he said, "Maybe you should call the immigration woman now. I can back up. Usually, reception doesn't go to hell until I get to the gate."

But then he realized that turning around, driving toward Immokalee, might be a mistake. The woman from state immigration would want to know Tula's exact location. That would bring the cops, asking questions.

The girl made up his mind, saying, "The police will believe Father Jimenez. A priest? Of course they will believe him. Plus, I told Father Jimenez that you are a wonderful man. He wanted to meet you, but I told him you are shy about coming into churches."

Squires liked it when Tula said that. He began to relax a little and feel at ease as the girl added, "Do you now believe that the Maiden is watching over us? When you do God's work, good things happen to you!"

By then, they were at the gate to the hunting camp.

Squires began to suspect trouble when he realized there was a light on inside his RV, the vehicle sitting up on blocks in the darkness. He and Tula had just gotten out of the truck, which was when the big man placed his hand on the girl's shoulder, stopping her.

"Hold it, sis," he said as he stared at the light.

318

He knew he'd switched off the generator before leaving just in case he and the girl didn't return. Plus, he would've heard the little Honda engine running if it was on.

That meant that someone inside had a flashlight. Or had lit a candle, or an oil lamp maybe. But where was the person's truck?

Squire's head pivoted from the mountain of cypress trees to the west, then to the east, where there were shadowed pine flats and a distant halo glow that was Lauderdale.

There had to be a vehicle somewhere. No one in their right mind would hike cross-country through the Everglades, not this late. Not half an hour before midnight . . . unless . . . unless they had parked their vehicle behind the RV. Which was possible. But how could they have gotten through the gate? The gate had been locked when he and Tula had arrived just as he'd left it.

Thinking that gave Squires a prickly feeling along his spine. Frankie had the only other key.

Squires reached out, patted Tula's arm and whispered, "Hang on for a second, sis. Something ain't right about this."

He took a few slow steps toward the trailer, favoring his right leg, but then stopped abruptly when he saw what might have been a person moving in the shadows behind the trailer.

Squires couldn't be sure. He had left the truck running, lights on, so he could see to unlock the door to the generator shed. He didn't have a flashlight, so all he saw was a blur of movement like someone ducking for cover.

Squires was thinking about hurrying back to the truck and opening the hidden compartment to get his revolver and night vision binoculars. That's when Tula whispered, "There's someone here. I smell cigarette smoke. And perfume, too."

Squires thought, *Shit. It's Frankie.*

Yes, it was. The large woman appeared, standing in the RV's doorway, shining a flashlight in his eyes, then focused the beam on Tula. Squires was shielding his eyes when he heard Frankie say, "Well, well, look at what we have here. Harris, you dumb pile of shit, I don't know what to do first—have some fun with the pretty little wettail you brought me or call the cops and hope there's a reward for turning in a kidnapper."

The woman was very drunk and probably stoned. Squires could tell by the way she slurred her words. Frankie had to grab the railing as she started down the steps, adding, "Either way, I want the goddamn money you stole from me. Sixty thousand dollars in cash, you son of a bitch. You really thought I'd let you get away with it?"

For a woman, Frankie had the lowest voice Squires had ever heard. It was from using too much primobolan and shooting testosterone, which the woman lied about, too. But there was no disguising what steroids had done to her voice—and the female parts of her body, too.

Squires waved and called, "Hey, sugar babe, I was hoping you'd be here!" like he was glad to see the woman, but then he nudged Tula toward the truck, leaning to whisper, "Get in and lock the doors. Don't come out 'til I tell you."

Tula yanked her arm away, though, being stubborn, and said, "I'm not leaving you! You're afraid of her, I can tell. I'm staying with you."

Frankie, on the grass now, wearing tight jeans, her breasts ballooning out of a tank top, was close enough to hear the girl, because she laughed, saying, "Now, isn't that sweet! You found yourself a loyal little *chula*. A cute young one, too. Harris, know what that tells me? It tells me you haven't screwed her yet. Even if she's a virgin, she wouldn't still be hanging with you. She'd be ready for someone bigger and better by now."

In a chiding voice, Frankie spoke to Tula, saying, "I'll bet you're still pure as the snow, aren't you, *niña*? Then this goddamn piece of white trash comes along and kidnaps you. But you don't have to be afraid of him now. Come here to Frankie"—the woman was patting her thigh as if calling a dog—"I'll make sure you're safe."

Squires felt Tula move close to him, throwing an arm around his bad leg for protection.

He wasn't afraid of Frankie—he'd never admitted it to himself, anyway—Tula was wrong about that. But the woman did make him nervous, particularly when she was as drunk as she was now.

Nervous, yes, that's the way Squires felt, but he could also feel a testosterone heat moving to his ears.

"You shut your mouth about this girl," Squires said to Frankie in a warning tone as he stepped in front of Tula. "She's not used to your garbage talk. And stop your damn swearing in front of her. This little girl's religious."

Frankie laughed, *"Priceless,"* as Squires continued, "You go on back inside the trailer. If you want to talk to me, I'll get the generator going and we'll talk. But you leave this girl alone."

Squires was lying about the generator. The moment Frankie closed the trailer door, he'd load Tula into the truck and they'd get the hell out of there.

Go where, though? Frankie knew what she was talking about when she'd mentioned kidnapping. Even if the priest told the cops that everything was okay, a call from Frankie might put them back on the alert. The woman would drop the dime on him the moment he left, Squires was sure of it.

Or would she?

Mismatched details were going through Squires's mind as he tried to view the situation clearly. Maybe Frankie didn't have so much leverage over him after all, he decided. Once he was in jail, how could the woman force him to give back the money he'd taken? She'd have to admit to the feds that they'd piled up a ton of cash selling steroids. They hadn't paid a dime in taxes, either.

No, Frankie couldn't risk that.

The woman was drunk. She was a vicious twat, but she was smart. She'd realize that getting the sixty grand was the most important thing, once he reminded her. It caused Squires to wonder if maybe he should offer the woman some kind of deal . . . which is when he heard an engine start in the distance.

A second later, a truck loaded with men came fishtailing out from behind the trailer, the truck's lights blinding him and the girl. In the same instant, a Mexican voice from behind Squires said, "Hey there, jelly boy! You stand real still or I'll blow your damn head off.

Squires turned.

Christ! There was Laziro Victorino, grinning at him with his gold teeth. And pointing a shotgun at him—a Browning Maxus 12-gauge that Squires had kept locked in the trailer gun closet.

Victorino and Frankie together?

323

It took Squires a slow, stunned moment to realize what had happened. Yeah . . . it had to be. Frankie and the gangbanger had teamed up. That was the only explanation. Frankie had somehow hooked up with the V-man, probably today at Red Citrus. After the woman had discovered the money missing, she would have been in the perfect mood to seduce someone like Victorino, a guy who could help her get what she wanted.

Even so, this surprised Squires, because Frankie was the most racist person he'd ever met. But here it was, staring him right in the face. And the two of them had been at it for a while, sharing some fun together, judging from the confidential looks Victorino and Frankie were now exchanging. Both of them drunk and probably cocaine crazy.

Squires had seen the woman like this many times. And the V-man was no different, he guessed—probably worse. Drunk as they were, neither one of them gave a damn about what they did or the consequences. They wanted the cash. But the V-man probably wanted Tula more or he wouldn't have wasted his time—a girl Tula's age was worth a lot more than sixty thousand to a business shark like him.

And they would kill him, Squires realized. They had to. Use the shotgun, but, more likely, Victorino's box cutter. He'd do it slowly to impress Frankie, a woman probably twisted enough to video the whole thing.

That made Squires feel sort of queasy. Then he felt worse when he realized that, no, Victorino and his gangbangers would be the ones to video his murder. Get it all on their iPhones and add another snuff film to their collection.

This was all shocking information for Squires to process. He didn't expect loyalty from Frankie, but he didn't expect her to help a Mexican dude murder him, either. He and the redhead had spent more than four years together, most of it either screwing or screaming at each other, but they'd had some good times, too. Could Frankie let go of all that so fast?

Squires got his answer when Frankie called to Victorino, "Don't shoot him now, dumbass! Get them in the cookshack, I've got the camera all set. Hurry up, it's almost midnight!"

Cameras in the steroid shack—this was another surprise to Squires. Why not the trailer, where they had already built a porno set complete with lights and a computer?

The V-man was wagging an index finger at Tula as he pointed the shotgun at Squires, saying something in Spanish to the girl—probably ordering her into the steroid shack—before telling Frankie, "What's the rush, now? Bring some duct tape. I'll hold the gun on your boyfriend while you tape him."

The woman replied, "The greaser genius giving orders again," sounding sloppy drunk now. But still sober enough to remember that Victorino enjoyed killing women, because she added, "Duct tape. Check. I'd love to tape that worthless piece of shit."

Squires watched the redhead walk toward the RV but then stop near the steps, where she reached down into a box. When he heard Tula scream, "Don't you touch that!" he remembered the fledgling bird the girl had saved. Could the thing still be alive?

Yes, it was. The egret was squawking and flapping its bare wings as Frankie held the bird up in the light. The woman was grinning as she said to Victorino, "Do you Mexicans like to eat squab? I think we've got a bottle of champagne around her someplace." Before the man could reply, though, the woman said, "Ouch! The little bastard just bit me!" and hurled the bird hard against the aluminum siding of the RV.

Tula gave a little shriek and swung her head away, but Victorino thought it was pretty funny, the hard-assed redhead getting bit by a bird.

Staring at Squires, the V-man grinned as he said to Frankie, "See? We're having ourselves some fun now. What's the hurry? Come back with the duct tape, then we gonna have more fun making movies. Hell, this dumbass probably has the money on him, maybe stashed somewhere inside his truck. It won't be hard to find."

As Tula sobbed, Squires was thinking, *The hell it won't.*

He'd built the hidden compartment himself, using a cutting torch and the help of a magic mechanic friend of his. Frankie didn't know about the compartment, because while she sometimes drove his Ford Roush, she never messed with his hunting truck.

More pressing on Squires's mind was the fact that Victorino and Frankie had planned this out together. Cameras and duct tape? Those were the principal props in the few snuff films that Squires had seen. They were sickening things to watch, although he'd never admitted that to Frankie, who always had a glassy, heated look on her face by the time one of those videos ended.

Thinking about it caused Squires's heart to pound, a slow fury building in him. Victorino would use that shitty hardware-store knife on him. He felt certain of it. And then he and Frankie would have more fun together by raping the girl, probably filming that, too.

Then an even worse scenario flashed into Squires's mind: They would video what they did to Tula first, just to piss him off. Make him watch the whole sick business before they got around to killing him.

Again the question came into Squires's mind:

327

Why the cookshack, a room that was all chemicals and propane tanks but no bed?

A moment later, Victorino's gangbanger buddies were jumping out of the truck—a Dodge Ram—as it skidded to a stop, running toward Squires and Tula. The V-man took a few quick steps, his eyes still fixed on Squires, and scooped the girl up in his left arm.

Tula screamed for help, yelling, "He has me, make him let me go!"

Squires took a step but then stopped, frozen by the gun and what was happening.

Now the girl was hollering to her invisible friend, "Jehanne! I need your help, Jehanne!" as she slapped at Victorino with her hands. Then the skinny girl shot a heartbreaking look into Squires's eyes, pleading, "Don't let him hurt me. All I want is my mother!"

Without even thinking about it, Squires began limping toward the V-man. Slow at first, then faster, taking long strides despite his bad hamstring.

Squires knew that the shotgun was loaded with bird shot, which was what he and his buddies used to hunt dove and quail. Little tiny pellets half the size of match heads. Hell, he'd been hit by more than a few of those pellets when he and his drunken buddies shot at birds in a cross fire. They didn't hurt much, and it took almost a direct hit to break the skin.

Not that it mattered, because inside Squires's brain something had snapped. He felt an invincible cerebral combustion surging through him. It caused the steroid oils, and the D-bombs he'd swallowed, to engorge his monster face with blood.

Laziro Victorino screamed a warning as Squires moved toward him, dragging his right leg with every step. The gangbanger screamed again as he hurled the girl to the ground, pointed the shotgun and this time pulled the trigger.

Squires jolted, grunting at the stinging impact. But that didn't matter, either. The giant stumbled, regained his balance and kept coming.

Arms outstretched, Harris Squires was hell-bent on getting his fingers around the V-man's neck because now the little saint was calling for his help again, screaming, "Please, *please,* Harris! Don't let these men take me away from you!"

THIRTEEN

THE REASON I TURNED EAST, TOWARD what turned out to be Harris Squires's hunting camp, was because after touring Immokalee, seeing a helicopter and a half dozen cops parked outside a church, I decided that my detective friend might be wrong when he told me that

Squires and Tula had left Immokalee and were now on their way back to Red Citrus trailer park.

It was 11:20 p.m. when Leroy Melinski called my cell to give me what he believed was the good news. I had cruised Immokalee's slow streets and then headed out of town, occasionally glancing at the satellite aerial that showed Squires's four hundred acres of what was probably saw grass and cypress trees.

"The girl wasn't kidnapped," the detective explained when I answered. "She told a bunch of people—including a priest and one of her aunts—that Squires volunteered to drive her around and help her find her mother. So there you have it, Doc. Turns out your kidnapper is just being a Good Samaritan."

The reception on my phone was fuzzy, so I said, "You've got to be kidding. Say that again."

Melinski told me, "Harris Squires and the girl stopped at some church, a pretty big one, so there's confirmation on all this. A couple hundred people listened to her give a speech or a sermon, whatever you call it. Squires got out of his truck to listen, but he didn't come inside."

I said, "People on the scene told you this?"

The detective said, "Squires even made nice with some gangbangers who gave him a hard time. Not Latin Kings. Probably MS-13 from Guatemala, who are bloodthirsty little shits. But even they must have been convinced."

I told him, "This just doesn't mesh with what I know about Harris Squires," as Melinski talked over me, saying, "I know, I know, it's hard to believe, but I've heard enough to be convinced. So you can relax, okay? Go back to your test tubes or have a beer. I'm going to bed."

I said, "Some minister lets a thirteen-year-old girl, a stranger, get up in front of the whole congregation? Why?"

"It happened," Melinski replied, sounding impatient, "that's all that matters. I talked to the priest myself. He's worked in Immokalee for nine years, which means he's heard every possible combination of bullshit story. According to him, the girl walked in and said she had something important to say, so he let her talk. He described her as happy and relaxed, which is not the way a kidnapped kid acts."

"The priest," I said.

"Along with several local women, too. They offered her a place to stay, but the girl refused. Squires may have something to do with the dead body we found, who knows? But the girl's with him because she wants to be with him. End of story."

I said, "Harris Squires wouldn't lift a finger to help anyone—not unless he expected to get something out of it."

Melinski told me, "We'll find out more when they get back to the trailer park. The girl told the priest that was their next stop, so we've got some uniforms there waiting."

I had to ask, "Did your hostage-rescue people call his cell?"

"That's the only part that bothers me," Melinski told me. "They tried but no answer. Reception's bad around Immokalee, which could explain it. The priest said, at first, he didn't like the idea of a Guatemalan girl being with a *gringo* guy that age. He tried to talk her into staying, but the girl was so sure of what she was doing, he decided it was okay. At least for the hour or so it takes them to get back to the trailer park. Red Citrus? Yeah, Red Citrus. Maybe a little longer because the girl told the priest they might get something to eat first."

"What time did they leave?" I asked. "I hope you have cops checking the local restaurants."

Melinski told me, "They pulled out at little before eleven, so they should be at the trailer park in half an hour or so." With exaggerated tolerance, he then added, "Have you heard anything I said? You can stop worrying. The priest told me some pretty wild stuff about the kid. So, finally, I maybe understand why you've taken an interest. You didn't tell me the Latinos consider her some kind of saint or something."

"The priest said that?" I asked.

"The guy sounded a little in awe of the girl, in fact. He said there were women crying, people waiting in line to ask the girl's blessing. 'God has taken the girl by the hand'—this is the priest talking, not me. But the man was serious. So there's no need to worry, according to him. The priest's exact words almost, and more than nine years he's been working with immigrants."

I said, "If God took missing girls by the hand, there would be a lot fewer missing girls. Please tell me you're not buying into this baloney."

I was relived that Tula and Squires had been spotted. But I was also feeling too restless to allow myself to be convinced. I didn't admit this to Melinski, of course, and pretended to be satisfied when he promised to call when he got word the girl was safely back at Red Citrus.

After I hung up, I checked the luminous face of my dive watch: 11:25 p.m. I was approaching the intersection of Immokalee Road and what I guessed was Route 846, where Squires owned the four hundred acres. Continue straight and I would take yet another lap through Immokalee, then north to home—or maybe Emily's place, if I could get her on the phone. Make a right, I would have to drive at least forty miles, round-trip, out of my way—and probably for no reason.

In my mind, though, I suddenly pictured the Mayan girl looking through the window of Squires's trucking, seeing a sign that read IMMOKALEE 22 MILES, then texting the infor- mation to Tomlinson, a man she trusted. The image was so strong that I actually shook my head to get rid of it.

As I neared the intersection, I hesitated, my intellect telling me one thing, my instincts telling me something else. Normally, that's seldom a cause for indecision—which is why I was a little surprised when I found myself following my intuition. I turned right onto the narrow two-lane that vectored eastward into the Everglades.

Something else my intellect and instincts argued about was whether I should call Tomlinson. If he had gone to Red Citrus, as expected, I should tell him to wait there to make sure Tula arrived.

It only made sense that I call him, but I had settled into a comfortable cocoon of solitude, focused laserlike on finding the girl. For me, that cocoon is a place rarely enjoyed when I'm Florida and I didn't want to leave it.

It had to do with my shadow life. Solitude is what I enjoy most about it. I travel alone to Third World countries, to Everglades-dark places, and I find people. I then track those people. I become familiar with their schedules, their habits.

For the period of a week—sometimes two, depending on the importance of the assignment —I charted the subtle movements and inter-actions of a stranger's life. I did it invisibly, with a laboratory precision that in the end allowed me to segregate that person from his surroundings as effectively as using tweezers to remove a bee, undetected, from its colony.

That was my specialty—my genius, Tomlinson might have called it, had he ever learned the truth. What I do, however, doesn't demand genius. I have no illusions about my own gifts, other than to acknowledge that, since I was very young, I have had an obsessive need to identify, then define, orderly patterns in what most would dismiss as chaos.

We all have our quirks.

That's my job when out of the country: to discern order in the chaos. To create a precision target. As creator, I am also tasked with finding the most effective method of displacing that target from his surroundings.

I am good at it.

After wrestling with the decision for a mile, I decided I wasn't in the mood for a conversation with Tomlinson. Instead, I pulled over long enough to send a text:

Tula and Squires to arrive at Red Citrus by midnight, cops waiting. Let me know. If you're drinking, stop now. Don't piss off cops!

After a moment of thought, I added, *Is Emily safe?* then sent the text with a slow *Whoosh!* that told me reception was getting worse.

I got out of the truck long enough to urinate, then got back in, but left the dome light on. Out of long habit—or, perhaps, just to reestablish my focus—I took inventory of my equipment bag. First, I popped the magazines of both pistols to make certain they were loaded, although I knew they were.

I am not a gun fancier or collector, but the precision tolerances of fine machinery appeals to the same sensibilities that cause me to linger over a fine microscope. It was true of my Sig Sauer P226 pistol. The Sig was one of the first issued after the Joint Service Small Arms test trials of 1985, and I have trusted my life to it since that time. I had recently purchased a new magazine that held fifteen rounds instead of only ten. I had also added Tritium night sights, which I had yet to try on a range.

I held the Sig's magazine in my hand, testing the mobility of the rounds with my thumb, the odor of Hoppe's No. 9 gun solvent spreading a lingering sweetness through the cab of my truck. It reminded me of Tomlinson's crack about smelling gun oil in the lab whenever I felt restless. An inside joke? Or was it a veiled reminder that, one way or another, my relationship with Emily was doomed as long as I continued to live my shadow life.

Whether a dig or a warning, what he'd said was true: When I get restless, it shows. After a month or two without a new mission, I find myself studying maps. I find myself at night sitting within easy reach of my Trans-Oceanic Radio, recleaning my weapons as if that private ceremony was an incantation that would bring a call from my handler.

After inspecting the Sig Sauer, I took the much smaller, lighter Kahr pistol in hand. It was black-matte stainless, comfortable to hold. After so many years trusting the Sig, it was tough to admit that this was now my weapon of choice. It wasn't as tiny as another favorite—a Seecamp .380—but the Kahr slipped just as easily out of the pocket. And it could be hidden almost as completely in the palm of my hand. Firing the Kahr, though, was a pleasure, and it had more stopping power than the Seecamp.

Like the Sig, the Kahr was loaded with federal Hydra-Shok hollow points. But the Kahr had the added advantage of a built-in laser sight that was activated whenever I gripped the thing to fire.

Unlike the high-tech Dazer Guardian, also in the bag, the laser sight was red, not green.

It was unlikely that I would use any of these weapons, just as I knew there was very little chance now that I would stumble onto Harris Squires and the Guatemalan girl. He and Tula were on their way to Red Citrus while I was out here wasting time on back roads east of Immokalee.

It didn't matter. I was in a certain mood. To

rationalize wasting time, I told myself this was training, a way to stay sharp.

I leaned to roll down the passenger window, and drove on.

Tomlinson is right. I'm not a fast driver. I slowed even more whenever I switched on the dome light and checked the satellite aerial. My pal had used a highlighter to square off the boundaries of Squires's property, but it still wasn't easy to pick out landmarks. I was driving through a shadowed mesa of cypress that I guessed was Owl Hammock. It meant I had at least fifteen miles to go.

Thus far, I hadn't passed a car. Not one.

Alternately squinting at the aerial, then accelerating, my headlights tunneled through a starry silence, toward a horizon abloom with the nuclear glow of Fort Lauderdale, eighty miles to the east.

I passed through the precise geometrics of tomato fields and citrus orchards. Then more cypress domes that exited into plains of myrtle and saw grass. My eyes moved from the road, to the satellite aerial, then to my watch.

11:45 p.m.

Training exercise or not, my mind wandered back to Emily. My reaction to her had been a surprise. A shock, in fact, and now it was a new source of restlessness that was pleasure mixed with angst.

I had left Tomlinson alone with Emily for a reason—a deceit that Tomlinson had guessed correctly. It was a test. He suspected it, I knew it. I was subjecting myself, my new lover and my old friend to yet another of my relentless personal evaluations.

"Why do you set traps for people you care about when you're the one who is inevitably hurt?" a smart but troubled woman had once asked me.

I had no answer then. I had no answer now.

It was an uncomfortable truth to admit, but that was balanced by something I believed with equal honesty: Emily Marston could be trusted. There was no rational explanation for why I trusted her, but I did. Attraction is commonplace. A visceral, indefinable unity is not. The chemistry that links two people is comprised of elements too subtle to survive dissection, too complex to permit inspection.

It was unlike me to ponder the exigencies of romance, but that's exactly what I was doing as the miles clicked by. My mind returned to the bedroom, where I had used every gentleness to follow Emily's physical signals, then fine-tuned what I was doing to match her respiratory and moaning guidance. Our rhythms escalated until, finally, she had tumbled over a sheer apex, crying out, then sobbing, a woman so disoriented even minutes later that she seemed as vulnerable as a creature newly born.

I'd like to believe I am a competent lover, but I knew my skills did not account for an eruption of such magnitude. It was Emily, uniquely Emily, her physical release so explosive that it was as unmistakably visual as it was audible—a jettisoning fact that only made her sob harder, and voice her embarrassment.

"That's why I've always been so careful about men," she had whispered. "I can't help how my body reacts, and it's goddamn embarrassing. It creeped Paul out, I think, so I almost never really let myself go. Tonight, *Christ!* I got carried away, I guess. I'm so sorry."

Sorry? I had just experienced one of the most sensual couplings of my life. I did my best to reassure her and succeeded, apparently, because half an hour later it happened again.

To equate sexual release with trust was as irrational—or as sensible—as any other aspect of love play between male and female. But there it was. It was the way I felt.

Just by thinking it through, I felt better about coming to Immokalee alone. After only a day together, I had no right to expect fidelity from the woman nor a reason to demand trust. If Tomlinson or anyone else could lure Emily away, so be it. I would be disappointed. *Very* disappointed. But I also knew that I would be secretly relieved. Discovering the truth tonight might spare me a more painful surprise down

340

the road—no doubt the reason why I set such traps in the first place.

It was refreshing to be able to admit that to myself. Freeing, in its way. So I closed a mental door on the subject and focused my attention on what I was doing.

A good thing, too.

By then, in the lights of my truck, I could see a curvature of tree line that indicated a bend in the road. According to the satellite aerial, it was where County Road 846 turned north as County Road 857—and marked the midway point of Squires's acreage. To the south was saw grass and swamp. To the north, more of the fertilized geometrics that define Florida agriculture.

I slowed enough to poke my head out the window and checked an east-facing road sign that drifted past. I was not surprised by its message. It was the same sign I'd seen in my odd vision of the girl.

IMMOKALEE 22 MILES.

Almost concurrently, two Hispanic-looking men on the Everglades side of the road caught my attention. They were standing by a gate, smoking cigarettes, no vehicle in sight. The gate was chained, I noted. I also noted the way the men turned their faces away from my headlights, shielding their identities, as I drove past.

They were spotters, I decided. They were standing watch. If Squires had indeed driven Tula

341

Choimha home to Red Citrus, why were these two guarding the gate to his Everglades acreage?

It suggested to me that I had indeed seen some kind of structure beneath the trees in the aerial photo. It suggested to me that Squires and the girl were nearby.

Slowing to a crawl, I gave the men a mild wave. In response, one of them flipped his middle finger, then turned his back. His reaction was more than just aggressive. It was stupid. Why would he invite a confrontation down here in redneck country, where a lot of pickup trucks still had gun racks?

I decided the guy was either drunk or he was aggressive for a reason. Was there something happening beyond that metal gate he couldn't risk anyone seeing or hearing?

I shifted into neutral, letting the truck coast, as I picked up my phone to call Leroy Melinski. It was the reasonable thing to do even though I didn't want to do it. Perversely, I hoped there was no reception or that I got the man's voice mail. Leaving the detective out of the loop would allow me to remain invisible.

I liked the potential of that. Neither Melinski nor anyone else knew where I was. The two men at the gate had no idea who *I* was. I could talk to the men or slip by unnoticed and search the area alone. Do it right and no one would ever know I had been there.

I got my wish. No reception.

I lifted my gear bag onto the passenger's seat as I shifted into reverse and swung the truck around. By the time I got to the gate, both men were standing in the road, dark bandannas now covering their faces like bank robbers in a TV western, their body language communicating a rapper's insolence. The bandannas and the tattoos told me they were members of a Latin gang—*pandilleros*, in Spanish slang.

Should I stop? Or should I park a mile up the road and jog back?

I foot-flicked my high beams on long enough to convince myself that neither man was palming a weapon. It gave me a reason to stop, which is exactly what I wanted to do—another perverse preference. I can tolerate stupidity because it is a biological condition. Ignorance and arrogance are choices, though.

I got out of the truck, engine running, lights on and my gear bag within easy reach if I needed it.

Beside the bag was the palm-sized laser I'd brought along, the Dazer Guardian. Because I had demonstrated the weapon to Emily earlier, I'd already overridden the twenty-four-hour security timer, which meant the weapon was operational, ready to use at the touch of a button.

I gave the thing a long last look, then almost stuck it in my pocket before I swung the door closed. But then I reminded myself I had never tried the light on a shark, let alone a couple of two-legged gangbangers, and now was not the time to risk a disappointing first test.

I felt confident I wouldn't need it, or any of the other weapons in my bag.

I was wrong.

Because both men assumed I didn't speak Spanish, I listened to them exchange nervous and profane assessments of me as I walked toward them.

I was a homosexual cowboy who had lost his hat as well as a horse that I abused anally. I was a drunken Gomer—a welfare redneck—who was too poor to buy a truck that was not inhabited by rats.

Hearing that caused me to take a closer look at the lane beyond the gate, wondering about their truck. It was all tree shadows and darkness, but my headlights were bright enough that I should have seen reflectors on their vehicle.

I did not. It confirmed what I had suspected: The dirt road led to a cabin or some sort of area where these two had parked.

Maybe Squires and the girl were there now. If not, someone else was there, because I heard radio static and then watched one of the men pull a little VHF from his pocket, saying in Spanish, "Don't bother us now. We got a visitor. Some white Gomer—he's probably pissed because Dedos just flipped him off."

Latin gang members use nicknames. Dedos was appropriate. It meant "Fingers."

The radio crackled in reply, a voice saying, "Tell that *pendejo* to stop causing us problems! A white dude? Jesus Christ, get rid of him! What kind of car? You call me back if there's any trouble, you hear me, Calavero?"

Calavero—another graphic nickname.

"A truck. An old redneck piece of shit, don't worry about it," Calavero said, looking at me now as he shoved the radio into his pocket. Then he said in pretty good English, "What you doing way out here, Gomer? You lost or something? Hell, man, my homey, he was just using his finger to point to the best direction for you to go. Straight up, unless you want to drive through a bunch of cow shit."

The man laughed, glancing at his partner, Dedos, then used his chin to motion toward me. It was a signal to separate, possibly, because Calavero started moving to my left as Dedos took a couple of steps toward the truck's passenger side.

I had stopped midway between the men and my truck, a hazed silhouette to them because of my headlights. If they hadn't separated, I would have continued to assume they weren't armed. But movement was all the warning I needed. So I maximized my Florida accent, saying, "I'm lookin' for an ol' boy named Harris Squires.

You boys know where I can find him?"

That stopped them. I used their momentary surprise to take a long step back, then leaned a hip comfortably against my truck, close enough to get to the door fast if I needed to.

Calavero was the talker, and I listened to him reply, "*Amigo*, we can't even see your face 'cause of them lights. How we supposed to answer a question like that? I suggest you get back in your truck and get the fuck outta here, man."

I planned to. But not yet.

"It's a pretty simple question," I said. "He's a great big guy, Harris Squires. I met him last night. He's not the one who said it, but I heard he has something for sale out here I might want to buy. Why don't you call him and let him know I'm here?"

I could only guess at what Squires might have to sell, but the *pandilleros* knew.

In Spanish Dedos said to Calavero, "He wants to buy steroids from jelly boy this time of night? Or maybe the V-man's right. Maybe they been running our girls outta here. Call Chapo, tell him we got to speak to the V-man right now."

Chapo—the voice on the radio and another nickname. *Shorty.*

It didn't tell me everything I wanted to know, but it told me enough—enough to get a rough estimate of how many people I was dealing with. Also, that there was an established pecking order. There were at least two more *pandillero.* beyond the gate, including a boss man named V-man. Plus Squires and, hopefully, the Guatemalan girl.

I had also learned that Squires wasn't a friend of the gang—perhaps he was even their captive. It was unlikely but a possibility. Referring over the radio to a man the size of Squires as "jelly boy" required a controlled environment or some firepower to back it up.

It was time for me to get going, I decided. Time to drive fast to an area where there was phone reception because I'd walked into something bigger than I had ever anticipated. This situation required the police—a whole squad of pros, including a chopper. In another country where there were fewer laws, maybe, just maybe, I would have tried to handle it on my own. But not here. And not when there was a chance that Tula Choimha was alive and still in danger.

Because I didn't want the men to know what I'd learned, I said, "I don't have time to stand around listening to you boys talking Mexican. If you see Squires, tell him I stopped by. But don't blame me when he gets pissed off 'cause he didn't make a sale."

I stood and turned my back to them, paying close attention as the two bickered about whether they should let me go or not. Because the exchange was in Spanish, they believed there was no need to keep their voices low. Dedos was the violent one, but Calavero was the boss.

"Stab him with a knife, that's just stupid!" he hissed at Dedos. "For what, to rob him? He don't have any money, look at his goddamn truck! We gonna have enough bodies to deal with!"

I almost stopped when he said that but forced myself to keep moving.

Dedos's response: "Man, we can't just let him go—the Gomer knows Squires! Call the V-man. The dude could bring the cops the moment he's out of here. Then what's the V-man gonna say?"

It wasn't until my hand was on the open door, my foot on the running board, that I allowed myself to risk a glance over my shoulder.

My timing could have been better.

Dedos was fast and quiet. He had closed the distance between us, suddenly only one long stride away from the truck. His arm was extended, something in his hand. A cell phone, I thought at first, but his partner was yelling, "Don't shoot him, you idiot!" so I knew that I was mistaken.

I threw my hands up, a defensive response, as I dived into the cab of my truck. At the same instant, I heard a percussion-cap *BANG!* then a brief whistling noise. A microsecond later, I felt a dazzling impact of something metallic that glanced off my left shoulder, then clanged hard against the truck's cab.

It took me a moment to realize I'd been tasered with an electroshock weapon. The thing produced a crackling burst of pain that radiated through my spine, down the sciatic nerves of my legs. Zapped by several thousand volts, my brain flashed with what might have been the white schematic of my own cerebral synapses.

Then the wild sensation was gone.

My body lay immobile on the seat for an instant, as my brain worked it through. Dedos had used an older taser, with a steel dart attached to a wire. But the dart hadn't hit me squarely. It had plowed a furrow of blood across my left shoulder, then skipped out, hitting the truck, steel on steel.

Now Calavero was calling, "Grab him, *pendejo!* We got no choice now!" as he also yelled into the radio, calling for help, but didn't seem to be getting a response.

I was dazed, my glasses hanging by fishing line around my neck, as Dedos grabbed me by the ankles, trying to pull me out onto the road. I kicked back hard . . . missed . . . then kicked again and heard the man make an encouraging *Woofing* sound that told me I had connected with his groin.

I got my left hand on the steering wheel and was pulling myself into the truck when Calavero joined the attack. He used his boots to kick my calves and thigh muscles numb as he ordered

Dedos, "Get on your feet, you drunken fool! Use the radio, tell them we need help 'cause you did something stupid again."

My equipment bag was in the middle of the seat, not quite within reach. The palm-sized laser was close enough, though. I grabbed the thing as, once again, I felt my body being dragged out of the cab.

I had experimented enough with the laser to know that the rubberized cap was an instant-on switch, much like a flashlight. But the system was far more complex. There was another switch that cycled through various ranges of effectiveness, from one yard to almost a quarter mile.

To impress Emily, I had dialed the thing to three hundred yards and then painted distant mangroves with its luminous green beam—"searchlight mode," according to the literature. Stupidly, I hadn't taken the time to switch the laser back to close-quarters-combat range. Would searchlight mode have any effect on men only a few yards away?

Calavero had a gun in his hand now, I realized. A little chrome-coated derringer, with sizable over-under barrels that told me it was heavy caliber. He was using the butt of the gun to bang at my knee, looking for an opening to put a bullet into me. My truck was about to become a killing field, and all I wanted to do was get the hell out of there and start over.

Probably because I have never been shot in the stomach or chest, an odd, slow thought moved through my mind, oblivious to the panic I felt. *Pain or impact?* Which would I feel as a bullet splintered my ribs?

I tried to kick my legs free so Calavero couldn't get a clean shot. It caused him to pocket the weapon long enough to concentrate on his grip. As he pulled me from the truck, my head banged hard on the running board, then I landed, back first, on the asphalt.

I fumbled the Dazer upon impact but managed to recover as Calavero gave me another numbing kick to the thigh. My glasses were still around my neck, but I could see well enough to know he was reaching for the derringer again. If I didn't disable the man soon, he would shoot me, then keep shooting until I was dead.

I used the laser.

When I brought the Dazer up to fire, I told myself, *Keep your finger off the damn switch until you've aimed!*

I had been told that surprise was an important aspect of the laser's effectiveness. So I waited . . . waited until I had the weapon in both hands, leveled at the man's face. I was sighting down the little metal tube as if it were a gun when I touched the button.

When contact was ignited, I got my answer

about the Dazer's effectiveness. The *pandillero* was stunned.

In Calavero's corneal reflection, I saw a bolt of green fire that flared like a welding torch. There was an instant of shocked silence, Calavero's eyes wide, his face contorted, then a scream as he released his grip on me and tried to claw his eyes free of the pain.

I jumped to my feet, hearing Dedos yelling, "Pull him out from behind the truck, I'll shoot him!"

The partner was armed now, I realized. I couldn't deal with both men at the same time, so I ducked low behind the door, holding the Dazer like a roll of quarters. I drew my arm back and swung hard from the hips, hitting Calavero twice in the ribs with my fist, hearing the distinctive *pop* of thin bones breaking.

Making a grotesque wheezing noise, the man collapsed beneath my left arm, blind and unable to take a full breath. To make sure he was disabled, I gave his eyes another laser burst, his scream not so loud this time because he was semiconscious.

It took a moment to balance Calavero's body against my chest, then get the Dazer positioned correctly in my right hand. When I was ready, I dragged Calavero away from the door, using him as a shield, until I had a clear view of his partner, Dedos, who had taken a few steps back.

The man was crouched in a shooter's stance, hands gripping a black semiauto pistol. Its laser sight created a smoky red beam that I realized connected the pistol with a dot that painted my forehead. I ducked lower, closer to the door, as the beam bounced, then searched for me.

Dedos's hands weren't steady. He was probably spooked by how easily I had disabled his partner. Yes . . . that was the reason, because he decided to bargain.

"Man, I don't want this kind of trouble," he called to me. "Tell you what. You throw that green-light thing you got on the ground, I'll do the same. I promise, man. You can stand up now —*seriously*. You want, I'll count to three. I count to three, we both throw our shit on the road at the same time. How about that?"

From behind the door, I said, "I don't want to have to kill you. Put your weapon on the ground and put your hands behind your head. Show me your hands, you won't get hurt."

The man answered with a forced laugh, saying, "You sound like a cop, the way you say that. But you ain't no cop. You just a cowboy redneck, talking big."

I didn't respond. Instead, I switched the Dazer's range to close-quarters combat, then took a second to check Calavero's pockets. I found an ornate pocketknife and the VHF radio—lucky for me because I realized that the volume had been turned low. I adjusted the volume so I could hear the *pandilleros'* friends if they called, then jammed the knife and the radio in a pocket of my fishing khakis.

A moment later, Dedos hollered, "Kill me with a light, man? How dumb you think I am? A light can't kill nobody, man!"

I'd kept my left arm locked around Calavero's throat. To keep him from responding, I squeezed his windpipe closed as I replied to Dedos, saying, "Then why's your friend dead? You tell me."

Calavero's body thrashed briefly until I reduced pressure, listening for his partner's quiet feet. I heard nothing, so I risked a look.

With one eye to the driver's-side window, I watched Dedos take another nervous step backward before he yelled in Spanish, "Calavero, hey! You okay? *Answer* me."

I watched until I saw that Dedos had lowered his weapon just enough for me to make a move. Using the door as a shield, I stood, aimed the Dazer at the man's face and pressed the button. As I did, I averted my own eyes, but not until I witnessed Dedos's face contorted by a searing, ocular virescence. It was simultaneous with his shrill scream.

The pistol went flying as Dedos covered his eyes. It didn't help because I kept the laser beam focused on his face, using the door to steady my aim. Dazer literature claims that green is four times more visible to the human eye than other colors. It claims that a laser of this wattage could pierce human flesh, including finger and eyelids.

"It feels like a knife through the orbital socket," one of the Dazer techs—who had experienced the pain—told me. At the time, I had assumed it was a mild exaggeration to get me interested in testing the company's product.

I believed the tech now, particularly when Dedos began to roll on the ground. After a few seconds, he gagged and then vomited. Nausea is a common reaction to being blinded by the laser, according to what I had been told.

I felt confident enough to take a quick look at my shoulder. The dart had plowed a small furrow of flesh. It was bleeding but not badly. Next, I switched off the Dazer long enough to crawl into the truck and grab my equipment bag. In those few seconds, I formulated a plan. I needed information *now*. Where was Tula Choimha? If the men didn't volunteer that information, I would have to force it out of them.

And I knew exactly how to make that happen.

Bag over my shoulder, I dragged Calavero to the front of my truck, positioning his head under the bumper. Alternately, I zapped both men with the laser even though they showed no readiness to fight back.

Next, I kicked Dedos's pistol away, then dragged him near his partner, but closer to my truck's right front tire. When he saw where I'd positioned him, the man became combative. To quiet him, I hammered my elbow into his nose. After one blow, Dedos pretended to be unconscious.

Then I stood and looked far down the road, first to the west, then to the east. How close would a driver have to be before he noticed the two men?

Not very close, I decided, which told me I needed to get moving. When the *pandilleros* had first attacked me, I'd desperately hoped a car would turn down this remote road. Not now. An eyewitness was the last thing I wanted. Unless I was willing to detain an innocent passerby, the plan forming in my head would have to be abandoned.

I didn't want to risk making that decision. Not that I was incapable of eliminating an eyewitness —I have done it before in my life. But I have never taken the life of a wholly innocent witness. Not knowingly, anyway. And never, ever in my own country.

"What have you done to my eyes?" Calavero moaned as I used duct tape on his ankles, then his wrists.

"Maybe this will help," I replied, then stripped off more tape and wrapped it around his head as a blindfold.

When I had both men bound, I repositioned them so they could both feel next to their faces the tread of my front tires. My truck was still running, which scared them. Even though they lapsed into a machismo silence, their expressions were easy enough to read in the headlights.

I knew that what the *pandilleros* were imagining was far more terrifying than what they would have experienced had I not taped their eyes. Which was all part of the plan.

I had set up a variation of an interrogation technique that, unlike waterboarding, is unknown to the public. I had been with a special ops team years ago in Libya when I witnessed just how effective—and fast—the technique was at extracting information from an enemy.

I knelt between the men and spoke in English, saying, "I'll give you one chance to answer questions. Refuse, get smart with me, I'll crush your heads with the truck. If you lie, same thing. You're roadkill. I'll leave you here for vultures."

"Don't tell him anything," Calavero said to his partner in fast Spanish. "His voice is different now, hear the difference? The accent. He *is* a cop. But he's not going to hurt us. Cops aren't allowed to hurt people in the States, you'll see."

Dedos didn't sound convinced when he answered, "My nose is broken, man, I could strangle on my own blood if he doesn't let me sit up." Then in English he added, speaking to me, "We don't know anything! But what do you want to know? Hurry up, I'm dying here!"

I asked the men about the girl. I asked about Harris Squires. I asked how many more of their gangbanger friends were waiting down this rutted drive?

Their reply was a smug silence that infuriated me. Two punks, secure in the rights guaranteed by their adopted country, were playing hardass. Two bottom-feeders who profited from the misery of others, dealers of drugs and flesh.

I zapped them both with the Dazer, but the duct tape mitigated the pain. I leaned closer and lasered them again, but they only squirmed and thrashed their heads in response.

"Why is this asshole doing this to us?" Dedos yelled in Spanish, getting mad. "I'm going to die, I'm choking! Even if he is a cop, how's he know so much about Squires and the little virgin?"

Voice steady, Calavero replied, "Shut up. The V-man will have us out of jail by morning. Tell him anything, you're dead, *pendejo*."

Dedos's words, "the little virgin," answered one of my questions. It told me that Tula Choimha was here and maybe still alive. Or had been, the last time these two saw her. Which couldn't have been long ago. According to Melinski, Squires and the girl had left Immokalee a little before eleven p.m.

I checked my watch. *Midnight.*

I was tempted to drag the two into the ditch and get moving, but I had to have more information. How many *pandilleros* and how were they armed? Was Squires a captive or working with the gang?

Calavero was telling Dedos, "My ribs are broken, you don't hear me whining, you pathetic woman—" when I interrupted him, saying in English, "No more talk. You have five seconds to answer my questions."

I began counting as I squatted to confirm the heads of both men were positioned directly in front of my tires.

"Why are you doing this? Who *are* you?" Dedos wailed, coughing blood as he tried to sit up.

With my foot, I forced the man to the ground. Then gave it a beat before I told them both in Spanish, "No more time. You assholes have no idea who I am. But you're about to find out." To convince them my Spanish was good, I added an insult that's common in Mexico.

I heard Calavero swear, groaning, "The Gomer understood us. Everything we said!" as I swung into the truck, limping a little because my leg muscles were beginning to knot from being kicked.

As I positioned myself behind the wheel, the VHF radio beside me crackled, and I adjusted the squelch to hear, "Calavero! Get your fingers out of your ass. Why haven't you called?"

I hit the button and replied, "I tried. Where were you?"

"Don't give me your shit. What happened to the Gomer? That's all I want to know."

I kept the radio a foot from my mouth and tried to make my voice higher and hoarser, to imitate Calavero. "Dedos is an idiot, but the white guy is gone. How much longer?"

I didn't want to risk his suspicion by saying more.

The man—Chapo, I guessed—was suspicious anyway.

"What's wrong with your voice? You sound different."

I snapped, "I'm bored shitless, I'm thirsty. Maybe you'd rather talk to Dedos."

The voice paused . . . more suspicious now? Even when the man laughed, saying, "Dedos is an asshole. What else is new?" I wasn't convinced.

I kept an eye on the wooded road, expecting Chapo, or his partners, to come and check things out for themselves.

The interrogation technique we'd used in Libya is called the Spare Tire Switch, although I have never heard the term again as it relates to intelligence gathering. It was called that by CIA officers running the operation—presumably CIA, because such information is never offered.

A spare tire, handled by two quiet men, is bumped against the head of a blindfolded enemy. A third team member sits next to them in a truck, engine running, that alternately accelerates, then decelerates, as the spare tire rocks in sync, as if attempting to climb over the enemy's face.

The interrogation subject, of course, doesn't know it's a spare tire. He's convinced he is lying under the truck. It is a powerful motivator.

My variation worked well.

When I got my truck into first gear, I accelerated slowly forward until I felt the first hint of resistance. It was accompanied by a duo of howls from Dedos and Calavero.

Instantly, I shifted to neutral, then stepped quietly out of the truck.

Using my left hand on the doorframe, my right on the accelerator, I began to rock the truck forward and back. With my hand, I added more gas with each forward thrust. The terror the two men endured—and the pain they imagined—was caused by the engine noise that grew progressively louder. It was the noise that convinced them their skulls were about to crack like eggs.

After just a few seconds of this, Calavero was begging me to stop.

"Anything," he pleaded, "I'll tell you anything."

He did, too. But he wasn't nearly as eager to share as Dedos, who I had to threaten just to shut him up.

"Crazy with fear" is just a cliché—until you have actually interacted with someone whose brain has been addled by terror. They weep, they slobber. Their sense of time and balance has been scrambled.

"Sick with fear" is another cliché, yet it accurately described the visceral dread I felt after what the two men confessed to me.

They were members of the Latin Kings. The Kings were killers and proud of it. Members were holding Squires and the girl captive at a hunting camp that consisted of an RV and a couple of outbuildings, half a mile away through the woods. There, a man named Victorino—a Latin King captain—and a woman called Frankie were filming a sex video, using Tula Choimha as their victim.

It made no sense to me when Dedos explained that the woman was Squires's girlfriend, but I didn't press for details. I grabbed the radio after a moment of indecision, pressed the transmit button and called, "Chapo! Stop everything! I think maybe the cops are here. Chapo?"

I waited . . . called again, but no reply. It was maddening.

Dedos referred to the girl as *la chula virgen*. The Mexican slang he used to describe how she would be raped was particularly disgusting: *Romper el tamor con sangre.*

His boss was going to bust through the girl's screen in search of blood.

Equally disgusting was the indifference with

which Dedos offered details. He wasn't referring to a teenage girl. He was discussing a worthless object, a young Guatemalan, no better than an animal.

It was not uncommon in the racial hierarchy of Mexican gangs. He mentioned Tula, in fact, as an unimportant aside after Calavero had told me about Harris Squires.

"This person—we call him jelly boy—he disrespected the reputation of our organization," Calavero said. "For this, he is being punished. How, I do not know. That is up to our *jefe*. Now, stop this bullshit! Arrest us, if you want. We'll be out by tomorrow, what do I care? I'm not guilty of anything but being too stupid to kill you when I had the chance."

Calavero was lying about Squires, and I knew it. When I threatened to put them under the truck again, Dedos was more forthcoming. Squires was to be the victim in a snuff film, he said. With a camera rolling, Squires would be murdered— "Slow, like a kind of ceremony," Dedos said —then his body would be burned.

"If he's still alive," Dedos added. "He attacked the V-man, so the V-man shot him in self-defense. With a shotgun, but I don't know how bad. When they sent us out to watch the road, jelly boy was still alive. He was bleeding from the face and chest, but the man is big as a mountain, so who knows? I only do what I am told. I have nothing to do with anything that happens at the hunting camp."

It was then that Dedos told me about the girl.

That's when I tried the radio. Then again.

Nothing but static.

I felt a panicked need to hurry even though I was unclear about the timing. Had Tula already been raped or was it happening now? More threats didn't make it any clearer, and I couldn't waste any more time.

Shock affects different people in different ways. Into my mind came an analytical clarity: I had to do whatever was required to help the girl —do it in a way that didn't risk my future freedom, if possible, but saving the girl came first.

There is a maxim that applied. At least, I wanted it to apply, because it excused the extreme behavior that might be required of me. An old friend and I had pounded out the truism together long ago in a distant jungle:

In any conflict, the boundaries of behavior are defined by the party who cares least about morality.

The Latin Kings cared nothing of morality. They'd made that clear.

I gave myself a second to review. No one knew I was here. The *pandilleros* had no idea who I was. They wouldn't expect a hostile visitor, particularly someone with my training and background. And, tonight, there were no rules, no boundaries of behavior.

Thinking that transformed my strange, restless mood into a resolute calm. I had made the decision to act before giving it conscious thought. The decision tunneled my vision. Thoughts of legalities and guilt—even my fears for the girl—vanished. They were replaced by the necessity of operating in the moment. Of acting and reacting with an indifferent precision.

It was a familiar feeling, a cold clarity that originated from the very core of who I am. I might have been in North Africa or the jungles of Central America. Nothing existed but my targets—threats which I must now find and neutralize.

There were three targets, according to Dedos, not counting Squires or the woman named Frankie, whose role was still unclear. Two fellow gangbangers plus their boss, Victorino—or the V-man, as they called him. All men were armed with handguns and knives. Two carried fully automatic weapons—"T-9s," Dedos told me.

He was referring to one of the cheapest machine pistols on the market, a Tec-9. Cheap or not, the thing could spit out twenty or thirty rounds in only a couple of seconds, then fire again with the quick change of a magazine.

Daunting. But yet another reason not to hesitate when my targets were in sight.

I was hurrying now, but methodically. From my equipment bag, I took a pair of leather gloves and put them on. The night was warm, but I pulled on a black watch cap, too. Roll it down, it became a ski mask.

I looked at my leather boat shoes. The tread was distinctive, so I found rubber dive boots in my truck.

When I had changed shoes, I tried calling Chapo on the radio again—nothing but static. Then I frisked Dedos and Calavero more thoroughly.

Dedos had pointed a .45 caliber Glock at me, fifteen rounds in the magazine, one in the chamber. Because Glocks have no safety—and I don't trust the weapon, anyway—I chose not to slide it into my belt.

That would come later.

Calavero's derringer was a .357. The recoil had to be horrendous, but it was a manstopper at close range. I slipped it into my back pocket.

I found a key to the gate and keys to what Dedos said was a Dodge Ram pickup hidden in the trees fifty yards down the hunting camp road. Because a priority was getting my own truck out of sight, I opened the gate, backed my truck into the shadows, then jogged back to Calavero and Dedos. I used my Randall knife to free their ankles—but not their hands—then ripped the tape from their eyes.

"Get up, get moving," I told them, pointing

Dedos's Glock at them. If I was going to shoot someone, I wanted the medical examiner to find rounds from a gangbanger's gun, not mine.

"Show me you where you parked your truck," I ordered them. "You can lay in the back while I look for the girl. Or stay here if you want. Let the ants eat you, that's your choice."

It was a lie. They were going with me.

From my equipment bag, I removed the night vision monocular, then hid the bag behind the seat of my truck. The monocular is fitted on a headband that holds the lens flush over one eye.

When I flicked the switch, the gloom of the woodland ahead vanished. I was in an eerie green daylight world, details sharp. My right eye is dominant, yet I prefer to shoot using natural night vision, which is why I wore the monocular over my left eye. It is a personal preference that wouldn't have held true were I carrying a rifle or a full automatic.

As we jogged toward the hunting camp—I had to literally kick both men in the butt to get them going—I stayed behind them off to the side. Because I couldn't get Chapo on the radio, I had no choice now but to go into the hunting camp fast and hard.

Twice, I told Calavero to shut up, stop talking, but he continued to goad me. Breathing heavily, he made threats about what the V-man would do when I found him, then said, "When our lawyer

gets you in court, man, how you gonna explain to the judge about my broken ribs? Dedos's fucked-up face? You going to jail, faggot. Police brutality. We got lots of Latin King brothers in the joint, they'll love meeting you. Man, those brothers gonna have some *fun*!"

That caused him to laugh, imagining what they would do to me.

By then, I could see the grille of their Dodge hidden in trees. To silence Calavero, I considered hammering him in the back of the head with the Glock but didn't. Pointless demonstrations of power—like anger—is for amateurs.

Instead, I timed his steps, kicked his right foot into his left ankle, then brought my knee down hard, between his shoulders when he fell. I taped his mouth, then pulled the man to his feet. As I forced Calavero to lean his head against the fender of the truck, I told Dedos, "You seem like the smart one. Keep your mouth shut until I tell you to speak."

Dedos nodded eagerly, his face through the night vision lens a misshapen montage of silver eyes and glittering blood.

Dedos got his chance to speak sooner than expected. As I forced Calavero, then Dedos, into the passenger side of the Dodge, the radio squelched with a muffled voice. Pulling the radio from my pocket, I heard a man say, "Calavero, you there, man? Come in."

It wasn't Chapo's voice.

I touched the transmit button and replied, "Hang on a minute. Talk to Dedos."

Then I pressed the radio to my chest and told Dedos, "Tell him cops just busted through the gate. In a truck. Tell him to leave the girl where she is and run. But"—I slapped him behind the ear for emphasis—"*listen* to what I'm telling you. If you screw this up, if they hurt that girl, I'll kill you. I'll shoot you in the back of the head."

To make my point, I touched the Glock to his temple, mildly amused that, beside him, Calavero leaned toward the dashboard so he wouldn't be hit if the bullet exited his partner's head.

Dedos looked at me as if I were crazy. "You kidding, man. The *truth?* That's what you want me to say to my boys?"

I replied, "Do it!" then held the radio up to Dedos's mouth.

Dedos was so frightened, his voice had a hysterical edge, the pitch of nervous laughter.

"The hell you talking about?" the *pandillero* replied. "Stop with your joking. V-man is sick of that little virgin, so we need something in the truck. The chain saw. Check, make sure it's there."

I took a deep breath, steadying myself. As I did, the man spoke again, saying, "Wait a minute.

You serious? Put Calavero on. You're joking about cops, right?"

I ignored him, thinking it through. If they needed a chain saw, it was to dismember Tula's body. And if the girl was already dead, I was better off going in quietly. It was safer, cleaner. Take the men by surprise, one by one. Or just wait for them to finish up and jump them as they left the camp.

But what if they were killing her *now?*

I held the radio to my face for a moment, undecided. Then I touched the transmit button and said in English, "If you hurt that girl, you're dead. Understand me? Tell Victorino. Tell him to stop everything and throw your weapons on the ground. We're coming in. You've got three minutes, then you're going to jail."

There was a shocked pause before the man responded in English, saying, "The fuck you talking about? Who *is* this?"

Hoping the gangbangers would abandon the girl and scatter, I told him, "We've got your names, we know where you live. We'll come to your houses if you run. But don't hurt that girl —or you'll be sitting on death row."

The pandillero was replying as I sprinted around to the driver's side, saying, "I don't know nothing about no girl, man! We having a party, that's all . . . ," but I didn't listen to more.

I tossed the radio into Calavero's lap as I started

the Dodge, put it in drive, then transferred the Glock to my right hand. Because I knew I might need the emergency break, I tested it to make sure it worked. Then I floored the accelerator, fishtailing toward the hunting camp.

Dedos was hollering at me, calling me crazy, saying, "I can't see nothing, man! You're gonna kill us all!" because I drove with the lights off.

I could see fine. Through the night vision lens, my world was sharp and clear. It was, to me, a familiar world, where shadows are unambiguous, a place without shades of gray.

Dedos was right about one thing, though. If Tula Choimha was dead, I would kill them all.

FOURTEEN

WHEN THE MEXICAN MAN WITH GOLD teeth shot Harris Squires with a rifle, Tula Choimha collapsed on the ground, in shock for a moment, regressing back to the child that life had never allowed her to be.

The lone exception: the night she had watched her father die in flames.

Tula screamed, drawing her body into a fetal position, as her eyes continued to watch what was happening. She screamed again when she saw that blood peppered the giant's face and chest. But when the big man stumbled . . . almost fell . . . then somehow found the strength to keep moving forward, toward the man with gold teeth, Tula's hysteria was displaced by her concern for Harris Squires.

The girl got to her feet, yelling in Spanish, "Stop hurting him! Don't shoot him again!" Then she ran toward the Mexican, her fists clenched.

The Mexican was laughing at Squires, taunting him. He was motioning with his hand for the giant to keep coming. With every step, though, the Mexican took a step backward, staying just out of the giant's reach.

Behind Tula, the redheaded woman was enjoying herself, calling, "V-man . . . Hey, Vic! Try to shoot him in the balls. See what kind of marksman you are!"

The rifle the man carried, Tula noticed, had two barrels. So maybe the rifle was a shotgun, although Tula wasn't sure of the difference. Was the V-man carrying the gun in the crook of his arm because both barrels had been fired with one shot?

If so, Tula believed the giant might survive because his spirit was still strong despite the blood that now soaked his pretty blue shirt. The girl could tell because Squires was saying to the Mexican, "Is that your best shot, *chilie*? That the best you can do, douche bag?" his voice flinching with pain at each step but his eyes aflame, focused on the V-man.

372

Suddenly, it was as if the Mexican was done having fun, because he took two fast steps backward. Then he pointed the shotgun at Squires's pelvis, saying, "I want to do this slow, jelly boy. Maybe shoot off your *penga*, that'll make you smile for the camera. *Then* I'll use the knife."

Still grinning, the V-man looked toward the redhead as if seeking her approval . . . but then his expression changed. His attention shifted to Tula, who, still running and only a few strides away, screamed, "No-o-o-o!" a word that she had transformed into a sustained shriek.

The resonance of a young girl's scream is fine-tuned by eons of adaptation to repel attackers, particularly human males. The V-man winced, his ears aching, and his awareness of Harris Squires was momentarily jammed. Then he had to stick a hand out to stop Tula, who crashed into his thigh, her fingernails flailing, as she tried to sink her teeth into the man's arm.

Victorino's Latin King soldiers had been pillaging the RV. But two of them were now sprinting to help as the V-man hollered, "Ouch, goddamn you!" Then: "Get this little bitch off me!"

Victorino swung his open hand at the girl's face but missed. "Damn brat!" he hissed, then swung again and connected hard. Tula went sprawling, her nose bloody.

An instant later, the V-man's attention returned

to Squires, who was suddenly towering over him, his right fist drawn back. Victorino noticed just in time to roll his face away from the sledgehammer impact, a glancing blow that would have crushed his face. Instead, Victorino backpedaled several steps, still holding the shotgun, then went down hard on his butt.

Squires kept coming, the grin on his face grotesque because of the blood. But then the giant wasn't grinning anymore because the V-man's soldiers, Chapo and Zopilote, tackled him from behind.

Chapo had a small crowbar in his hand—he'd probably been looking for a secret stash inside the RV. And he began hammering at Squires's back and butt with the bar to immobilize the man.

Victorino was dazed but still coherent enough to yell to Chapo, "Cripple him, but don't kill him! Leave him for me!"

Then, standing, testing his balance, Victorino had to yell again, warning Chapo, "Watch out for the little cougar!" because the girl had a rock in her hand and was sprinting to help Squires.

Frankie intercepted the girl, though. She did it on the run, even with a drink in her hand, sweeping the skinny child up with her muscles, then swinging her around as if playing a game.

The redhead was still in a playful mood, the V-man could see it, which provided him an optimistic boost. So far, tonight hadn't been nearly as much fun as he'd hoped. On the drive to the hunting camp, he'd pictured how it would go in his mind, first impressing the redhead by killing Squires with a flourish, then the two of them getting it on in front of the camera, being real sexy-dirty with the cute little *chula*.

But this *chula* was a street cat, not a whimpering child like most. And jelly boy had proven he had balls after all, almost humiliating him in front of Frankie.

Shit—Victorino was looking at his wrist where the girl had bitten him to the bone—the *puta* would have to pay for this. He'd make an example of her. Not kill her—a girl her age was too valuable—but maybe tie her up and use a razor like the Muslims did. Cut her body so she'd never be able to enjoy a man even when she was old and not getting paid for it.

Yeah, get it on camera. Victorino was wiping blood on his jeans as he pictured how it would go. Give the redhead a private warning by letting her watch him use the box cutter on the girl, then show the video to new *chulas* when they arrived in Florida desperate enough to do anything for money.

Tell the new girls: *See what happens when you disobey the V-man?*

But that would come later. *After* he and the redhead had enjoyed themselves a little, just as planned.

It would happen.

Victorino felt his confidence returning as he watched Frankie touch her fingernails to the little virgin's throat and whisper something into the girl's ear.

The *chula* had been screaming but instantly stopped, her face paling as if she was about to be sick.

It caused Frankie to beam at the V-man and brag, "You're an idiot when it comes to girls, know that? To make a spoiled brat behave, you have to understand it's all an act. Screaming, not putting out, whatever. It's because they *want* something. Figure out what it is, then threaten to take it away. That's how you handle a *puta*. Just about any girl, if she's cute at all. They're all the same."

Frankie laughed into the *chula*'s face, adding, "Aren't you, darling? *Aren't* you?" Then looked at Victorino, smiling. "I think the two of us are gonna get along just fine. You ready to have some fun?"

Spooky, the V-man decided, the way the redhead said that. *They're* all the same. But kind of sexy, too, like Frankie was different from other women.

And maybe she was. But the bitch was already insulting him in front of his soldiers, calling him an idiot in her superior way. Which had to stop.

Victorino watched Frankie brush the girl's hair back very gently as if playing with a doll, then he turned his head and told Chapo and Zopilote in Spanish, "Tie up jelly boy, we'll deal with him later. Then search his truck. The tall *gringa* and me want some privacy for maybe an hour, with the girl. Find the money wherever jelly boy hid it. Then get the gas cans out, soak everything so the whole fucking place goes up when we're ready. Afterward, I'll give you the redhead as a present."

In reply to their surprised expressions, he added, "*Seriously.* Have yourselves some fun with those big *chichis* of hers tonight because tomorrow, maybe next day at the latest, I'm cutting them off."

What Frankie whispered into Tula's ear was, "Listen, you spoiled little bitch. If Harris dies tonight, it's *your* fault. So shut your mouth . . . or God's gonna blame you for killing your new sweetheart."

It shocked Tula that a woman with eyes as black with fog as Frankie's could speak of God in such a knowing, confident way.

And also that the woman was able to look into Tula's heart and recognize the sudden affection she felt for Squires.

Never in her life had a man done so much to protect her. Not since her father had died. The giant had not only tried to save Tula, he had continued to fight for her safety even after having been shot, then beaten. It squeezed the girl's heart now, seeing him lying on the ground, bleeding and humiliated, after risking so much to help her. She wondered how many bullets were in his body and if he was dying.

He is our warrior, the Maiden said into Tula's mind when she stopped struggling against the tall woman's muscles. *He is our knight. You must do whatever you can to help him.*

As if reading Tula's thoughts, the redhead surprised the girl again by saying, "Harris is kind of cute, isn't he? Like a big stupid animal who's eager to please. Trust me"—the woman laughed into the girl's face, her breath foul with smoke and alcohol—"I know exactly what you're thinking."

Into Tula's mind flashed the image of the sad bear in the zoo as Frankie swung her toward the RV, bragging, "Know how I do it? I understand how women think. All their sneaky, catty ways. Plus, we're a lot alike, me and tomboys like you. The first time I saw you, I could tell. *A boy, my ass.*

"Difference between us, you're still hiding behind God. Me, I got smart quick and joined the other side. That's where the fun is and the power. It's all about power, *niña.* Power and money-money-money."

Then the woman stumbled, slurring, "*Shit—* you spilled my drink! Look at what you did. And your goddamn blood's all over my new tank top!"

They were at the door to the RV now, and Tula was looking over the woman's shoulder, seeing two men use tape on the giant's wrists as the Mexican with gold teeth watched, holding the shotgun over his shoulder like a soldier who was tired of marching. In the lights of the pickup truck, Victorino's face appeared swollen, misshapen, which reminded Tula of her own throbbing nose.

She pushed herself away from the woman and said, "I can't breathe, please put me down. I need to blow my nose because the man hit me."

The woman dropped Tula without warning— like a practical joke. When the girl's head banged the steel steps to the trailer, it evoked a snort of laughter from Frankie.

"Good," she said. "Knock some sense into you."

The woman had found a tissue in her jeans and was rubbing at the blood on her shirt, her balance unsteady, getting madder as she smeared the blood. Then she gave up and hurled the tissue at Tula. "Stop fighting me! If you don't, I'll tell that Mexican to kill your boyfriend. How'd you like that?"

Tula was on her feet, sniffling, trying to stop her nose from bleeding, but her eyes were focused on Squires, who was still on his back, hands folded across his belly like a corpse because of the tape. The two men had the doors to the giant's truck open. They were leaning inside, throwing things out onto the ground, while the Mexican with the gold teeth walked toward the RV, a bandy-legged man trying to appear taller than he was.

Frankie looked away from Tula long enough to grin at the V-man, who was close enough for her to call, "Does my Mexican stallion need a drinkie?"

Then the woman stabbed her fingernails under the girl's chin, lifting Tula's face, and whispered, "How's a little saint like you gonna feel? Murdering your sweetie when God knows you could've stopped it."

Tula could barely hear the woman's words because, suddenly, the Maiden was in her head, voice firm, telling her what to do, what to say. The girl's heart was pounding, but she wasn't afraid —not for herself, anyway—but she ached for Squires, who lay on the ground, breathing fast, shallow breaths. She watched him turn his head to the side and cough, something bubbling out of his mouth and nose.

Blood, Tula realized.

Inside the girl's head, the Maiden's voice warned, "He has a bullet in his lungs. To save him, God will forgive you for anything you must do. I lied to my Inquisitors. *Remember?*"

Tula remembered. Jehanne had even warned the vigilante priests that she would mislead them, if necessary, to spare her warrior knights. It was in the book Tula had left back at the trailer park.

I would rather have you cut my throat than betray my knights by telling you the truth, the saint had vowed.

Lying to an enemy wasn't a lie—it was a weapon. And it made Tula furious to see the giant lying on the ground, vulnerable and in pain. It caused her to remember that she had weapons of her own.

You were born to do this, the Maiden whispered over the noise of Frankie's voice. *You were born to fight evil, to smite the devil down.*

Evil. This woman, Frankie, *was* evil. Tula had known it from their first meeting. In Harris Squires, the girl had recognized the scars of the redheaded woman's sins. A wickedness so pervading that it had clouded the man's goodness. It clung to him like an odor.

That odor filled the air now, stronger than Frankie's drunken breath, as Tula looked into the woman's face and said, "I'm sorry . . . I don't want you to be mad at me. I'm sorry about your blouse—you're so beautiful, it's a shame. Because of the way you look, a woman so tall and pretty, it scares someone like me. That's why I tried to get away."

The woman appeared startled. It took her a drunken moment to process what the girl had said. "You're goddamn right you should be sorry. But maybe the stains'll come out if I don't let it dry. I've heard if you use warm water—"

Abruptly, Frankie stopped, as if she'd just realized something. She had been looking at her tank top, pulling it away from her breasts, but then grabbed Tula by the hair and tilted her face upward. "Hey! Where'd you learn to speak such good English? Don't get the idea you can fool me, you're not smart enough."

The girl stared at Frankie, wanting the red-headed woman's eyes to concentrate on her, only her. At the convent, Sister Lionza had taught her that focus was required if she hoped to influence a person's thoughts.

Tula winced because the woman was hurting her but maintained eye contact, saying, "I don't blame you for being suspicious, but there's something you don't understand." The girl lowered her voice as if to whisper a secret. "I've never had anyone say the things you just said to me. It's like you were inside my mind. You understand my thoughts. Do you really? It would be nice to know that someone really understood. I feel guilty sometimes—and alone."

Slowly, the woman released Tula's hair, looking at her, her expression puzzled. She watched the girl's posture change, noting the girlish cant of hips, the innocent dark eyes, before asking, "What I said about not killing Harris, you mean? Or about the tomboy thing?"

By then, Victorino was close enough for Tula to glance at the man, then say to Frankie, "Maybe later we can talk—just us together? It's . . . it's not easy for me to trust anyone, but you seem . . . different than other women."

Victorino arrived, throwing his arm around Frankie's waist, asking, "What's the problem with the little bitch now?"

The woman disentangled herself from the man and gave him a shove, demanding, "Where's the money? Did you find it?"

The V-man couldn't believe what he was hearing, the woman mad at him again for no reason. "You been watching the whole time," he said. "What the hell you think? My boys are doing that job right now, stop worrying. I give them an order, you can bet they gonna do it."

"Priceless," the woman muttered, "a regular genius," as she placed her hand on Tula's shoulder. When the girl felt Frankie's fingernails on her skin—their questioning pressure—Tula walked her hand across the small of the woman's back and leaned her weight against Frankie's thigh despite the welling disgust inside her.

Tula was concentrating on Squires, sending the giant strong thoughts, telling him, *Stay alive . . . stay alive . . . stay alive,* as Frankie said to

V-man, "Tell me something—why'd you have to slap this girl? You're so goddamn dumb, I'd slap you myself if your face wasn't already such a mess."

The man thrust his wrist out, saying, "The bitch bit me, what you expect?"

Frankie didn't even bother to look. She leaned her nose toward Victorino, standing on her toes, Tula noticed, to tower over the man. "Big tough Mexican stud," she said loud enough for everyone to hear. "Harris almost kicked your ass, that's what really happened. So you went and did *this*." The woman nodded toward Tula.

"A girl with a face as cute as hers, now I'm going to have to take her inside and get some ice. Why'd you do it? It make you feel like your dick's bigger to bloody up some defenseless girl? Well, it hasn't done much for you so far, *amigo*."

Victorino was glaring at the woman, pretending not to notice that one of his soldiers had stopped to listen, while the shorter one—Chapo—held a VHF radio to his mouth, talking to someone.

As Frankie took the girl's hand, turning her toward the open door, Chapo called to V-man in Spanish, saying, "Hey! Calavero says some white dude stopped, he's asking for jelly boy. A redneck in a truck."

Tula's attention vectored, thinking, *Tomlinson?*

The girl shook her hand free from the woman, senses probing the darkness beyond the silhouettes of trees. Her mind was alert for the aura of godliness that accompanied the strange man with long hair. Instead, she discerned an unexpected force—something cold out there beneath the stars. It was a focused energy, dispassionate, moving her way. And human . . . Or was it?

Tula tilted her head, hoping the Maiden would provide confirmation, but received only a vague premonition of violence.

The V-man had his back to Tula and Frankie, relieved to be conversing with Chapo. A *gringo* stranger was easier to deal with than the red-head's nasty attitude. Victorino called in reply, "The Gomer asked for jelly boy by name? What's a redneck dude want, coming out here this time of night?"

Frankie, Victorino realized, had stopped at the top of the steps for a reason. Probably waiting until Chapo was done talking so she'd have everyone's attention before insulting him again. Victorino was so pissed off by the shit the woman had said, he considered walking over and kicking Squires in the ribs—blow off some steam—then demand to know if jelly boy had told anyone that he'd be at the camp tonight.

Chapo spoke into the radio again, then called, "Dedos flipped the Gomer the finger, I guess.

Pissed him off. So maybe the white dude's a local and that's why he turned around."

Victorino said, "Turned around?" but then realized what Chapo meant. He said, "Don't waste your time worrying about rednecks. Tell Calavero don't bother us unless he's got a real problem. Search jelly boy's truck, then get to work doing the other shit I told you to do."

Chapo nodded, forgetting that the woman didn't speak Spanish. He'd already been told the V-man didn't want her to know about the cans of gas they'd brought and the bag of rags so they could torch the hunting camp.

Frankie, still watching, waited as Victorino changed his mind, saying, "No. First you two help me drag jelly boy in there . . ." With his chin, he indicated the wooden steroid shack. Then changed his mind again, saying, "Shit, you haven't found the money yet? You two drag his fat ass by yourselves. *I'll* search the truck."

The woman turned to confirm that Tula was inside the RV, doing something in the kitchen—looking for a towel because of her nose, she guessed. Frankie swung the door closed, stepped down onto the sand and wiggled her index finger, motioning Victorino closer.

"The hell you want?" The man took a couple of careful steps toward the RV, expecting the redhead to take a swing at him or launch into another tirade.

Instead, Frankie produced a joint, lit it, then offered it to the V-man, her *chichis* sticking out because she was holding her breath after taking a big hit.

Man, that *banano* grass smelled good. A couple tokes of coke-soaked weed, that's exactly what he needed. Victorino leaned so Frankie could put the cigarette between his lips.

"The girl has a thing for me," the woman finally said, exhaling and keeping her voice low. "She wants me to be her teacher—sort of sweet, really. You wouldn't understand. But all the signs are there."

Victorino said, "Probably because you talk to her so sweet," being sarcastic.

The woman shook her head. "Don't take it personally. I said all that nasty shit to convince her I'm on her side. But I knew you were smart enough to figure it out. I'd have made a hell of an actress, huh?"

The expression of confusion on the Mexican's face. *Priceless.*

Frankie grinned, holding her hand out impatiently for the joint as Victorino replied, "Then we still gonna do it, huh? In front of the camera?"

"Don't worry. You'll get your share."

Victorino took a second hit of the *banano* as he watched the bodybuilder's head disappear into the shack, the two *pandilleros* dragging the man by his feet. He said, "What about jelly boy? Do him later or after you have your fun?"

"Get his clothes off him—at least his pants." Frankie said, taking the joint from Victorino's hand. "You meant what you said, didn't you?"

Cut the man's nuts off.

The V-man replied, "A dude disrespects the Latin Kings—I got no choice in the matter." He was studying the woman's face, hoping to see that hungry look again. And there it was: Frankie flicking her tongue to moisten her lips, eyes bright.

The V-man couldn't help himself. He kissed the woman, enjoying how she exhaled the last of the *banano* smoke into his mouth. Frankie let him slip his hand under her bloodstained shirt, too, then drew back and said, "I just wish you made better movies. Last one, you taped the girl's mouth—you couldn't hear her scream! What's the point of that?"

Now the know-it-all woman was being nasty again, telling Victorino that he sucked at making movies, too.

The V-man was thinking, *This is one very crazy gringa.* High from smoking coke and grass, and probably thirsty for more Crown Royal, the woman's mood swings were really pissing him off.

In that instant, Victorino decided he was done with Frankie. As of tonight. Wait any longer, he realized, and she would want part of the sixty grand, once they found it. No . . . she would want it all.

The realization made Victorino want to smile. He was picturing himself using the box cutter on Frankie, too, but only after reminding her why it was better if he didn't tape her mouth.

You're the one told me how to make movies, he would tell the woman. No . . . he'd say, *I could make it easier on you, but I don't want to disappoint my audience.*

But the V-man kept that to himself, playing it cool, even when Frankie asked him, "What arc you grinning at? You look like the cat that just ate the bird."

Whatever the hell that meant.

She started to walk to the RV. "I'm going to see the girl. Get started on Harris. When I hear him screaming, I'll know it's time to come out and play."

Tula was inside the RV, rushing to follow the Maiden's instructions and also trying to come up with some ideas of her own. She had to escape and save Harris Squires. But how?

It was dark inside the trailer, even with the lights of the truck tunneling through the curtains, so first Tula found three candles, lit them, then got busy. Everywhere she went, everything she did, she ran. There was no telling how long Frankie would be out there talking to Victorino. Soon, the woman would come inside, expecting the girl to share her secrets—and her body, too.

Tula had known from the start what Frankie wanted. The same with Victorino, with his vicious gold teeth. The two of them were plotting together, probably outside right now, forging an agreement about who would take her body first.

It made Tula queasy, the thought of Frankie or the Mexican touching her. But she was now aware that she might have to allow it to happen. Jehanne had already promised Tula God's forgiveness. Whatever was required to win the redheaded woman's protection, and her help, was permissible.

The thought of submitting herself to Frankie, though, was disgusting. But her feelings no longer mattered. Tula was resolved to do whatever was necessary to save Squires and find a way for the two of them to escape. It was what the Maiden was telling her to do.

However, the Maiden's written words were also strong in the girl's mind: *I would rather die than to do what I know is a sin.*

Tula had repeated the phrase so often that it was part of who she was. She believed she could endure anything rather than disappoint God. But those words, even when whispered as a vow, did not apply to the life of another human being.

Allow Harris Squires to die just to spare herself embarrassment and pain?

Tula couldn't do that. If she could save the giant by surrendering her body to evil, she would. In the meantime, her brain was working hard to devise another way.

The RV door had a tiny window, and the girl stood on her toes long enough to confirm that Frankie and Victorino had moved away from the RV so no one could hear them. The woman was just lighting a marijuana cigarette, which suggested that she was in no hurry. Tula knew that it was marijuana because many people smoked *mota* in her village, even married women if they were suffering cramps during their periods. That's what the women claimed, anyway, although the girl was dubious.

Tula thought about locking the door, then decided against it. Frankie had believed her lie about wanting to speak privately. It would only make her suspicious. So the girl hurried to the kitchenette to search for weapons.

Help yourself, and God will help you, Jehanne had written. *Act, and God will act through you,* she had counseled her knights.

Tula was looking in cupboards, opening drawers, hoping to find an ax or a large knife, or even a gun. Although she had never fired a weapon, the girl was willing to try. But could she kill another human being? Tula tried to imagine how it would feel, as the Maiden reminded her, *These are our enemies. You must fight.*

That was as true, and as real, as the revulsion Tula felt for the redheaded woman. Still . . . to sin against God by hurting another human being. It was a difficult decision to make.

But then Tula reminded herself that the Maiden had carried the equivalent of a gun—a sword she had found behind the altar of a church and carried into battle. Jehanne had told her inquisitors that her sword had never shed blood, yet she had also warned that she would lie to them, if necessary. And there were witnesses who swore the Maiden had used her sword to kill Englishmen, and also to punish prostitutes.

Tula pictured herself stabbing Frankie . . . then imagined the woman lying on the ground, dying, as the evil inside her bled out onto the sand.

If it meant saving herself and the man who had fought for her, the girl told herself that she would have to do it. Even so, she still wasn't convinced she actually could.

Tula didn't find an ax, or a gun, but the paring knife she had used earlier was in the sink, the blade bent but sharp. The girl wrapped a dishrag around the blade and hid the thing in her back pocket.

Squires's wrists and ankles had been taped. She would need a knife to free the man—if she could invent an excuse to be alone with him. But why would Frankie or Victorino allow such a thing?

Thinking about it was discouraging, until the Maiden's voice spoke again, telling the girl, *God is with you. He will show you the way.*

Cupping a candle in her hands, Tula trotted down the hall to the bedroom. There, a steel locker had been broken open—Victorino's men had done it, she guessed—but there were only boxes of shotgun shells, no weapons.

Next, reluctantly, she checked the strange room with the bed and mirrors where there had been a video camera and a stack of obscene photos.

Victorino's men had been there, too. The camera was gone. The photos were scattered across the floor, dozens of them. Tula tried not to look at them as she searched under the bed, then a tiny closet, but she didn't want to step on the pictures, either—it was like walking on someone's grave.

As she moved through the room, Tula winced at each new obscenity. The eyes of unknown women peered up at her, communicating a secret agony that was as apparent to Tula as the grotesque poses the women affected for the lens. They were young girls, some not much older than herself, each brown face forever trapped in a frozen silence from which Tula perceived screams of pain, of fear, of desperation.

Then, suddenly, the girl's legs went out from under her, and she found herself sitting on the floor, weeping, holding the candle in one hand, a photo in the other.

From the photograph, despite the woman's nakedness and despite her leering mask, a familiar face stared back at Tula. In disbelief, the girl turned away from the picture, then looked at it again, hoping to discover that she was wrong.

No . . . her eyes hadn't tricked her. What Tula saw was a loving likeness of herself, the girl's own first memories of home and kindness and safety.

It was her mother.

Still pinned to Tula's shirt was the miniature doll that she had found earlier. The girl touched her fingers to the doll as she studied the photograph, her mind trying to ignore her mother's shocking nakedness by focusing on the face she loved so much. Familiar odors came into the girl's mind, then memories of her mother's touch. Tula had been crying softly, but now she began to sob.

How had this happened?

Tula remembered the woman at the church in Immokalee saying her mother had gone to work for a man who made movies. But her mother never would have consented to something like this. Trade her dignity . . . her very soul . . . for money? No, impossible. Even more impossible because, also in the photo, a man's reflection was visible in a mirror—not his face but his naked anatomy.

Not since Tula's father died had the girl witnessed anything more painful. In a way, this was even more traumatic because her mother had encouraged by example Tula's devotion to God and the Church. Never had there been such a good and loving women—even the villagers said it was true. To Tula, she represented all that was godly and clean, a woman who had vowed to be forever faithful to her husband even though he had been dead for a year when Tula heard her make the promise.

It was beyond the girl's ability to comprehend. Here, though, was the truth—an obscene infidelity that seemed to debase the children of all loving mothers and mocked Tula's deepest convictions.

The Maiden came into Tula's head, then, reminding her, *Only God's eyes know the truth. The truth is lasting but often hidden from us. Even though we see, we remain blind.*

Jehanne had written those words centuries ago, but it was if they were intended to comfort Tula at this very moment. The words were true. This photograph represented only a moment in time. It proved nothing other than it had happened.

But *why* had it happened?

Her mother had been forced to participate in this profanity, Tula decided. In fear for her life, probably. It was the only explanation that made sense. Perhaps the naked man in the photo was holding a gun. Or the man behind the camera. Only minutes ago, Tula realized, she herself had made the decision to submit to sin if it meant saving herself or the life of Harris Squires.

Gradually, the girl felt her faith returning. Her mother had been the victim of threats and violence. The girl felt certain of it now. Her mother would confirm the truth of what had happened when Tula found her. Or . . . should she even mention the photo when they were finally face-to-face?

No, Tula decided. She would never speak of it. Not to her mother, not to her family, not to anyone. It would only add to the humiliation her mother had suffered. Her mother had given Tula life—like God. And like with God, Tula knew, she would never doubt her mother's goodness again.

This photo . . . it felt so light and meaningless between the girl's fingers now. Yet it was a final justification for the mission on which God had sent her—to rescue her family, to lead her people home from this terrible sinful land.

Then, as she held the photo, another realization came into the girl's mind, but not as shocking. Her mother had been *here,* at the hunting camp.

The photo had been taken in this very room. Tula confirmed it by comparing the background with the bedroom's walls and the mirror hanging above the bed.

Harris Squires, she realized, hadn't lied about knowing her mother. It had only sounded like a lie because the man honestly didn't remember meeting her. Tula felt certain of it, just as she felt sure the giant would have remembered her mother if she had worked for him.

No . . . Harris hadn't forced his mother to do this. He might have played a small role, he might even have been aware that it was happening—but only because he was under the spell of someone more powerful. Someone evil.

Tula could hear her pulse thudding as her thoughts verified what she had sensed from the beginning: Frankie was to blame for this. The drunken woman with her man's voice, her tattoos, her viciousness. Carlson had seen her giving Tula's mother a cell phone how many months ago?

The girl couldn't remember, but she now knew in her heart the truth of what had happened. The redheaded woman had victimized her mother. Only one of many. Frankie's many sins lay scattered on the trailer floor, these profane photographs like discarded souls. The woman was *evil*.

Her body shaking, Tula got to her feet, aware

that Frankie could return to the RV at any second. She had to get herself under control. For Tula to allow Frankie to see her weak and in tears would only give the woman more power over her.

She couldn't allow that to happen. She *wouldn't* allow it to happen.

Tula considered tearing the photo of her mother into tiny pieces. Instead, she folded it and put it into her back pocket, while, inside her, the revulsion she felt for Frankie was transformed into hatred, then rage. She had never experienced the emotion before. It created inside her a determination and fearlessness that was unsettling because, in that instant, Tula understood why soldiers in battle were so eager to kill.

As the girl hurried down the hall toward the kitchenette, it was difficult to keep her hand off the paring knife. She wanted to use the knife now. She wanted what she had imagined to happen: Frankie on the ground, the evil bleeding out of her.

Which was when the Maiden's voice surprised Tula by saying, *What about the stove? The giant showed you how to turn the gas on.*

The girl was confused for a moment. To be so passionately focused on one subject, it was difficult to concentrate on anything else. But she tried, wondering, *The stove?* Of what use was the gas stove now?

Then she understood. Frankie had been smoking a cigarette. If the woman was still smoking when she walked into a room filled with propane, she would die.

For a moment, Tula was excited. But the Maiden rebuked her, telling the girl that the stove was better used as a diversion, because it was smarter.

The girl was disappointed, but she understood. If the RV caught fire, Victorino's men, and Frankie, would be so surprised they might forget about Harris Squires for a few minutes. Maybe they would leave the giant alone long enough for Tula to free him, then they could escape together down the lane to the road.

No . . . not the dirt lane. Tula remembered that Victorino had sent two men to watch the road, so she and the giant would have to escape through the woods.

But escape without confronting Frankie? That seemed cowardly after what that evil woman had done to Tula's mother.

The Maiden entered the girl's head and comforted her, saying, *God will judge her. Can there be anything more terrible than His wrath?*

Tula wasn't convinced. As always, though, she obeyed. Equipping herself for a hike through the woods, the girl put matches, two candles and a bottle of mosquito repellent in her pockets.

Then she knelt beneath the sink and turned the gas valve until it was wide open.

At the stove, however, the girl hesitated. She had extinguished the candle she was carrying, but there were still two burning candles in the room. Secretly, she wanted to blow out the candles and hope Frankie was still smoking a cigarette when she opened the door. But there were no secrets with the Maiden, who told Tula, *Hurry . . . the woman's coming. Do it now!*

Tula opened both valves on the stove, then ran down the hall, pulling doors shut to isolate the propane, including the door to the bedroom she entered, maybe slamming it too hard, but it was too late to worry now.

On the far wall was a window. Tiny, but big enough to wiggle through. Tula bounced over the bed to the wall, then flipped the lock, expecting the window to open easily.

It didn't. The window frame was aluminum. Maybe it was corroded shut. Tula used all her strength, pushing with her legs, then tried cutting around the edges of the window with the paring knife.

It still wouldn't open. As the girl stood there, breathing heavily, she could smell propane gas seeping under the door. She would have been less surprised by smoke and flames. Had the candles gone out, extinguished by the doors she had slammed? Or did the concentration of gas have to be higher before the candles would ignite it?

Tula didn't know. She knew only that she had to escape from the trailer before Frankie came in, smelled the propane and realized that a trap had been set for her.

Next to the bed was a lamp. Tula grabbed it and swung the base of the lamp against the Plexiglas window, expecting it to shatter with the first blow. It made a sound like a gunshot, but the glass didn't break.

Panicked because she had made so much noise, Tula began hammering at the window. Finally, it cracked, but the girl had to pull the Plexiglas out in shards, piece by piece, before the window was finally wide enough for her to crawl through.

She draped a towel over the opening so she wouldn't cut herself, then dropped to the ground, feeling an overwhelming sense of relief to be free.

The feeling lasted only a few seconds.

As Tula got to her feet and turned toward the shack where she'd last seen Squires, a low voice from the shadows surprised her, saying, "You sneaky little slut. What did you use to break the window, a damn sledgehammer? I didn't even have to go inside, it was so obvious."

Frankie was standing at the corner of the RV, a towering shape silhouetted by headlights. Not smoking now but a pack of cigarettes in her hand.

Tula's fingers moved to her back pocket, feeling the lump that was the paring knife. An edge of her mother's photograph was sticking out, too.

"It's because you scare me," the girl said, trying to sound reasonable. "What I told you was true. I want to talk to you, tell you things I've never been able to tell anyone. But my body's afraid because of the way you look. Why would someone as beautiful as you waste time helping someone like me?"

With her deep voice, the woman said, "Liar! The whole time, you were lying," sounding furious but undecided as if she wanted to be proven wrong.

Tula focused her eyes on the woman's black eyes, hand inside her back pocket, saying, "We should go inside and let me wash your blouse. I know how to get bloodstains out. Where I lived in the mountains, that was one of my jobs, washing clothes."

In her mind, Tula was picturing Frankie pausing at the steps of the RV to light a cigarette, then opening the door.

The woman was staring back, perhaps feeling the images that Tula was projecting because, for a moment, the woman's anger wavered. But then the woman caught herself, visibly shook her head as if to clear it and yelled, "What the hell's *wrong* with me? You're lying again! Don't tell me what to do!"

Then the big woman charged at Tula, whose hand suddenly felt frozen, unable to draw the knife from her pocket, so the girl turned and ran.

Frankie sprinted after her, yelling, "Come back her, you lying brat! Just wait 'til I get my hands on you!"

For a woman her age and size, Frankie was quicker than Tula could have imagined. After only a few steps, the girl felt a jarring impact on the back of her head. Then she was on the ground, Frankie kneeling over her, using a right fist to hit the girl so hard that Tula didn't regain full consciousness until she awoke, minutes or hours later, in the cookshack.

Woozy and dreamlike—that's the way Tula felt when she opened her eyes. Nauseous, too. It took the girl several seconds to organize what she was seeing as her eyes moved slowly around the room. Overhead were bars of neon light. The sound of a motor running confirmed that the generator had been started. There was a strong odor of gasoline, too.

Tula wondered about that, making the distinction between the smell of gasoline and the smell of propane, which struck her as important for some reason.

Tula lifted her head to study her body, then lay back again, eyes closed. She was tied, unable to move, her wrists taped to the legs of a heavy table. They had used short pieces of rope on her ankles, securing her legs in a way that suggested they intended to cut her jeans and shirt off next. The owl-shaped jade amulet and her Joan of Arc medallion were missing, she realized, but the girl could still feel the shape of the paring knife hidden in her back pocket. Even so, in her entire life, she had never felt so naked and defenseless.

Could this really be happening?

Yes . . . it was as real as the blood Tula could now taste in her mouth. The girl strained against the tape again. The table moved a little, but her legs were spread between a stationary counter. Freeing herself was impossible, so she lay back to think, her mind still putting it all together.

Frankie and the Mexican with gold teeth were standing nearby but not looking at her. The woman was concentrating on a camera mounted on a tripod, angry about something—impatient with the camera, Tula decided. Then Frankie spoke to Victorino, muttering, "I told you the battery was in wrong. Stupid wetbacks, if it's anything more complicated than a knife, you can't deal with it."

A moment later, though, the woman swore, and said, "This battery's no good—probably because of the way you did it. In the RV, I've got a camera bag full of shit. Send one of your pals to go get it."

Tula's brain was fogged, but mentioning the RV was of interest to her. She had just escaped from the RV, she remembered, where she had left the stove valves open to fill the trailer with propane.

Slowly, the girl's attention shifted to Victorino, who was wearing surgical gloves for some reason. The gloves and the man's wrists were stained with blood. He was glaring at Frankie with dead, drunken eyes, and seemed too preoccupied to respond.

It was because of what a second Mexican had just said to Victorino. Even before Tula had opened her eyes, she had heard the man speaking Spanish, but her mind had not translated his words yet his phrases lingered. What the man had said was important for a reason, Tula was sure of it, yet her brain had yet to unravel his meaning.

Poli—she had heard him use the word. *Poli* was Mexican slang, the equivalent of "cop." If so, then it *was* important. But why had the man mentioned police? Tula strained to recall. She squeezed her eyes closed, her brain scanning for details.

Yes . . . it was coming back to her. The man had said something that sounded like *The cop said don't hurt the girl. They're coming in.* Words close to that. "The girl" referred to her. It had to . . . didn't it? *Don't hurt the girl.* It suggested to

405

Tula that the police were coming to save her.

Tula wanted to believe it, but what was happening around her was so surreal that she didn't trust her judgment. Hope was such a tenuous, flimsy thing, after the photograph she had found in the RV, after what she was now experiencing.

The Mexican who had mentioned police was standing in the doorway, holding a radio. He sounded worried. "We dumped all the gas just like you said. Why don't we torch the place now and go?"

Gasoline . . . it explained the odor, which Tula filed away as the man, getting very serious, added, "The redheaded witch, she doesn't understand a word of what we're saying, right? So leave her here with the girl. Get the woman's fingerprints on your box cutter and let the cops arrest her for jelly boy. Hell, maybe they'll think they got into a fight or something. Cut jelly boy free, too— he's not going anywhere. You know, a steroids war. Let the cops figure it out."

The man was referring to Harris Squires. Tula had momentarily forgotten about the giant, but events were flooding back now. But arrest the woman for what? What had happened to Harris?

Confused, her mind working in slow motion, Tula moved her eyes to where the Mexican was looking. He was staring at something to her left. But to see, she would have to move her head and risk alerting Frankie that she was conscious.

Into the girl's mind, the Maiden spoke, saying, *Be fearless. You were born to do this! I have not forsaken you!*

To hear Jehanne's voice at such a moment caused the girl's eyes to flood with tears. Because she was crying when she turned her head, she was unable at first to decipher what she was seeing. A massive pale shape was lying next to her. Tula squinted tears away, and the shape acquired detail. Even then, it took her several seconds to understand what she was seeing.

It was Harris Squires. After what they had done to the man, Tula didn't want to believe it was actually the giant. His body appeared shrunken, deflated. Harris was naked, legs tied wide, just as they had tied her legs. His chest was peppered with shotgun BBs, his ivory skin patched with blood.

Beneath the giant's hips, the blood had pooled like oil. Tula didn't want to look any closer but she forced herself. Her brother was the only male she had ever seen naked, so it took the girl a moment to understand what had happened Victorino had mutilated the giant.

Tula grimaced and turned away, comforted only by the fact that Squires was unconscious, no longer in pain, and also that he was still breathing.

When the girl opened her eyes again, Frankie was standing over her, staring down. The woman

407

smiled and said, "Well, well, well! My sleeping cutie is finally awake."

Then, turning to Victorino, she asked, "What are you two yapping about? What's wrong?"

Victorino was ripping off the rubber gloves, suddenly in a hurry, as he asked the Mexican man in Spanish, "Where's my Tec-9? Chapo's got the other one—is he ready? Goddamn it, he should've been in contact! We got to be ready for anything anytime!"

The Mexican took a boxy-looking gun from the bag on his shoulder and handed it to Victorinio, saying, "It bothers me that we haven't heard a word from Calavero or Dedos, either. Dedos, he's probably passed out. But Calavero, if the cops grabbed him—"

Victorino interrupted, "That's what I'm *telling* you," as he ejected the magazine from the weapon, checked it, then slammed it back. "Shit," he said, "for all we know, it's not the cops. It's some *La Mara* bangers from Immokalee. Why would cops call and warn us they're coming? You know, Guatemalan punks talking English because they figure we're so rich, we got lazy and stupid."

In Guatemala City, Tula had heard of the street gang, *Mara Salvatrucha. La Mara*, for short, or MS-13. It was a murderous gang, always at war with Mexican gangs. She lay back, taking in details, as the V-man asked Frankie, "You and jelly boy ever do any business with *La Mara*? Maybe that's who it is."

Frankie got taller on her toes again as Victorino slipped by her, the woman yelling, "What kinda shit are you trying to pull now? I don't know anyone named *La Mara*! You and your greasers found the money, *didn't you?* Now you're feeding me some bullshit excuse about why you have to run."

Holding the box cutter in his hand, the V-man leaned over Squires for a moment, then pushed the razor toward Frankie, saying, "Cut his hands and legs free. Someone finds him, we want them to wonder what happened."

Tula remembered what the Mexican had said about fingerprints. Frankie took the knife in her right hand and, for a moment, Tula thought the woman was going to stab the blade at Victorino. The man took a step back, thinking the same thing, which was when the Mexican warned Frankie from the doorway, saying, "Don't even think about it, *puta*. It'll be like shooting balloons at the fair. Like back when I was a kid."

The Mexican was pointing a pistol at Frankie, holding the weapon steady until the woman muttered, "A couple of big tough wetbacks, that's what you are," then dropped the razor, too unconcerned to watch where it landed.

Tula was watching, though. She kept her eyes on the razor even as Frankie collected her cigarettes and pushed past the Mexican, outside, pausing only to tell Victorino, "I need a drink. Either of you disappear while I'm getting it, I'll have *your* nuts!"

Then, without waiting for a reply, she was walking toward the RV, hips swinging. Tula could see the woman plainly through the open door. The girl focused her eyes on the back of Frankie's head, then pictured the woman on the RV steps. Tula was telegraphing images, thinking over and over, *Light a cigarette . . . Light a cigarette.*

Tula could also see Victorino standing in the doorway, the weapon in both hands, his concentration intense. Maybe he hadn't heard the woman's insult. No . . . he'd heard, because as his eyes swept the darkness he called after the redhead, "You can burn in hell, for all I care—" but then stopped abruptly and crouched.

A second passed, then another, before he whispered to the Mexican, "Hey—there's a vehicle coming down the road. See it? No lights, but it's headed this way. How the hell they get past Calavero and Dedos?"

The Mexican started to say, "Our two guys— maybe that's who it is. See them through the window?" then stopped talking as he watched the truck fishtail, then drift into a slow spin.

Now on his knees, the V-man was yelling, "Shit—that's our Dodge! Those aren't cops. They stole our goddamn truck!"

Beside him, the Mexican tried to mention Calavero and Dedos again but was interrupted by two consecutive gunshots, *WHAP-WHAP!* very close.

Victorino ducked his head back, hissing, "Shit, they firing on us, man! Shooting at us from our own truck!" Then he took a quick look out the door and decided, "We've got to get to jelly boy's truck. Four-wheel drive, we can drive through the goddamn swamp if we need to."

The Mexican sounded dubious, saying, "I don't know, man, that shit's wet out there."

"Our goddamn truck's got the road blocked, man!" Victorino said, getting mad. "You don't got eyes in your head? Plus, they probably got more dudes waiting for us as we leave. We gotta take jelly boy's truck and get the hell out of here." The man peeked out the door again, asking, "You ready with the thing I told you about?"

The Mexican showed Victorino the lighter in his hand, saying, "You want me to wait until the *gringa* is inside the RV? Unless you think we don't have time."

Smiling, the V-man replied, "I warned the bitch. You heard me warn her. Let's go!"

Both men took off running, the Mexican firing three shots at something, then Victorino opening up, his weapon making a continuous ratcheting sound, loud, but not as loud as the pistol.

411

From outside came the sound of more gunshots —maybe Victorino's men. Maybe someone else.

Tula's mind was too busy thinking to notice or care.

Sensing the room's sudden emptiness, Tula lay back for a moment, concentrating on breathing into her belly to calm herself. Then she attempted to communicate with the Maiden.

They poured gasoline, I can smell it. This building might catch on fire. Please don't let me burn.

Jehanne didn't reply, but into Tula's head came words Joan of Arc had written, words the girl had committed to memory: *Help yourself, and God will help you. Act, and God will act through you.*

Tula raised her head. Through the open doorway, she could see that Frankie was on the steps to the RV but crouched low because of the gunshots. Maybe the woman would seek cover inside the trailer and light a cigarette later to calm herself. Revenge wasn't a priority in Tula's mind now, though.

Her eyes moved to the razor Frankie had dropped. The box cutter had landed only inches from Harris Squires's right hand. The giant no longer reminded the girl of Hercules or polished stone. Only a few hours ago, the veins of his body had resembled blue rivers, tracing the contours of his biceps, the muscles of his chest and calves.

Now the rivers had been drained. The giant appeared shrunken inside his own skin, a mountain of pale, dead flesh, although the man's chest continued to move.

Tula watched Squires's chest lift and fall, his breathing shallow. As she stared at him, the girl focused all of her attention on the man's unconscious skull, seeking the spirit that lived inside.

Open your eyes. God will save us. Open your eyes. You are the strongest man I have ever met, open your eyes . . .

For more than a minute, Tula repeated those phrases, but then was stopped by more gunshots, then a *Woofing* detonation that shook the floor beneath her. It was a firestorm explosion so close that it sucked air from the room, replacing it with heat so intense that it felt like needles on the girl's face and arms.

Through the doorway, Tula saw a wave of fire rolling toward her, the flames so wild and high that the RV was screened from view.

Had the trailer exploded?

The fate of the redhead seemed unimportant now, and Tula threw her head back, screaming, "Jehanne? Jehanne!" then strained to use her teeth on the tape that bound her wrists. The table to which her hands were tied moved a few inches with each effort, but the angle was impossible.

As the girl convulsed her body, trying to tear herself free, the memory of her father's last moments came into her mind, an image so stark, so sobering, that it caused Tula to stop screaming long enough to hear a voice calling to her. When she tilted her head to listen, the voice summoned her again, a soft voice, barely audible.

Tula became motionless, head up, eyes wide, listening for what she expected to be the Maiden offering advice . . . or, at the very least, comfort.

Instead, she heard a man's voice beside her say, "Sis . . . Sis! Shut your mouth long enough to answer me. Are those assholes gone?"

Tula turned to see Harris Squires looking at her, his eyes two dull slits. On his face was an inexplicable smile that gave the girl hope even though she knew it was because the man was in shock, probably delirious, he was so near death.

Tula began crying, she couldn't help herself, and talking too fast as she replied, "Harris! I am so sorry they hurt you. But you'll get better. I will take care of you myself. I will take you home to the mountains and make sure no one ever hurts you again. I promise!"

No . . . the giant wasn't delirious. He was alert enough to look toward the door, see the fire, then say, "Shit! This place will go up like a bomb. I've got to get you out of here!"

That possibility stayed with the man for a second, but then he realized the hopelessness of

414

what was happening. Squire's face contorted, then he slammed his head back and began to sob. "Did you see what those sons of bitches did to me?" he moaned. "I fought and fought, but I couldn't stop them. I'm sorry, I'm so sorry. I'm no good to anyone now."

Tula yelled, "Harris, *stop it,* you're wrong!" to snap the man out of his misery. Then she used her head to motion toward the box cutter, telling him, "We have a knife, Harris! If I can pull myself close enough, maybe you can cut the tape on my wrists."

Squires opened his eyes as the girl added, "Don't leave me again, Harris. Stay strong, *please.* God will help us—but we have to help ourselves first."

The giant appeared to be fighting unconsciousness, his voice barely audible as he replied, "My guardian angel, I forgot." Then, gaining focus, he asked, "What knife?"

Because of all the blood on the floor, Tula wondered how the man found the strength to open his fingers and take the box cutter into his huge right hand.

Inch by inch, Tula dragged the table closer to the giant. He held the razor, fighting unconsciousness as he waited. Two minutes passed, then four minutes. From the doorway, the girl could hear the roaring energy of combustion as the fire drew closer, feeding itself on gasoline fumes and grass. Soon heat and smoke made it difficult to breathe, but the girl continued to fight the weight of the table.

Squires watched her, struggling to remain focused after losing so much blood. Every minute or so, he would awaken himself by telling Tula, "Don't give up! Just a couple more!" These were phrases he had spoken so many times in weight rooms while spotting partners that he repeated the words by rote.

Even so, the giant's determination was an inspiration to Tula, but his terrible wounds also caused the girl's heart to ache.

When Tula realized the roof of the wooden shack had caught fire, she began to lose hope. She was dizzy from breathing smoke and her arms ached. For a few seconds, the girl paused to rest, and also to gauge the distance remaining before Squires might be able to cut the tape on her left wrist.

Two feet . . . a little less. The wooden building was burning so ferociously, though, it might as well have been two miles.

Tula closed her eyes and summoned the Maiden, resigned now that she and her warrior giant were probably going to burn to death. No . . . the smoke would kill them first, the girl reminded herself. In books she had read about Joan of Arc, witnesses all agreed that the saint had died from smoke inhalation before flames despoiled her flesh.

In a way, Tula found the recollection comforting, but she wasn't ready to give up. Before
yanking at the table once again, she spoke to her
patron saint. A request.

*Give us time. Just a few more minutes. If not,
please grant me just one wish. Spare this good
man from more suffering and pain.*

FIFTEEN

THROUGH THE NIGHT VISION MONOCULAR
I saw two men kneeling in the doorway of a
wooden shack, guns drawn, as I steered the
Dodge truck, headlights off, toward an RV
where a tall woman was approaching the
steps, presumably about to enter.

Isolated beneath a macrodome of Everglades
stars, the detailed images of the woman, the men
and both structures were as sharply defined as if
looking through a well-focused microscope.

The men heard our truck approaching, then
singled us out in the darkness. The woman did
not. She appeared oblivious, standing with her
back to the road, patting her pockets for something, probably looking for a flashlight or maybe
cigarettes.

Beside me, Calavero, his mouth taped, made
grunting noises of disapproval while, beside
him, Dedos told me, *"There*—that's the redhead

bitch. It was all her idea, her and that asshole bodybuilder."

Because the truck's windows were closed, air conditioner on, the man didn't have to raise his voice to be heard. It also guaranteed that his fellow gangbangers wouldn't hear him if he decided to call a warning or yell for help.

For the last half mile, Dedos, my new best friend, had been supplying me with information as we bounced through the woods at forty miles an hour, the heads of both men banging off the ceiling more than once.

I had only slowed long enough to transform my wool watch cap into a full-faced ski mask, then fit the night vision monocular over it.

I had also experimented with the vehicle's cruise control. It worked fine at twenty-five mph, but I needed more speed to skid the truck into a combat turn—which is what I intended to do. On pavement, I would've needed to be doing at least sixty. On this dirt lane, though, forty would work—even with the Dodge's antilock brakes.

Antilock brakes have become the bane of tactical driving schools worldwide. I've been through enough of those schools to know.

As we closed on the hunting camp, I noted a redneck-looking pickup truck, off to the left. The doors were open, junk strewn all around, which made no sense. But it was the sort of truck a guy like Harris Squires would drive and it gave me hope that he and Tula Choimha were still here.

I kept my eyes focused on the men in the doorway, paying close attention to the orientation of their weapons. One man held a pistol—a long-barreled revolver, it looked like. The other, a fully automatic Tec-9 that Dedos had mentioned. Maybe he was the gang leader—V-man, they called him, or Victorino—but that was too early to confirm. If Dedos had told me the truth, the math was neither difficult nor comforting. One gangbanger was missing. So was a second Tec-9.

Where?

Time for careful observation was over. We were speeding toward the clearing, and I had to make my moves fast and clean. In preparation, as I drove, I opened my door and held it open with my left foot. Because I had already switched off the truck's dome light, the cab remained dark.

With cruise control locked in at forty, I was free to move my right foot to the emergency brake. Pointing the Glock at the men in the doorway, I waited . . . waited until I saw one of the men stand, bringing his weapon up to fire, and that's when I jammed the emergency brake to the floor.

The cruise control disengaged instantly, the wheels didn't lock, but the truck had enough momentum to bounce into a skid, then do a slow-motion right turn as I guided the wheel. My left foot was already searching for the chrome step to the ground when the door flew open.

A "modified boot-turn," is the tactical term. The turn is used to effect a hasty retreat from roadblocks or a trigger-happy enemy. The technique dates back to the days of bootleggers.

Crouched low, I waited as the truck skidded. Then, as it slowed, I closed the door quietly and stepped off the running board while the Dodge was still moving. For a second or two, I trotted along behind the truck, using the bed to screen me from sight.

By the time the Dodge had come to a stop, I was several paces into the woods. In the doorway of the shack, both men were on their feet now. The temptation was to take a wild shot at them. For an expert marksman, eighty feet was manageable. But I am only a competent shot with a handgun, plus I was using a stranger's weapon, the Glock. I wasn't going to risk giving away my location to a man carrying a full automatic.

Besides, I had already committed myself to an extraction plan and I was determined to stick with it. It was the simplest plan I could devise, and it didn't include engaging gangbangers in a running gun battle.

I had whittled the strategy down to three priorities: If possible, I wanted to block the exit to the road so they couldn't pack Tula into a vehicle and run. Next, I would locate and mobilize the girl. Finally, I would have to eliminate witnesses who might be able to identify me later.

As far as Dedos and Calavero were concerned, the last priority came first. They had seen my face, they could ID my truck. I could have killed them myself. Later, I would do just that *if* they survived the scenario I had just contrived. Surprise, panic and confusion—these are all linking elements in the majority of deaths from friendly fire. Using the gangbangers' own radio and vehicle, I had combined the elements into a volatile combination.

Kneeling behind a tree, I provided what I hoped was an effective catalyst. I took aim and fired two shots, targeting the Dodge's rear tires. Maybe the tires ruptured, maybe they didn't, but I didn't stick around to confirm that I had or had not temporarily immobilized the truck and blocked the exit to the road.

Instantly, I was on my feet and running. The structures which comprised the hunting camp were luminous green through the night vision monocular. They flickered past, bracketed by trees, as I gave careful attention to each building. As I ran, I did a hostage assessment, trying to determine the girl's most likely location. That's when the men in the doorway opened fire.

I dropped to the ground and remained motionless for a moment. Then I lifted my head, hoping to confirm that they were firing at the Dodge.

They were. The Tec-9 sounded like a fiberglass machine gun firing plastic bullets. The report of the revolver was flat and heavy. Combined, they created a chorus of breaking glass and punctured metal as slugs hammered through the Dodge.

In less than five seconds, the men had fired twenty, maybe thirty rounds. Then there was an abrupt silence that left the night sky echoing with the squawks of outraged birds and the trilling of indifferent frogs.

I crawled toward the Dodge, then lifted my head again. I could see only the back of the truck. The silhouettes of Dedos and Calavero were no longer visible through the shattered rear window. It seemed impossible that they hadn't been hit, but that was something I would have to confirm later. Judging from the vehicle's tilted angle and the steam spiraling from the engine, the blockade I'd hoped to create was now solidly in place.

I got to my knees, my attention on the two gangbangers. They weren't heading for the safety of the RV as I'd assumed. They sprinted past the trailer, indifferent to the woman cowering near the steps, and I watched as one of the men took something from a bag and handed it to the man carrying the Tec-9.

A fresh magazine, I realized.

As the two men slowed to reload, I heard one of them holler, "Chapo! Where are you? Chapo, get your ass over here now! We're going!"

The woman looked unsteady as she got to her feet, one hand on the stair railing. She screamed, "What the hell is happening?" then added a string of profanities, calling the men cowards for leaving her. Her language became more graphic as she demanded money they owed her.

She mentioned a figure: sixty thousand cash.

Interesting, but my mind was on Chapo, the missing *pandillero*. His was the voice I had heard on the VHF. Presumably, he was the gangbanger carrying the other Tec-9.

Was he in the RV, guarding Tula Choimha? Or in the shack? Until proven otherwise, I would have to handle myself as if either could be true.

The man carrying the Tec-9 was the V-man, the gang's leader, I decided. I was sure of it when he summoned Chapo again, yelling, "You better get your ass in gear, man, 'cause we're leaving now!"

The men didn't wait for an answer and neither did I. As they took off running, I shadowed their pace, keeping trees between us. They were headed for what I assumed to be Squires's truck. It was a massive vehicle, built for the swamps, with deepwater tires, an industrial winch and banks of lights mounted overhead on a roll bar.

A mudder, Floridians might have called it, a swamp buggy, to uninformed outsiders.

I had a head full of adrenaline, and my first instinct was to disable the truck so the men couldn't escape. A vehicle that size could bull-doze the Dodge aside, then make a clean break for the road.

Ahead was a tangle of swamp tupelo, then a stand of bald cypress, the trees wide enough to provide cover and thick enough to shield me from bullets. It was a marshy area. I knew it even before I was ankle-deep in water, but the trees gave me an ideal angle, a clean side view of Squires's truck. The Glock held fourteen more rounds. I was tempted to put a couple of slugs into the tires, then a few more into the engine. Do it right, have some luck, and the gangbangers wouldn't be going anywhere. Not fast, at least.

As I pressed myself against one of the trees, though, my training and experience took over. An emotional response is for amateurs. Anger is a liability that signals a lack of discipline.

Priorities, I reminded myself. *Stick to the plan.*

Engaging an enemy with superior firepower was not only dangerous, it was a waste of time. And pointless. So far, these two gangbangers had not seen me. Killing them—or even stopping them from escaping—was unimportant.

In certain circles, there was a maxim that has saved many lives and taken more than a few.

Keep it simple, stupid.

That's exactly what I intended to do.

I shifted my focus to one objective and one objective only: Find the girl, then get her out safely.

My second priority was also important—leave no witnesses—but it was still a secondary consideration. If the V-man and his partner made it to the road, that was a problem for the police. Dedos and Calavero were a different story, but they weren't going anywhere. If they weren't dead, they were at least wounded and could be dealt with later.

The girl was foremost in my mind. I had to find the girl. I might also have to deal with Chapo, I reminded myself, the man who carried the second Tec-9. Or the tall woman who Dedos had accused of orchestrating Tula's abduction and rape. In my lifetime, I have encountered at least two women who were as dangerous as any man. Maybe this woman was as dangerous or maybe she was just a masochistic freak. If the time came, I would find out. The fact that she was female would not save her if circumstances required me to act.

Shielded by the cypress tree, I knelt and took a closer look at Squires's truck. It was a supersized model, and all four doors were open, dome light on. So much junk lay scattered around the truck, I got the impression that it had been ransacked. The woman's reference to sixty thousand dollars came into my mind, but I didn't linger on the implications.

I wanted to be absolutely certain that the girl wasn't being held captive in the truck. I could see clearly enough through my night vision to confirm she wasn't in the cab. But what about the bed?

The truck bed wasn't covered, and it seemed unlikely the gangbangers would have left her there. To be sure, I watched both men closely as they approached the truck. It took a while. They appeared worried about what was hidden in the trees behind them, close to the smoking Dodge.

Finally, it was V-man, carrying the Tec-9, who told me what I needed to know. As he approached the driver's side of the truck, he didn't bother to glance into the open bed. Same with the man carrying the revolver.

Had Squires or the girl been lying there, they would have at least taken a quick look to make sure their captives were still secured. Instead, the men climbed up into the truck, then the engine started.

Surprisingly, as I watched, the gang leader didn't turn toward the exit road as expected—maybe he didn't want to be slowed by the disabled Dodge or possibly because he feared an ambush. Instead, he accelerated fast over ruts and through tall sedge, the truck's headlights bouncing northwest toward what to me appeared to be swamp, judging from the hillock of cypress trees in the distance.

Maybe Victorino was familiar with the area and knew of a lumberman's trail not visible on the satellite photo. I had studied the photo pretty thoroughly, though, and was doubtful. But the fate of the gang boss and his partner was no longer my concern.

The girl wasn't in the truck, that's all I needed to know. It told me that Tula was being held in the RV or the wooden shack—unless they had already killed her and disposed of her body someplace in the woods.

I turned and began retracing my steps toward the Dodge, studying the two buildings, but also keeping an eye on the tall woman who was still watching the truck as if hoping the gangbangers would change their minds and return. She had been yelling a stream of profanities and threats even as the men drove away, but now she punctuated it all by screaming, "Come back here, you assholes!"

After a few moments of silence, as the woman cupped her hands to light a cigarette, a man's voice surprised both of us, calling, "Don't worry, Señorita Frankie! They comin' back right now. I just talked to the V-man."

I recognized the voice, the heavy Mexican accent, and began trotting faster toward the disabled truck. Because of the rubber dive boots I wore, I moved quietly, using night vision to pick the cleanest, shortest path. I had the Glock in my right hand, my gloved index finger ready, resting parallel to the barrel. In my left hand, I carried the Dazer.

It was Chapo's voice. Finally, I had located the man armed with the second Tec-9. He had played it smart, I realized. Instead of panicking, he had remained in the shadows, trying to figure out what was happening before making a move. It was a sensible thing to do. Chapo had a VHF. He knew that Victorino or his partner had a radio, too. So why should he risk making his position known?

My brain assembled all of this data automatically, then warned me that dealing with this man might require special care.

Startled by Chapo's voice, the woman shouted, "Jesus Christ! You scared the hell out of me!" Then she stood taller, exhaling smoke, and searched the darkness before calling, "Where are you? What was all that shooting about? No one tells me shit around here!"

To the northwest, I noticed, the truck was already turning—but having some trouble from the way it looked, rocking back and forth in what might have been mud. I allowed myself only a glance, though, because I was still moving fast.

I changed my heading slightly when I heard Chapo reply to the woman, saying, "I wanted to be sure of something before getting V-man on the radio. Now I'm sure. You better go on inside the trailer 'til you can come out."

The woman was drunk, I realized. She puffed on the cigarette and took a couple of careful steps in the direction of the truck before Chapo stopped her, dropping his pretense of politeness. "No closer, *puta*—you'll get yourself hurt. I'll shoot anyone, they get too close. Do what I say. Get your ass inside that trailer until it's safe to come out."

The woman hollered back, "For Christ's sake, at least tell me what's happening! Is it the cops?"

I was zeroing in on the man's hiding place, deciding maybe Chapo wasn't so smart after all because he continued to respond, saying, "We got us a visitor, *señorita*. He's around here somewhere. Hell, maybe he's got a gun pointed at you right now."

Chapo laughed, then tried to bait me by adding, "But it's no big deal. It's only a dumb redneck— sorta like jelly boy. And you saw what happened to jelly boy. V-man and us will take care of this Gomer. I bet he can hear me right now!"

No, Chapo had his shrewd moments, but he wasn't smart. He had just provided me with important intel. Jelly boy? He was referring to Squires, I decided. They had ransacked the bodybuilder's truck, probably looking for money, then they had killed him. Or tortured him at the very least. Chapo had also let it slip that Dedos or Calavero had told him about their visitor. Maybe just before they had died . . . or maybe both men had survived.

If so, their minutes were numbered because now I was close enough to the Dodge to see where Chapo had hidden himself. The *pandilleros* hadn't told him I was wearing night vision, apparently . . . or the man wasn't aware that he'd done a bad job of concealing his feet.

Just as his nickname suggested, Chapo was a little man. The first thing I spotted were his two child-sized cowboy boots. He had positioned himself under the truck, feet visible beneath the passenger's side, the barrel of the Tec-9 and a portion of his head protruding from beneath the driver's side. It provided him a panoramic view of the buildings and the clearing while the truck's chassis protected him on three borders.

Or so he thought.

As I approached, I considered yelling to get his attention, then using the Dazer. A bad idea, I decided. Even bat blind, a man with an automatic weapon can cover a lot of area by spraying bullets.

Instead, I got to my knees, then to my belly. I crawled for a short distance but then stopped. I was approaching from the back of the truck, which wasn't ideal. It gave me a decent shot at the man's lower body, but that's not where I needed to hit him.

I had to try something different and I had to make up my mind fast. Unless the gangbangers had mired Squires's truck up to the axles, they might soon return, although I thought it unlikely.

Peripherally, I was aware that the woman was now on the steps of the RV, reaching for the door, when I decided to surprise Chapo by doing the unexpected. I bounced to my feet, already running, and reached the bumper of the Dodge after three long strides. When I dropped down into the bed of the truck, I could hear Chapo yelling, "Hey! Who's up there?" his question nonsensical because he was so startled.

I was looking down at the man, seeing the back of his head, holding the Glock steady in both hands. Only because it might provide me a larger target, I answered the man, hoping he would turn. I told Chapo, "Up here, it's Gomer. Take a look."

He replied, *"Who?"* maybe trying to buy some time as he tilted his face to see but also attempting to aim the Tec-9 upward without shooting himself in the chin.

Twice I shot Chapo: Once above the jaw hinge,

although I had aimed at his temple. And once at the base of the skull.

A moment later, I heard Dedos's frail voice call from inside the cab, saying, "*Amigo!* I need a doctor, I'm hurt!"

I looked to confirm that Chapo wasn't moving, then I knelt to peer through the shattered back window. The truck was a chaos of glass, debris and blood.

Dedos was staring at me from the front seat, his hands somehow free, maybe from broken glass or possibly Chapo had cut the tape. When the man realized who I was, he thrust one arm toward me, palm outstretched, a classic defensive response when a man sees a gun aimed at his face.

Dedos spoke again, saying, "It's me, *amigo*. I helped you. Remember?" His voice had a pleading quality but also an edge of resignation that I have heard more than once.

Speaking to myself, not Dedos, I replied softly, "This is necessary—I'm sorry," a phrase I have spoken many times under similar circumstances before squeezing a trigger or snapping a man's neck.

We are a species that relies on ceremony to provide order, yet I have never allowed myself to explore or inspect my habit of apologizing before killing a man.

When I fired the Glock, the round severed a portion of Dedos's hand before piercing his forehead. I shot him once more, then turned my attention to Calavero, whose body was splayed sideways between the front and back seats.

Through it all, the man hadn't moved. Maybe Calavero had died more quickly because his mouth was taped. I didn't know—or care. If Calavero was still alive, though, he would be able to identify me later. I couldn't risk that.

Because I was aware that this would soon be a crime scene that demanded close inspection, I knelt, placed the Glock next to my feet, then took Calavero's own .357 derringer from my back pocket. When the medical examiner recovered slugs of different calibers from these bodies, it would suggest to police that there had been more than one shooter.

Recent headlines had inspired the crime scene I was now manipulating. Eighteen people killed, execution style, by a gang in Ensenada. A dozen in Chiapas forced to kneel, then shot in the back of the head. It was not something a respected marine biologist from Sanibel Island would be party to.

I had to lean through the back window to position myself closer to Calavero. I wanted to get a clean angle, close to the man's left ear. Because the gun was so small and the caliber of the cartridge so large, I anticipated the terrible recoil. When I pulled the trigger, though, I was the one who felt as if he'd been shot.

It wasn't because of the derringer's recoil. Simultaneously, as I pulled the trigger, there was a thunderous explosion to my left. I was thrown sideways, the derringer still in my hand, aware there were flames boiling in the sky above me.

I landed hard on my shoulder but got quickly to my feet, holding the Glock again, unsure of what had happened. Nearby—close enough to feel the heat—what had once been a recreational vehicle was now a mushroom cloud of smoke and fire. Flames were radiating outward, toward where Squires's truck had been parked, and also toward the wooden shack, traveling in a line like a lighted fuse.

Someone had poured a gas track, that was obvious. It was arson. But what had caused the explosion?

I remembered the tall woman standing at the door to the RV, a cigarette in her hand. RVs, like many oceangoing vessels, use propane. It was all the explanation I needed.

Then, as if to confirm my theory, the woman suddenly reappeared from the flames. She was screaming for help, slapping wildly at her clothing even though her clothes didn't appear to be on fire. I watched her spin in a panicked circle, then sprint toward the cooling darkness that lay beyond the inferno. Soon, she disappeared into a veil of smoke that separated what was left of the RV and the wooden shack.

If Dedos hadn't told me the woman had orchestrated the Guatemalan girl's abduction, I might have gone after her. Instead, I tossed the derringer into the cab of the Dodge, then vaulted to the ground.

Running hard, I headed toward the flames, yelling Tula's name.

To my right, the wooden structure hadn't caught fire yet. It soon would, but I had to check the RV first because, as I had already decided, it was the most likely place to keep a captive girl.

There was a light breeze out of the northeast. It was enough to change the angle of the flames and channel the flow of smoke, so I had to circle to the back of the trailer before I could get a good look at what was left of the structure.

There wasn't much. The westernmost section of the trailer, though, was still intact. I noticed two small windows there—bedroom windows, perhaps—that had been shattered by the explosion. The darkness within told me flames hadn't reached one of the rooms yet, so I ran to take a look.

As I got closer, the heat was so intense that I had to get down on the ground and crawl. It seemed impossible that anyone inside could still be alive, but I had to make sure. I took a deep breath, put both gloved hands on the frame of the windows and pulled myself up to take a look.

Smoke was boiling from the plywood door, the floor was a scattered mess of photographs, some of them already curling from the heat. There was an oversized bed and so many shattered mirrors that I would have guessed the room had been used to film pornography even if I hadn't noted the tiresome, repetitive content of the photos. A camera tripod lying on the floor was additional confirmation.

Tula had been in this room. I sensed it—a belief which, by definition, had no validity. Yet, I also knew intellectually that if the tall woman and her gangbanger accomplices had planned to rape the girl, this is the place they would have chosen.

I screamed Tula's name. I tried to wedge my shoulders through the window and call for her again.

Tula!

The window was too small to fit my body through, the heat suffocating, and I was finally forced to drop to the ground just to take another full breath.

I squatted there, breathing heavily, trying to decide what to do. I told myself the girl couldn't possibly be alive, yet I pulled myself up to the window for a final look.

There was a closet, but the door was open wide enough to convince me the girl hadn't taken refuge inside. I called Tula's name over and over, but when I smelled the stink of my own burning hair I dropped to the ground, then jogged away in search of a fresh breath.

I was furious with myself. It was irrational anger, but to come so close to saving the girl's life only to fall short and lose her to fire was maddening. I also couldn't delude myself of the truth: I probably could have forced my shoulders through the window and made a more thorough search of the RV had I really tried.

The fact was, I was afraid.

Like the other primary elements wind, air and water, fire can assume an incorruptible momentum that is a reality—and a fear—hardwired into our genetic memories over fifty million years of trying to domesticate nature's most indifferent killer.

That's what I was thinking as I ran toward the wooden building, my attention focused on the building's roof that was now ablaze, instead of noticing what was going on around me—a mistake. With my night vision system, I owned the darkness, yet instead of looping around through the shadows I stupidly sprinted straight toward the burning building—in plain sight of Victorino and his partner, I soon realized, as Squires's truck skidded to a stop only thirty yards to my right.

Because of the fire's combustive roar, I hadn't heard the engine approaching. Nor had I been listening for it. My last memory of the two men was of them bogged in mud, trying to escape.

That all changed when I heard a gunshot, then the telltale sizzle of a bullet passing close to my ear. It was an electric sensation punctuated by a vacuum of awareness—a sound once heard, never forgotten.

I ducked and turned, seeing one of the gang-bangers using an open door to steady the gun he was holding. Thirty yards is a long distance for a revolver, but the man had come close. I was already diving toward the ground when he fired a second round.

I was shooting back at him with the Glock even before I hit the ground, squeezing the trigger rapid-fire, my rounds puckering the door's sheet metal, then shattering the glass window.

I heard the man bellow as he ducked from view, but I kept firing, while my left hand searched for the Dazer that was in my back pocket. I didn't aim, I shot instinctually, letting muscle memory control my right hand. Nor did I count the rounds —something I always do—because I had been taken so totally by surprise, and also because I had allowed myself to panic.

There was a valid reason to be afraid. I could see Victorino behind the driver's-side door, slapping at the Tec-9, getting ready to open fire. Maybe he hadn't seen me until his partner had drawn his weapon and fired. Or maybe the Tec-9 had jammed—they are notoriously undependable.

Whatever the reason, I knew that if he got the machine pistol working, I was dead.

When Victorino's partner suddenly reappeared, he was beneath the passenger's-side door on his back, chest pulsing a geyser of blood. At least one of my rounds had hit him.

Because there was no cover nearby, I got to my feet and charged the truck. I had the Dazer in my left hand, the Glock in my right. It seemed impossible that the gun's magazine had more than one or two rounds left, and I was tempted to dump the weapon and reach for my Kahr 9mm—the pistol I had used to kill the gator. It was in my hip pocket, fully loaded.

Victorino was bringing the Tec-9 up to fire, though, his head and shoulders framed by the driver's-side window. A wasted second would have killed me. I was pointing the Glock at the man, screaming, "Drop it! Drop it!" as I squeezed the trigger.

Instead of a gunshot, I heard *Click.*

Absurdly, I tried the trigger again. *Click-Click-Click.*

The Glock was empty.

Victorino had ducked involuntarily when he saw me sprinting toward him, aiming the pistol. But now that he realized I was out of ammunition, I watched the man appear to grow taller as he stepped away from the truck. He was taking his time now, grinning at me with what might have been gold teeth, the machine pistol held at chest level.

I had stopped running. The Glock was useless, so I dropped the thing at my feet, hoping the man was egocentric enough not to shoot me immediately, which is what a professional would have done. Maybe he would offer some smart-ass remark, provide me with a few seconds to think while he gloated over his triumph before killing me.

As if surrendering, I thrust my hands in the air, as Victorino took charge, his ego on display. He told me, "The flashlight, too. Drop the flashlight, jelly boy. Who the fuck you think you are, coming in here causing so much trouble? And take off that goddamn ski mask!"

I was holding the Dazer in my left hand, my thumb on the pressure switch. My heart was pounding. Even if I had the laser aimed accurately, even if I blinded him instantly, the man would still be able to fire twenty or thirty rounds in the space of a couple of seconds. It was my only hope, though. Drop the Dazer without at least trying, I would be dead.

Victorino took a step toward me and yelled, "Do it now, *cabrón*!"

As I reached to remove my watch cap, I mashed the pressure switch and collapsed to my knees. My aim was off only slightly, and I saw a shock of green light pierce the man's eyes. In sync with Victorino's shriek of surprise, I rolled to the ground, anticipating a long volley of gunfire. Instead, a three-round burst kicked the sand nearby, then the gun went silent while the man continued to howl, trying to shield his eyes with his left hand but still jabbing the machine pistol at me with his right.

The Tec-9 had jammed again, I realized.

I took a long, deep breath and got to my feet, still aiming the laser. Until the weapon's fouled chamber had been cleared, the thing was probably harmless, yet there was also a possibility that Victorino had somehow activated the safety —a mistake he might correct at any moment.

Holding the laser in both hands, I kept it focused on Victorino's face as I dodged out of his probable line of fire. I was yelling, "Drop the weapon, get down on your belly!" repeating the commands over and over as I approached. But the man was in such obvious pain, I doubted if my words registered.

When I was close enough, I slapped the machine pistol out of Victorino's hands. When he tried to take a blind swing at me, I grabbed him by the collar, kicked his legs from beneath him, then pinned the man to the ground.

I had one knee on Victorino's chest as I jammed the Dazer hard into the socket of his left eye. The laser's megawattage was radiating heat through its aluminum casing that even I could feel despite my leather gloves.

I held the gang leader there for several seconds, ignoring his screaming pleas, his wild promises, until I was certain he had had enough. Then I switched off the laser, pressed my nose close to his and said, "Tula Choimha. The Guatemalan girl you abducted—where is she?"

Victorino started to tell me, "I don't know nothing about no—" but I didn't let him finish.

I speared the Dazer into the socket of the man's right eye and held the pressure switch, full power, as he tried to wrestle away. Even when he had stopped fighting me and was screaming, "I'll tell you anything! Anything!" I kept his head pinned to the ground. I held him there for another few seconds before switching off the laser, then I tried again.

"Where's the girl?" I asked the man. "Did you kill her?"

In the stark light of the inferno, Victorino was crying now—perhaps an involuntary ocular response to the laser or because he was afraid. The teardrop tattoo beneath his left eye glistened with real tears. The irony might have struck me as vaguely amusing had I been in a different mood.

I placed a finger on Victorino's Adam's apple, my thumb on his carotid artery. As I squeezed, I said, "I'm not going to ask you again. Where is she?" and then I lifted until the gang leader was on his feet.

He didn't try to fight me. "You blinded me, man," he said. "I can't see! How the hell you expect me to answer questions when I can't see nothing?"

When I squeezed his throat harder, though, Victorino opened his eyes and blinked a few times before telling me, "Okay, okay. Everything's real blurry, man. And my eyes fucking hurt, man. It's like you stuck a knife in my brain. You got to give me a minute."

I gave him a shake and said, "Tell me where you have her—the girl. And what happened to Harris Squires?"

I released the man long enough to confirm his partner was dead. Beside the body was a .44 Smith & Wesson, a small cannon that caused my pants to sag when I stuck it in the back of my belt.

My attention had shifted to the wooden building, flames shooting out the door now. It caused Victorino to turn his head, and I felt myself cringe when he finally answered my question. "Last time I saw that little girl," he said, "she was in there."

I got behind the gang leader and shoved him toward the flames. If Tula Choimha was still alive, she wouldn't last long.

We had to hurry.

I slapped Victorino in the back of the head, then pushed him harder toward the building, yelling, "The girl might still be alive. Run! Help me get her out, I won't kill you!"

The man replied, "You serious?"

When I pulled my hand back to hit him again, Victorino took off running.

Together, we sprinted toward the wooden structure, the heat from the burning RV so intense that we had to circle away before angling toward the door of the shack. As we ran, I took the Kahr semiautomatic from my pocket, already aware that Victorino was faster than I and he might decide to keep running.

That's exactly what he had decided to do— until I stopped him by skipping two rounds near his feet.

"Goddamn it, man!" he yelled. "I'm not escaping, I'm trying to get to the back side of this place. I think there might be a window there."

Victorino had long black hair. I grabbed a fistful, then used it like a leash to steer him, saying, "We check the door first. Get as close as you can and take a look."

I gave the man a shove toward the opening as my brain scanned frantically for a better way to clear the building. For a moment, I considered the possibility of ramming one of the walls with

Squires's truck—but that might bring the blazing ceiling down on the girl, if she was still alive inside.

But Tula wasn't alive. She couldn't be. I knew it was impossible, as my eyes shifted from the truck to the building that was now a roaring conflagration of smoke and flames.

Twenty feet from the door, Victorino dropped to his belly because of the heat. He yelled, "There's something you don't know, man! This place"—he gestured toward the building—"it's a cookshack for steroids. It's got a bunch of propane tanks all lined up. Any second, they're gonna start—"

There was no need for him to continue because that's when the first propane canister exploded. Then three more followed in staccato succession, each shooting a fireworks tapestry of sparks into the night sky.

When Victorino got to his feet and tried to sprint to safety, I caught him by the hair again and yelled, "We check that window next. I'm not giving up until I'm sure."

From the expression on the gang leader's face, I knew there was no window. He had been lying. Even so, I herded him to the back of the building, where a small section of the wall had been blown outward. From a distance of thirty yards—that was as close as we could get—I could at least see inside the place.

I was positive then. No living thing could have survived that fire.

For several seconds, I stood there numbly, taking in the scene. Had I arrived a few minutes earlier, spent less time interrogating Dedos and Calavero, maybe I could have saved the girl. It wasn't the first time my obsession for detail had thwarted a larger objective. But it was the first time an innocent person had died because I could not govern what secretly I have always known is a form of mania—or rage.

Obsession *is* rage, a Dinkin's Bay neighbor had once told me—a man who also happens to be a Ph.D. expert on brain chemistry and human behavior.

The fact was, I was doing it now—obsessing—and I forced myself to concentrate. Later, I could wallow in the knowledge of my inadequacies. Tonight, I still had work to do.

There were a lot of unanswered questions. Unless I was willing to risk prison, I had to understand what had happened here. Obsessive or not, details are vital when manipulating a crime scene.

I asked Victorino, "Is Squires in there, too?" The wooden building, I meant.

I knew the man wasn't telling me the whole truth when he replied, "I think so. Him and that woman, Frankie, they did some weird, kinky shit. But she got pissed off at him. That Frankie is crazy."

446

I watched Victorino's head swivel. "Where the hell that woman go? She's the one you ought to be hammering on, man. Not me."

When I told him the woman had been in the RV when it exploded, he did a poor job of hiding his reaction—a mix of relief and perverse satisfaction.

Victorino and Frankie had been sexually involved at one time, I guessed. Hatred is often catalyzed by the pain of previous intimacies—or infidelities.

I asked, "Were his hands tied? His feet? What about Squires?"

I was trying to assemble a better overview of who had done what to whom. Before crime scene police could understand who the bad guys were, I had to understand it myself.

Victorino replied, "Man, I had nothing to do with that shit." When he saw my expression change, though, he added quickly, "But, yeah, I'm pretty sure Frankie had them both tied pretty good. She was getting ready to do a video deal, you know? So later she could have fun watching herself do shit to the girl, and her old boyfriend, too. A freak, man. I already told you."

The truth of what had happened was becoming clearer in my mind despite Victorino's dissembling. As the man continued talking, inventing details, I was studying the portion of wall that had been blown open. It was a narrow section of planking wide enough for me to see inside, if the angle was right, but not large in comparison with the rest of the structure.

It bothered me for some reason. What I was seeing didn't mesh with my knowledge of explosives and the complex dynamics involved. At that instant, as if to illustrate, another propane canister exploded, and we both ducked instinctively, watching a column of red sparks shoot skyward.

Victorino was telling me, "My boys and me, we sold them grass, coke, whatever. Sometimes moved some of the muscle juice shit they made —strictly business, you understand. That's the only reason we come out here tonight. Then this shit happened."

What bothered me about the hole in the wall, I realized, was that the boards had shattered geometrically, yet it was a random displacement of matter in an otherwise solid wall.

What I was seeing made no sense. An explosive force creates a rapidly expanding wave of pressure slightly larger than the volume of the explosive. It expands with predictable symmetry —a three-dimensional sphere capped by a matrix of superheated gases and particles. The matrix created by the exploding propane takes was rocketing upward. Why had this small space been blown *outward?*

But then I decided that the anomaly could be

explained in many ways. A weakness in the structure, an absence of bracing because the hole had once been a window or a door. The shack looked homemade, sturdy but inconsistent. What I was doing, I realized, was fishing for hope—hope that the girl and Squires had managed to crash their way through the wall and escape.

The fire had started so suddenly, though, the heat and flames so intense that the pair would have had very little time to knock a hole in what had been a very solid wall. And they had both been tied, hands and legs.

"The bitch *invited* us," Victorino told me. "She told me they had a new batch of muscle juice. Only reason my boys and me were here tonight. And we got certain security procedures we follow. Two guards at the gate, two of my best men with me riding shotgun. A dude they don't know shows up, they're trained to take certain steps. It was nothing personal. You understand."

I waited, watching Victorino's eyes move from the fire to the shattered windows of the Dodge pickup, aware that at least two of his men were dead inside. The truck appearing animated in the oscillating light. I wondered if the man would have the nerve to ask what he was aching to know. He finally tried.

"Maybe you know something about the steroid trade yourself?" I watched Victorino grin, showing his gold teeth. He wasn't a bad-looking guy,

449

actually. He had a good chin, a strong Aztec nose and cheeks. Had the man made different decisions—or been born in a different setting— he might have succeeded in a legitimate business.

Staring into the fire, I said, "Her name was Tula Choimha—the surname dates back to the time of the Maya. She was thirteen years old, two thousand miles from home, and the girl had no one to protect her from scum like you. That's why I'm here."

Victorino chose not to respond.

Slowly, I backed away from the heat. Victorino backed away, too, but he was gradually creating more distance between us, I noticed, until I hollered at him to stop. I used the pistol to wave him closer, before telling him, "Let's get in the truck and get the hell out of here. You drive."

It surprised the man. He replied, "Both of us you mean?" unsure if he had less to fear or more to fear.

"A plane or a helicopter's going to spot the flames," I told him. "Cops and firefighters will be coming soon. Maybe park rangers—we're close enough to the Everglades. I don't want to be here when they show up. How about you?"

I had taken off the night vision headgear, and Victorino jerked his head away when he realized I was going to remove the ski mask, too.

Mask up—but not off—my face pouring sweat, I told the man, "It's okay. You can look."

Victorino was three steps ahead of me, facing the truck. I could see his mind working, wondering what was going on.

The man stood frozen for what seemed like several seconds. Perhaps because I began to whisper to myself, repeating a private liturgy, he finally turned to look at me.

When he did, I asked, "Where's the money? Sixty thousand dollars cash." I didn't know if the drunken woman was telling the truth, but I was thinking about Tula Choimha's determination to lead her family home to Guatemala. They would need money.

Victorino's eyes revealed the money's location, but I waited until he lied to me, replying, "Money? What money?" the staged look of confusion still on the man's face when I shot him in the chest. A few seconds later, I shot him at close range in the back of the head.

His partner's .44 Smith & Wesson made a thud when it landed on the ground beside Victorino's body.

I wasn't going to invest much time searching for the money—if it existed. What I had told Victorino was true. The hunting camp was in one of the most remote regions in Florida, yet a fire of that magnitude might still attract attention.

I found the cash in a canvas gym bag on the floor of Squires's truck, along with a .357 Ruger

Blackhawk revolver. The temptation was to get behind the wheel of the truck, and drive as fast as I could back to the main road. But then I remembered that the Dodge blocked the exit. Bulldozing the thing out of the way would take time and would make a lot of noise. It would also prove that at least one of the shooters had escaped.

It was safer, cleaner, if I returned on foot.

To add further confusion to the scene, I tossed the Blackhawk under the truck, then took off, jogging toward the darkness, gym bag over my shoulder, as I repositioned the night vision monocular over my left eye.

I had learned my lesson. Until I was close enough to my truck to risk stepping into the open, I would stay in the shadows. To me, darkness— and open water—have always represented safety.

I am a stubborn man, though. Because the anomalous hole in the wall still bothered me and because it would be the driest route back to my truck, I chose to run past the burning shack before turning into the woods. There, the topography was upland pine. Plenty of cover but lots of open ground, unlike the swamp to my right. It would be a hell of a lot easier to parallel the hunting camp road before angling to the gate where my truck was hidden.

There was a third reason: I also believed that if Squires and the girl had managed to escape, they would have had to travel a similar path to safety. It was unlikely that they had survived, but it would satisfy my mania for thoroughness while also providing an ironic last hope that my obssessiveness hadn't cost a young girl her life.

It happened.

Fifty yards into the woods, north of where the shack was still burning, I heard a mewing sound. It was soft, rhythmic, a noise so similar to the sound of wind in the pine canopy that I would have dismissed it as a feral cat had I not been wearing night vision.

After only a few more steps, I could discern the source of the noise. It was Tula Choimha. She was kneeling over a massive shape that I soon realized was the body of Harris Squires.

I had been moving so quietly, the girl hadn't heard me. I didn't want to frighten her, but I also realized that I couldn't allow her to see my face. I lowered the ski mask, readjusted the monocular, then knelt before calling to her softly, "Tomlinson sent me. Don't be afraid. Your friend Tomlinson wants me to help you."

It was as if I had spoken a secret password. Instead of being startled, the girl jumped to her feet and ran to me, sobbing, then threw herself into my arms. Only when she noticed my strange headgear did she recoil, but I patted her between the shoulders as I held her and spoke into her ear, saying, "I'm taking you home. Please don't ask me any questions. Okay? But it's true, I'm taking you home."

Through the lens, the girl's face was as radiant as phosphorus, but I could also see that her nose was swollen, her face bruised. She stared at me for a moment, and I sensed she knew exactly who I was, although she had only seen me briefly after the alligator attack at Red Citrus.

"You're Tomlinson's friend?" she asked, but there was a complexity to her intonation that signaled she was asking far more than that simple question.

"I'm taking you home," I repeated. "That's all I can tell you. But first I need to know how badly you're hurt. Someone hit you in the face, I can see that. But were you burned? It's important that you tell me the truth."

My mind was already scanning our options. If Tula needed emergency attention, the decision was easy. I would call 911 and risk the fallout—claim to have found her wandering in the woods, which was true. If she was okay, I would park in the shadows at Red Citrus and not let her out of my truck until Tomlinson had arrived and found her "officially."

But the girl replied, "I have a headache, that's all. Some of my hair got singed. The only reason I'm not hurt is because"—her head pivoted toward Squires—"because the giant saved me. I have never met a man so strong—stronger than

454

Hercules, even. We were in a building, there was a fire, so he picked me up like a bear, then we both crashed through a wall."

Carrying the girl in my arms, I walked toward Squires. What I saw was unexpected. The man appeared to be badly burned on his shoulders, yes, but he had also been peppered with a shotgun and castrated. It caused me to remember what Victorino had said about the woman I had seen running from the RV, batting at imaginary flames.

"That Frankie is crazy," he had told me.

It was a rare nugget of truth from the gang leader.

"Please," the girl told me after several seconds. "You shouldn't look at Harris anymore. He's not covered. God is with him now, but we still need to show respect. I'll come back later. I'll pray for Harris and then cover him with a shroud."

I wasn't surprised that Tula was in shock. But I also wondered if she was delusional—something I had suspected from the first—because she leaned her mouth close to my ear as if to whisper a secret, saying, "Jehanne already told me that you were coming. That you would be wearing a helmet like a knight. I expected it to be made of steel"—the girl touched her fingers to my ski mask—"but this is the armor that Jehanne spoke of. I understand now. You are the warrior knight God sent to save me. That's why I understand I cannot ask you questions."

455

"Jehanne," I said gently even though I had never heard the name. "Yes . . . that was good of her. I'm glad she told you because I didn't want you to be afraid."

Cradling the girl in my arms, I turned and began walking in the direction of my truck. Tula laid her head against my shoulder and began to cry. After a few steps, though, she pulled away and plucked at an oversized polo shirt that covered her like a dress, saying, "Normally, I'm not so weak, but I can't help myself. It's hard for me to leave Harris all alone because he fought for me so hard. He even gave me his shirt to wear. And he found my amulets—my shields."

The girl was cupping what looked like a necklace, as she continued, "Once I was wearing my amulet, I thought everything was going to be okay, that God would heal him. That we would live in the mountains together, where I could take care of him. But then . . . but then . . ."

I felt the girl's body shudder, and I expected her to say that it was then that Squires had died.

Instead, Tula turned to look at something I hadn't yet noticed. It was an elongated form lying in the distance, difficult to decipher details even with night vision. I began walking toward the shape as I listened to the girl explain, "But even God can't control evil. The power it has over people—a giant like Harris, it makes no

456

difference. I wonder sometimes if even Jehanne understands."

The girl nodded toward the shape, her expression fierce, then turned away before telling me, "Evil. That's what killed Harris—even though I fought to save him just like he fought for me. She came out of the darkness, screaming profanities, and running. It surprised us. Both of us. I fought back. But Harris lost his strength and died."

Carefully, I placed the girl on the ground, her back turned, and I walked to the body of the woman I had seen fleeing the RV. It was Frankie, I realized.

I knelt, then risked moving the woman's arms to assess her injuries as best I could. To be certain, I even used a small LED light to check her legs, her face, a portion of her abdomen.

The flames might not have been imaginary, but Frankie's body had only minor burns. Some blistering on her arms and a head of singed red hair. Maybe the explosion had blown the woman clear of the fire—possible, if she had been standing in an open doorway when a cigarette ignited the propane.

I knew from what I'd witnessed that the woman was already drunk. Alcohol could have contributed to her hysteria, so Frankie had assumed the worst, panicked and sprinted into the woods. Maybe the woman had tripped and fallen. Or collapsed from exhaustion—but only after surprising the Guatemalan girl and her injured bodybuilder protector.

What my careful scenario didn't explain was the blood that soaked the woman's tube top . . . and the paring knife protruding from Frankie's throat.

"She was evil," Tula said to me, her back still turned. "She wanted to kill Harris and she finally did. But not his goodness. That's what I was trying to save."

My mind was working fast, already anticipating the questioning the girl would have to endure. Tula Choimha needed an out. Something real. Something she had witnessed with her own eyes so she could speak honestly of it later.

I said to Tula, "I want you to watch something. It won't be pleasant. Later, though—when people ask you about what happened—you'll be able to tell them honestly what you saw. Other things . . . things that happened earlier tonight . . . you'll probably want to forget."

I waited until I was certain that the girl had turned to look. Then I used the paring knife on Frankie—several times—before leaving the knife just as I had found it, in her throat.

We walked in silence then, the girl in my arms. It wasn't until we were almost back to my truck that Tula looked up into my masked face and said, "Do you remember the goodness that was in you as a child? God's goodness, I'm talking about."

I replied, "Sure. Everyone does," because I thought it might make her feel better or reassure her at the very least.

I had underestimated the Guatemalan girl's strength, however, and her maturity. It was Tula who then provided me with a more tangible form of reassurance, saying, "That doesn't mean warriors shouldn't lie to protect other warriors. Joan of Arc did it many times to protect her knights. The Maiden has promised me it's true—Dr. Ford."

EPILOGUE

ON THE SECOND SUNDAY IN MARCH, which is when daylight savings adds an hour of light to winter's darkness, I drove my truck to the West Wind Inn, a mile from Dinkin's Bay, and was on the beach in time to watch the sunrise.

It was 6:43 a.m. The sun had not yet appeared above the Sanibel Lighthouse, but clouds to the west were fire laced, tinged with pink and edged with turquoise from a sky that melded blue with the green of an old morning sea.

I had just taken possession of a custom surfboard, designed by surf icon Steve Brom and shipped from the Florida Panhandle by YOLO Boards of Santa Rosa Beach.

It was Tomlinson who had discovered the

fledgling company, perhaps charmed by the YOLO acronym: *You Only Live Once.*

As my friend pointed out, the name didn't mesh with his convictions about reincarnation or life after death, but, as he explained, "You gotta love the kick-ass spirit it represents."

I was unmoved until I had tried one. The next afternoon, I spoke to Brom and ordered a board specifically for my needs. After discussing what I wanted, I then provided the man with my height and weight.

Amused, the California surf guru had told me, "I don't expect to see you on the pro circuit any-time soon. But this might be my chance to create a board that even a gorilla could use, maybe even learn to shred."

Funny guy.

The board—a stand-up paddleboard, by definition —had arrived yesterday, a Saturday, just as I had finished separating a new batch of specimens, sea horses and filefish in one tank, two dozen anemones in another. After I had unboxed the board, I had leaned it against the outside wall of my lab, then trotted down the steps to get a better view from the deck.

There is something iconic about the shape of a surf board. It gave me pleasure just looking at it. The body was laminated bamboo, rails classically arched, the bottom painted deuce-coupe yellow. The board was more than eleven feet long, the ends symmetrically rounded, and I amused myself by deciding it would have appeared equally at home on Easter Island, guarding a seaward bluff, or sliding down a North Shore wave.

Waves. That's why I had come to the beach. It's why I had done only an abbreviated morning workout, then headed straight to the West Wind after checking the weather report.

Sanibel Island isn't known for its surf, but this morning was different. Wind was blowing low over the Gulf, rolling waves from the southwest, their crests finally peaking as they soldiered toward the beach after a five-hundred-mile journey from the Yucatán, Mexico.

Just beyond the second sandbar, fifty yards from shore, a translucent green beach break was curling with a symmetry so consistent that I realized my hands were shaking a little as I strapped the leash around my ankle, then carried the board to the water.

To my left, to my right, there were early-morning beach strollers and shellers and young honeymooners walking hand in hand. Decade after decade on the islands, the faces differ, but the beaches continue to provide a safe conduit to the infinite, narrow galleries of sand that illustrate relentless change.

The surf line, though, was as empty as the horizon.

Waves were waiting. And so was something else I needed: solitude. I craved it. Craved it so intensely that, since I had rescued the Guatemalan girl eleven days earlier, I had been avoiding people. It is the same when I return from an overseas assignment. I view it as decompression time, a period of slow reacclimatization after surfacing from the depths.

At the gate to my boardwalk, I had hung the NO VISITORS PLEASE sign. I retreated to my lab, ignoring e-mails, refusing phone calls, and I had even skipped Dinkin's Bay Marina's traditional Friday-night party.

I worked out every morning and afternoon, then spent most of the day in my flats skiff or in my little trawler, dragging nets. My only companions were the sea creatures that inhabited my aquaria, my telescope and the marina's self-important cat, Crunch & Des, who spent an unusual amount of time gifting me with an unusual amount of attention.

Two people I made a special effort to avoid were Tomlinson and Emily Marston.

The only person I spoke with daily—almost daily, anyway—and visited whenever I could, was Tula Choimha. I had wrestled with the possibility that interacting with the girl might cause police to be suspicious. As I got to know her better, however, and because I paid close attention to how law enforcement types reacted when I was around, I was soon convinced that the opposite was true.

More important, I was convinced of something more compelling: Tula could be trusted. We never discussed what had happened. The girl was savvy enough to understand that any mention of that night could mean years in jail for me.

Instead, we spoke of her brother and her aunts and how eager she was to return to Guatemala. Her mother, though, was never mentioned. I didn't pry because of something Tula had shared with me that night during our long drive. "My mother is dead," the girl told me. After several minutes of silence, she explained, "Harris confessed something to me that I can never speak of again. I love them both and I forgive them both. Because I love them, the truth of how my mother died will die with me."

A safer topic for our daily talks included the hundreds of Central Americans who visited the girl's hospital daily, waiting patiently and offering prayers, even though they knew they would not be allowed to see the patient they revered.

It required special patience for me to pretend to accept Tula's explanation. "They're aware that God has sent them a message through me. My people don't belong here. No amount of money is worth the homes and families they abandoned. On their cell phones, I know they probably exaggerate what I suffered—some of the crazy stories the nurses have told me! But the fire was real, and so was the evil. God wants me to keep spreading His message. And I will."

What transpired the night I rescued Tula was on my mind hour after hour, day after day. From it sprouted additional worries and realizations. I had saved the girl. It made me responsible for her in some ways. I also felt a growing affection for Tula that was beyond anything I had anticipated. It matched my admiration for Tula's intellect, her maturity and her decency.

In the bag I had taken from Squires's truck, I had counted out more than fifty-three thousand, mostly in hundreds, fifties and twenties. Cash of that amount would invite scrutiny, and I was still investigating the best way to create an account in Tula Choimha's name.

Responsibility is a petri dish of worry.

But now as I waded into the Gulf, then paddled toward the surf line, my earth-linked worries faded, becoming incrementally smaller with every freeing stroke.

Nine days after the missing Guatemalan girl made headlines by suddenly reappearing at Red Citrus RV Park dazed and injured, she was released from the hospital with the blessings of the Florida Department of Law Enforcement, but only after several interrogation sessions plus

four days of medical tests and psychologic
evaluations.

"The child is suffering from shock and what
may be post-traumatic amnesia," a department
spokesman was quoted as saying. "But she is a
resilient child, very brave, and the information
she has provided is so detailed that we believe
we have a firm grasp on the facts regarding how
she disappeared and the murders she may have
witnessed."

Because of the girl's age, thankfully, the reports
never revealed Tula's name.

Unlike Tomlinson, who is a *New York Times*
junkie, I avoid newspapers. Reading a litany of
human outrages, I believe, is a damn dark way to
start what in Florida is usually a consistently
bright day. Because I had a personal stake in
how the investigation unfolded, however, I spent
those ten days paying close attention.

Especially nerve-racking were the afternoons
that I knew Tula was being interrogated.

At any moment, day or night, the police could
come tapping at my door. Paranoia isn't irrationa
when fears are well founded or when guilt is t
burden of someone who is truly guilty. It wa
new experience for me—while living within
normally safe borders of the United St
anyway—and not pleasant.

Not that I suffered from pangs of g
didn't. If a shrink somehow learned th

about my life, if he was provided details of some of the things I have done, he might conclude that I am a sociopath, incapable of remorse or guilt.

The shrink would be wrong. I am sufficiently objective to acknowledge that I am less affected by emotion than most people, yet I suffer guilt and regret on a daily basis just like everyone else. I am aware that too many times I have behaved thoughtlessly, stupidly and childishly. I have hurt people I care about and I have said words that will forever make me wince.

The difference between myself and a sociopath is this: When I executed those five men, I did it while in full control of my emotional and intellectual facilities. I didn't pull the trigger because I wanted to do it. I killed those men because it was *necessary*—required, in fact, by the circumstances and the exigencies of their own violent behaviors. Pyromania is to arson what murder is to assassination.

"Strictly business," Victorino might have explained it, and the man would have been correct for once.

When I replayed the events of that night in my mind, I felt no guilt for the same reason I felt no perverse thrill or any emotional satisfaction. Even so, what had happened was on my mind constantly. So I followed the news reports.

The St. Pete *Times* referred to the incident as

The Immokalee Slayings, which for that excellent newspaper was an understandable hedge because Immokalee was the nearest town and also because three of the seven victims resided within the city limits.

Laziro Victorino, I was not surprised to learn, had chosen upscale locations—a riverfront home in Cape Coral and a condo near Tampa.

"Police believe the homicides are gang related," one of the stories read. "Mass killings have become commonplace in Mexico, and the ceremonial nature of the Immokalee slayings suggests that gang violence has finally arrived in South Florida. Four victims were shot execution style. The body of a fifth victim was mutilated, although authorities refuse to provide specific details."

Because police had found steroid-manufacturing apparatus at Harris Squires's hunting camp and also a small facility at his Red Citrus double-wide, the news reports implied what police had yet to confirm: The killings had something to do with a turf war over the sale of illegal steroids.

"Such turf wars date back to the days of Prohibition," one newspaper editorial read. "Illegal drugs spawn murderous behavior. To members of a warring gang, killing an enemy is viewed as a right of passage."

Six consecutive days the slayings dominated headlines, but the few known facts didn't vary much. It wasn't until the ninth day that some enterprising reporter hammered away at an obvious question until some unknown source provided an answer. How exactly did a teenage Guatemalan girl escape the carnage only to be found forty miles away, wandering the shrimp docks near Tomlinson's rum bar, bayside, Fort Myers Beach?

According to a source familiar with statements made by the abductee, the reporter wrote, *the girl was rescued by a person she described as a "Spanish-speaking man who drove a truck."*

Because the man wore a ski mask, the girl was unable to provide a physical description of her rescuer, although she described him as "kind and gentle" in at least two of her statements. In a third statement, the girl told investigators that the man's truck must have been almost new because it was so quiet that she was able to fall asleep as the masked man drove.

The story continued, *Although it cannot be confirmed, at least some investigators believe the man may be a member of one of the warring gangs whose conscience would not allow him to execute a young girl. A Collier County psychologist, often consulted in homicide cases, has suggested the man may be the father of a girl who is of similar age. Police are cross-referencing the information in search of the suspect, although investigators believe that most, if not all, of the warring gang members were killed on the night the incident occurred. The exception, of course, is the man who drove the girl to safety.*

A Spanish-speaking masked man. Tula had found a way to effectively distance me from the case by providing her interrogators with very specific truths.

After five days, heartened by the reactions of police and the news report I read, I began to enjoy a tenuous confidence that I had manipulated the crime scene convincingly. After seven days had passed, the only cop who had bothered to contact me was my detective friend, Leroy Melinski. And the only reason he called was to congratulate me on Tula's rescue.

Well . . . to congratulate Tomlinson. Not me.

"I've got to give your crazy hippie friend credit," Lee had said. "All night, our guys had been staking out that trailer park, but it's your pal who happens to find the girl wandering the streets and brings her in. 'Psychic intuition,' he told our guys. He claimed that's how he knew where to find her. The first thing they did, of course, was check his vehicle for weapons and a ski mask. And he also had a very solid alibi— he'd spent the entire evening with a woman biologist that Tomlinson claims you know. So maybe there's something to that mystic bullshit after all."

I didn't comment on Melinski's reference to Emily, although I was tempted to tell him he was right about the bullshit but wrong about the rest of it.

Tomlinson's "psychic intuition" had nothing whatsoever to do with him finding Tula.

Truth was, Tomlinson was so drunk and stoned by the time I reached him on his cell phone that I judged him incapable of driving to Red Citrus. Because I couldn't depend on him, I hung up without mentioning that Tula was with me.

I was disappointed in the guy, of course, but I wasn't shocked. I *was* shocked, however, when I dialed Emily Marston as a backup and suddenly I was talking to Tomlinson once again.

For a moment, I was confused. Had I or had I not dialed Emily's cell phone?

Yes, I had.

"Ms. Marston is temporarily indisposed," Tomlinson answered formally, unaware he was speaking to me. Because he tried hard to sound sober, he only sounded drunker when he added, "May I help you? Or you can wait for Emily— she's a pretty quick little spliff roller."

By then, Tula and I were only twenty minutes from Red Citrus. I had driven the distance with particular care for obvious reasons, and now the girl was asleep, her head in my lap. So as not to wake her, I had to move my right arm gently to get a look at my watch.

1:30 a.m.

My best friend, it turned out, was still guarding the safety of my new lover, Emily, the quick little spliff roller. The temptation was to nail Tomlinson with a very valid question: What in the hell, exactly, was going on?

Instead, I remained calm. I had to because I needed his help. Someone had to be close to Red Citrus, waiting, when I dropped off the girl. Someone I trusted. Not inside the park because cops might still be posted. If police saw the exchange, if they suspected I was the one who had driven Tula to safety, they would search my truck and correctly associate me with the murders I had just committed.

Phone to my ear, I took a slow breath and said, "Tomlinson, if you care anything about our friendship, please don't say a word. Just listen."

The instant he tried to respond I stopped him, saying, "I'm warning you, this is serious. And please don't use my name—or tell Emily it's me."

After a reassuring silence, I told him, "I need your help. I'm counting on you." Because it was true, I added, "You're the only person I trust with my life."

During another long pause, I imagined the man's mind trying to rally. Tomlinson claims that his brain conceals what he calls "a sober lifeguard twin" who comes to his rescue in demanding situations no matter how wasted he happens to be. He claims his ever-sober twin has saved him from suspicious cops and freak storms at sea.

Because of my tone, I suspected that Tomlinson was summoning that lifeguard now.

Finally, he said, "Anything you want. You can count on me."

As he spoke, I could hear Emily in the background, asking, "Is it for me? Why are you using my phone?" The woman, at least, sounded sober, but I wasn't going to entrust her with what had to happen next.

As I spoke to Tomlinson, I used short sentences. I kept my directions concise. Lifeguard twin or not, the man still sounded slobbering drunk.

Half an hour later, I sat in my truck in the shadows of the boatyard that adjoins Tomlinson's rum bar. The bar's party lights and its underwater lights were still on, but the place was closed.

Twice, cop cars cruised past, probably changing watches at Red Citrus, I guessed. Each time, as my knuckles whitened on the steering wheel, I felt Tula pat my arm, trying to calm me.

When a Yellow Taxi finally appeared, pulling beneath the security light near Hanson's Shrimp Yards—exactly as I had instructed Tomlinson— I leaned, kissed Tula's singed hair and told her, "You're safe now. Tomlinson's waiting. He won't ask you any questions. He promised me— and I trust him."

Then I sat back and watched the girl run toward the security light into my pal's waiting arms.

Aside from a few accidental meetings at the marina—"awkward" would describe our exchanges —it was the last time I saw the man until that early Sunday morning when I noticed two familiar figures appear from the strand of sea oats that separate the West Wind Inn from the beach.

I was a hundred yards from shore, waiting for a good wave. I watched the figures stop . . . scan the water . . . and then both people waved.

It was Tomlinson, looking absurd in a pink sarong. Emily was beside him.

I had been avoiding the couple, it was true. But I waved in reply, anyway, because petty demonstrations of anger are, in my opinion, the equivalent of cancerous little cells that eat away at the quality of a person's life.

Why not? I was feeling pretty good because I'd already had some fun. Waves had tumbled me and humbled me, confirming, with supreme indifference, that I still had a lot to learn about paddleboard surfing.

My ego is still sufficiently adolescent, though, that I became determined to make my final ride to the beach stylish enough to impress Tomlinson and, more important, Emily.

Maybe I tried too hard. That's probably what

happened. Only a few seconds into the ride, the board nose-dived, then pearled. I went flying.

Because I deserved it, I expected both Emily and my pal to be laughing as I carried the board to the beach. Not derisive laughter. The variety that comforts a friend after he has looked foolish.

Instead, they both appeared oddly serious as I approached. It became more serious—and confusing—when the woman marched toward me, then took my face in her hands. She stared into my eyes for a moment before saying, "This is an intervention! That's why we're here."

More confused, I said, "Huh?"

The woman explained, "An *intervention*. It's a sort of last-resort tactic that's supposed to work on alcoholics and habitual gamblers. So we decided that maybe, just maybe, it would work on someone as obsessively stubborn, bullheaded and downright dumb as you."

I replied, "*We* decided?" moving my head to look at Tomlinson.

The man rolled his eyes and shrugged as if to distance himself from what was happening. "I wouldn't call Doc dumb," he said. "The rest of it's true, yeah. Especially the 'obsessive-stubborn' deal. But 'dumb,' that's taking it a little too far."

I replied, "*Thanks,* pal," and broke away from Emily's grip long enough to place my board on the sand.

A moment later, though, she was cupping my face in her hands again. There were tears, I noticed, welling in her eyes, so I stood quietly and paid attention.

"We both know what you've been thinking about Tomlinson and me, and you're wrong," the woman said. "I've called you more than a dozen times. I sent you e-mails, trying to explain. I came to the marina twice, but each time you were off somewhere doing God knows what on your boat. It's been more than ten days, damn it!"

Emily's hands dropped to her sides and formed fists to illustrate her frustration. "I thought you cared about me, Doc! I wanted to talk with you. No . . . I *needed* to talk with you! The night you called my cell phone, the night Tomlinson answered, why didn't you at least have the courtesy to explain to me that you were in trouble? If you'd told me you the truth, that you were in trouble and needed help, I would have been there for you, damn it!"

I tried to remain expressionless as slowly, very slowly, I shifted my attention to Tomlinson. My throat was tight as I asked the man, "You *told* her about what happened that night?"

Even when he's stoned, Tomlinson has wise old eyes, a prophet's eyes, some say. He stared back at me now, though, with clear eyes, his gaze steady. "I didn't tell her the specifics," he replied. "Just enough so she would understand."

I said, "Well, discretion has never been your strong suit," not caring now if Emily realized that I was suddenly furious.

Sounding unflappable, Tomlinson continued, "I figured it would be okay. So I explained that your truck broke down in Immokalee and a couple of the rednecks were giving you a hard time. But I didn't mention the cops—or the drunken waitress at the barbecue place."

Emily said, "What drunken waitress?" as I studied the man's face in surprise, wondering how any human being could lie so effortlessly.

I exhaled a slow breath, very relieved. "It was an ugly scene," I told Emily. "There was no reason to get you involved."

I expected the lie to calm the woman. Instead, it made her madder. Emily put her hands on her hips and leaned toward me, saying, "No, the truth is, you thought your buddy and I had something going on that night. Didn't you? Just because he answered my phone at one-thirty in the morning. That we both got stoned and jumped in the sack or something—like I'm some sort of easy tramp. That's why you didn't want me to help you. That's why you've been avoiding both of us. Tell the truth, Doc."

Glancing at Tomlinson, I did tell the truth. "It wouldn't be the first time that it's happened," I said.

Smiling, Tomlinson was walking toward us. "I

476

explained that to her, Doc," he said. "I'm a sinner, God knows it, and now Emily knows it. But what you need to understand is that my premonition of fire almost came true. That's why I was still there at Emily's house. Trust me, she couldn't get rid of me fast enough."

The woman was protesting, "That's not *exactly* true," as Tomlinson continued, "Remember that old drawing I showed you, the woman falling into a wall of flames? I followed Emily back to her place just like you told me. Just as I was pulling away, she came running out, saying maybe she smelled smoke."

To Emily I said, "Is he serious?"

The woman replied, "I told you about the house I own, out near Alva. It's built of old Florida pine. It took us a while to figure it out, but one of my electrical breakers was bad, just starting to spark. If we'd gotten there a few minutes later, the whole place would have gone off like a bomb."

"There's nothing more calming than a bud of Captiva-grown weed," Tomlinson added. "That's what we were doing when you called. I was already shit-faced, of course, but her"— Tomlinson nodded his chin toward the woman —"she was as about as loose as a nun at a Viagra convention. Because I was there after midnight, though, I don't blame Doc for assuming the worst. Later, I tried to explain to her why you

477

don't trust me and probably never will."

To survive the awkward silence that followed, Tomlinson looked around, saw the waves, then focused on my new surf board. "Very cool," he said. "An eleven-six? Really sweet rockers."

I was staring at the man, tempted to ask if he remembered what I'd said to him eleven nights earlier about trusting him with my life. Not actually say the words but just jog his memory in case he'd been too sloshed to remember.

Instead, I put my arm around Emily. It seemed a wiser, safer choice. As Tomlinson leaned to study the YOLO graphics, I touched my lips to the woman's cheek, then suggested that we walk back to my stilt house, where I could apologize in private.

"But what about your new surf board?" she asked, trying to look over her shoulder as we walked toward the sea oats that fringed the beach.

I replied, "Don't worry, Tomlinson has it. Sooner or later, he would've taken it, anyway."